WESTERN

Small towns. Rugged ranchers. Big hearts.

The Maverick's Promise
Melissa Senate

Big Sky Bachelor
JoAnna Sims

MILLS & BOON

Melissa Senate is acknowledged as the author of this work
THE MAVERICK'S PROMISE
© 2025 by Haelequin Enterprises ULC
Philippine Copyright 2025
Australian Copyright 2025
New Zealand Copyright 2025

First Published 2025
First Australian Paperback Edition 2025
ISBN 978 1 038 94061 2

BIG SKY BACHELOR
© 2025 by JoAnna Sims
Philippine Copyright 2025
Australian Copyright 2025
New Zealand Copyright 2025

First Published 2025
First Australian Paperback Edition 2025
ISBN 978 1 038 94061 2

MIX
Paper | Supporting
responsible forestry
FSC® C001695
www.fsc.org

Published by
Harlequin Mills & Boon
An imprint of Harlequin Enterprises (Australia) Pty Limited
(ABN 47 001 180 918), a subsidiary of HarperCollins
Publishers Australia Pty Limited
(ABN 36 009 913 517)
Level 19, 201 Elizabeth Street
SYDNEY NSW 2000 AUSTRALIA

Cover art used by arrangement with Harlequin Books S.A.. All rights reserved.

Printed and bound in Australia by McPherson's Printing Group

The Maverick's Promise

Melissa Senate

MILLS & BOON

Melissa Senate has written many novels for Harlequin and other publishers, including her debut, *See Jane Date*, which was made into a TV movie. She also wrote seven books for Harlequin Special Edition under the pen name Meg Maxwell. Her novels have been published in over twenty-five countries. Melissa lives on the coast of Maine with her son; their rescue shepherd mix, Flash; and a lap cat named Cleo. For more information, please visit her website, melissasenate.com.

Books by Melissa Senate

Montana Mavericks: The Anniversary Gift

A Lullaby for the Maverick

Montana Mavericks: The Tenacity Social Club

The Maverick's Promise

Dawson Family Ranch

The Long-Awaited Christmas Wish
Wyoming Cinderella
Wyoming Matchmaker
His Baby No Matter What
Heir to the Ranch
Santa's Twin Surprise
The Cowboy's Mistaken Identity
Seven Birthday Wishes
Snowbound with a Baby
Triplets Under the Tree
The Rancher Hits the Road
The Cowboy's Christmas Redemption

Visit the Author Profile page
at millsandboon.com.au for more titles.

Dear Reader,

Cowboy Diego Sanchez is known around Tenacity, Montana, for being unwilling to commit to a serious relationship. He *has* his reasons. But when he finds himself snowbound overnight with a struggling widowed mom and her adorable baby, everything changes.

Jenna Lattimore is so drawn to the handsome, helpful cowboy who tends to her baby daughter with such care and tenderness that she can almost see him beside her for life. But Jenna has already lost so much and knows better than to believe there's such a thing as forever...

Luckily for Diego and Jenna, the Sanchez family— including beloved Uncle Stanley and his ninetysomething psychic bride, Winona Cobbs—is around to share a few lessons about love. I hope you enjoy *The Maverick's Promise*!

Warm Regards,

Melissa Senate

CHAPTER ONE

"WHICH SANCHEZ WILL be the next to say 'I do'?"

Don't look at me, Diego Sanchez was thinking as his great-uncle Stanley—eightysomething years old and a newlywed himself—asked the group.

The entire family was sitting around a bunch of tables put together in the Tenacity Social Club. Diego's sister Marisa—the youngest of the five siblings—had gotten married today. When the reception had wound down at 10:00 p.m., the Sanchezes were still in celebration mode and had moved the party there. Even Diego, hardly a romantic, had gotten a little choked up at the ceremony at the Goodness & Mercy Nondenominational Church. And watching Marisa and her new husband, Dawson John, slow dance at the reception at the Tenacity Inn, gazing into each other's eyes with such love, had Diego nodding. If you *were* going to get married, it should look like that.

At thirty-three, Diego had long stopped believing in all that for himself. But his family was everything to him, and Marisa's happiness really touched him.

"Nina? Maybe Luca? How about Diego?" Stanley asked with a smile as he wiggled his bushy gray eyebrows and looked across the table at his great-nieces and -nephews.

"I think we can safely say that Julian is next," Diego said, popping a chili-topped nacho into his mouth from the platter in the center of the table. Julian was the eldest of the siblings and very seriously involved. Diego hadn't seen *that* coming, especially since Julian's love, Ruby McKinley, who was sitting beside him, was a single mother with young children. His brother, a father figure? To a four-year-old and a baby? Diego had seen with his own eyes how much Julian loved Ruby and the kids. His brother had become a true family man—and very recently had become the first of the Tenacity Sanchezes to buy land for a ranch of his own. People could surprise you—no one knew that better than Diego.

"*Obviously,*" Stanley said. "I'm just so happy—for myself, for Julian, for Marisa—that I want every one of my great-nieces and -nephews to find their forever love." His dark eyes misting, he put his arm around his bride, ninetysomething-year-old Winona Cobbs-Sanchez.

Darn it. Even Diego might get teary. Stanley and Winona had been *through* it. Last summer, the family had gathered to watch the elderly lovebirds get married. But Winona hadn't shown up. No one had been sure if she'd gotten cold feet or if something had happened—and man, had something happened. She'd been injured and was suffering from amnesia when a psychopath kidnapped her and convinced Winona—for months— that she was his wife—despite her notorious psychic gifts. But thanks to Stanley's determination, he'd found her when no one else could. The power of love, his great-uncle had insisted. The two had finally married to much celebration.

Winona was now staring hard at Diego, her blue eyes boring into him. Chills—in both a good way and a scary way—skittered up his spine. Winona really was psychic. Diego had never believed much in *that* either, but his new great-aunt's gifts could not be denied. She *knew* things. *What* she knew was a secret, though, because she never said much. What she did say was usually so cryptic that no one could understand what she meant— until her pronouncements came true weeks or months later.

"Diego's the second oldest, so I say *he's* next," his sister Nina said with a grin as she pushed her long dark hair behind her shoulders. "Then again, he's not even dating anyone right now, so maybe not."

"Yeah, that part—the maybe not," Diego half mumbled. "Anyone up for old-school pinball?" he asked, desperately hoping to change the subject as he looked around the club for escape from the conversation. The place doubled as a teen hangout during the day—with the alcohol under lock and key until after 7pm.

"I wouldn't count him out," Julian said, not taking the hint as he scooped nachos on his plate. "When love comes along, that's that." He looked at his girlfriend, who leaned over with puckered lips. Julian and Ruby kissed, then fed each other nachos with their arms entwined.

Love won't be coming my way, Diego wanted to say. *Because I'll block it like I always do.* He kept that thought to himself.

He'd been down that treacherous road, he thought, the old flicker of bitterness burning in his gut. He'd gotten hurt bad when he was twenty-six and all these years later, he wasn't over it. He dated, but when the relationship never got to exclusivity, let alone a proposal, a diamond ring and talk of forever and kids, the woman invariably got tired of waiting and said goodbye. Nina, who'd fixed him up a time or two, would shake her head and tell him that someday, someone was going to steal his heart no matter how good he was at dodging his feelings.

Honestly, Diego hoped so. If his brother and sister were right about love, he supposed it would be that powerful. He might be prickly on the subject, but he certainly didn't want to *die* alone. At the same time, he couldn't imagine feeling so strongly about anyone to the point that he'd propose.

Also your fault, Nina had insisted. *You keep all your dates and girlfriends at a football field distance.*

He supposed he did. But anytime he thought about the future, he could hear his ex, whom he'd loved, telling him she was ending things. *You'll never be more than just a cowboy on some middling ranch. You'll never own your own place. And that's where the money is. Sorry, Diego, you're a good guy and hot as hell, but I've got dreams.*

Dagger to the heart. Owning his own ranch had never been *his* dream. Maybe that was why instead of Caroline's words lighting a fire in him, instead of trying to prove her wrong, something in him had deflated with what had felt like truth. Even if he wanted his own ranch, all it demanded financially just wasn't in the cards. His parents had been renting their house, a good-sized cabin, really, on the big ranch where his dad had worked as a hand for decades—and still did. Diego worked right beside his father as a cowboy. It had been more important over the years for Diego to help support his family, something he'd been doing since he was a teenager. He'd managed to save up some money and could *probably* buy a small fixer-upper ranch, but it was either land or livestock, livestock or equipment.

So yes, Diego had lived up to his ex's assessment. And he figured any woman would feel the same way. He didn't exactly have much to offer. Caroline had married a businessman in a nearby town so at least he didn't have to see her around Tenacity. Reminding him that he hadn't been good enough—and still wasn't at thirty-three.

So no, he definitely wasn't next to say "I do."

"I'd never count out Diego," Stanley said, reaching across the table to pat his great-nephew's hand. The pride on his great-uncle's face scratched at Diego's heart. He didn't like to let people down but he was who he was.

Diego tipped his cowboy hat at *Tio* Stanley. He might be in a suit for the wedding, but he rarely went anywhere without a cowboy hat, and tonight he wore his one Stetson, a gift from his parents when he'd graduated from high school. He had on his good cowboy boots for the occasion too.

"Winona, *you* tell us who's next," Nina said. Her voice was light, but Diego could see the wistfulness on his sister's face. Same look she'd had during Marisa and Dawson's wedding ceremony earlier. Nina was twenty-nine and had had romantic relationships, but had never settled down herself.

"The answer is out there," Winona said calmly.

Nina tilted her head. "Out there?"

Diego watched his sister bite her lip. She seemed to be lost in thought about something.

Or someone.

"You know," Nina said, spending a good twenty seconds heaping a bunch of nachos on her plate. "I, um, I've been thinking about Barrett Deroy lately. Just wondering about why he left town so suddenly."

Ah. Of course. Barrett Deroy. Her first love. Her childhood love. He and his family had left Tenacity under mysterious circumstances when he was sixteen. Poof, gone, no forwarding address, no contact. Diego had a feeling that no man would ever come close to meaning to Nina what Barrett had.

"I mean, it's been fifteen years," Nina added, biting her lip again. "I just have so many questions, you know?" She glanced at Stanley. "Maybe you could look into it?" she asked the amateur detective. "To find out more about what happened all those years ago to make the family leave. The 'incident.'"

Diego wondered about that. The incident? He couldn't remember why the Deroys had packed up and left so suddenly. But he could tell by Nina's expression that she wasn't up for questions. Just answers.

"The Deroys don't seem to be on social media at all," Nina added.

Which meant she'd tried to find them—and Barrett.

"I've got you, *mi gran sobrina*," Stanley said with a warm smile. "I'm up for the challenge."

Winona was now staring at Nina. Diego much preferred that to those shrewd blue eyes on him. "The answer is closer than you think," the elderly psychic said, but her attention turned to the bar.

Diego glanced over. Winona didn't often turn her head, so he was curious. There weren't many people here this late, so the long wooden bar with a bunch of stools was almost empty. Winona seemed to be looking at the expanse of wood with initials carved into it. Couples tradition here in Tenacity. His ex had liked fancier places so they'd never come here together— their initials were not among the hundreds covering the bartop.

Diego was about to turn his attention back to the table when he saw a gorgeous woman who'd just come in approach the bar. She was wearing a big pink parka, her cheeks a bit reddened from the cold. Even a few seconds out in the frigid February cold was too much. She pulled down her hood to display long silky red hair. When she turned slightly, he realized she was holding a baby. The tiny human was encased in a pale yellow snowsuit with some kind of animal ears.

Figured. The first woman to turn his head in months had a baby. And was probably married. Just as well. He wasn't looking for anything anyway. At his age, the women he dated were ready to settle down. He might not want to die alone but at this rate he'd be ready for a relationship when he was Stanley's age. At least he knew a shot at love would be possible then.

Still, he couldn't stop watching the woman. She seemed... stressed, which was evident in her body language. Even under that parka he could see she was coiled tight. Her beautiful face was etched with something like worry but not quite that. He couldn't put his finger on it. She was upset, though. He didn't recall ever seeing her before. Maybe she was new in town. Then again, Diego worked hard, hung with his family at home over going out in town, so it was possible that he'd just never run into her.

He watched the bartender, who Diego didn't know, come around the long bar toward the woman. She carefully handed him the baby. Her husband?

Lucky guy, he thought, then froze. *Lucky guy?* Being a husband and father? Where had that come from all of a sudden?

Lucky because the redheaded beauty is his. That's all, Diego corrected himself.

"Hi, Robbie!" he heard a young voice say. Diego noticed a little boy, seven or eight, maybe, had come out of a room beside the bar, and smile up at the baby, clearly Robbie, and then the woman. Normally it wasn't the kind of place children hung out, but during this kind of celebration, The Tenacity Social Club was so family friendly that clearly a kid was not out of place.

"You okay, Jenna?" the bartender asked the woman as he pulled down the yellow hood to reveal a headful of wispy auburn curls. He kissed the little forehead, then rocked the baby a bit as he peered at the woman—with concern. Husbandly concern.

So her name was Jenna.

If Jenna responded, Diego couldn't hear. Suddenly she pivoted and rushed out.

Whoa. What was that about? The bartender didn't seem affected. He was lifting the baby up and down in a round of Upsy-Daisy, the little boy giggling and holding up his arms.

"Can you even lift me anymore?" the boy asked with a grin. "I *am* eight."

Hmm, were they a family? Of four? The mysterious, beautiful Jenna was a mother of two?

"I'll always be able to lift you, buddy," the bartender said, his gaze soft on the boy.

Diego watched the very sweet scene, wondering why such a caring man didn't seem to care about his wife, who'd run out with all that stress on her face.

Diego forced his attention back to the table, where talk had turned to the differences between Tenacity and Bronco, another Montana town where Stanley and Winona lived half the time. The Sanchezes had relatives there, but it was a good distance away.

Diego glanced toward the door, then back to the bartender, who was rocking the baby and humming a lullaby.

He couldn't stop thinking of Jenna's face—troubled. Not like: *My baby won't stop crying and it's driving me bonkers.* Or: *I'm so tired and need a twenty-minute nap.* Something was really bothering the woman. Diego wondered what.

Why *he* was so concerned about a stranger he'd seen for less than a minute was beyond him.

But he did care. Was she outside, leaning against the building covering her face with her hands, worrying about something? Was she pacing? Or had she left?

It was really cold out there. February in Montana. At night.

Diego was only half paying attention to conversation at the table—Stanley was saying it was time to go, that octogenarians and nonagenarians turned into pumpkins at ten thirty. The group started getting up, everyone hugging Marisa and Dawson, again saying what a beautiful wedding it had been.

Ah, time to go anyway. The perfect opportunity to check on Jenna.

And make sure she was okay. But if she wasn't out there, if she'd left, he'd worry about her all night.

Sometimes Diego really surprised himself. And this was one of those times.

JENNA LATTIMORE SAT in her car in the parking lot of the Tenacity Social Club, staring at the puffs of air her breath was making in the cold. She was freezing but didn't turn on the ignition for heat. She couldn't move, couldn't think. She didn't want to think—that was the point.

Would this ever get easier?

Between the cold and the forecast—snow for the next couple of days, including a possible blizzard—Jenna couldn't stop the barrage of painful memories. Over a year ago, on a frigid December day, Jenna had lost her husband when a storm had turned into a blizzard and the whiteout had sent Rob Lattimore's pickup careening into a tree. He'd been going slow but it hadn't mattered. Just like that, he was gone.

A wife had lost her husband. A baby who hadn't even been born yet had lost her daddy.

Thirty minutes ago, Jenna had been standing with baby Robbie at the sliding doors to the patio in her house, pointing out the evergreens in the yard and explaining how they never lost their green needles. The weather forecast on the TV news she'd had on in the background had suddenly caught her attention. The meteorologist was talking about the impending blizzard. A chill had snaked up her spine, and she'd been frozen in place just as she was now.

Then sorrow had overtaken her. A heavy, suffocating sadness—with her precious daughter in her arms. Jenna had made a promise to herself, to Rob's memory and to their baby that she wouldn't ever lose it in front of little Robbie. Her best friend, Mike Cooper, had told her that if her anxiety got the best of her, she should bundle up Robbie and bring her to him so that Jenna could just sit with the pain until it passed. It never did quite pass, not exactly, but day by day, week by week, month by month, she'd been able to focus on remembrance instead of sorrow. Except for days like today. When the smell of snow in the air, the forecast of a blizzard, gripped her hard.

In an instant, two lives had changed. That added to the fear. That at any moment...

She'd gotten Robbie into her snowsuit and had driven over to the Tenacity Social Club, where Mike, a rancher, moonlighted as a bartender two to three times a week for extra money. One look at her face, knowledge of the coming storm, and he'd known she needed just fifteen minutes, a half hour, to get ahold of herself. He'd watch Robbie until her anxiety passed, until she was ready to come back in and get the baby girl and take her back home.

Jenna picked up her phone from the console and stared at the photo on her lock screen of her precious daughter. That helped ground her. She eyed the time. Just before 11:00 p.m. She'd sit here just a bit longer, then go back in. Mike was working and had his nephew with him; the last thing the man needed was a baby to rock while trying to pour a draft for a customer.

And Jenna needed to get home; she didn't want to be out on the roads with even *hours* to spare before the first flake fell in the morning.

She didn't drive in snow anymore.

Extra deep breath, like in Lamaze class, she told herself, hearing her mom's words. Her parents lived an hour and a half away in Bronco, where Jenna had grown up, but Jenna spoke to her mother every day. Sometimes, when she was scared about the future, about the here and now, she'd need to hear that soothing voice telling her she would be okay, that she could always move back home. To take a deep breath, feel what she felt and just wait it out. That the memories would always hurt but that she had people who loved her who were ready with a hug at any time.

She couldn't see moving back home with her folks—despite her money troubles. Rob hadn't had life insurance. They'd talked about it, and when they got the happy news that Jenna was pregnant, Rob had made an appointment with an insurance agent. But it was for the day *after* the accident. Jenna had the small, sweet Cape Cod–style house they'd painstakingly saved for. She couldn't imagine selling it and downsizing even further. The home was where she felt safe, and it was Robbie's legacy. She couldn't leave. Her job at a daycare center didn't pay all that well, but it covered her bills and she had free childcare, plus two great bosses. She just got by, and she was grateful she did.

Besides, Tenacity was home—and she felt comfortable here. For lots of reasons. A hardscrabble, blue-collar town, full of hard-working people—ranchers, mostly—many of whom barely scraped by. Most young people couldn't wait to escape it. But there was something to be said for a small town where everyone knew your history and loved you in spite of it. Those who chose to stay recognized the value of family and friendship and staying true to your word. Jenna liked that. She vaguely remembered that there had been some big to-do about fifteen years ago—a family that had been run out of Tenacity over what she wasn't sure. Back then she'd been too worried about making the grades to get a scholarship to pay attention to local gossip.

Now, she leaned her head back and took that Lamaze-like deep breath.

Okay. She would go back inside. She would get her beloved little girl and go home.

A tap on the window startled her and Jenna almost jumped.

She turned to see a very good-looking man bending down beside the window. The black suede Stetson gave him away as a cowboy. He was dressed up in a wool overcoat, a bolo tie against a white shirt just visible. Jenna was pretty sure he'd been sitting with the big group in the club when she'd gone inside. They'd all been dressed to the nines. Jenna couldn't remember the last time she'd been out of jeans or yoga pants.

Some people came out of the club, and a woman joined the cowboy, peering in through the window at her.

What was this about? Jenna sighed and opened the door and got out. It was time to go in anyway. She closed the car door and locked up, then eyed the cowboy.

"I'm Diego Sanchez and this is my sister Nina," he said. "I just wondered if you need help since you were sitting in the car without the engine even running. And it's cold out here." He gave a shiver. "Is the car not starting?"

Jenna's eyes misted with tears. Darn it. The kindness undid

her. She wasn't used to someone making a fuss over her like this. And to Jenna, this constituted a fuss. She had her bestie Mike here in Tenacity, of course, but she'd kept to herself the past year. She had a few friends, though, including her bosses at the daycare. But for the most part, she shied away from people, afraid to get close, to care.

"Should I go get your husband?" Diego asked, peering at her with such concern.

"I don't have a husband," she said, the words still sounding so wrong after more than a year. She stared down at the ground, a numbness saving her from crying in front of the cowboy.

He winced as though embarrassed that he'd made an assumption. "Your boyfriend, then—the bartender."

Ah. He'd clearly seen her talking to Mike and handing over Robbie to him, but two and two didn't equal four in this case. Jenna was still so overwhelmed that she didn't have it in her to explain who Mike was to her. "I'm fine," she said. "I was just heading back in to pick up my daughter."

Diego's head tilted. He seemed to be taking in what she'd said, thinking about something, and trying to reach a conclusion.

Nina wrapped her arm around the cowboy's. "We'd better get going. Everyone's waiting." She gave Jenna a sympathetic look as though she understood that Jenna needed to be alone. Women had a way of reading one another.

"If you're sure," Diego said to Jenna, still assessing her. He was looking at her so intently, with even deepened concern in his eyes. She'd wonder why he was so interested in the first place, but he'd seen her rush into a bar with her baby, hand her over to the bartender and then rush out to sit in her car in the cold without even turning on the ignition for heat. Of course he wanted to make sure she was all right.

Get it together, Jenna, she told herself. *You're making total strangers nervous for you.*

She nodded and tried to put something of a smile on her face, but she was sure she looked awkward.

Nina's own smile was warm when she said, "We'll just make sure you get inside okay."

There was that kindness again, which clearly ran in the family. Jenna looked at them both and nodded once more, then hurried toward the entrance as a few more people came out. Someone held the door open for her, and she turned back to see Diego holding up a hand in goodbye.

She was struck by it to the point that she couldn't move for a moment.

Without even meaning to, she held up her hand too. He smiled—a big, warm smile—but didn't move. She finally realized he was waiting for her to go inside first.

The cowboy's creed. The guy was a gentleman. And kind. Between that and the breathtaking smile, Jenna actually felt better, a little stronger. She was ready to get her daughter, to be present for her.

Thank you, Diego. She didn't know why, exactly, but something about him, about his kindness, about the way he looked at her like he really saw her, made her feel okay again tonight.

Yes—thank you, Diego Sanchez. Even though she was sure she'd never see him again.

CHAPTER TWO

"So DO YOU and Ruby hang out at the Tenacity Social Club often?" Diego asked his brother Julian the next morning—with an ulterior motive. They were inside the barn on the ranch where Diego and his father worked, but Will Sanchez wasn't feeling well so Julian was pitching in since he wanted to go over the plans for his new ranch afterward. The barn was heated just enough that coats and gloves weren't necessary.

"The only place we hang out *often* is home," Julian said, pausing in his raking. "I like the social club, but it's more for teens than families during the day. And with the kids, we're not having many date nights. Last night was the first time we've been out in a while."

Diego nodded, trying to figure out another way to ask his brother if he knew anything about the bartender without out-right asking. That would lead to questions. At this point, Diego only wanted answers when it came to Jenna. He wasn't even sure why he couldn't stop thinking about her. Wondering how she was doing. He didn't know a thing about her, other than that she had a baby. Maybe a son too. And that she sat in her car in dark, cold parking lots at night.

Her face rose to mind. He hadn't known she had such blue eyes until they'd been face-to-face outside. Blue eyes filled with something he couldn't figure out. Unease for sure, though.

Oh hell. He was just going to have come out and ask. "The bartender? Nice that the club is so family friendly—he even had his kids with him at work last night."

Julian looked puzzled. "Mike Cooper? He doesn't have kids. Oh—wait, he kind of does right now. He's guardian of his eight-year-old nephew while the boy's mom is working out of the country. Cody, I think his name is."

Nephew. Huh. So not Jenna's son.

"And he was holding a baby for a while there," Diego said. "Is the baby his? His girlfriend came in—long red hair?—and gave him the baby to hold for a while."

Again his brother looked puzzled. "Girlfriend? Mike? Definitely not since he's gay. I've seen the redhead around town with the baby and with Mike a few times. If anything, they're just friends."

Gay. Just friends.

A strange sense of relief came over him that Mike wasn't her boyfriend. Because Diego was interested and had been the minute he'd seen her.

He wanted to know more about her. He *had* to know more.

"What's with the twenty questions?" Julian asked, resuming raking. He stopped and stared at Diego for a long moment. "Wait a minute. Is this why you've been single for a while? Why you always say no to blind dates?"

Huh? Now Diego paused from raking the straw. He turned to his brother. "What are you talking about?"

"You're clearly interested in Mike."

"I'm interested in *Jenna*," Diego said. "The redhead."

"Ah." Julian continued raking, stepping farther into the stall. "Single mom with a baby. Didn't see that coming for you."

"Nothing's coming for me," Diego muttered. "I'm just... I don't know. She seemed upset last night. And then Nina and I talked to her outside the club for a bit. Jenna just seemed so stressed. I want to make sure she got home okay."

"Such a Good Samaritan," Julian teased.

"All right, dammit, I'm interested. Something about her..."

Something that had kept him up last night. He'd thought

about Jenna on the way home. *At* home. When he'd gone to bed. When he'd woken up at just after 2:15 a.m., his throat parched.

Last night, when he and Nina had watched Jenna go inside the club, his sister had said, *Diego, you're such a good guy. The woman who finally wins your heart will be very lucky.*

He'd waited a beat to see if she'd laugh and sock him in the arm or something. But she didn't. He must have looked at her like she had three heads because she'd added, *Yes, I'm being serious. You should settle down, Diego. It's time. Yeah, you got hurt. But it was years ago now. Don't let that dictate the rest of your life.*

Luckily just then, their sister Marisa pulled Nina away for a hug; the newlyweds were heading out for their honeymoon. The conversation had thankfully ended.

Was it time? Would it ever be time? When some relatives were surprised that Uncle Stanley had fallen in love again after being widowed, the starry-eyed octogenarian had said: *You know what you know when you know it—and I know it.* Diego had understood. Except when it came to himself. At the moment he didn't feel much ready for anything other than a strong cup of coffee.

Julian was grinning now. "Well, little brother, let me help you out. I'm pretty sure her last name is Larrimore. No—*Lattimore.* With t's."

"Jenna Lattimore," he repeated. He'd look her up. Phone numbers and addresses were easy to find online. He'd call or even stop by. Just to check on her.

"Diego, when you need to know where to get diapers on sale or the best lullabies to sing a cranky baby to sleep, just ask." Julian started whistling a lullaby and resumed raking.

"Let's not get a million miles ahead of ourselves," Diego said, moving to the next stall. Good. He needed a little distance from what his brother was saying. Diapers? Lullabies? Come on.

Diego could hear a vehicle pulling up, so they both leaned their rakes against a post and put on their jackets, then went outside to see who it was. It was just flurrying now, but they were expecting a couple of inches by tonight and a storm tomorrow. He and Julian had started out even earlier than the usual pre-rooster crowing to make sure they'd get everything taken care of.

Luca, the youngest of the Sanchez brothers, got out of his pickup. He looked a lot like Diego and Julian. Same dark hair and eyes. Tall and muscular from years of ranch work.

"Hey," Luca said as he approached them outside the barn. "Thought I'd come see if you needed any help. Dad mentioned you were filling in for him this morning." One of the benefits to living on the ranch where two Sanchezes worked was that if one was having an off day, another Sanchez was always willing to help out.

"Appreciate that," Diego said. "It's about time to get the cattle moved closer in." They started walking toward the barn to saddle up the horses.

"Oh and by the way, Luca," Julian said. "Diego's interested in a single woman with a baby." He shot Luca a grin.

Luca stopped in his tracks. "Good one," he said on a laugh.

Julian laughed. "I kid you not. He just said so himself."

Diego was the only one not smiling here. "I don't even know her! I'm just...curious about her. That's all."

At this point.

"Well, that's how it starts," Luca said. "And this from the guy who gave Julian a hard time about dating a single mother?" He clapped an arm around Diego.

"We both gave him a hard time," Diego reminded Luca. "And I wouldn't even call it that. We just pointed out that his life would change—hard and fast. That dating a single mother came with big responsibilities."

"Well, we'll tell *you* that now," Luca said. He turned to Julian as they each picked up a saddle. "Any words of wisdom for a guy who hasn't even had a *relationship* in years?"

"Hey, I've dated," Diego said.

"Yeah, maybe you've gone out with the same woman three times at most. And I can't recall any single or divorced mothers in the mix. So who's the lady? How old is her kid?"

Diego sighed and told Luca what happened last night to get him off his back. "So I'm just concerned about her. Maybe she needs help. Or a friend."

Both brothers smiled. "Well, you go check up on Jenna," Julian said. "Remember what I said about the diapers and lullabies. You'll be asking in a matter of days."

Luca cracked up.

Diego laid the saddle over the mare. He took in a deep breath, the familiar scent of the barn, of any barn, grounding him a bit in this unfamiliar territory. Of being unusually interested in someone. A single mother, at that.

You know what you know when you know it...

The only thing *he* knew for sure right now was that he would go check up on Jenna Lattimore.

He *had* to. He just wouldn't explore the why of that too deeply.

DIEGO HAD GONE home for his twenty minute break—to think about calling Jenna. *Think* because every time he started to press in her number, which was as easy to find online as he'd figured, he stopped before the fourth number.

He sat on his bed and stared at the phone. *It's just a hello. A how are you? Just checking in since last night...* That wouldn't lead anywhere but her *I'm fine, thanks*, the rote answer to that question, and they'd probably not run into each other again.

Which was for the best. Diapers? Lullabies? *What?*

Those were words that weren't in Diego's immediate future. Maybe a few years down the road?

He could hear Julian and Luca now. *A few years down the road or now if you meet the right woman.*

Well, Jenna Lattimore couldn't be the right woman. She was a package deal. She had responsibilities. No way would she be interested in "just a cowboy."

Would he ever get that voice out of his head? Probably not.

Well, then he had no reason not to check in. To just hear that she was okay so he could somehow force himself to stop thinking about her.

Yes. Once he knew she was all right, that she'd just had a bad night, he'd go back to his regular old thoughts. His job. His family.

That he just might die alone, after all.

Dammit.

The problem with forcing himself not to think about Jenna was that she was so fully present in his mind. Her face, those beautiful eyes. Something about her had captured his attention. That was how attraction and chemistry worked—whether he liked it or not. Whether she was a single mother of a baby or not—not a carefree woman who might say yes to a date.

A date. That was something else he couldn't stop thinking about. Sitting across from Jenna at a restaurant. Having a drink, a good meal, talking, getting to know each other.

Oh yeah, he would like that.

But.

She'd find out during the *so what do you do* small talk on their date that he was "just a cowboy," and she'd rule him out.

He got up and sat back down. *What is with you? You saw this woman for like 5 minutes once in your life! Get a grip!*

Except it *was* just five minutes—and she'd made *that* much of an impression.

Just call her. Check in. The call won't go anywhere. You'll go back to work. You'll wonder what Tio *Stanley is making for dinner, if it's his turn. You'll fix the broken hinge on the back door. You'll put Jenna out of your mind.*

He pressed in the numbers. All of them this time.

Voice mail. Ah, perfect. He hadn't even considered that, but he was calling her landline and she was probably off somewhere, town or at work.

He really liked the sound of her voice.

Leave a message after the beep and I'll return your call as soon as I can. Thanks!

"Hi, Jenna, it's Diego. Sanchez. We met last night outside the Tenacity Social Club. I was the nosy one wondering if you were okay? I guess I'm still wondering and just want to hear you got home fine and all is well with you. How about this, if all is well, no need to call me back. If you could use a friend, feel free to call me back." He left his number and then disconnected the call.

His heart was beating a little too fast. He stood up again and paced. He thought he'd gotten that voice mail right. No pressure to call him back.

Honestly, he didn't know which he preferred. A call back. Or not.

JENNA HAD BEEN home on her afternoon off, sitting in the kitchen with a mug of coffee and her laptop while Robbie was napping when her phone had rung. The landline. Caller ID showed it was an unknown number.

She'd let it go to voicemail, but the second she heard Diego's voice, heard him say his name, she'd almost jumped.

With nerves. And a little excitement. His very good looking face came to mind, his dark hair and dark eyes, the kindness in his expression. That he'd managed to actually register at all during all that anxiety was something. In a moment when she needed a strong hug, Diego Sanchez's gallantry had pretty much rescued her from herself.

There'd been a time or two or three even, when she'd been that anxious at a very inopportune time, like in the supermarket with a full cart, and a man had come over in the produce section to ask if she was okay, that she looked…stricken. She'd forced whatever pleasant expression she could and said she was fine and hurried off. No one had ever made an impression on her, except to appreciate a nice gesture toward her.

So why had Diego Sanchez managed to get in her head? Why was she picturing his face? Why had she listened to the voice mail a *second* time?

She was okay now. So there was no need to call him back.

She bit her lip. She *wanted* to call him back. The awareness of that jolted her and she stood up and paced some more.

What did this mean? She certainly couldn't be interested in him, right?

Sure felt that way, though. Those happy little feelings for a little crush. She'd had plenty of that in high school. Before she'd fallen hard for Rob Lattimore.

Her late husband's name in her thoughts had her sitting back down.

She bit her lip again.

There it was—she wasn't really okay. She'd lost her first and only love. Dating wasn't on her radar.

You're scared to even consider it, a voice said.

Yeah, for good reason. How could she ever start dating when any man who could possibly turn her head would also have the power to destroy her if something happened to him?

Exactly, she thought, shaking her head. She'd never make it back a second time.

And she had Robbie to think about.

And that had to be that.

She sipped her coffee, which had gone cold. If this was all settled in her mind now, if she would not call him back because she *was* okay and needed to stay that way for her daughter's sake, then why couldn't she stop thinking about Diego?

He was so kind and she should be kind back by calling him to say thanks. But that would possibly open up some kind of... *something*. She didn't know what. Friendship? Friendship was good.

But what if he asked her out?

A small burst of butterflies suddenly fluttered in her belly. Could she possibly *want* him to?

She did, she realized. *You don't have to say yes. You probably won't say yes.* But the idea of it had a warmth now spreading in her chest.

She knew what to do. She would *not* call him back. If "Unknown Number" called again, then she'd answer. If he did ask her out, she'd…see how she felt in the moment.

She was sure she'd say no—politely, nicely. She wasn't ready to date. Certainly not a man who'd managed to actually turn her head.

Luckily, Robbie chose that moment to wake from her nap with a hearty cry. Jenna vowed not to think about Diego again—if he did he call, she'd…see what happened.

But he probably wouldn't. He only expected her to call if she wasn't okay, if she needed a friend. If she didn't call to acknowledge that he'd left that nice voicemail, he wouldn't reach out again.

And as she picked up her baby girl, cuddling her close with a soft pat on her back, Jenna realized with a shocking burst of clarity that she hoped he *would* call again.

CHAPTER THREE

THE NEXT DAY, with Robbie down for her morning nap, Jenna sat at the round table by the window in the kitchen with her laptop, phone and a mug of coffee—just like yesterday except the phone hadn't rung with an unknown number.

She was actually relieved.

And slightly disappointed.

Not that she had the right to be.

Focus, Jenna, she ordered herself. She had the morning off and was going over her budget to see where she could cut back. She glanced at her banking portal at her paltry savings, then at her checking account balance, low after paying the first of the month's bills. She also needed to bring in more money. She'd asked the owners of the daycare about taking on a couple more hours a day, but they were fully staffed and so that wasn't an option.

Mortgage. Phone. Electric. Gas. The forty bucks a storm she paid the cowboy down the road for plowing snow from her driveway—and in winter, those added up. Homeowner's insurance. Health insurance. She'd already canceled her internet and cable service since she had Wi-fi on her cell phone. She didn't see what else she could scale back. The car was paid for and upkeep wasn't too bad. She got her dental cleanings at the local university's dental school for 40 percent off the typical cost.

She clipped digital coupons for the grocery store and shopped wisely. Babies were expensive, but Jenna had done well with some secondhand items in great condition, and Robbie had what she needed. Jenna bought diapers and baby food in bulk when she did a monthly shopping at a big box store a few towns over.

She took a sip of her coffee and pulled her laptop closer. She opened a Word document she'd started a few weeks ago. *Possible Side Gigs I Can Do at Home* was the heading. The list wasn't long. Hand-knitted items. Pies. Custom pizzas. Playlists.

She sighed. There was hardly a market in Tenacity for hand-knitted baby booties or caps. Or for specialty pizzas with every imaginable topping when everyone was fine with the plain and pepperoni at Pete's Pizza. And the Silver Spur Café always had a few pie choices every day and wasn't looking for freelance bakers either—she'd asked. Forget about her worst idea of making playlists for joggers or car rides or podcast lists by interest when folks could easily do that themselves with a few clicks.

At least she *did* get by. She could pay her bills. There just wasn't money for extras. Like the lullaby-playing bouncer she wished she could buy for Robbie, let alone an extra pacifier to keep upstairs. $4.99 for a plain pink binky was a no-go when money was tight and she had a perfectly good one.

Jenna's gaze drifted out the window, the flurries not getting to her. Surprised, she sat up straight and stared out at the pretty white flakes drifting and settling on the evergreen out front. When was the last time she'd thought of snow as pretty?

Granted, it wasn't snowing hard by any stretch. But the day before yesterday, just the mention of the storm coming had sent Jenna into a downward spiral of memories and fear.

It's the cowboy.

Diego Sanchez.

His good will—his and his sister's kindness—had stayed with her. As had his follow-up call and voice mail.

And warm dark eyes. It was the darndest thing, but on the way home two nights ago from the Tenacity Social Club with Robbie safely buckled into her rear-facing car seat, and for hours afterward, any time Jenna would get nervous about the forecast, Diego's face would float into her mind and she'd feel a little better.

She pulled her long green cardigan more tightly around her. She wasn't sure why he'd made such an impression. Yes, he'd been nice. But it was more than that. If she was being honest with herself, she'd admit to...finding him attractive. Very much so. To the point that last night, as she'd lain in bed, she'd wondered what it would be like for those strong cowboy arms to hold her.

She sucked in a breath. Jenna hadn't thought about dating at all—not once. Rob Lattimore had been a great guy, a great husband. They'd been together since college, where she'd also met Mike Cooper. At first Rob had been jealous of her growing friendship with the tall, handsome guy until Jenna had shared that Mike's romantic interests were elsewhere—like on the cute guy in their history class.

Both Rob and Mike were from Tenacity but hadn't known each other despite how small the town was. Different circles. Rob had wanted to settle down in Tenacity because his widowed mom had been ill, so they had, but unfortunately, they'd lost her soon after they bought the house. Rob had felt the connection to his parents strongly in town, so they'd stayed, and since Mike lived there too, Jenna had even more reason not to fight for moving to Bronco, where she'd grown up. It was just far enough away at an hour and a half to make it difficult to see her parents, for them to see their grandbaby. But in the year that Rob had been gone, she couldn't imagine leaving. Not only was the house her baby's legacy, but she felt settled here.

She loved Tenacity. Here and there over the years, some stores had closed, but those that had managed to stay in business were beloved by the ranching community. While Tenacity was a town used to hard times, it was still a place where neighbors helped each other.

She felt safe here. She had Mike, and her job, and nice neighbors. And she'd recently made a new friend. Renee Trent owned a mobile dog grooming business and had clients on this road. They'd started chatting when Renee had been giving a huge poodle a bath in the yard a couple houses down. One day, Jenna would get a puppy to add to the family. That was all the extra love she'd be up for.

She was *not* ready to date.

She looked out the window at the flurries, coming down a bit harder now. She was a Big Sky girl, and there was no getting away from snow—and lots of it—in Montana. She'd have to make peace with it. Somehow. But as the wind began whipping the flurries around, she started getting that panicky feeling again.

Diego Sanchez's good-looking face, his strong shoulders in that wool overcoat, came to mind and she felt herself relaxing.

He was like her own secret talisman of sorts. She had a sudden urge to tell him how grateful she was for the way he and his sister had been so kind that night. For caring. For asking. For being there. For watching her go inside, safe and sound. The way her husband would have.

She bit her lip. She sure seemed interested in this man. In a *romantic* way.

Was that what these feeling were about? And was that okay?

She grabbed her phone and called Mike. He'd be working on his family ranch right now, his nephew in school. Especially with his twin sister away, Mike had his hands full, and he'd confided in Jenna that times were tough for Cooper Ranch. He often told her he appreciated being able to take a break when he got a call. If he was busy with cattle or a horse or riding fences, he'd let her know he'd have to call her back.

"Hey, Jenna," Mike said. "I was just about to check in with you. You doing okay?"

When she'd gotten home from the club the other night she'd texted him to let him know she'd arrived and he'd asked that same question. You doing okay? She'd texted back that she was. And for the first time in a long while, that had actually been the truth.

"Strangest thing, Mike," she said. Should she even say it out loud? Wasn't that what best friends were for? To really talk to? "I, uh, met someone that night. In the half hour between dropping off Robbie and picking her up."

"You *did* seem a lot calmer when you came back in to get

her," Mike said. "The color was back in your face. And not from the cold, either. But how did you possibly meet someone by sitting in your car in the parking lot?"

She told him the story. The knock on the window. The Sanchezes, all dressed up. The care and kindness. Diego holding up a hand in a wave as he'd waited for her to go in the club.

She didn't mention her attraction. She wasn't quite ready to say that aloud. Or to believe it herself, really.

Mike was quiet for a moment. "I don't know Diego personally, but I've heard a few women at the bar talking about him over the years," he finally said. Kind of cautiously. As though he was holding back.

"And saying what?" she asked. Mike always kept mum about what he overheard at the bar—or was told directly by a forlorn customer—but he'd mentioned more than once that the things he heard on a weekly basis sometimes made him glad he was single.

She swallowed around the sudden lump in her throat. Her very first foray into feeling the slightest bit of attraction for another man—and he was trouble?

"Okay, Jenna, you know I don't gossip. I don't talk about what I overhear. But you're my best friend. And so I'm just going to tell you that I've heard a few different women say that Diego Sanchez doesn't commit, that he never goes out with the same woman more than a couple times."

Her heart plummeted. "He's a player?"

"I don't know about that, necessarily, but apparently, he's not looking for a relationship."

"Oh," she said.

Well, I'm not either, right?

"I do know he comes from a great family. I'm not surprised he and his sister came to your rescue. But maybe he's not someone to get interested in."

That was coming a little late.

"Well, I'm hardly ready for a relationship," she said. "Maybe a first step back into that world with someone gorgeous and sexy and kind is what I need. Then when our two or three dates are up, we go our separate ways."

"Listen, honey. It's not that I don't think you're ready to start thinking about dating. But your heart is delicate, Jenna. You need someone who'll be careful with it."

That was probably true too.

Robbie let out a cry. Jenna waited a beat since the baby girl had gotten adept at soothing herself back to sleep if something woke her up. *"Waah! Waah!"*

"I hear my favorite baby," Mike said.

"I'd better go get her. I'll talk to you later."

"Jenna, sorry if I was the bearer of bad news. I just love you, you know?"

Her heart swelled. "I know, Mike. And I love you too."

They disconnected and she headed down the hall to the nursery. Robbie's room was small but sweet, painted a pale yellow since she and Rob had wanted to be surprised with the sex. When it came time to paint the room, Jenna had opted for a neutral color scheme. Rob had never gotten to know his baby was a girl.

One more fussy cry came from the crib. Jenna reached in and scooped up her daughter, cuddling her close.

"Well, maybe it's for the best that Diego Sanchez isn't up for a relationship," she said to Robbie as she laid her down on the changing table. "Because I'm not either."

With Robbie's diaper changed, she brought the baby into the living room. Her phone rang—the landline.

Unknown caller.

Jenna's heart was practically bursting out of her chest.

She set Robbie in her playpen and sucked in a breath—and then picked up the receiver.

Oh God. "Hello?" she said, wondering if she sounded nervous. For all she knew it wasn't even him. Maybe it was a spam call.

"Hi, Jenna, it's Diego Sanchez. We met two nights ago?"

She almost gasped. Not spam. *Him.*

I was just talking about you... Ears burning, maybe?

"Hi," she said. "I'm glad you called back."

"Oh?"

"I wanted to thank you for the other night. For being concerned. You and your sister. I really appreciated it. I was in a bad way and your kindness snapped me out of it. I was okay yesterday and that's why I didn't call back. But thank you."

"You're welcome. And I'm extra glad I went to check on you in your car." Diego was silent for a moment, as though he was waiting for her to elaborate, fill in some missing information. But she was kind of speechless at the moment. A little shocked that he'd called just when she'd been talking about him. Thinking about him. For two days now.

"I'm sorry for being so curt," she said. "You would have no way of knowing this but—"

She stopped talking, her heart suddenly pounding. She wasn't sure what was going on. Nerves, probably. The attraction. And what Mike had said.

"Knowing what?" he asked.

She bit her lip. "That... I'm a widow. I lost my husband in a car accident a little over a year ago. In a snowstorm. I heard the forecast, and I got so anxious." She explained how they had an understanding that when she felt that way, she'd bring Robbie to him so she could get through the difficult moment without her daughter in her arms.

"Oh, Jenna. I'm so sorry. Everything about that night makes sense now."

She took in a deep breath.

"My family's in Bronco. And Rob—my late husband—his family is gone. So it's just me and Robbie. And Mike, thank heavens. I'm just trying to figure things out, you know? How to get by."

"I understand," Diego said. "Getting by is tough when your heart is broken and the world feels tilted. When you wake up and put on a brave face but feel scared inside."

She almost gasped again. "Yes, that's exactly how I feel." How could he know that? She hadn't even been able to articulate to her parents how she'd been feeling all these months. Maybe because she didn't want to worry them. And here she was telling a near stranger her most private thoughts. Making herself vulnerable. And he got it.

"You've lost someone close to you?" she asked, knowing he had. In some way or another.

"Not like you," he said. "Let's just say I've had my heart handed back to me. Cruelly."

She winced. She barely knew Diego Sanchez, and she'd felt that *cruelly* in all her nerve endings. He'd been hurt bad. "I'm sorry about that," she said.

"It was a while ago. You'd think I'd be over it but—" He stopped. "Now wait a minute. I've known you for barely two days. I've talked to you for like ten minutes total. And I'm spilling my guts? What secret powers do you have, Jenna Lattimore?"

He knew her last name. Which meant he'd done a little work to track her down, find her number.

He'd reached out *again* too.

She felt her smile in her toes.

"I could say the same for you, Diego."

They talked some more, about the Tenacity Social Club and how it had once been a speakeasy, like a hundred years ago. That he'd been there only twice, the first time because his uncle Stanley had insisted the whole family go for karaoke night, and then just yesterday for a nightcap celebration after his sister's wedding.

"I have to say, the nachos were pretty good," Diego said.

"Mike's nephew Cody loves those nachos," she said. And suddenly there were talking about their favorite places in Tenacity, both agreeing there weren't many options but that the Silver Spur Café had good burgers and pie, but they were only open for breakfast and lunch.

"I have a question for you," he said.

Butterflies let loose in her stomach. She liked Diego Sanchez a little too much if she was excited by a pending random question. "I'm all ears."

"I'd like to take you out," he said. "To dinner. Or whatever you might like. I guess that's more a statement than a question. But I'm asking you on a date, Jenna. I'd suggest a casual walk in the park but it's freezing and—"

And a snowstorm is coming. She could hear him about to

say it and then remembering what she'd said earlier about how snowstorms affected her.

A snowstorm *was* coming. And maybe this was all just moving too fast.

Who was she kidding about being ready for any of this? Even flirting was apparently too much for her.

"I, uh, it's probably, um…" *Oh God, Jenna. Just speak.* "A formal date might be too much. But a walk in the park is out too. So it's probably a sign that…" She trailed off, not quite ready to say no entirely either.

She *did* like this man. Yesterday, after his voice mail, she'd tried so hard to put him out of her head. But she kept seeing his handsome face, hearing his voice.

"I know just the thing, then," he said, clearly running with the opening she'd given him. "I'll bring over dinner. We can sit on the sofa with our plates on our laps. Watch a sitcom or a movie. And Robbie is invited too, of course. I can even bring a jar of her favorite baby food."

Her toes tingled again. She liked that idea. A lot.

"Robbie does like pureed sweet potatoes," she said.

He laughed. "Don't we all."

She heard herself laugh too. She didn't do much of that these days.

"It's a date then," she said, then swallowed, the word sounding so formal. "Or something," she added fast.

"Or something," he repeated, his voice warm. "How about Thursday night?"

The day after tomorrow. "Sure."

If they did get a bad snowstorm, he'd cancel. Then she could breathe easy. Either way, it was win-win.

A baby step into almost dating—*or something.*

CHAPTER FOUR

THAT NIGHT, THE SANCHEZES were together again—minus Marisa who was away on her honeymoon—this time for dinner at the family home. Sometimes Diego wondered how the seven of them—his mom, dad and the five kids—had fit into this house. There were three bedrooms—the girls had shared one room, the boys another, and his parents had the primary. There were two bathrooms, at least, not that his sisters in particular had found two enough. But step outside on the ranch and they had all the space they needed. The place might not be theirs—Will and Nicole had long rented the "large hands cabin"—but they'd turned it into a cozy home, and all that land and sky out the front door, the mountains in the background, felt like it stretched on forever.

"So what's this I hear about Diego dating a single mom of a baby?" Nina asked, mirth in her eyes. She twirled a forkful of pasta.

Uh-oh. Diego was not interested in being the topic of conversation again. His appetite for his mother's always scrumptious meatballs and linguini was waning.

And how could this possibly have gotten out? He hadn't told anyone about the date.

Luca had the decency to look guilty. "Hey, I only said he was *interested* in Jenna Lattimore." He turned to Diego. "I ran into Nina and Mom in town earlier and it just popped out."

"Oh, I'm sure," Diego said, shaking his head with a smile. "But if you must know, we *do* have a date. Thursday night."

Nina gasped. "Thursday night? Really? Wow."

Diego frowned, his fork paused midway to his mouth. "What's the big deal about Thursday?" He'd always thought weekend nights were the biggies for dates.

"Even *I* know what the big deal is," Luca said, taking a piece of garlic bread from the basket in the center of the table. "And I don't have a date."

"Well, someone fill me in," Diego said, staring around the table at his relatives. They were all looking at him like he was from another planet.

"Thursday," Ruby said, "is Valentine's Day."

Now it was Diego's turn to gasp. "Oh. *Ohhh.*"

"Yeah," Nina continued. "A first date on Valentine's Day? Unusual unless both parties are *really* into each other." She wiggled her eyebrows at him.

"You must really like this woman," Nicole Sanchez said, something like relief in his mother's dark eyes. She'd made it clear she wanted to see all her children happy and settled. Two down, three to go.

He had to change the subject—fast. That this was the topic of conversation was bad enough, but the date was scheduled for Valentine's Day? Why hadn't he checked a calendar first?

Then again, Jenna hadn't seemed to know either—or care. She'd been widowed just over a year ago. Valentine's Day was probably the last thing on her mind. Unless it *was*—and added to her sadness the other night.

His heart lurched for her.

Diego had loved and lost hard—but not to that degree. Not a spouse. He glanced at his uncle Stanley, who was clearly enjoying the conversation. Diego would never forget how devastated his uncle had been when he'd lost his wife of sixty years. Sixty years! Not to mention the gut-wrenching pain he'd gone through when he thought he'd lost Winona last year after she'd vanished without a trace on their wedding day. But now here

Stanley was, his arm around his bride, happiness on Stanley's lined face that lifted Diego's spirits on a daily basis. There were second chances at love. If you were willing and open.

He wondered if Jenna was.

Was *he*? All he knew was that he was very interested in Jenna.

"So maybe Diego will be the next Sanchez to walk down the aisle, after all," Uncle Stanley said. He raised his glass, and everyone else did too, clinking away while Diego felt a punch to his stomach.

Marriage? Well, that was taking things a giant step too far. What did he have to offer a single mother with the huge responsibility of a baby? He didn't have his own home. He didn't have his own ranch.

You'll always be just a cowboy on some middling ranch...
I have big dreams...

Diego slunk down in his chair, his appetite gone.

Maybe this was a mistake. But there was no way he'd cancel the date when she'd already accepted.

Over their cheeseburgers or turkey clubs on her sofa tomorrow night, she'd very likely bring up at some opportune point that she wasn't interested in anything beyond friendship, that she needed a different kind of man. A family man. A man who could make her feel safe, secure. A man with something to offer a widow and her baby.

Yes. He was getting ahead of himself again. But for good reason. She'd shut this down at the end of the date and they'd be friends.

Except there was no way he could see being platonic with beautiful, sexy Jenna Lattimore.

FROM THE MOMENT Jenna had ended the call with Diego Sanchez yesterday to now she'd been going back and forth about the date. *I should cancel. I should not cancel. It's too much. It's just enough.*

As she stood at a big round table in the Little Cowpokes Daycare Center, collecting crayons the kiddos had left scattered during arts and crafts, she made a final decision. She wasn't canceling.

She'd learned over the years that when she was on the fence about something, she should just accept that something was holding her back for a reason.

So she hadn't picked up her phone to call him and say she just wasn't ready.

She wasn't—but she wanted to take that baby step. Not in general. *That* she did understand.

With Diego. Specifically.

There was just something special about him. Something she couldn't ignore if she wanted to.

She'd see how it went, minute by minute. How it felt to have a man in her house. On her sofa. Sharing a meal while watching a comedy. If it was too much, she'd know and be honest with herself and with Diego.

"The flurries are coming down harder," one of her bosses, Angela Corey, said, her gaze out the window. Seventy-two-year-old Angela, who Jenna adored, co-owned the daycare with Elaina Bernard, who was leading an end-of-day sing-along in the back room. Jenna glanced out the window, which she'd been avoiding since a light snow had started a half hour ago. Barely an inch of snow covered the grounds, the roads reasonably clear but dusted. Tomorrow's storm had been scaled back from potential storm to a few inches of snow. Which would hardly ever just be basic to her. She was glad she'd have company tomorrow night, when the roads should be kept clear. "Head home, honey," Angela said. "Elaina and I have it covered."

Relief swept through Jenna. "You sure?"

"Positive. And if it's bad tomorrow, don't even think about coming in. You hear?"

Thank God for Angela and Elaina, both so warm and compassionate. They knew about Jenna's loss and whenever it so much as flurried, they were by her side, checking in, offering a soothing cup of tea, making sure she was all right—as they'd been doing all day. She'd been wrong to think that Rob had been the last to make a fuss over her, to care if she got home safely. Yes, he'd been the last to make that fuss from a place of romantic love, but she knew how lucky she was to have this job with such wonderful bosses who'd become friends. She also knew she had to work on not letting the snow get to her.

After saying her goodbyes to the children now getting ready for pickup, Jenna bundled up Robbie and headed out. She looked up at the sky, the white flakes falling all around her. Once she'd found snow so beautiful. She hoped she would again.

All in time, she told herself.

Yesterday she'd thought the flurries were pretty. A good start. The blossoming of possibilities.

A few minutes later, driving five miles an hour down Central Avenue, Jenna was feeling less friendly toward the snow. The wind picked up and a few times she'd had to use her windshield wipers just to see past the blowing flakes. Her chest tightened.

Honk!

Jenna almost jumped and glanced in the rearview mirror. A small dark car was too close. Jerk! She put on her blinker and pulled over to the shoulder so they could pass. As the car peeled off as though the roads were perfectly dry, Jenna sucked in a few sharp breaths, looking in the back seat to check on Robbie. But since the car seat was rear-facing she couldn't see her daughter's face. She needed to. Just see her sweet face. Jenna quickly got out and went to the back door, opening it up and peering in. Her baby girl was looking at her, curious and alert, happy. Jenna took a calming breath. *Everything is okay. You're okay. Just drive slowly.*

She was about to get back in her car when a pickup truck pulled up behind her, the door opening and someone hurrying out toward her.

A tall, muscular man in a dark brown cowboy hat, the snow collecting on the brim and the broad shoulders of his navy blue down jacket.

Diego Sanchez.

"Jenna! I recognized your car. Are you okay? Did your car slide off the road?" He stopped close by, peering at her, then studying her car, checking the tires. Checking her face, her eyes. He suddenly looked in the rear window at the car seat, and the concern on his face truly moved her.

"I'm fine," she quickly assured him. "As is Robbie. The car is fine too. I was going so slow a car honked at me, and I pulled over to let him pass and then..." She bit her lip. Tears sprung to her eyes. She hated how she sounded. Weak. Like a woman who couldn't handle herself, her life. She was someone's mother, this baby's only parent. She had to be better than this, stronger. "I'm fine, really."

But she wasn't. She was trying, but she wasn't fine.

There were flurries on her eyelashes. On her nose. She wanted to cry.

He reached for her hand and gave it a quick squeeze. "I'll follow you home. Just to make sure you get there safe."

Relief came over her, unknotting her shoulders. "I hate to trouble you, Diego. But I won't say no to that. Thank you."

He smiled. That warm, dazzling smile that for just a moment made her completely forget everything, that she was standing outside on the side of the road, the snow coming down steadily now, despite the forecast calling for it to start later. "Of course. And if anyone honks me, I'll make sure their license plate appears in that online gossip column, the *Tenacity Tattler,* in a not-so-blind item about jerk drivers."

She actually managed to laugh. Oh, Diego. She got back in her car, feeling warm and safe—and not alone. She turned on her blinker and pulled out, driving super slow. Diego stayed a good two cars distance behind her. There were a few cars behind him too, and maybe it was the big pickup or the tall, strong cowboy who owned it, but no one dared honk at *him.*

It took an extra ten minutes to get home. She pulled in her driveway, again flooded with relief. She was home safe. Her own hero cowboy pulling in beside her.

But then she noticed the tree down and half blocking the road a few houses up the road Were those power lines dangling by it?

That panicky feeling returned, her chest tightening again, her shoulders bunching up.

She stepped out into the windy night, the snow whipping around. She carefully got Robbie and shielded her face.

Diego stepped from his pickup and hurried over, holding up his phone. The screen was dark. "I'd just sent a text to my mom that I followed a friend home out of caution so not to expect me for dinner, but it looks like the wind and the wet snow took out cell service right after. And judging from the dark houses," he added, looking across the street, "the power might be out too."

Chills ran up her spine and she sucked in a breath. "The good news is that I have a fireplace and a good amount of logs piled up. And a bunch of flashlights. The house is small enough that it'll warm up fast."

A low heavy branch of the big tree in the yard was swaying near the driveway. Jenna almost screamed.

"You two head inside," he said, glancing up at the tree, then back at her. "I'll take care of that branch. I have tools in my truck."

Jenna hurried the baby to the porch, got her key in the lock and opened the door. The power had clearly gone out recently because it was still warm inside. That was a relief, even if it was dark.

She got Robbie out of her snowsuit and cuddled her then went to the kitchen for a flashlight. She settled Robbie in her baby seat near the sofa while she lit a few candles on the mantel, the coffee table and in the kitchen. That was better. She scooped Robbie back up and moved to the window, watching as Diego carried some items from his truck over to the tree in the front yard near the driveway.

The snow, mixed with sleet, was coming down harder, the wind merciless. Diego had to be soaked, even in that down jacket and his cowboy hat. He had on a hard hat with a light in the center, a stepladder set up, and then used a big pair of clippers to take off the branch. A minute later, he was back, dripping wet on her doorstep, still in the hard hat.

"Hurry in," she said, shutting the door behind him.

He set the hard hat with the light shining on the narrow bench by the door, illuminating the small entryway and living room beyond.

She ran to the bathroom for a thick towel. As she watched him hang his hat on the coat rack and then use the towel on his face and wet hair, she suddenly envisioned him in the shower. Naked.

Whoa. What the heck?

She was going to have to accept that she was *very* attracted to Diego if she was picturing him naked in the middle of a snowstorm and power outage. Normally, she'd be fretting and pacing, despite her collection of flashlights and nonperishables and the fireplace.

He hung up the towel, then got out of his coat. He wore a dark green Henley shirt that showed off his broad shoulders, worn jeans and work boots.

At least she was more focused on him than on the storm. Not that it was doing all that much for her heart rate and stress. Could she actually be interested in another man? All signs said yes. Maybe this was how it happened. Every day pretty much like the last until you met someone who changed everything by just appearing.

She cleared her throat, trying to clear her head as well. "This is Robbie," she said, giving the baby a little bounce in her arms. "She'll be seven months tomorrow."

Valentine's Day.

She swallowed.

Tomorrow was Valentine's Day!

Their date. A very casual one, but still. She hadn't been thinking. Clearly, neither had he.

It's just take-out on the sofa, she reminded herself.

The warm smile Diego bestowed on the baby went straight to her heart. "Hi, sweetie. What a beauty you are." He covered his face with his hands, then opened them in a round of peekaboo. "Peekaboo, I see you!"

Robbie stared at him with those curious blue eyes and batted her hand toward him. "Ba! La!"

Jenna laughed. "She's been babbling for a couple of months now. I can't wait till she says *mama*!"

He smiled and very gently "shook" Robbie's hand with two fingers. "I'm Diego. It's very nice to meet you."

"You're good with babies!" The man might not be up for a relationship, according to Mike, but he was nice to kids. Duly noted.

"From visiting my soon-to-be baby nephew and little niece,"

he said. "My brother Julian's girlfriend is a single mom with a four-year-old daughter, Emery, and she's in the process of adopting an adorable baby named Jay. I've been helping Julian plan out a ranch on land he just bought, so I've gotten to spend a lot of time with them the past couple of weeks."

Jenna smiled. "I've definitely seen them around town and at the playground. Last summer and fall I took Robbie to the playground a lot even though she couldn't exactly leave her stroller. It's just nice to sit on the bench in the sun among the other families."

Except that it was hard to watch daddies lift up their children into the baby swings. Wait by the bottom of the slide for their toddler to come happily shrieking down.

The wind was gusting so loudly that they both looked toward the living room window, where the trees were swaying, the snow whipping fast and furious.

"Diego, I know the plan was for you to come over tomorrow night, but since you're here and it's so bad out, how about I make us dinner? I'd feel better knowing you weren't out there driving."

"Only if you let me help," he said.

"Deal." Goose bumps broke out on her arm. "Though without power, we'll have to stick with sandwiches. You can choose between slathering the bread with the peanut butter or the jelly."

He laughed. "I'll do the jelly."

She laughed too. "Do you mind holding Robbie while I get the fire going?"

Did he wince slightly or was she imagining that? The discomfort on his face was gone before she could study him closely. She'd gotten the sense he was used to holding baby Jay and was comfortable or she wouldn't have put him on the spot.

"Sure," he said, reaching his arms out.

Robbie went right to him, no fuss and she was often fussy about people she wasn't familiar with. Her blue eyes latched on to him so fiercely that he smiled.

"She likes me," he said, his dark eyes sparkling with surprise. *Who wouldn't?* she almost blurted out but thankfully didn't.

In a couple of hours, it would be Robbie's bedtime and then

it would be just the two of them. Having that almost-a-date a night early.

With a blazing fire, which she was now lighting in the fireplace. On the sofa with their peanut butter and jelly sandwiches, cozy and warm and safe from the storm.

And now, her nerves had less to do with the snow than the fact that she was on what felt very much like a date.

CHAPTER FIVE

THE MOMENT DIEGO had little Robbie in his arms he felt a surge of protectiveness he hadn't expected. Similar to what watching Jenna in the Tenacity Social Club had engendered in him. Seeing her sitting in her cold dark car in the parking lot. And standing outside next to her car on Central Avenue earlier. With the snow coming down.

But this was something else. Something more. Probably because Robbie was a baby. Most likely because he was *holding* the baby.

Yes, that had to be what this was about. When he'd held Ruby's baby Jay, when he'd picked up little Emery to show her the star on the family's Christmas tree, he'd been hit with: *If you ever need anything, Uncle Diego is there. Anything at all.* And they weren't even officially his niece and nephew yet.

He'd better not so much as hug Jenna for ten seconds because he'd be a goner.

"You mommy is good at lighting a fire," he said to Robbie as he watched the flames begin to roar to life. Then he wished he hadn't said that aloud. Jenna had lit something inside him—that was for sure.

He quickly started telling Robbie how his dad had taught him and his siblings to light a fire while they'd been camping far out on the ranch as children. Maybe Jenna wouldn't have taken what he'd said as an innuendo, anyway. He shouldn't be flirting with Jenna like that, not that he'd meant to. He had a great deal of respect for where she was right now, what she was going through.

Jenna turned and smiled, then gave the logs one last jab with the iron poker. She stood and walked over. "I'll take her."

He couldn't tell from her expression if he'd offended her. Maybe that meant he had.

He was about to make some awkward attempt at apology when she reached out her arms, but the second he'd handed the baby over he felt Robbie's absence and missed the sturdy little weight.

"Ready for a sandwich?" she asked him, giving the baby a kiss on top of her head. She smiled at him then, warmly. Relief unbunched his shoulders. She was letting the comment go. And so would he.

"Starving, actually." He grabbed the hard hat with the built-in light. "So we can see what we're doing." *So I can see your beautiful face*, he added silently.

She led the way to the kitchen, where she set Robbie down in her baby bouncer in the corner. Jenna gave Robbie a teething toy, which she began nibbling.

He set the hard hat on the counter and watched her take out the loaf of bread, the jars of peanut butter and strawberry jelly. He moved beside her as she set out two plates and two knives.

She placed two pieces of bread on each of their plates. "I like a lot of jelly, by the way."

"Me too," he said, and generously slathered both slices of the bread with jelly as she did the same with the peanut butter.

She laid both her pieces on top of his. "Voilà."

He cut both sandwiches in half, and took a bite. "Delicious. Never fails. Like french fries."

Jenna nodded and also took a bite. "Agree. I'm always surprised when pizza is bad. Like bad frozen pizza, I mean. It should always be good."

"Exactly," he said.

She looked too beautiful in the dimly lit kitchen. He could stand here and take in every bit of her, from her long silky red

hair to her blue eyes and lush lips. She had delicate features
and a sexy, lush figure. He had such an urge to take her in his
arms and kiss her.

"I have to keep the fridge closed just in case the power
doesn't come back on soon," she said, shaking him out of his
trance. "But I have a bottle of sparkling water in the pantry if
you'd like some."

"That sounds great."

She got out the bottle and poured two glasses.

He held up his glass. "To silver linings."

Surprise lit her eyes. "What's the silver lining here?"

"Bad storm. No power. But I'm exactly where I want to be.
Doing exactly what I want to be doing."

She smiled. "Eating peanut butter and jelly in the dark—
while standing at my kitchen counter?" Her smile faded a bit,
and she was barely looking at him.

She's afraid, he realized. *This is all new to her. Be gentle.*

"With you," he said. There it was. Yeah, he'd asked her out,
so she knew he was interested. But he'd made something very
clear just now. To both of them.

Prepare yourself to hear that she's not ready, he told himself. *It's likely what she's about to say.*

She bit her lip and looked at him, holding up her glass to his.

He realized he was holding his breath.

"To silver linings," she said, and clinked her glass with his.

He was so happily surprised that he wanted to step closer
and reach a hand to her face, that urge to touch her, to *kiss* her,
so strong.

But she took a sip of her water just then, her lips busy. He
sipped too. Then she carried her plate to the table and sat down,
so he did the same. There were four chairs at the round table
and he opted for one right next to her.

It's better that you don't make a move, he told himself. *Jenna
Lattimore isn't the typical woman you'd date. She's a widowed
mother. Tread very carefully here.*

"Robbie sure likes that teether," he said, eyeing the baby
gnawing away at the translucent green rubbery star.

"Loves it. Her first tooth is coming in. I'm so excited for her first word. I do hope it's *mama*, but I've heard some babies say all sorts of other words first, like *duck*."

"What was your first word?" he asked, then took a bite of his sandwich.

She smiled. "I actually know because my mother told me a few weeks ago when we were talking about exactly this. It was *dada*. She said her feelings were a little hurt." She laughed, but then stopped suddenly, her smile fading hard. "I guess that won't be Robbie's first word, though." She put her sandwich down and looked toward her lap, a sadness overtaking her face.

"Hey," he said gently. "Robbie's father is always going to be with her here." He tapped his chest in the region of his heart. "So it very well might be her first word. Don't get offended like your mom, though," he teased.

She brightened a bit and looked at him. "I hope you're right."

"I'm sure you tell Robbie about her daddy all the time," he said. "While you're feeding her, you probably mention her father loved applesauce or scrambled eggs. And while you're bundling her up in her cute little yellow snowsuit, you probably tell her that he loved the color yellow."

"He did," she said with a hint of smile. "It's why I chose that snowsuit."

He reached his hand over and gave hers a squeeze. "He's with her all the time because of you."

She burst into tears, which he hadn't been expecting. He got up and knelt down in front her.

"I'm sorry, Jenna. I shouldn't be saying anything." *Idiot*, he chastised himself. He had no business talking to a widowed mother about her late husband or her baby. Like he knew anything about what she was going through or feeling. Especially during a snowstorm.

She shook her head, wiping her eyes. She leaned toward him and wrapped her arms around him, resting her head on his shoulder.

He almost gasped at the intimacy of the gesture, the moment. Once again, he was holding his breath, unable to move a muscle.

"They're not sad tears," she said. "You said exactly the right thing. I'm just very touched and a little emotional."

He felt himself loosening just then and hugged her back, vaguely aware of the scent of her shampoo. He could stay like this for hours.

But unfortunately, she lifted her head and sat back in her chair. He stood and went back to his.

She cleared her throat, and he knew she too needed a moment. "Thank you, Diego."

"Of course," he said. "And thank you for dinner."

She glanced at him before taking a sip of her water. "You're so…good at this. I'm surprised you're not married with three kids."

"Good at what?" he asked, tilting his head—and having no idea what she was going to say.

"People. Knowing when someone needs a kind word, a tender look, a squeeze of the hand. A hug."

"My siblings would be looking at you like you were from another planet," he said with a smile. "My brothers especially."

"Well, I speak from personal experience."

A warmth spread inside him. "I appreciate that."

She took a bite of her sandwich. "I really am surprised you're single, Diego Sanchez. You're a serious catch."

He winced and hoped it wasn't too evident. "I don't know about that. I thought I was headed in that direction once. But things didn't work out."

"You proposed?"

"Didn't get that far," he said. "We dated for six months, but I wasn't what she was looking for, so…"

She was staring at him intently. "What was she looking for?"

He wasn't expecting that question. Nor did he want to answer it. She'd know he was the same guy he was back then. Living at his family home, doing the same job. Seven years later, nothing had changed. His ex had been right.

At twenty-six, he'd had the excuse of still being young. At thirty-three, he was proving his ex right. Her friends must see him around town and think, *Wow, at first we thought she was being snobby, but turns out she was right. Dodged a bullet there…*

Diego Sanchez had nothing much to offer a woman—especially a single mother of a baby—except maybe that compassion Jenna had been talking about moments ago. That and fifty cents...

Luckily, Robbie started fussing and he'd never been so happy to hear a sharp cry come out of a baby. Saved by the shriek. Robbie rubbed her eyes as her mom picked her up.

"Someone's ready for bed," Jenna said, patting her daughter's back and murmuring to her. "It's a little early but tired is tired. I guess I'll move her bassinet into the living room where it'll be warm all night."

"I'll go get it," he said, shooting up.

"Upstairs, second door on the left. And thanks."

He headed up. The nursery was a soft yellow with stenciled white stars and moons on the walls. On the dresser was a photo of Jenna with a good-looking man with light brown hair and blue eyes. In a suit. Not a cowboy. Or blue collar. He could tell the photo had captured them as they usually were, because Jenna wore jeans and a T-shirt, so they weren't at an event that required dressing up.

He let himself look at the photo for a while. A widow with a baby who'd been married to a successful man needed a different kind of guy than Diego. He'd known that before he saw the photo, but it was all the more reason to not date Jenna Lattimore. Not fall for her. Because if he did—and he could see that happening—she'd get realistic in a couple of months and tell him she had a child to think about, sorry.

He waited for the usual bitterness to settle in his gut but all he felt was...disappointment. Not in Jenna. In *himself.*

He sucked in a breath and then picked up the bassinet and its stand and carried them downstairs.

"You're my hero, Diego Sanchez," she said. "You've come to my aid quite a few times for someone I just met two days ago."

I wish I could be your hero, he thought, then froze for a second. He knew he liked Jenna. That he was very attracted to her. That he felt protective toward her and Robbie. But would he be ready to date a woman with a child anyway?

If he were thirty-three and not a cowboy on someone *else's* ranch, sure. He'd have something to give, a home, roots, a legacy.

Robbie brought up a little fist and rubbed her eyes again. He shook away his thoughts. He might not be their hero, but he could help while he was here.

"Where would you like this?" he asked.

"How about that corner," she said, pointing. "She'll stay warm but won't be too close to the flames. And I can keep an eye on her. I'm always happiest when I can see her little face, you know?"

"I'll bet," he said, taking the bassinet over to the corner.

"I'll go get her changed. Make yourself comfortable. Back in a few."

As she went up the stairs with a flashlight in one hand and Robbie against her other hip, he had to force himself not to stare at her.

He went to the kitchen and popped the last bite of his sandwich into his mouth, then brought the plates to the dishwasher. He put away the peanut butter and jelly and the bread and gave the counter a spritz with her lemon-scented cleaner. Then he brought their glasses to the coffee table and sat down, appreciating the extra warmth from the fire, his gaze going to the photos on her mantel. They were mostly of Robbie, one of Jenna hugely pregnant, and one with her, Robbie and her parents, he assumed, her mother holding the baby.

None of her husband. They were likely too hard to look at, to pass by every day and see him. Diego could understand why she'd keep the one in the nursery, though. That was for Robbie—a photo of her parents.

Diego took a sip of his sparkling water and walked over to the sliding glass doors, the snow coming down fast and furious. He focused on the awful weather to clear his head—until something occurred to him.

There was no way he could drive in this storm—the wind was creating whiteout conditions. And even if it had been the usual Montana snowstorm, he wouldn't want to leave Jenna and Robbie on their own. He wouldn't want a glance out the window to bring on her anxiety. And the lack of power would have him worried about her all night.

That he cared about her was clear. If he could just think of her as a friend... See her as a buddy...

A few minutes later, Jenna was back with Robbie in a pair of cowgirl pj's. She snuggled the baby, pressing a few kisses on her head, then laid her down.

Diego came over and pressed a kiss to his fingertips and then to Robbie's forehead. "Good night, little one. Sweet dreams."

Jenna smiled so warmly at him that his knees actually wobbled. He needed the sofa, pronto.

He sat down and picked up his glass, taking a long sip.

"Diego, I dared a peek outside when I was upstairs. There's no way you can drive home in that." Her gaze moved to the sliding glass doors, which were covered by plastered wet snow. "You can stay here."

He swallowed. He'd figured he wouldn't be going anywhere tonight, but her acknowledgment and the invitation was having some kind of crazy effect on him. He'd be staying at her place. "Are you sure you're comfortable with that?"

"I'm well aware that we hardly know each other," she said, "but I consider myself a pretty good judge of character, and you're a pretty wonderful guy."

He smiled. "Well, thank you. I always keep a go bag in my truck just in case—change of clothes, toiletries so at least I won't have to sleep in my jeans. Oh, and you can rest assured I'm not an axe murderer."

Jenna laughed. "The sofa is yours. I'll take the love seat, since I often curl up on it anyway. Sometimes it's hard to sleep in my bed." Her voice was practically a whisper on that last part. She picked up her glass. "And sometimes I overshare." She sighed, then looked at him. "Actually that's not true. It's just with you that I seem to say stuff I'd normally keep to myself."

"Ditto. You're very easy to talk to, Jenna Lattimore."

She glanced up at him with those beautiful blue eyes and smiled.

Diego couldn't take *his* eyes off her.

And he was spending the night. In the same room.

JENNA FELT SO safe and cared for and supported that she barely noticed the snow whipping around out the windows. Granted, it was dark and there were no outside lights to illuminate the rough weather. But she knew a storm was raging, and it wasn't getting to her the way it normally would.

Because of Diego Sanchez. The man sitting on her sofa.

Even the littlest thing, such as discovering he'd cleared the table and put the plates and knives in the dishwasher, had touched her. And how he'd pressed a kiss to her baby's forehead and wished Robbie sweet dreams.

The man had even clipped a perilous branch in her front yard so it wouldn't land on her car—or her and Robbie while they were in the driveway.

When she was a teenager in Bronco, making a list with her best friend about what they wanted in a boyfriend, *a good heart* had topped Jenna's. Her friend's top line was *cute*, followed by *sweet*. She'd married a very cute, very sweet guy, so all had worked out there. Even if Diego wasn't so attractive, that big heart of his would make him gorgeous to Jenna. And minute by minute, he'd shown her just what a caring person he was.

An hour after she'd put Robbie to bed in the bassinet, the baby had let out a cry in her sleep, and Diego had practically jumped. *Is she okay? Does she need something?*

He *cared*. That was who he was.

And he was so darn good-looking. That face. Once she was looking at him it was very hard to look away. Those dark, dark eyes and long lashes. The short dark hair. And his body. She mentally fanned herself. Tall and muscular with lean hips and broad shoulders. The way his Henley skimmed his chest. More than once she'd found her gaze going to his bronze belt buckle, a cowboy silhouetted on a horse. She really hoped he hadn't noticed.

Even the thought that he might have made her cheeks burn. She was mentally fanning herself again.

Yes, she liked Diego Sanchez. She just had to accept it. Last Christmas, her mom had told her that one of her wishes for Jenna was that one day, she'd find someone very special, someone who'd make a great father figure for Robbie. When

Jenna got back home after spending the holiday in Bronco with her parents, she'd told Mike what her mom said and how surprised Jenna was that she hadn't immediately discounted it. That maybe in a couple of years, she *would* be ready to date again, find that person. Mike had said it was definitely a sign that she was ready, maybe even sooner than she thought. *That* Jenna had discounted. Finding a guy as wonderful as Rob had been? Come on. She'd gotten very lucky the first time around.

But quite possibly, here that special guy was. Early.

And Jenna wanted to know more about him. Personal things.

She took a sip of her water and tried to adopt a casual expression. Like she was just making conversation. They were at opposite ends of the three-seater sofa, facing each other, Jenna's legs tucked up beneath her, Diego's right foot across his left knee. A good distance—not too close, but just close enough. "I guess we're having that date a day early," she said as an opener. Going right for it.

He shook his head. "Nope. The plans for our date included me bringing dinner over and watching a funny show or movie. Spreading jelly on sandwiches doesn't count as bringing you dinner—or making it. And no power means no TV. So..."

So...they were still on for tomorrow night. She had to try very hard to keep a smile from breaking out on her face. She didn't want to seem *that* excited.

But as she looked at him, she thought she saw his expression change for a moment, as though he was thinking hard about something. Second-guessing himself, maybe. Diego was such an upstanding guy that she could see him sticking to their plan for tomorrow even though they were not only having the date impromptu right now—but that it had gotten surprisingly intimate.

The conversation in the kitchen. The hug. How she'd leaned her head on his shoulder.

A chill skittered up her spine—and she recognized it as plain old fear. She was scared of what she was feeling for this man. It might just be interest and attraction and appreciation and red-hot desire, but this wasn't just some crush on a nice and handsome guy who'd done her a solid. A few solids. She was really starting to like Diego. A lot.

Just ask him what you want to know, she told herself.

"So you know that this is my first foray into dating in a very long time," she said. "Since I was nineteen and I'm now twenty-eight. But what about you? When was your last relationship?"

His expression *definitely* changed this time. Impossible to miss. "A long time ago too. I date, but I don't get serious about anyone." Did he pointedly look at her on that last word? Seemed so. It had been *so* long since she'd dated that she was reading into every little thing, trying to get a handle on her emotions. Feel in control.

But that was just it about dating. And romance. And love. No one was in control. The heart was.

Tonight, the weather was.

Her heart deflated a little and she forced herself to not look toward the windows or sliding glass door, which was completely covered by snow.

She remembered something her father had said over Christmas. *You might never feel ready, sweetie. But your heart will know otherwise and gently nudge you toward letting someone in.*

Right now, because of that comment *I don't get serious about anyone*, her heart was telling her *not* to let this man in. Not to fall for him.

Because when you loved, you lost.

It was hard enough to risk loving *anyone* again. But a man who was telling her he didn't, wouldn't, couldn't commit?

That was a blinking neon warning sign. The red flag of red flags.

Dammit.

She thought about all Mike had told her—and grabbed her glass to chug down some sparkling water.

Pay attention to what he says, Jenna. And heed it.

Except he wasn't saying anything. He seemed a little uncomfortable, and now she felt bad about asking. He'd gotten hurt, that much she knew. He'd said he wasn't what his ex had wanted.

"I'm sorry, Diego. I didn't mean to put you on the spot."

"It's okay. Really." But she had a feeling he was just saying that to let her off the hook. He looked down for a minute.

"I mentioned things didn't end well with my last relationship. I was hoping you wouldn't ask about it because I didn't want you to know the truth. But I think it's better that you *do* know."

She sat up a little straighter, intensely curious. "Why?"

"Because we're not a match, Jenna. It's obvious that I'm interested in you—I asked you out, after all. And I'm very attracted to you. But I'm not the guy for you." She felt everything else inside her deflate. She was about to question him when he added, "Can I ask a personal question?"

That was unexpected. "I'm not sure about answering, but you can certainly ask."

"What did your husband do for a living?"

Huh. She wondered why he wanted to know. "Rob was a real estate agent. He loved his job and was good at it."

Diego was nodding slowly.

"Why did you want to know?" she asked.

"It has to do with why I'm not the man for you. And never will be."

She let out a little gasp; she couldn't help it. Never will be? "How? I mean, in what way?"

"I noticed the photo of Rob in the nursery. He was wearing a suit."

She nodded. "Every day. Usually men complain about wearing suits, but he loved putting on a tie every morning."

Again with the slow nodding. "My last serious girlfriend—seven years ago—broke up with me because she didn't think I'd amount to anything. Back then, I was living in the family home, working as a cowboy on the ranch where my parents have been renting a house for years. She said I'd never own my own ranch, that I'd always be just a cowboy."

Just a cowboy? Jenna was still trying to figure out where he was going with the comment about the suit, but the *just* echoed in her head. "What on earth is wrong with being a cowboy? First of all, it's hard work, honest work, and requires brains and brawn in equal measure. And, yeah, I'll say it—there's something about a man in a cowboy hat. On horseback." She smiled, hoping to add a little levity since his expression had gotten so...serious.

"She was right, though. About me. I *still* live in my family home. The same bedroom I had growing up—and I have a roommate, my brother Luca. Like old times. And I'm still just a cowboy, doing the same job I was seven years ago."

Just a cowboy, she thought again, shaking her head. "And?" she asked. "Why shouldn't you be?"

He glanced at her, then leaned his head back against the sofa cushion. "My brother Julian bought land here in Tenacity last month. He's going to get his own ranch up and going. My parents are so proud of him. *I'm* so proud of him."

"That's great for him," she said. "Is that *your* dream? To have your own ranch?"

He shook his head. "No. My dream has always been to be a cowboy, actually. From the time I was four, five years old. I wanted to be just like my dad. I work alongside him." He brightened just a bit. "I've loved that. My father and I have gotten so close over the years."

"That is really wonderful, Diego. And it sounds to me like you're doing exactly what you want to be doing."

"It's not enough, though," he said.

She tilted her head. "For who?"

"For any woman who'd get serious about me. And why would any woman? What can I offer? Yeah, I work hard, I have some money in the bank, but..." He trailed off and leaned forward, running a hand over his face, through his hair. "Take you, for instance. I have no business being on a date with you. A widow with a baby to raise. You need—" He let out a breath and stopped talking.

"A man in a suit?" she offered. Now she understood why he'd brought up what Rob had done for a living. He'd seen the photo in the nursery. Rob in his suit, arm slung around Jenna.

"Yes, exactly. I might work hard and put money away every month, but I also help my parents. And I'll be helping Julian get his ranch off the ground. I'm just a cowboy on a middling ranch, like my ex said seven years ago. What do I have to offer a family? Nothing."

She felt her mouth drop open. "Diego, I didn't fall in love with Rob because of a suit or a job. I fell in love with him when

I was nineteen because he was a very good person. Kind, caring, funny. When it rained when we were in college, he'd hold his textbooks over my head. He made me tea when I got colds. He'd go for a morning run and come back with my favorite muffins. He was so happy when I told him I was pregnant, so excited. He was a good man, Diego, and he showed me he loved me every day. I'll choose that over a fancy car any day."

He seemed to be taking all that in. "But you've got a baby to think about, Jenna. You can't date someone who can't provide for the two of you."

She bit her lip. She had an aunt who liked to rattle off that old saying: *It's just as easy to fall in love with a rich man as a poor one.* First of all, Jenna wouldn't know. And yeah, if Diego, the only man she'd been interested in since she'd lost Rob, were rich, that would make life easy. But that lullaby-playing new bouncer she coveted but couldn't afford wasn't a necessity; she had a basic one that Robbie liked fine. And her house might be small, but it had a solid roof and good foundation and everything she needed. Diego got by just like she did and that was how it was. That was absolutely fine with her.

But this was all beside the point because it wasn't like she was planning a future with the man.

A future. Rob Lattimore's face came to mind. She felt a burst of sadness. Rob had considered this house a "starter home" and had said, *One day, we'll have our forever home but* we're *forever, so all's good.*

Oh, Rob.

She wondered what he'd want for her. To not even think about dating for a good five years? Ten?

No. That didn't sound right.

What she did know was that Rob had loved her and had always prioritized her happiness, which had come easy with him by her side.

If I met someone who seemed special, who actually captured my interest, who was sweet and attentive to Robbie, Rob would smile down on me.

He would, she knew. But she was getting way ahead of herself.

And she should be setting Diego Sanchez straight right now, anyway about the person she was.

"I'll always prioritize love and character and kindness over money, over dinner out and a big house. That's what I care about."

She could hear his silent rebuttal. *What you care about and what you need are two different things. And because I care about you, I'm stepping out.*

Not literally, thank heavens. Into the snowstorm.

That she wouldn't be able to handle. And she also knew that because he *was* so caring, he'd never leave her in the middle of a whiteout storm to worry over him getting home safely.

He'd stick it out on the sofa as planned.

"Waah!"

Again Diego practically jumped at Robbie's sudden cry, concern on his handsome face as he looked toward the bassinet in the corner of the room. "Is she okay? What's wrong?"

"She's a baby, that's what." Jenna smiled and extended her hand to him, surprising herself. Given that Mike's worry about him as someone who wouldn't commit was now proven true from Diego himself, she shouldn't be touching him, which would only make her feel closer to him.

He looked at her in confusion, but took her hand and stood. She led him to the bassinet and gave his hand a squeeze then let go, though she sure had liked how it had felt for those ten seconds.

Robbie was fussing, moving her head, scrunching up her face, kicking her little legs. *"Waah!"*

"I've got you, sweet stuff," she cooed, picking up her daughter and bringing her vertically against her chest as she rubbed Robbie's back. "She's started to sleep through the night last month, but she still wakes up occasionally. Sometimes she goes right back to sleep and other times she needs a little soothing."

Diego nodded and took a step back. He looked out the window at the whipping snow, probably wishing he could leave. Get away from all this intimacy. From the "needy" widowed mother and baby.

But he was stuck here.

Jenna might not have two nickels to rub together, but she did have a voice. And she was going to try to make Diego Sanchez see that he had so much to offer. Himself.

CHAPTER SIX

ONCE AGAIN, SAVED by the baby. At least that hard conversation had come to a halt. Robbie had gone back to sleep in five minutes and Diego was relieved when Jenna asked him if he wanted a room-temperature cranberry juice from the pantry. And chocolate chip cookies.

He said yes to both, glad coffee wasn't an option. Staying awake all night from a caffeine infusion was a no-go. He'd be mere feet away from Jenna, watching her sleep, itching to push back strands of her red hair from her face, add another blanket to make sure she was warm enough.

And he'd be checking on the baby every ten minutes.

He'd be a wreck come morning and he had to work tomorrow. A whiteout snowstorm might keep him off the roads for several hours, but when the sun rose, he'd need to head out.

They sat at the kitchen table again, both drinking their cranberry juice, a plate of cookies between them. He took one. Home-baked and delicious.

"My uncle Stanley makes amazing chocolate chip cookies. You'll have to try them some time."

She smiled at that. "I think I know who your uncle is. I saw a couple walking down Central Avenue a couple of weeks ago. Both elderly. The woman wore a purple parka down to her ankles with silver fur on the hood. She was arm in arm with a tall man. I heard a few people calling out hellos to them by name. Stanley and Winona."

Diego laughed. "Yup, that was definitely them. Winona's in her nineties. And they're newlyweds."

Jenna's mouth dropped open, her eyes twinkling. "Really?"

"Yup. Stanley was widowed a few years ago—married sixty years. And Winona had gone through some very tough times. But they met and that was that."

That wasn't that, since they'd both been through hell and back to walk down the aisle. But they'd done it.

"Sometimes, at a family dinner or the other night at the wedding and after-party," Diego said, "I look at them and think anything's possible. A second chance at love when you're eightysomething and ninetysomething."

"So Winona's an older woman?" Jenna asked. She pressed a hand to her heart. "I'm very happy for them. Second chances at love *are* possible, no matter what the prior circumstance. I definitely believe it."

"You're ready to jump in, whole hog?" he asked.

She sipped her tea. "I don't know. I'm ready to stick a *toe* in. It's why I said yes to you."

And here he was, closing a door. Idiot. Jerk. After what she'd been through, after saying yes to even a casual date when it must have been hard, *he'd* said he didn't get serious about women he dated.

But he was a jerk for good reason. It was a fact that he had nothing to offer. Most especially to a widowed mom. A woman who claimed not to care about a man's bank account. And he believed her. But he still wouldn't saddle her with himself. She had a baby to raise. She had to be practical.

They barely knew each other, even if it felt like he'd known her forever. They could go their separate ways in the morning, be friends. He wanted to be there for her, even if she wasn't someone he could date.

Stab to the heart—and twisting.

"Want to play cards by hard hat lamp?" she asked on a laugh. "Crazy Eights? Rummy? Or maybe Scrabble? I know, real exciting. But I do love Scrabble." She looked at him with those warm blue eyes, and it was so hard not to stare at her. Jenna was so beautiful. She'd changed the subject, suggesting something lighthearted to do because she'd clearly seen his expression change.

"I'm terrible at Scrabble," he admitted. "Well, I'm terrible at *spelling*."

Jenna laughed. "Crazy Eights, it is."

"You'll have to remind me how to play. It's been a long time since I've played cards. Like twenty years, maybe."

She faux punched him on the arm. "Lucky for you, I know the rules."

For the next forty-five minutes, they ate cookies and played Crazy Eights, and Diego had to force himself not to lean over and touch her, her face or her hair or even her hand. He wanted to kiss her so badly it physically hurt.

Keep off, he told himself as she dealt the next round of cards.

To take his mind off her pretty face and how her long pink sweater skimmed over her body, her full breasts making him swallow, he glanced at the snow-plastered window, hoping the storm really would stop by 3:00 a.m., as forecasted. Tenacity had a few municipal trucks with snowplows for the roads, but most folks, like Jenna, hired cowboys with pickups rigged with snowplows to clear their driveways before sunrise. He'd be able to get home, to work. He'd never wanted to leave somewhere and stay so badly at the same time.

Diego suddenly realized Jenna was watching him and quickly looked from the window down at the cards in his hand. He could have kicked himself. She didn't need to be reminded of the storm.

"Diego," she said, then clamped her mouth shut.

He looked at her and waited.

She seemed a little shy all of a sudden. "I don't think you know what you've done for me tonight. For the past few hours, I normally would have been a wreck. And this time, because of the whiteout, I wouldn't have been able to get Robbie to Mike so that I could tremble for twenty minutes solo in my car and work it out." She reached a hand to his forearm. "Because of you, I wasn't as affected. I know the storm's out there, but I felt...protected somehow."

He put his cards down and laid his hand atop hers on his arm. He couldn't take his eyes off her if he wanted to.

She leaned forward. So he leaned forward.

She tilted her head left. He tilted right.

And they both leaned forward some more—until their lips met.

Fireworks. Parade. Magic.

Diego had not been expecting that kind of intense reaction to a simple, short kiss, but maybe he should have. From the moment he'd laid eyes on Jenna Lattimore, he'd been affected by her.

The kiss lasted all of three seconds. When he opened his eyes, hers were still closed.

"I'm glad that happened," she whispered, looking at him now.

"Me too," he said. "Because I couldn't stop thinking about it. Now I can—" He shut up fast, glad he didn't blurt out what he'd been about to say.

She winced and sat up straight. "Now you can...stop thinking about it because you got it out of your system?"

She sounded hurt. Dammit.

"I... What I said before... I'm not the man for you, Jenna. You and Robbie need someone who can give you the world."

She seemed about to say something, then stopped and got up. She collected the plates and put the two cups on top, then brought them over to the sink. Normally he'd jump up to help, but his entire body felt like a lead weight.

This was complicated. As the saying went, the silence was deafening.

She was loading the dishwasher. She wouldn't be able to run it, but it got the dishes out the way. He tried to make himself useful by gathering the cards and sliding them into the box.

"Jenna, I..." he began, standing up. But she didn't turn around and he sat back down.

Dammit. He didn't even know what he was going to say. He'd screwed up here.

Because Jenna didn't need a man to hurt her feelings or

dangle something in front of her, like the date, and then snatch away any promise from it. He felt terrible.

If she dragged him to the door and literally kicked him out with a sharp kick, he'd understand.

"I'll, uh, go get our blankets and pillows," she said, then practically ran down the hall.

How was he going to fix this when there *was* no fix?

JENNA SHUT HER bedroom door behind her, hit with the chill of the cold air. When she'd first gotten home, she'd closed all the doors, except the bathroom, to reserve the heat from the fireplace. The cold felt good, though. Right now she needed the opposite of a warm hug. She needed reality.

She sucked in a breath, then sat down on her bed, grabbing a throw pillow and holding it against her belly. Reality was exactly what Diego had been saying tonight. *Not the man for you.*

She knew she'd been right about what he'd been about to say—or thinking. *Can stop thinking about kissing you... Got it out of my system...*

Nothing she particularly wanted to hear, but right now, she was focused on the kiss itself.

She'd *kissed* someone.

Another man.

For the first time since she was nineteen.

She'd kissed Diego Sanchez—and she'd liked it.

For a man who'd decided that he couldn't date her because she supposedly needed things he couldn't give her, *he'd* kissed her too. And sorry, Diego, but she wasn't buying what he'd said about being able to stop thinking about it now.

It was a short, sweet kiss, but there was nothing platonic about it. It was no peck on the lips. There was attraction and interest and desire and excitement in everything about the meeting of their lips. That was what the kiss had been about. And Diego had been right there.

There was no taking away that kiss. No backtracking. She knew it. And he did too.

You didn't get someone out of your system by kissing them.

That was how you got them *embedded*, actually. One kiss would only make a person want more.

She smiled, but it faded fast. Because she was scared. Excited but scared. No matter what else was going on, Jenna had done something brand-new and brave—she'd accepted a date, she'd kissed a man. She needed to focus on that. Forward motion.

She stood up and went to the mirror above her dresser and leaned forward to peer at her lips. They looked different. *She* looked different.

She looked *hopeful*. Yes, that was how she'd describe her expression, her eyes. Hopeful. That she could do this. That she could be interested in and attracted to another man. That she could go for it.

She could hear Mike Cooper now. *Jenna, he told you he's not the man for you. He told you he has nothing to offer you. Believe him!*

Oh yeah. She knew that was exactly what Mike would say.

The problem was, she didn't want to kiss anyone but Diego.

Oh boy. Diego was probably wondering if she was okay in the cold bedroom, why she was taking so long. She got up and grabbed two down comforters from the top of her closet and two pillows. She went to the door but with her full arms she couldn't open it.

"Hello? Diego?"

She barely got his name out before the door opened, Diego standing there, concern in his dark eyes. He'd probably had his ear against the door, listening for any tearful sounds, worried about her state of mind.

"Are you okay? What happened?" he asked, peering at her.

Oh, Diego. Stop being so there for me.

No, actually don't stop.

"I just couldn't open the door cuz of this," she said, lifting the armload.

He looked at her. She looked at him. Their gazes were locked. There were so many emotions in his eyes, all warring.

If she weren't holding the comforters and pillows, they'd kiss again and she knew it.

"Oh. Here, let me help," he said, taking everything from her.

He turned and headed to the living room. He set the stack on the coffee table while she got two sheets from the linen closet and covered the cushions of the sofa and love seat, then spread a comforter on each and set a pillow at one end.

Jenna smoothed the comforter on the sofa, imagining Diego lying naked under it, not that he'd be naked in her house, for Pete's sake. She wondered what it would feel like to lie with him, snuggled up, spooning, keeping warm, trading body heat.

Kissing more.

His hands on her face, in her hair, on her body…

Okay, she was getting way ahead of herself. For a three-second kiss, it had sure been potent.

"Jenna, I—" he began, sounding hesitant. And worried. Like about whether he'd hurt her feelings.

"It's okay," she said. "We need to be honest with each other. I'd rather hear how you really feel than some sweet words you don't mean. Or worse, now that I think about it, you not saying anything at all."

He studied her for a moment, then finally nodded. "Can I do anything? Check anything? The fire's burning bright."

They both turned to it, the orange flames leaping, the occasional soothing crackle. The living room was warm. Silver lining to a small house.

"I think we're all set. Robbie is fast asleep." She walked over to the bassinet and put the back of her hand to the baby's cheek. Her soft skin wasn't cold at all. She looked at her daughter in her fleece pj's and light cap, her heart overflowing.

Diego was suddenly beside her, looking down at the sleeping baby. "Hope you're having sweet dreams, Robbie."

Jenna smiled at him, wishing she could take his hand and just hold it. Lean her head on his broad shoulder.

But she didn't want to scare the man down the hall and into one of the cold rooms to get away from her and her lips.

She let out an unexpected yawn and realized she was bone-tired.

"I second that," he said. "Long day, long night."

"Thank you for everything, Diego. No matter what, please know that."

No matter what. Even she wasn't sure what exactly she'd meant by that.

He gave her something of a smile, then said, "I'll just go change." He grabbed the go bag he'd braved the storm to get from his pickup a little while ago and disappeared into the bathroom.

He returned five minutes later wearing a long-sleeved T-shirt with *Bronco Summer Family Rodeo* across the front and navy sweats.

Jenna smiled. "I used to go to that every year. I grew up in Bronco. What's your connection?"

"I have family there, an aunt and uncle and cousins. Stanley and Winona split their time between Tenacity and Bronco. Bronco is where they met."

"Small world," she said. "I left Bronco officially right after college when Rob and I moved here. But every summer we went back for the rodeo."

"Maybe we can go this summer," he said, then kind of froze.

She almost smiled. The man was truly in a fight with himself. Saying things he meant but that didn't support his case that they weren't going to be a couple. Yeah, they could go as friends. But...

Summer was the *future*.

"Maybe," she said, giving him the easy out.

He gave her a tight smile and went to the sofa and stretched out. She tried not to stare. He settled the comforter over himself, which helped since she couldn't see his hot body.

Jenna took a last look at Robbie, sleeping peacefully, then curled up on the love seat and pulled the comforter over herself.

This was one of those times that Jenna wished she could go into her bedroom with her cell phone and call her best friend, Mike, or her mom.

She'd kissed someone.

And God help her, she'd *really* liked it.

She must have dozed off because the next thing she knew, she was opening her eyes and felt cold. The comforter was half on the floor. Before she could even move to get it, Diego was lifting the comforter and putting it over her.

He almost jumped when he realized she was awake.

"Something woke me up and I saw that you weren't covered," he said, then visibly swallowed, his eyes locked on hers. He tucked her in, smoothing the overturned top of the comforter. "You can't be comfortable on this love seat. It's too short for a kid, let alone an adult stretching out. I'll switch with you."

She smiled. "Diego, you just said…" She shook her head. He'd twist himself into a pretzel just so she could be comfortable. Without thinking she said, "The sofa is plenty big. We could share. I'm a side sleeper anyway, and you could sack out on your back. We'll conserve body heat."

"Are you sure? I'll be a perfect gentleman, of course."

She suddenly realized what she'd offered, and now it was her turn to swallow. It was one thing to kiss—and a short kiss at that. To imagine his hands roaming all over her. It was another to suddenly be lying on a sofa with him—under a comforter. There was no way their bodies *wouldn't* touch.

That might be just a little too much for her. A little too fast. Spending the night was big in itself.

You must be ready, though, she thought. *To take these steps. After all, you made the offer.*

He'd find an excuse and move to the love seat, she told herself.

Except he wasn't saying anything. He was just looking at her. With warmth in his eyes. And…something else. Something that didn't scare her. In fact, it had the opposite effect.

You are changing before your eyes, she realized. Huh.

"I'm sure," she said.

"Then I am too." He still didn't move, though. Maybe *he* was scared. Of getting that close physically. They'd spent the evening developing quite an emotional connection. Opening up. Sharing. Kissing.

She moved to the sofa and lifted the comforter to welcome him.

CHAPTER SEVEN

DIEGO WOKE UP to the sound of snowplows. The room was dark, but it was comfortably warm despite the fire having gone out at some point in the wee hours. The power must have come back on. He'd get up and go look out the window to see if lights were on in nearby houses, but there was no way he was moving.

Jenna was sleeping on her side facing him, a swath of red hair in her face.

God, she was exquisite. He moved the hair, carefully, trying not to wake her.

"Morning," she whispered, opening her eyes.

Diego usually woke up every morning to a rooster or two crowing and his brother Luca doing push-ups, clapping between them, next to his bed on the other side of the room.

This was much, much better.

"Morning," he said. "Power's back."

"Oh, good! Is that why I'm not freezing?" She eyed the fireplace, just embers.

"Yup. Snowplows are out on the streets. Can't mistake that sound."

Which meant he'd be able to leave soon, within an hour.

He wasn't getting up so fast, though. He liked where he was. And the view of Jenna's lovely face.

He was also rock-hard and if he even turned slightly, she'd

feel his erection brush against her. That would not fall under being a perfect gentleman.

And he'd been one all night.

Last night, once she'd lifted the comforter and he'd slipped in beside her, on his back, she'd settled her head on his chest.

"That okay?" she'd whispered.

No, he'd thought. *Not okay. Because something is happening under your head. In the region of my heart.*

You just care about her, he'd reminded himself. *You feel protective. She's a widow with a baby. Her family is over an hour away. And yeah, she has her best friend, Mike, but he's got two jobs and is guardian to his nephew while his sister is away.*

She could use another good friend, he'd thought.

That he could be to Jenna. A friend just needed to be there. To step up. He could and would do that.

Except the word *friend* didn't sound right to him, though. Not where Jenna Lattimore was concerned.

Because he wanted more.

"Of course," he'd whispered back, barely able to speak, as her head snuggled against him, her silky hair trailing on his arm.

Within a few minutes, she was asleep.

Whereas Diego had been wide awake, lying there stock-still. Trying to normalize his heart rate.

It had taken him a while to drift off.

And now, this morning, lying face-to-face… He wanted her so *bad that he was going to have to move anyway.*

"Waah! Waah!"

Bless you, Robbie, he thought. Saved by the baby yet again. He owed that little girl.

"I'll go to her," he said, slowly shifting.

"Really?"

He turned to her and nodded. "I'm closer."

He got up and walked over to the bassinet, eyeing the little squirming creature, giving her legs and arms some pumps. She sure wanted out of bed.

"She's seven months today!" Jenna said excitedly, sitting up.

He reached in and carefully picked her up, her big blue eyes locked on his face. He instinctively took off her cap and tossed it on the coffee table. She didn't need it now that the heat was back on. "Happy seven months on earth," he said.

"She's staring so hard at you!" Jenna said on a laugh. "She must like your face."

"Do you?" he asked Robbie, leaning his face closer to her.

She promptly grabbed his nose, then let go and went for his ear.

"That's a good grip," he said. "She might be a champion bull rider one day."

"Oh God, don't say that. Even kidding!"

He laughed. "Sorry."

She got up and came over, standing beside him as she reached up on tiptoe to give Robbie a kiss. "Morning, sunshine. Let's get you out of your fleece pj's finally." She smothered the baby's forehead in kisses.

This is what family life would be like, he suddenly realized. Waking up with a woman you treasured, kissing your baby's forehead, changing her into fresh clothes. Making breakfast. Shoveling the porch and steps. Having coffee.

Nice. Very nice. He understood, just last night, why his brother Julian found it all irresistible.

But Julian had a plan and now he had land, Diego thought. And he shared a room with his younger brother in the rented family house he'd lived in his whole life.

"I'll go give her a bath," Jenna said. "Feel free to make coffee."

As she headed into the bathroom with Robbie, he went into the kitchen and got the coffee going, then went to the front door and opened it. The storm door was still coated with stuck-on snow. He pushed it open and looked around. The sun wasn't up yet, but it was nice to see lights back on in houses and streetlamps. Five, maybe six inches of wet, clumpy snow was on the ground and in the trees, but the winds had managed to really whip it around. A plow truck headed up the street for another pass. And next door, a pickup with a plow had just cleared that driveway and was now pulling into Jenna's.

He breathed a sigh of relief. He'd leave. He'd wait till Jenna came back, of course. Say a proper goodbye to her and Robbie.

For good? he wondered, but the fact that it was a question told him that was a big no.

He poured a cup of coffee and rooted around the fridge for the cream, which he figured was fine since they hadn't opened the door since the power went out. He took a long drink, then checked his phone. A few texts from his siblings from this morning, checking in that he'd fared okay with the storm. One from his sister Nina:

Happy Valentine's Day. I'll want deets on tonight's date!

He froze.

Valentine's Day.

Date.

Given the storm and all that happened last night, he'd forgotten all about it. Not the date, but the significance of the day.

The bathroom door opened, and Jenna emerged with Robbie wrapped in a pink towel with cat ears. She stood in the kitchen doorway, giving the air a sniff.

"You did make coffee—thanks," she said. "I could sure use a cup."

Diego took out another mug and poured for her.

"Will you hold this cutie while I fix my coffee?" she asked.

The lump in his throat settled in his stomach. "Uh, sure." She passed over Robbie, who smelled like baby shampoo. Robbie's arms were covered by the towel so she couldn't grab his ear this time.

Jenna added cream and a sugar packet to her coffee, then took a sip. "Ah," she said. "Hits the spot."

"It's Valentine's Day," he said—as if he were in a trance.

She tilted her head, then her expression became what he could only describe as wistful. "I'd actually forgotten all about that—more like I blocked it."

"I can understand that," he said. She'd been with her husband for almost ten years. That was a lot of Valentine's Days to celebrate their love.

"When you and I talked about Thursday," she said, "I didn't realize… But then yesterday, I got a huge reminder at work."

She smiled as if recalling something sweet. "When you work in a daycare center, the love holiday is big. So yesterday, I was helping the kiddos make cards for one another and their families and the staff. Lots of hearts and stickers and glitter."

Diego hadn't celebrated Valentine's Day in seven years. His mom had a tradition of making a giant heart-shaped chocolate chip cookie for the family, and Diego always enjoyed his share. But otherwise, he spent Valentine's night catching up on TV.

"That sounds really nice," he said. "I can see the kids now— glitter on their noses, stickers on their fingers. So proud of their sweet cards."

She smiled. "They're all so great, from the toddlers to the school-aged kids that it took me out of my head. But then I got a flash of memory and—" She wrapped her hands around the mug and looked away for a second. "It's my second Valentine's Day as a widow, but I still got sad yesterday while we were working on Valentines. I went to the infant room and held Robbie close and told her that we're each other's Valentine, and I felt okay. Happy even. Plus the fact that she's a *fourteenth* baby takes precedence anyway."

As if Robbie knew her mom was talking about her, a little arm shot out from under the towel and grabbed his nose.

I always did say you had great timing, Robbie. Letting me know while my knees are kinda shaky that I'd better get over myself and give both you and your mommy a special Valentine's Day.

He wanted to do something for her. Why not stick to their plans, even if they'd basically done just that last night? "Hey, what about our date? I was thinking of bringing over a pizza from Pete's Pizza. Or maybe Mexican from Castillo's. I love that place. Their steak fajitas—so good."

She didn't say anything. She wasn't looking at him, either. Or Robbie. She seemed a bit lost in thought. She put her mug down on the counter and held out her arms to take the baby. He handed Robbie over and she snuggled her daughter against her, resting her head atop the cat ears.

She still didn't respond.

"Or not," he said fast, feeling his cheeks burning. "We can

play it by ear. If you're up for company again, great. If not, that's fine. I haven't had Valentine's Day plans in seven years so..."

She bit her lip. "Oh Diego. I'd give you a great big hug right now if my arms weren't full."

"Probably better that you don't," he said with too much emotion in his voice. He stood there, unable to take his eyes off her. "I could give you a ride to work."

"Oh, that's okay, but thanks. I'm not due in until noon today. The roads will be perfectly clear by then."

He held her gaze for a moment, then drained the rest of his coffee. "I'd better get going." He glanced out the window, still dark. "Cowboy hours—crack of dawn."

She walked over to him and took his hand with her free one. "Thank you, Diego. From the bottom of my heart. For everything."

That sounded like goodbye. Which was good, right? He'd told her, after *kissing* her, that he wasn't the man for her. She *should* be saying goodbye, not spending Valentine's Day with him.

He felt like hell. "Anytime," he said, his voice sounding off to him. He ran a finger down the baby's soft cheek. "Happy seven-month birthday," he said to her, then gave Jenna one last smile.

Diego grabbed his bag, got his coat and boots on, and headed out. He shoveled her porch and steps and the path to the driveway, then cleaned off both their vehicles.

Once he was in his pickup, he let out one hell of a breath and started the ignition. But it took him a good few minutes to actually leave, drive off.

He missed Jenna and Robbie the moment he'd walked out the front door.

This couldn't be goodbye.

MIKE INSISTED ON picking up Jenna at 11:45 a.m. and driving her to work—not because of the roads, which were all clear now. But because when he'd called to check in with her this morning to see how she'd fared in the storm, she'd told him she'd had company throughout the entire thing. Very good-looking, sexy company. She'd told him all about their night, including the sleeping arrangements in the end. How Diego had—no surprise to her—shoveled her porch and cleaned off her car.

For a moment, there'd been silence. Then: *Well, it was incredibly good of him to follow you home and stay with you during the storm. And help you out the way he did. But I'm not gonna lie, Jenna. I'm worried.*

He was still worried when he arrived in her driveway. Jenna had known Mike a long time and could tell by his expression.

At the moment, though, he was busy getting Robbie into her car seat and playing a round of peekaboo. She wouldn't mention that Diego had done that too.

She watched him entertain her daughter while double-checking that the car seat was properly latched. "You're gonna make some guy a great husband, Mike."

"Don't change the subject," he said, mock narrowing his greenish-gold eyes at her. He double-checked Robbie's harness was buckled correctly, then opened the passenger door for Jenna. Such a gentleman. She was so lucky to have Mike in her life.

"Let's get going and we'll talk," she said. They both got in and buckled up.

"I don't like that he kissed you and then said he wasn't the guy for you. You're a widow on your first date. He shouldn't be playing games."

"I truly don't think he is," Jenna said. "I know he's not. He was pretty open about why he doesn't commit. I told you a little about his past relationship—I guess I just understand where he's coming from."

He ran a hand through his curly brown hair. "Me too. I'm on your side, no matter what. That's all I can really say."

She smiled and touched his arm. "And last night wasn't a date. That's *tonight*." She bit her lip, wondering why she'd said that. She hadn't decided to say yes. Mike was absolutely right about him kissing her and then reiterating that he had nothing to offer her and Robbie. If he believed that, he should keep his lips to himself, not confuse her and send her mixed signals.

But she had a good feeling that Diego Sanchez was the confused one. That his cautious head and bruised heart were ganging up on him. He liked her—she knew that. He was attracted to her—no doubt. But he was worried that where he was in life meant that he wasn't husband material for a widowed mother.

"So you're gonna let him come over? With dinner and roses?"

"More like pizza and a new toy for Robbie, I'm sure. She's seven months today."

Mike smiled and peered in his rearview mirror even though the car seat was rear-facing. "Happy seven-month birthday, Robbie! I know you're smiling even if I can't see your adorable face."

Jenna laughed. "I like him, Mike. Really like him. But I hear you. And I'm listening. I'll be careful. If he keeps saying we can't be a couple, but keeps asking me out on dates, then I'll know I need to stop this."

"Good. If he hurts you, I'll…"

"I think Diego himself is worried enough about hurting me for all of us," she said as Mike turned onto Central Avenue. They passed the Silver Spur Café and Tenacity Feed and Seed, plenty of folks out and about.

"He really was good with Robbie?" Mike asked.

"Attentive, holding her, playing peekaboo, laughing when she grabbed his nose and ear."

Mike sighed. "Fine. If Robbie likes him, I'll give him a chance. A *cautious* chance."

Jenna smiled. "Good. Because I think I am going to say yes to tonight. I want to give this a try. Because I do like him so much. I'm going in duly warned by the man himself. But I just have a feeling about him—and that Rob would give me his blessing to take this small step."

Mike pulled into the parking lot for the Little Cowpokes Daycare, then turned to her. "That's really big, Jenna. I'm happy for you. You deserve the world."

She gasped. "That's what Diego said. That Robbie and I deserve the world. It's why he thinks he has nothing to offer us. Because he's 'just a cowboy.'" She shook her head.

"Sounds like Diego has to start accepting himself."

"Maybe I can help. Hey, if I supposedly deserve the world and I want to date him, then…"

"Hopefully he's not too stubborn. You said the ex who'd gutted him was seven years ago? That's a long time. Is he using it as an excuse to not get serious about anyone? Maybe he just can't or won't commit."

Jenna's heart deflated. "Maybe," she said, feeling really crummy all of a sudden.

"Hey," he said, taking her hand. "I'm sorry. I don't have to voice my every worry to you. He sounds like a good guy. He's nice to Robbie. He was there for you, in a very big way, when you needed someone. I'm okay with giving him a chance."

Jenna's heart puffed back up. "Oh, thanks." She gave him a playful sock in the arm. "Seriously, though, I appreciate you, Mike. With all my heart."

He smiled. "Two minutes to noon," he said, gesturing at the dashboard clock. "Better get in there with all those kiddies. Oh, and Happy Valentine's Day, Jenna. I might have skipped saying that to you, but I think you *will* have a happy Valentine's Day."

Jenna did too. Even if her stomach was full of fluttering butterflies.

CHAPTER EIGHT

SEVEN LONG HOURS had passed since Diego had left Jenna's house. He sat at the kitchen table of the family home with his brother Julian, both of them breaking off pieces of the big heart-shaped chocolate chip cookie their mom had baked. Once the roads were clear, Julian had stopped by to see if he could help out with snow removal around the house, but Diego and Luca had taken care of that early this morning. After lunch, their dad had gone back to work early to see to an ailing bull, Luca tagging along, and his mom had gone upstairs to put the finishing touches on a dress someone had hired her at the last minute to take in for a special date tonight.

Valentine's Day.

He wondered when he'd hear from Jenna. *If* he'd hear.

"Where you taking Jenna tonight?" Julian asked.

"Honestly, I'm not even sure we're still on."

"Because the plans are up in the air or because you're not sure about dating a widow with a baby?"

Diego frowned. "Both?"

His brother studied him. "I'm just not sure where you're going with this."

Well, neither did he. Diego took a drink of his coffee, and then glanced out the window, nothing but snow-covered evergreens in the distance.

"Oh hell, I might as well just tell you." But he clamped his mouth shut. He wanted advice. He *needed* advice. But he also didn't love the idea of Julian knowing such personal stuff about him. Close as they were.

Julian grinned. "Out with it, bro."

He started with spotting Jenna beside her car on Central Avenue, the snow just starting to come down then. He ended with their awkward conversation about tonight. Valentine's Day.

He mentioned the kiss.

Waking up nose to nose.

And holding Robbie. Twice.

"Okay, that's the equivalent of ten dates in one night," Julian said, slowly shaking his head and then letting out a low whistle.

"Technically, tonight's our first date."

Julian nodded slowly. "Castillo's? Tenacity Inn?"

"I'm thinking the inn. I saw a post on social media that they're having a special Valentine's menu." Usually the inn just served a basic weekday breakfast buffet for their guests. But for holidays they sometimes went all out and turned the event room into a special dining room.

"Sounds good. Plus, if you suggested Castillo's and she said she didn't like Mexican food, you'd have to break up with her."

Diego laughed. "That would solve the problem, though."

"And the problem is that she has a baby?"

"That's part of it. For years now I've felt like I have nothing to offer a woman—and Jenna has a baby to raise. But there's just something special about her." He paused for a moment. "And something feels like it's shifting in me." He shook his head. "I don't know what I'm saying. Just that maybe I've been holding back from committing for the wrong reasons."

Julian clapped him on the back. "Well, duh, *mano*. I mean, I'm trying to picture my life right now if I'd turned away from Ruby and Emery and Jay."

"What was it like, becoming an instant father?" Diego asked, breaking off another piece of cookie and practically crushing it between his fingers. "I mean, I know you and Ruby aren't officially engaged, but you're clearly headed in that direction."

Julian nodded. "All I can say is that it was out of my hands.

At least, it felt that way. Those kids had my heart, Diego. As did Ruby. I was powerless." He chuckled. "I laugh but it's true."

Diego nodded. "I care about her—and the baby. But how can I take on a family? It's not like I have any experience. How do I know if I'm even cut out to be a dad? Especially to a little girl who lost hers? And what *do* I have to offer? I'm a cowboy living at home, working someone else's ranch."

"I did for years, Diego. Dad has for years. Being a cowboy, helping your parents by living at home, all good things. But what you need to figure out is if you *want* to take on a family. Because if you don't, you have no business dating Jenna. She's lost too much."

"It's a good thing she hasn't gotten back to me about tonight. She's probably decided it's better that we're just friends." He let out hard breath and dropped his head back. "Jeez, I am gonna die alone."

Julian clamped a hand on his shoulder and smiled. "I don't see that happening. For one, we're having this conversation in the first place. When's the last time you talked to any of us about a woman you're interested in?"

Never.

"Listen, Diego. Your ex was money and status obsessed and said a crappy, hurtful thing. It stung you bad and I get it. But not every woman is like that. You do know that, right? I can name names if I have to. Women you're well familiar with. Starting with Mom."

"It's more that I lived up to what she said I was. 'Just a cowboy on a middling ranch.'"

His brother gaped at him. "You saying what's good enough for Dad isn't good enough for you? He's been happily married for forty years. Raised five good kids and gave us everything we needed by working on this so-called middling ranch. And because you're making me say it, Mom and Dad gave us the most important thing of all—a strong foundation of love, family, commitment, values. Come on, Diego, you know what's important."

Except love and values wouldn't buy Robbie a new stroller when she outgrew hers. Love wouldn't pay for braces. Or her wedding.

Okay, even *he* knew he was getting way ahead of himself.

If he cared about the Lattimore duo this much already, after knowing them a few days... He'd want to give them everything, be the provider they deserved, and he'd fall short.

Julian's phone buzzed. "Ah, gotta head out. Think about what I said, okay?"

Diego nodded but everything he'd heard in the last twenty minutes was all a big jumble in his confused head.

At the door, Julian turned. "You know, hanging on to what your ex said seven years ago gives you an out. You break up with every woman who wants more, a commitment. Maybe what you're really scared of is the love part."

"Scared? Of love? No. Weren't you just talking about the excellent role models we had in that department?"

"So why aren't you married at thirty-three, Diego?"

Diego scowled. He'd just said why. *Because I have nothing to offer...*

It wasn't an excuse. It wasn't.

Diego's phone dinged.

"I'll talk to you later," Julian said, and headed out the door.

Diego was still scowling—until he saw Jenna had texted him.

He grabbed his phone.

Hope we're still on for tonight. Followed by a smiling emoji wearing a cowboy hat.

His frown had most definitely turned upside down.

But then he recalled what Julian had said, about not getting too close to a widowed mom if he didn't intend to get serious about her.

What he *intended* didn't feel entirely in his hands. What had Julian said about being powerless against what was going on inside him? Maybe it was like that.

We are most definitely on, he texted back. I'd like to treat you and the newly turned seven-month-old cutie to the Tenacity Inn's Valentine's Day menu. Pick you up at 6:45?

Three dots appeared and disappeared. She was texting and deleting. For a good fifteen seconds.

Uh-oh. Was she changing her mind? His felt a little pinch in his chest. Disappointment.

Three more dots appeared.

See you then! she texted.

Well, whatever had been going on there, the exclamation point was a good sign.

Diego smiled and tucked his phone in the pocket of his flannel shirt. He popped another piece of cookie in his mouth and finished his coffee. Goose bumps trailed up his arms at the thought of picking up Jenna and taking her out.

He might not be able to answer Julian's questions, but he did know he'd never looked forward to anything more than tonight.

JENNA HAD MADE a big decision about tonight. If she was going to date Diego Sanchez, she wanted to get to know him without Robbie as a buffer or as a point of comfort. Or source of conversation. When he'd texted the invitation to include Robbie, she'd been touched, but a one-on-one date felt right.

Mike and his nephew, Cody, were coming over at 6:50 to babysit—and her best friend would meet Diego for the first time. She had no doubt he'd like Diego immediately; it was impossible not to, even if you were very protective of your bestie.

Jenna glanced at her phone on the top of her dresser: 6:38. Butterflies started fluttering around in her belly.

She looked at herself in the full-length mirror in the corner of her bedroom. The past hour, Jenna had spent a little too much time in her closet, trying to figure out just the right outfit for tonight. She'd bypassed her jeans. And her two dresses, one a sundress, the other something appropriate for a wedding. She'd been going for just right—not too dressy and not too casual.

Casual black pants paired with the elegant black mohair sweater her parents had given her this past Christmas—perfect for tonight. She'd added her black leather ankle boots, a delicate gold necklace with a ruby heart to fall in the V-neck, and hoop earrings. A light application of makeup, her hair loose down her back, and a little dab of perfume, and she was ready.

Her first date in almost ten years.

Suddenly, the butterflies started flapping their wings like crazy and she had to sit down on her bed. *You'll be fine*, she told herself. Last night was like a first date on steroids—and it had been impromptu. A planned date... That was a different story because instead of the casual takeout from the Silver Spur Café or Castillo's and some TV, they were going out—on a very romantic holiday.

Diego's handsome face flashed into her mind, and she got excited all over again. *I'm ready in more ways than one*, she reminded herself.

She turned to Robbie, sitting in her bouncer and chewing on her teether. "What do you think, sweets? How do I look?" The baby's gaze went to her mother and she smiled. Jenna decided her daughter was giving a thumbs-up.

She got up and moved over to the bouncer to unbuckle Robbie. Baby in her arms, Jenna headed into the living room to await the ringing of the doorbell. "It's just about showtime." She was equally nervous and excited. "I feel good about this, Robbie." Just as she kissed her daughter's cheek, the doorbell rang.

She sucked in a breath. Gave herself a last once-over in the oval mirror above the console table, and then opened the door.

Her knees actually wobbled.

Diego Sanchez stood on her doorstep. Holding a bouquet of red roses wrapped in beautiful paper in one hand and a bakery box with a tied white ribbon in the other. And wow, did he look amazing. He wore the black overcoat he'd had on when she'd met him in the parking lot of the Tenacity Social Club. The coat was open to reveal a dark gray sweater over black pants. He might not think *they* were a match, but their outfits sure were.

"Come on in," she said. "It's cold tonight."

He stepped in and she closed the door behind him. "You look lovely." She was aware that he was taking her in. That this man who she found so hot was equally attracted to her did wonders for her ego. She'd had a baby seven months ago, and she was soft where she used to be taut.

"Happy Valentine's Day to you, Jenna," he said. "And happy seven-month birthday to you, Robbie." He smiled at the baby and held up the bakery box. "This is for you, Big Cheeks. Just a little something to celebrate your special day." He looked at Jenna. "I'll switch with you," he said. "Flowers and bakery box for Robbie."

"This is so nice," she said, so touched that she had to take a second to let it all sink in.

He gave her the box to start and scooped up Robbie with one arm, then handed over the flowers. "You won't spit up on my sweater, will you, Robbie?" he asked on a chuckle.

Jenna laughed. "I was worried about that myself on the way from my bedroom to the door. All good."

He hoisted up Robbie and kissed her cheek. "Well, if you do barf all over me, that's okay. That's what babies do."

Robbie grabbed his ear and let out a giggle.

Her favorite sound on earth—her baby's laughter. "I see why she likes you so much."

His smile lit up his handsome face. "It's mutual."

Her heart was thudding so loud she worried he might hear it. "I love red roses so much," she said, taking an inhale of the beautiful flowers. "Thank you. Very thoughtful."

"My pleasure," he said, giving the baby a sway.

"Robbie, let's go put these gorgeous roses in water," she said. "And we can see what's in this delicious-smelling bakery box." There, she was doing it. Using Robbie as a buffer because the moment was…a lot. In a good way, but a lot. If she was going to date, she'd need to get used to all these new feelings.

She was so aware of Diego, holding her child, following her into the kitchen. She had such an urge to turn around and kiss him. For the kind gestures. For making a very sweet fuss. "So, it turns out I uninvited Robbie from our date tonight," she said as she headed to the cabinet under the sink where kept a few vases. "Mike and his nephew are coming over to babysit."

He glanced at the baby. "Well, Robbie, you're definitely not going to miss the Tenacity Inn's steak special, since you only have one tooth."

Jenna laughed and filled a tall glass vase with water, then arranged the roses and set them on the kitchen table. "So true! Robbie, let's open your surprise."

Diego sat down with the baby in his arms, her big blue eyes on the box. Jenna opened it to find three red velvet cupcakes nestled inside. Her hand went straight to her heart. "Oh, Diego, how sweet. Literally too. Thank you."

"You're very welcome. I figure we'll save our cupcakes for dessert later. But maybe Robbie can have some of hers now to celebrate being seven months today."

Her toes tingled. He was basically asking to come back here after dinner. To extend the date.

"Sounds perfect," she said. She went over to the drawer with Robbie's utensils and took out a little yellow plastic fork.

"Oh wait—can't forget this," he added, pulling a little yellow candle and a book of matches from his coat pocket.

Hand to the heart again. Of course he brought a candle and matches. "Look, Robbie, it's a candle!" Jenna said, coming back over to the table. She took a cupcake from the box, then inserted the candle, and lit it. "Make a wish, Robbie."

"My wish is for a big bite of that frosting, Mama!" Diego said in a singsong high-pitched voice.

Jenna laughed. "Oh yeah. That was definitely her wish."

"Time to blow out the candle, Robbie!" Diego said. "One. Two. Threeeee!"

He leaned close and together they blew out the candle. Jenna had the biggest urge to grab his gorgeous face and kiss him. She was deeply moved. By all of this.

So she quickly picked up the fork and scooped a small bite of frosting and cupcake, and held it to the baby's mouth, which opened wide.

Robbie gobbled it, her eyes lighting up, licking the little smear of frosting beside her lips.

Diego laughed. "I see I made the right choice in flavors."

"Definitely." Jenna gave Robbie one more little bite when the doorbell rang. "That's Mike and his nephew, Cody." She scooped up Robbie and they all headed to the door.

"Hi, Robbie!" Cody said, his brown eyes twinkling. "Hi, Jenna!"

"Hi, yourself," she said. "Mike Cooper and nephew Cody, meet Diego Sanchez."

The three shook hands, Mike giving Diego a serious once-over as he and his nephew stepped inside.

"Thanks for helping Uncle Mike babysit," Jenna said to Cody. "I really appreciate it."

Cody grinned. "I love hanging out with Robbie. She's so cute!"

Cody was such a great kid. Jenna knew he missed his mom while she was overseas. Especially because it was just the two of them—and Uncle Mike.

"Hey, Miss Seven Months," Mike said, leaning over to kiss Robbie on her head.

Jenna smiled. "She just had her very first bite of cupcake to celebrate and no surprise, she loved it. Diego brought it for her."

She had to stop beaming at the man. She could see Mike eyeing her. He missed nothing.

"I was at the Tenacity Social Club a few days back with my family," Diego said to Mike. "I recall seeing you and Cody there."

Mike nodded. "Great place. I moonlight there. My day job is on my family's ranch."

Jenna noticed Diego taking that in. A rancher. *Not just a cowboy.* Maybe she was reading into things, though.

They chatted a bit about the Tenacity Social Club, then the storm last night and how great the Tenacity public works department had been at taking care of business at the crack of dawn. Tenacity might be small and hardscrabble, but the town had the necessary, if most basic, services. And local cowboys were always on hand with their snow-plow-rigged pick-ups to help out.

"Well, you two go have fun," Mike said. "We'll hold down the fort." There was a slight edge in Mike's voice. A protective edge.

"I really appreciate this," Jenna said, handing Robbie to Mike. "Cody, you're awesome. Robbie loves when you help babysit." She turned to Digeo. "Shall we go?" she asked him, heading to the closet. Of course, when she got her coat, he took it from her and held it as she slipped in her arms. She gave her baby a last kiss on the head, said goodbye to her ace sitters, and she and Diego left.

And then they were in his pickup, driving off toward downtown Tenacity. When Jenna had first moved here, she'd been surprised by how few shops and businesses and restaurants there were. Bronco, where she'd grown up, wasn't a big town by any stretch, but Tenacity had just a grocery store, the Grizzly Bar, Castillo's Mexican restaurant, a lunch place that Jenna loved,

not that she could afford to go there more than once a month.
The one thing there were two of were feed supply stores due
to all the ranches. Tenacity Feed and Seed and Strom and Son
Feed and Farm Supply. Tenacity did have one hotel, the Tenacity Inn, where they were headed right now for dinner. And the
very special Tenacity Social Club, where teens could hang out
after school and on weekends, and nighttime brought open mike
performances and folks enjoying a casual night out to have a
drink and play some old-fashioned pinball.

"I just love Tenacity," she said, looking out the window as
they turned onto Central Avenue. She smiled as she saw at
least five men coming out of Tenacity Grocery with various
bouquets of flowers.

"Do you?" he asked, glancing at her. "I mean, I do too, but
you're from Bronco. I've been there to visit family, and even
on their side of town, which isn't the fancy section, there was
a lot going on. The town is full of restaurants, shops, baker-
ies, all kinds of businesses. Winona even has her own psychic
shop there. Right on the property of her nephew's ghost tours
business. Ghost tours, can you imagine? Tenacity doesn't even
have its own movie theater."

"True, but is there better Mexican food in Montana than
Castillo's? Yum. We have what we *need* in Tenacity. That's
what matters."

"That's true," he said. "That and the wide-open spaces and
good people are why I love it too. And I'm happy to hear you
like Mexican food. That would be big with my family. But
sorry, my uncle Stanley makes the best Mexican food in Tenacity, though Castillo's is second best. You'll have to come over
for dinner sometime."

"I'd love that," she said, that warm, happy feeling spreading
in her chest at the invitation.

He pulled into a spot at the inn, couples coming and going.
Now she was one of those pairs, out on the town on Valentine's
Day when she'd thought she'd be alone for quite a while.

Diego had the passenger-side door open before she could

blink. "My lady," he said with a warm smile, extending his arm for her to take.

She was actually doing this, going on a *real* date with Diego Sanchez, scary as that was.

CHAPTER NINE

LUCKILY DIEGO HAD thought to make a reservation, something that was never required in Tenacity except for holidays. Lots of folks were in the transformed lobby, which was festooned with red garland, twinkling white lights, and dangling paper hearts, some talking about whether they should go to the Grizzly Bar instead of waiting a half hour for a table. As he and Jenna stood in line to check in with the hostess, they read the chalkboard menu on an easel near the entrance to the dining room. Tonight was a limited menu, since it was catered: Filet mignon in peppercorn sauce. Grilled salmon. Heart-shaped pizza with various toppings. Raspberry cheesecake for dessert.

"Mmm, I'm definitely getting the salmon," Jenna said. "And with a side of risotto—my mouth is watering."

"I'm going for the filet mignon and steak fries. I already had a heart-shaped food today so I'll pass on the pizza."

Jenna smiled. "Oh right—you said your mom always bakes a giant heart-shaped cookie for her family. I love that. I want to do something sweet like that for Robbie. Maybe heart-shaped pancakes with red berries. A new family tradition."

Diego could just see toddler and teenaged Robbie enjoying her heart-shaped pancakes every February 14.

They inched closer to the hostess station and finally it was their turn. Diego let the woman know he'd made a reservation, but it would be five minutes until their table was ready.

"Hi, Jenna!"

They both glanced over toward the direction of the voice. A woman he'd seen around town driving a mobile dog grooming van with a funny name—Git Along Little Doggy—sat behind a table on the other side of the hostess stand. A banner hanging down read: *Loyal Companions Animal Rescue Fundraiser.* A yellow lab sat calmly by her side with a harness across his back indicating that he was a service animal.

Diego had noticed in the ads for tonight's dinner that Loyal Companions was sponsoring the dinner as part of their fundraising efforts. Great idea.

"Hi, Renee," Jenna said, smiling at the blond woman. "And hello there, beautiful pooch."

"This is Buddy, my service dog." Renee gave the golden a kiss on the head and got a lick on her cheek in return.

"Aww," Jenna said. "What a sweetheart."

Diego wasn't sure what Renee needed Buddy for, but he knew dogs could be trained to aid people in all sorts of important ways.

"You're fundraising for Loyal Companions?" Jenna asked.

"Yup. It's such a vital resource. Loyal Companions match and provide therapy and service dogs. Such as when someone is diabetic like me and needs a nudge when their blood sugar runs dangerously low. Loyal Companions does such vital work."

"Absolutely," Diego said. "And I'd like to contribute for me and Jenna." He took out his wallet and slipped a twenty dollar bill into the slot on the toolbox, which was decorated with paw prints.

"Thank you," Jenna said to him. "Renee, do you know Diego Sanchez?"

"I've definitely seen you around town, Diego. You have a big family. I know your sisters. I'll be sure and tell them how generous you were to Loyal Companions. Thank you so much. And Buddy here thanks you too."

He smiled. "My pleasure."

"I hope you two will come to the Loyal Companions Fur-Ball next month," Renee said.

You two. He liked the idea of someone assuming they were a couple, that Jenna was his.

As if Renee suddenly realized they might not be at the stage where they made plans a month in advance, she quickly added, "It's a good thing I'm single and have no plans tonight because there's been a ton of foot traffic. I had the right idea setting up here."

A few people stepped up to the table to slip cash into the donation box just as the hostess called out, "Sanchez, party of two."

"Oh, that's us," Jenna said to Renee. "Good luck, tonight. I hope you get lots of donations."

They followed the hostess through the dining room, both of them smiling and waving at several people they knew. Lots of people here tonight, a nice sight to see. Most folks in Tenacity didn't have the kind of disposable income to spend on dinners out, which was why there were few restaurants. But finding it in the budget to celebrate "love day" with a special meal at the inn was clearly important to many.

Diego felt eyes on him and glanced to his left. Uh-oh. A woman he'd dated for a month last summer was glaring at him. She sat a table with a man, and they were both dressed up, but she was paying more attention to Diego than her date.

"Um, Diego," Jenna said once they were seated at a table by a window and the hostess had left. "I couldn't help but notice that Wendy Bean was shooting daggers at you. Even I felt a little scared."

He frowned. "You know Wendy?"

"Well, just from around town. I don't know her personally."

That was a relief. Maybe he should tell Jenna about his breakup with Wendy as a good—and very bad—example of what he'd said last night and this morning. He didn't want to cast a pall over Jenna's Valentine's Day dinner before it had even begun, but being honest about who he was—that was important.

The waitress came by to bring the special menu, take drink

orders, and light the short candle at the side of the table, giving him a necessary minute.

He quickly glanced at where Wendy and her date were sitting across the room. They were drinking coffee, then her date left cash on top of the bill and they both got up, the guy helping Wendy with her coat and giving her a kiss before they left. With them gone, Diego felt better about rehashing the story.

"We dated last summer," he said. "For a month. We spent July Fourth together, which happened to be her birthday. But when the fireworks display ended, she seemed to be waiting for something." He frowned again, hating this part.

"Waiting for what?" Jenna asked.

Oh good—the waitress was back with a bread basket for the table and their drinks. Club soda with lime for Diego, since he'd be driving, and a white wine for Jenna. More time to delay telling this story. He rarely thought about it, but when he did, he got a pit in his stomach.

"I wasn't sure at first," he continued. "I'd already given her what I thought was a nice gift—a gift certificate to the yoga studio in a nearby town since she'd been saying she wanted to take up the practice. And flowers and a card. But after a few minutes of staring at me, she seemed really frustrated and upset. She finally said, 'Isn't there something you'd like to ask me?'" Diego took a sip of his club soda.

"Ohhh," Jenna said, making a wincing expression.

"I was confused at first. But then I had that *ohhh* just like you did now. I said, 'I like you a lot but we've only been dating a month and it's way too soon to be thinking about a proposal.' She glared at me much the way she did as we passed by her table and snapped, 'I'm just talking about being exclusive, jerk!'"

"Ohhh," Jenna said again, her voice dropping a register.

Diego nodded. "I did like her a lot. But I'd told her on our first date that I wasn't looking to get serious with anyone, and her response to that was 'Well, you wouldn't be here if that was the case. I mean, why bother dating at all?' I didn't really know how to answer that."

Jenna tilted her head. "It's a good question, though. She likely thought she could change your mind."

Yes. Like many of the women he'd dated. It was a problem he didn't know how to fix.

"Anyhoo," Jenna said, taking a sip of her wine. "How did things end with Wendy?"

He let out a sigh. "I gently reminded her that I'd been honest with her from the start. She stared at me for a few seconds, her expression going from angry to hurt. I felt like such hell. Then she got up and said, 'Thanks for ruining my birthday. Have a nice life without anyone to share it with.' And she stalked off."

"Well, I'm glad she found someone special," Jenna said, eyeing the table where Wendy and her date had been sitting. She took a piece of Italian bread and dipped it in the little dish of infused olive oil. "But tell me this, Diego. Why *do* you date?"

Oh hell. He hadn't expected the conversation to turn to this.

What could he say?

"You're too much of a gentleman to be in it for the sex," she said. "At least I think so. But I guess I don't really know you that well yet."

Dammit.

The waitress returned to take their orders. The steak for Diego and the salmon for Jenna. In those few moments to think, he still hadn't come up with a response for Jenna.

She tilted her head again. "Maybe Wendy, maybe *all* the women you've dated, have been right on both counts—asking why you bother dating and then thinking they can change your mind."

He was confused again. "What do you mean?" He grabbed a piece of bread to have something to do with his hands.

"I think you date because it *is* possible that your mind can be changed about getting serious. You don't strike me as cynical."

Except it had been seven years since he'd stopped dating with an open mind and open heart. He'd call that cynical. But he couldn't bear the thought of shutting a door when it came to Jenna Lattimore. That had to mean something too. Even if his feelings on the subject hadn't changed. "Well, I was just thinking the other day that I didn't want to die alone. So maybe you're right. I don't know, though."

"I guess what I'm really trying to say is that I'm being brave by just being here, Diego. So you should be too."

He smiled. She was absolutely right. But…

"What I said about the kiss and getting the thought of it out of my system? Hardly, Jenna. You've got me turned upside down. In a *good* way. What hasn't changed is my situation. And I don't see it changing in the near future, either. I would never want to make promises I can't keep."

Her mouth dropped open. "All I know is that you've been wonderful to me. Since the second I met you in the parking lot of the Tenacity Social Club. And you just hit the nail on the head—it's not the part about *not* getting serious that needs to change. It's your perception of yourself. And what you have to offer a woman."

Despite how much he liked Jenna, he didn't want to keep talking about this. He took in a breath, the little piece of bread sitting like cement in his stomach. "Shouldn't we be making first-date small talk?" he asked with a sort of smile.

She laughed and reached over to take his hand. "No. We're well past 'where did you grow up' and 'do you like to travel' and 'who are you rooting for in the Super Bowl.'"

"We definitely are," he said, giving her soft hand a squeeze. He searched her eyes, hoping to see that she was okay with his trying to drop the conversation.

"What I know for sure is that I'm glad I'm here. That *we're* here."

"Me too," he said without hesitation.

"But we can have *second* date conversation, even though technically this is like our third given that our first spanned a second morning."

He grinned. "Agreed. I *do* have questions."

"Oh?" she asked. "Like what?"

"I'm curious about your job. Did you always want to work with kids?"

She nodded. "I majored in early childhood education. I had this dream back in college that I'd be involved with policy some-how, setting standards for preschool, pre-K, that kind of thing. But it wasn't easy to find an entry level job, especially close to

Tenacity. My first position was in a preschool as an assistant teacher. I loved it. But I left when I got pregnant, thinking I could take a year off, maybe try to find a work-from-home job part-time. And then Rob died and…"

She stopped talking, her expression tight, and took a sip of her wine.

"And everything changed." He finished for her.

She nodded. "Everything changed. Rob didn't have life insurance, and we'd put our savings into the down payment for the house, so…" She bit her lip. "I was very lucky to get the job at Little Cowpokes. Especially because I could bring Robbie to work—free childcare is a serious perk. Without that, I don't know what I'd do. The cost of childcare would take my entire paycheck. I've been looking around for tutoring gigs, but they're not easy to come by for young kids."

Diego swallowed around the lump in his throat. He'd been worried about what he could offer when he didn't know she was in financial trouble. Now he felt his shoulders both tense up and then deflate. "That must be a huge weight off your shoulders to have a job where you can bring your daughter."

"It is. Because I can also see her all day. That's worth quite a lot too." She seemed lost in thought for a moment as she sipped her wine. "I love that you achieved your dream. To be a cowboy."

My dream is hardly able to give you and Robbie what you need. That pit in his stomach was back.

"Like your dad," she added.

Like my dad, he repeated silently, the words slamming into his head, his heart. Julian had raised the very point earlier today. Diego was damned proud of his father and held him in the highest regard. Will and Nicole Sanchez raised five children on a ranch hand's and a seamstress's salaries. Yes, times had always been tight, the budget strict. Diego never got the trendy sneakers he'd wanted as a tween and teenager. But even when he'd started working at fifteen and could afford them, he'd given that extra money to his parents to contribute to the household. The family had always had what they needed—and like Jenna had said earlier, having what you needed was what mattered.

Birthdays and holidays in the Sanchez household were always wonderful. Did each kid get five presents for Christmas like some of their friends? No. But they all got what was on top of their Santa lists, even if it had be to secondhand.

Diego had no business referring to himself as "just a cowboy" when he was so proud of his father. He had no greater respect for anyone. He'd never really thought about it that way as he'd applied those words to himself in his ex's voice and tone and disdain. His father wasn't "just a cowboy." He was a great man.

Still, when it came to taking on a family in need? A young widow in financial straits with a little baby to raise? That felt like a whole other story.

As if she knew he needed a minute to let her words sink in, she said, "I'll just check in with Mike about Robbie." She pulled out her phone and tapped on the little keyboard, then waited.

He knew from her happy smile that Mike had texted everything was okay.

This what was family life was about. Caring, worrying, loving, checking in, hoping. She was on her own with a baby. Without much money. She had a good support system, including right here in town with Mike, but she was a single parent. That had to be *very* tough. He was about to ask her about that when he realized something had caught her attention across the room.

"Oooh, that's Faith and Amy Hawkins!" Jenna said. "They're sitting with Faith's fiancé, Caleb Strom. You know how much I love the rodeo. The Hawkins Sisters—there are many sets of sisters and cousins—are so amazing. The rodeo stars in their family go back generations. They're so inspiring."

Diego nodded. "Absolutely. I always try to catch a show when they're in Bronco."

"I wonder what they're doing in Tenacity," Jenna said. "Maybe they have family here."

He glanced at the trio. Amy Hawkins was sitting across from the engaged couple, who had turned toward each other for a kiss. Diego caught the wistful expression on Amy's face. Maybe everyone had a complicated relationship when it came to matters of the heart.

The waitress came back with a tray holding their entrées.

Mmm, his filet mignon, smothered in peppercorn sauce, smelled so good.

"You should know something about me if we're going to date," Jenna said. "I'm a sharer. So you get the first bite of salmon."

"And you get the first bite of steak. I'll even throw in a steak fry."

They each cut a bite, leaned forward and held out their forks to the other.

It was sort of a romantic, personal gesture, and Diego liked it.

"Oh wow," Jenna said. "So delicious."

"The salmon is too. Thanks for being a sharer."

He was too, clearly. Except when it came to that kicked-around guarded thing beating in his chest.

"Told you so," said a dry voice from behind him.

Diego turned to see Winona coming their way, Uncle Stanley right behind her. Winona was in her trademark purple, a dress with silver fringe, and purple cowboy boots, her long white hair in a braid down one shoulder. Diego stood and Jenna did too.

"Diego!" Stanley said in his happy booming voice. "Nice to see you out on a night such as this!"

It *was* unusual. Diego rarely dated anyone around the holidays up to Valentine's Day to avoid any high expectations. "Winona, Stanley, this is Jenna Lattimore," Diego said. "Jenna, my great-uncle Stanley and his new bride, Winona Cobbs-Sanchez."

"I'm so glad to meet you both," Jenna said. "Congratulations on your marriage."

Stanley's eyes were positively twinkling. He took Jenna's hand with both of his and held it for a second. "Thank you, dear. And very nice to meet you!"

Winona gave Jenna a pleasant enough nod, then turned that stare back on Diego in that Winona way. Not smiling or frowning. Honestly, the woman could be a bit unnerving. He often heard her laughing and telling a funny story to Stanley in the backyard or while they were in the kitchen of the family home. And Stanley had such a big personality that they had to be a great match for them to work so well.

Told you so... Winona's words as she'd approached his table echoed in his head.

"Told me what, Winona?" he asked super casually, smile on his face. Winona *was* psychic. Had she said something cryptic to him at the family after-party at the social club? He couldn't remember. He thought it was his sister Nina who Winona had been talking to. Something in relation to Nina asking Stanley to look up the Deroy family—particularly Nina's first love, Barrett—and see what had become of them.

Winona wrapped her arm around Stanley's. "Have a lovely dinner. We won't keep you."

Guess she wasn't going to answer. *Told you so* could mean a whole bunch of things where Diego was concerned. Something about his date with Jenna, he assumed. But what? *Tell me*, he tried to telepathically communicate to Winona. If she heard him through the airwaves, she didn't let on.

Stanley clapped Diego so hard on the back he almost pitched forward. His uncle was beaming. Diego had no doubt part of that had to do with his grandnephew being out on a date on Valentine's Day. He shot Diego a wink, then the newlyweds left.

"Aww!" Jenna said. "I love them."

Diego smiled. "They do make a great case for second chances."

Jenna's eyes twinkled. "Aha. I was right. You *do* believe in possibilities."

"On a night like this, being here with you, it's hard not to, Jenna."

He almost couldn't believe he'd said it. He meant it. There was definitely *something* happening inside him, something... different. Changing? *That* he wasn't sure of.

Which meant it was time to change the subject yet again. He dipped a steak fry in ketchup. "Can't get these at home. I try to make my own version when it's my turn to cook, but they're either half raw inside or burned. I never get them right."

Jenna smiled. "I make great steak fries. Sweet potato or white."

"Well, *I'll* be the judge of that," he said on a chuckle.

She laughed. "I saw you trying to change the subject, but

look, you fell right into my evil trap of a fourth date. This *is* technically our third."

He felt so much for this warm, funny, smart, beautiful woman that every part of him was pulsating. Including his heart. She deserved a man who wouldn't change the subject from hard topics. And tonight, at least, he was her man. He put his fork down and reached across the table for her hand.

"I couldn't stay away if I wanted to, Jenna. I guess I've dug in my heels about where I am in life. I hate talking about this—especially with you. I don't know how to get my mind around it. Not being able to give you what I'd want. You and Robbie. So then I revert right back to not thinking we *shouldn't* date. And then back to that first thing I said about not being able to stay away. Conundrum. Except I can't and won't play games with you, Jenna."

She stared at him, looking anxious and hopeful at the same time. "Meaning? I'm here, Diego. Do you know how hard I've worked to let go of my fears enough to be here with you? And you're not even going to try?"

He felt that like a punch. But it was still a hard question.

"I'm here. On Valentine's Day. I'm absolutely trying too."

She visibly relaxed. "That's what I thought. But given your past, I shouldn't assume. I'm teasing you a little. But also serious. One day at a time, Diego."

"One day at a time," he said, holding up his glass to her.

They clinked and sipped. Things were okay. Better than okay. They were going to keep dating. What was that saying about necessity being the mother of invention? Diego would have to figure something out if he wanted to give Jenna and Robbie the world.

They were just about done with dinner. Then they'd go back to her house and have those red velvet cupcakes and their date would be over. There was no snowstorm to keep him at her place, though for Jenna's sake he was glad for that. He wanted to prolong the evening. But what could they do that didn't involve taking a walk in the cold, dark February chill? Nearest movie theater was a half hour away, and the show times might not work out anyway. Maybe the Tenacity Social

Club? Just didn't seem romantic enough with its dartboards and pinball machines.

And then he remembered something. A poster on the wall at the social club—for a Valentine's Dance at the Tenacity Town Hall. Slow dancing with Jenna? Yes, please.

"If you don't need to get home soon to relieve Mike and Cody," he said, "I thought we might go to the dance at the rec center."

Her face lit up. "I love that idea!" She pulled out her phone to check the time. "I'll just text Mike again to ask."

He watched her tap away.

"We're good to go," she said. "No curfew for us," she added with a laugh. "Cody will conk out early, but the kid sleeps through anything, including being carried out to Mike's truck in the cold and then being transported to his bed."

"I'm like that too. When I'm asleep, a herd of buffalo on the roof wouldn't wake me."

Jenna laughed. "I have Mama radar. I can be in the deepest sleep, but one tiny cry from Robbie and my eyes pop open. I might even hear her while we're at the dance. But I have a feeling I'll be very distracted by my handsome date. Good thing I have a trusted sitter."

Diego smiled. He hoped she wanted to forego coffee to get the dance as soon as possible. Because he couldn't wait another minute to have her in his arms.

CHAPTER TEN

AN EIGHTIES NEW-WAVE song that Jenna loved, Just Can't Get Enough by Depeche Mode, was playing when they arrived at the rec center, which was pretty crowded. People of all ages—from kids and teens to elderly couples—were on the dance floor. The place had been dolled up for the night and looked so festive. More red garland and many hand-drawn posters of hearts, some clearly done by children and adorable. There was a punch station with cups and many plates of heart-shaped sugar cookies with red sprinkles. Many chairs were dotted around the huge, square, dance area. Jenna spotted several kissing couples. She was so happy that Diego had suggested coming here. It was perfect.

Moonlighting as DJ for the event was the town clerk up on a small stage. A slow song by Beyoncé came on, and Diego took her hand.

"Shall we?" he asked.

"We shall," she said on a giggle.

They found a space on the dance floor and squeezed in, Jenna's arms going around Diego's neck, his hands at her waist, their gazes locked.

Pinch me, I'm dreaming, she thought. This entire night had been magical. From the cupcake Diego had brought Robbie with the yellow candle to the romantic dinner at the inn and all the honesty in their conversation to meeting his uncle Stanley and his new bride Winona, and now—swaying in a slow dance with a man who made her knees weak.

The song ended but Diego didn't move.

Neither did she.

Another slow one, this one by Tim McGraw, came on. A favorite of Rob's. A song they'd danced to at their wedding. At other weddings. At home.

Jenna froze.

"You okay?" Diego asked, concern in his dark eyes.

"I just, uh, need a minute. Find me by the punch in five minutes, okay?"

He tilted his head, studying her, trying to read her expression.

She fled, heading out of the event room and into the hallway. She leaned against the wall and sucked in a breath, her heart thudding. Tears misting her eyes.

This was all part of the sadness she sometimes felt, and it could strike without warning. The littlest thing could spark a memory of another time and place, when she'd been an entirely different person: a wife, happily married. She wrapped her arms around herself, suddenly cold.

"Jenna?"

She looked up to find Diego's uncle Stanley peering at her with the same concern Diego had a few moment ago.

"Winona's at the dance but asked me to run out to the car and get her shawl," Stanley said. "Is Diego here? Did something happen?"

Jenna couldn't speak for a second. Everything was jumbled.

"I... I was dancing with Diego," she said, her voice quavering. "And another song started. A favorite of my late husband's." She shut up fast, lest she start crying.

Compassion filled his gaze. "Ah, I understand, my dear. When I was first courting Winona, a song, a memory, a movie, the stars in the sky—so much would remind me of my first wife. It was a combination of sadness, unsettling guilt and the knowledge that she'd *want* me to love Winona, to be happy. But sometimes those moments..."

It was so comforting to talk to someone who understood. "This was the first time something so overtly reminded me of him. It wasn't so much that I was in another man's arms on the dance floor. But that I have strong feelings for that man, you know?"

"Losing someone we love so much is unspeakably painful," Stanley said. "Only you can know when you're ready. There's no rushing it."

That made her feel better. She didn't have to go in there and pretend she was fine when she wasn't. She knew she didn't have to do that with Diego.

"You've been a big help, Stanley. Thank you." She took his hand in both of hers.

"Any time you need to talk, you find me."

She smiled, and he headed down the hall toward the exit. What a kind man. Like granduncle, like grandnephew. She was so grateful that he'd come along when he did.

She looked toward the double doors to the event room, which had been propped open to let air circulate. Winona stood in her purple dress, staring at Jenna from the middle of the crowd. And unless Jenna was imaging it, Winona was giving her a nod. Then she turned and disappeared among the dancers.

Jenna had to smile. Winona, with her psychic gifts, had known Jenna was going through something in that moment, and had sent her husband for her shawl...right in Jenna's path.

Thank you, Winona, she said silently.

Feeling stronger, she headed back to the dance. She weaved through the crowed, easily spotting tall, gorgeous Diego by the refreshments table. Waiting for her. With a cup of punch in each hand.

Warmth spread in her chest. He made her feel safe. Cared for.

He smiled when he spotted her and walked toward her with two cups of punch.

"Just what I need," she said, taking the cup he held out.

"Would you like to leave? Whatever you need, Jenna."

She took a sip of the punch, then another and finished it off. It hit the spot.

He drained his cup too, then tossed them in the trash can.

"I don't want to leave," she said. "I'm okay now. Just had a moment there." She was about to tell him about "running into" his uncle, but decided to keep that sweet interlude to herself. Just like her earlier sadness. There would be times a memory of her marriage would get ahold of her, and she'd feel it and sit with it. She didn't want or need to bring the new man in her life into the thick of that. It felt private in a good way.

"Would you like to sit?" he asked, gesturing at two empty chairs, a rarity at the dance.

"Sure," she said. "I'll just quickly check in with Mike again." She took out her phone and glanced at it. "He hasn't called or texted, which means everything is fine, but I just need to hear him say it. Or see him text it, actually."

She had a feeling Diego knew that her need to hear that her baby girl was okay was tied to what had happened on the dance floor when she'd seized up and run out. That the song had reminded her of her husband. Of a family that had changed in an instant. She'd bet on it.

He gave her a soft smile. "While you do that, I'll round us up two of those heart-shaped sugar cookies with the red sprinkles."

"Perfect," she said. As Diego walked back toward the refreshments table, she sent Mike the text. Song got me all teary but I'm fine. Just checking in. How's my baby girl?

He texted back right away. Sleeping like a champ. Cody played around two hundred rounds of peekaboo and got the loudest laughter out of Robbie I've ever heard. He also read her five bedtime stories. She was asleep by page two of the first but he kept going in case she woke up.

She so appreciated having a friend who understood that she sorely needed a long, newsy, sweet text.

Aww. Be still my heart. You give that nephew of yours a kiss for me.

I would but he's out cold himself. See you whenever you get home.

Diego came back with two cookies on a small paper plate atop two more cups of punch. He handed her a cup and held out a napkin.

She took a bite of her cookie and so did he, then they sipped the punch.

"All's well with Robbie?" he asked.

She nodded. "Apparently Cody read her five bedtime stories. I have some really wonderful people in my life. Including an eight-year-old." She smiled. "Helps me count my blessings."

He nodded thoughtfully.

She pictured Robbie at home in her bassinet in the nursery, safe and sound, snug as a bug. Yet still... Jenna was here. She supposed she'd have to get used to this now that she was seeing someone. Someone who'd invited Robbie on their date, she reminded herself, brightening a bit, but there would be plenty of times it would be just her and Diego. Like that invitation to come for dinner at his house so that she could see that Stanley's cooking had the edge over Castillo's. She wouldn't bring Robbie, who could neither eat nor talk.

Plus bringing her baby daughter would imply she and Diego were serious. And they were just getting to know each other.

Dating had so many components.

"I'm so used to being with Robbie all the time," she continued. "Except for those twenty minutes here and there when Mike watches her for me. She comes with me to work and then at home. It's just us two. Always has been. It's a little weird to be away from her for so many hours like this."

Jeez, Jenna. A little much all at once. Then again, she and Diego had been nothing but open and honest all night. Letting themselves be vulnerable. She wasn't going to bounce back from that song and everything it had called up in her in ten minutes. And that was okay. Even when she was on a date.

She could *talk* to Diego. Really talk to him.

"It must be a lot to carry that load alone," he said. "A precious load, nonetheless."

"It is. I've been alone since the first trimester."

She saw him wince. Those days, those early weeks, were hard to call up and reach anymore because of how hard and painful that time had been. Her heart clenched for her parents and Mike, who'd listened to her howl and had held her tight as she'd sobbed, murmuring sweet things, rubbing her back, stroking her hair. They'd made sure she was eating, taking her prenatals, getting sunlight instead of lying shell-shocked under the covers in bed, clutching her blossoming belly. Mike had even been her Lamaze partner, and both he and her mom were in the delivery room.

Blessings.

Diego took both her hands in his. "I wish I could ease some of your worries, but I guess parents never stop worrying."

Jenna smiled. "I only have seven months' experience myself, but I know my folks are always thinking about me. They make that obvious."

"That's nice. Same with mine. And Uncle Stanley."

Again, a warmth spread across her chest. She shifted her hands so that she was holding Diego's. She never wanted to let go.

As if he could sense she was ready to leave, he stood. "How about one more dance and then I get you home?"

"Sounds good," she said in almost a whisper. She looked around to see if Winona and Stanley were still at the dance to say thank you for before, to just be in the midst of their beautiful second-chance love story, but the room was so big and crowded that she didn't spot them.

She and Diego swayed to a vintage Bee Gees song, their bodies so close. She could easily lift up her chin and press her lips to his.

But she'd wait. Until they were home. Or maybe she'd leave that alone. She'd had a big night, lots of emotions going on, and she could probably use some time alone to let it all settle.

A few minutes later, they had on their coats and were headed out to his pickup. The cold air was invigorating. On the drive home, they listened to music, Jenna feeling peaceful.

They arrived at her house, Jenna excited to see her baby. As they headed up the porch steps, Mike came to the door.

"Robbie's still fast asleep. Not a peep out of her all night."

Jenna grinned. "That's great. Imagine if you'd said she'd been fussy and shrieking and feverish. I'd never leave the house again."

"I can understand that," Diego said. "Which is why I'm glad

Robbie is sleeping peacefully." He smiled at her, then extended his hand to Mike, who shook it.

Mike seemed to like what Diego had said. So did Jenna. A hint at a future. That there would be another date.

"Well, let me go scoop up my nephew," Mike said. "I recall that being very easy until he was around four, maybe five. Now, it's like he lifts weights," he added on a chuckle. He went to the love seat, where sweet Cody was stretched out, a throw over him, a chapter book about a robot on the coffee table beside him.

Cody didn't stir, just like Mike had said he wouldn't, even when they all helped his arms into the sleeves of his down jacket and put his Montana Grizzlies hat on his head.

"You're the best, Mike," Jenna said. "Thanks a million."

"Anytime." He smiled, including Diego in it, and he headed out. Diego opened the back passenger door so that Mike could settle Cody in his booster seat. Then the two quickly shook hands again, and Mike was off.

Diego came back, and she shut the door behind him.

With Mike and Cody gone, the house seemed smaller, intimate. As she looked at Diego standing there, his dark eyes on her, she recalled what she'd said about moving more slowly tonight. No kissing? Oh, no, there would *definitely* be more kissing tonight.

"Jenna, I have to confess something," Diego said as he took off his coat and hung it on the rack.

Uh-oh. What was this?

He took her hands, which worried her. "I know we'd made plans to have those red velvet cupcakes when we got back here, but if I eat one more thing, my stomach will literally burst."

Jenna chuckled. Phew. "Same here." Except she suddenly realized that maybe he'd said that to make his getaway—kindly.

"I'd love some coffee, though," he added.

So he intended to stay. She felt goose bumps rise up her spine. "Me too," she whispered.

He bent his head slightly and kissed her.

The sweet passion of his kiss, how his arms wrapped around her, assured her he was exactly where he wanted to be.

DIEGO WAS STANDING by the sliding glass doors to the patio thinking about that kiss when Jenna came back from checking on Robbie. He'd enjoyed the kiss but he wanted more. Much more.

"Sleeping so peacefully as reported," Jenna said. "I'll go make us that coffee."

He swept her back into his arms. "I have another confession." He trailed kisses on Jenna's neck. Her soft skin smelled like flowers.

She leaned back a bit and looked up at him, her blue eyes sparkling. "Oh?"

"I don't want coffee either. I just want you."

Her smile told him everything he needed to know. "Same here," she said just as he captured her mouth again.

He could stay here, in this embrace, forever. How had Diego Sanchez gotten here? Because this woman in his arms had slowly chipped away at the brick he'd built around his heart. Chip, chip, chip. He wasn't sure of anything but that he didn't want this moment to end. And that he wanted a new beginning.

A new chance.

She took his hand and headed for the stairs. At the top, they passed the nursery, then she paused by the door to her bedroom, but kept walking. She went to the next door and inside what looked like a guest room. Diego followed.

Jenna seemed unsure of herself suddenly. She moved over to the windows and nudged the filmy curtains to look out. "I, uh, I...think... I—"

"Honey," he said, walking to the other side of the window to give her some space. He faced her, leaning against the wall with his hip. "It's okay. I completely understand. You don't have to explain or say anything."

He'd known right away in her hesitation to enter her room that she wasn't ready to bring another man into her marital bed. She might never be unless she replaced everything in her room, and it was no longer the bedroom she and her husband had shared, but a new, neutral space.

"Jenna, bypassing your bedroom and taking me in here might

be enough of a step for you tonight. A first step about letting someone into your life. No one says we have to rush this."

She gave her head a shake. "Everything about tonight has felt right. *Now* feels right. But yes, in here with this bedroom's lack of personal attachments and memories. The bed is just a bed. Comfy, even for a guest room." She smiled, but he could see she was emotional.

He gently pulled her to him and held her. He pushed aside the curtains and raised the blinds so they could look out at the stars and the moon, not quite a crescent. For a few moments they just stood there.

"Did you pick a star to wish on?" he asked.

She turned to him, surprise lighting her beautiful face. "Actually, yes. How'd you know?"

"Lucky guess. I did too. Made my wish already."

"I want to ask what it was but I won't," she said. "I just hope it comes true."

He did too but he'd leave it at that.

She closed her eyes, then opened them. "Okay, I made mine."

"I hope *yours* comes true."

She smiled and put a hand on either side of his face and kissed him. Tenderly at first. Then very passionately. Her hands were on the buttons of his shirt. Two undone. She was in a hurry, he thought with a smile.

She took his hand and walked him to the bed, then sat down. He sat beside her, the anticipation driving him wild. He'd go at her pace, though, let her run the show.

This was something of a new experience for him too. For the first time in seven years, he'd be with a woman he hadn't run from when she'd laid her expectations on the table.

I'm not here to practice getting back in the swing, Diego.

He'd promised her to try, to keep an open mind, an open heart about the possibilities.

And he was making good on that. One day at a time, like they'd agreed on.

She got up and slowly straddled him, her hands against his chest, and he wondered if she could feel his heart pounding out a beat.

"Just so there's no mistake, Diego Sanchez. I want this. I want *you*."

He didn't need to hear anything else. He laid her down on the bed, inching up her sweater to reveal her creamy soft stomach. His hands traveled upward to her lacy bra. Diego smiled when Jenna impatiently lifted up a bit to yank off her sweater and toss it on the upholstered chair in the corner.

The sight of her satin black bra, her lush breasts filling it, tightened every muscle in his body. His hands found the clasp and he slid the straps from her shoulders and flung it to the chair with her sweater. He couldn't wait for the rest of her clothing to join them.

Diego sucked in a breath as his hands gently caressed her, his mouth trailing over her nipples. Her breathy moans and arching back were making him harder and harder. Her hands found the button of his pants, then the zipper as he did the same with her pants. She worked on his shirt buttons until his own clothes were on the chair, leaving them both in only their underwear.

"Not exactly the sexiest undies you've ever seen," she whispered, her hand protectively moving to her belly. "Baby seven months ago," she added, her voice sounding a bit unsure.

"They *are* the sexiest undies I've ever seen. And you're the sexiest woman, Jenna. If you need proof of what you do to me," he said, "it's right there." He glanced down at the bulge in his boxer briefs.

"I need more proof," she whispered in a seductive voice, slipping her hand under the waistband to his rock-hard erection.

All he could do was groan and throw his head back, focusing on the feel of her cool hand and fighting to keep control.

She wrapped her hand firmly around his throbbing, heated erection and moved it up and down, up and down. He groaned again, wanting their underwear off *now*. She fused her mouth to his, her hands now in his hair, then her nails scraping up his back.

He slowly moved down her body, trailing kisses on her neck, her collarbone, her breasts, the path to her belly button, then used his mouth to nudge away the band of those black panties.

She gasped and arched her back as he explored every inch of her softness once her underwear was off. He quickly got rid of his.

"It's gonna kill me to move away from you, but the condom is in my wallet in my pants on the chair," he said.

She smiled. "I love being a femme fatale."

He went to the chair and found his wallet, removing the little square packet. He tore it open and sat down, about to roll it on when Jenna came over.

"I'll take that," she said, kneeling down in front of him.

He almost lost it right there.

She rolled the condom onto his hard length, then inched up to him, very slowly lowering her body on top of him, closing her eyes as they became one. Diego sucked in a breath and gripped the sides of the chair, fighting not to lose control.

She rocked against him, his hands and mouth on her breasts, on her neck.

"Oh, Diego," she moaned, panting, arching her back, her long silky red hair falling behind her. He knew she was close to release. He just had to hold on a few more seconds. A few more seconds as she writhed against him and began to scream, her hand flying to her mouth to muffle the sound.

And then he let go.

She collapsed against his chest, her head on his shoulder, a kiss pressing against his neck.

"That was amazing," she whispered, while catching her breath.

"The best ever," he whispered back.

He shifted and scooped her up and carried her to the bed. They got under the covers, her head on his chest, their hands entwined.

I could stay like this forever, he thought, actually feeling his heart widening, deepening. He cared so much about this woman, he wondered if he was already falling hard for her.

As if in answer, he felt his heart crack wide open.

CHAPTER ELEVEN

JENNA WOKE UP in the middle of the night, Diego fast asleep beside her. For a moment, she just lay there, remembering every second of their time on the chair in the corner. When he'd carried her to the bed and they'd snuggled together, she was so sated and spent and overwhelmed—in a good way—that she must have dozed off.

She turned slightly to look at him, this beautiful man with his dark hair that had tickled every inch of her body. Their lovemaking had been passionate and intense and full of promise. She'd felt his intentions in every kiss, every thrust. In the way he'd held her close afterward, kissing her cheek, her forehead. The tenderness almost made her cry.

That was when the trouble had started for her.

She bit her lip and turned to face away from him, needing to figure out what she was feeling, what was happening in her head, in her heart.

It was too much, too soon. She understood that. The passion, fine. The passion combined with the tenderness? Way too much.

I can't fall in love with him, she thought, tears misting her eyes. *I can't love someone else.*

And not because of Rob. Not because of guilt.

Because of *sorrow*. Of heartbreak so painful and wrenching she couldn't bear the thought of going through it again.

She'd loved with all her being and had lost hard. She could see herself falling in love with Diego and living in constant fear and worry every time he drove off in his pickup no matter the weather conditions. Every time he was out on the range on a steep ledge with the cattle. Every time he rode a horse.

I can't do this, she thought, a familiar panicky feeling echoing those words in her head.

She quietly slipped out of bed, piled Diego's clothes neatly on the chair, then collected her own and hurried from the room, closing the door behind her. When she entered her bedroom, the bedroom where she and Rob had made love endlessly, where they'd watched late night TV and movies afterward in bed. Where Rob munched on his favorite snack of red grapes and she knitted after a long day. She flashed back to their last night together, when she'd been working on yellow baby booties because she'd found out just a few days prior that she was expecting.

Rob had been beside himself with happiness.

The next day, he was gone.

Because that was how life was. It changed in an instant.

Like when she met Diego Sanchez in the parking lot of the Tenacity Social Club. Her whole life had changed with that tap on her car window, leading to that chair in her guest room.

She felt so much for him—to the point that he was able to even get in the guest room.

She closed her eyes and dropped down on her bed, staring out the window at the inky night, at the same stars she and Diego had looked at in the room next door just hours ago, each choosing a star and making a wish.

Her wish? That this wasn't a dream, that he'd change his mind about what he had to offer, that he'd be all in.

She'd dashed her own dream without even giving him a chance.

Tears stung her eyes again and she got up and went into the bathroom, her gaze falling on the baby monitor sitting on the counter. She moved to the shower and turned on the water. Part of her wanted to keep every imprint of his lips, every scent from their lovemaking on her. But a bigger part needed to wash it all away.

Her heart aching and heavy, she stepped under the hot spray of water, soaped up her body and hair, and cried hard.

When she emerged, wrapping a thick towel around her, another for her hair, her feet in her soft slippers, she felt much better. She wasn't scared anymore because she'd settled on a decision about Diego. They could be friends. Good friends. He'd understand, surely.

You should have come to this before you slept with him, she chastised herself.

Her heart clenched at that. She should have. But she wouldn't have gotten to this point, of understanding that she could not handle loving him, without having been brought to the brink of it.

I'm sorry, Diego, she thought sadly, facing herself in the mirror. She dried off her hair and tied it back into a ponytail, then got dressed in a long pale pink sweatshirt and gray yoga pants. She changed her slippers for fuzzy warm socks. She looked at herself long and hard in the mirror. Self-preservation, she told herself.

She stared at the baby monitor. Aside from being unwilling to experience the pain she'd suffered when she lost Rob Lattimore, a great man who'd never gotten the chance to meet his child, she needed to be a very present mother. She was worried enough about her financial situation without adding being a panicked mess every time Diego left her side. Robbie didn't need her sole parent to be distracted like that. She'd made promises to Robbie about being a good mother. And she'd keep them.

Jenna let out a deep breath and went to Robbie's nursery. Standing over her daughter's bassinet, she felt her resolve strengthen. Yes, this was what was most important. This baby. She pressed a fingertip to her lips and then to Robbie's soft auburn wisps.

Then Jenna curled up in the glider chair by the window, moving the cozy throw over her, and closed her eyes.

DIEGO WOKE WITH a smile on his face, his eyes still closed. Mmm, the memory of making love to Jenna was so fresh that he could replay it without missing one delicious thing. He opened his eyes, not wanting to wait another second before seeing Jenna's beautiful face.

Or to tell her that he was in this 100 percent. He understood now, because of Jenna herself, that his ex had been one woman with a particular mindset. No, he couldn't give *that* woman what she wanted or needed. What he wished he'd understood in hindsight was that he shouldn't want to give anything of himself to a woman who valued a job title and a bank balance over deep and abiding love.

His family had tried to tell him, but he'd shut everyone out on that subject. Shamed and bruised and battered.

Not anymore. Because of the depth of his feelings for Jenna, she'd gotten through. Julian's wise words yesterday about their dad had gotten through.

He got it now. He might not be able to buy out the baby department of a big box store, but he could provide for Jenna and Robbie. He finally understood that that was enough. That he was good enough, as he was.

Thank you, Jenna Lattimore.

He turned, but Jenna wasn't in bed with him. Her clothes were gone from the chair, his own stacked neatly.

The sun wasn't quite up yet so it was very early. He hadn't heard Robbie cry, but Jenna clearly had. He couldn't wait to see her, wrap her in his arms, hold that precious little baby to his chest. This was all just beginning, but he was ready for it. Ready to be what Jenna needed: a man she could trust, count on, who could support her and Robbie in all ways, including financially, though granted, not with a new car every few years like folks seem to have in Bronco Heights or vacations beyond camping every summer. Anyway, he could easily pick up an extra hour a day on the ranch and let a rainy-day fund grow. A family fund.

He quickly dressed and went in search of Jenna. She wasn't in the nursery. And the crib was empty too, so they must be downstairs. He rushed down, his heart practically bursting with how much he had to tell her.

He heard her talking to Robbie in the kitchen.

"We're gonna visit Grandma and Grandpa today in Bronco,"

she was saying. "They're gonna be so surprised and happy to see you, Robbie!"

He paused. Bronco. Three hours round trip. Then two to three hours there. She'd be gone all day. And it was clearly an impromptu visit—to get away. Or she would have mentioned it last night.

She stopped talking when he entered the room, her expression going from animated to...

Serious. Worried. Sad.

And she wasn't saying anything, like *Good morning* or *I had a great night's sleep* because of all that strenuous activity or coming over to kiss him and wrap her arms around him.

The way he wanted to do to her.

But he was immediately aware that he shouldn't. That something had changed.

His heart sank with the realization that not only had something changed, but that something was very wrong.

He wasn't going to put her on the spot. Not with Robbie in the high chair, enjoying the mashed banana Jenna was feeding her with a spoon.

"Morning," he said, attempting a slight smile. He wasn't successful.

She glanced at him, that strange expression still on her beautiful face, then back at Robbie. "Morning."

Give her the time she needs, he told himself. It was all he could do now.

"Wish I could stick around this morning," he said to let her know at least that, "but I need to hit the road, get to the ranch. Can I make you a cup of coffee before I go?" He wished he could tell her what last night had meant to him. What she and Robbie meant to him. But this wasn't the time.

Her expression remained strained. If she said yes to coffee, he'd know she wanted him to stay a bit. If she said "No, I had a cup already," he'd know she wanted him to leave right now. And that he was correct about the way she was feeling. Differently from last night, that was for sure.

"No, thanks," she said, his heart sinking. "I already had a

cup. Robbie woke even earlier than usual. All that good sleeping through the night last night."

He managed a smile at Robbie. "I'll get going then. Talk tonight?"

She was pushing the spoon into the banana and mashing it a bit. "Yes. Definitely."

He nodded and turned to go.

"Diego?" she called.

His heart lifted and he turned around.

"I... I just..." She bit her lip and stopped talking. She looked like a woman who didn't want to tell the man she'd just slept with that she was sorry but she couldn't do this after all.

Which dammit, he understood. She had every right to take this as it came, see how she felt. Sometimes you didn't know how you felt until you went too far. But what they had was so...special.

"Jenna, it's okay. No worries. No matter what, I care about you and Robbie. That'll never change, no matter what we are to each other."

It was true, but it stung. Because he'd just come around. In the other direction than she went.

She stood and put down the spoon and walked over to him, her expression a mixture of sad and resolute. "You're a wonderful person, Diego Sanchez. And I'm lucky to know you."

That sounded like goodbye. His chest tightened, his shoulders tensed. He wanted to fight for her but now was not the time. Not with Robbie having her breakfast. Not with Jenna needing some space between them. *Put her first*, he told himself.

"Ditto," he said, and gave her a fast hug back, relishing the feel and scent of her. Then he let go and turned again, heading to the coatrack. He needed air and some time to let this settle.

But dammit, it hurt.

THE MOMENT JENNA turned onto her parents' street, she relaxed. She hadn't lived in Bronco in ten years, but the sight of the house she'd grown up in, the familiar brick Cape with its welcoming red door and black shutters, did a weary heart good.

She knew that Diego had relatives in town, in Bronco Valley, the less affluent side of town where she grew up. Her mother was a longtime happy customer of hairstylist Denise Sanchez, who managed a salon nearby. Jenna was pretty sure Denise and her husband, Aaron, were Diego's aunt and uncle. It was a small world.

She couldn't stop thinking of the Sanchez in *her* life. His face when he'd stood in the doorway of the kitchen that morning. She'd had a script in her head for what to say, to avoid any real conversation in the moment with Robbie right there, eating her mashed banana. They'd talk later, she'd figured. But she'd been able to tell that he knew something had changed between the time they'd fallen asleep naked in each other's arms and when he'd awoken.

She felt terrible about it. And because Diego put others before himself, he'd understood and had quietly left.

Her heart still hurt.

As she was taking Robbie out of her car seat, her parents came out all bundled up. Her parents each hugged her, then her dad said he was taking his grandbaby to the nursery to put on a puppet show—they'd found an adorable little stage and puppets at a thrift sore—and to read her stories.

Code for: *so you and Mom can talk.*

They knew that Jenna didn't make impromptu midweek visits, an hour and a half away, unless she was needing her mom's advice and her dad's hugs and hot chocolate.

Inside, her dad got Robbie out of her snowsuit. "Give Mama a kiss before we go to the puppet show by yours truly."

Jenna kissed her daughter's baby-shampoo-scented head. "Enjoy the show, sweetie. And thanks, Dad."

Her father winked at her and headed upstairs. The house had three bedrooms, and they'd turned a guest room into a nursery with everything Robbie needed while they were visiting. Her dad had been able to pick up everything secondhand.

She and her mother smiled as her father chatted to Robbie the entire trip up the stairs. Her parents were the best.

"Difficult night?" her mom asked, voice full of compassion as they walked into the living room. Her mom knew all about difficult nights. Her parents had stayed with her for six weeks after she'd lost Rob; they'd been in the thick of it. In the months after, her mother would call every night, and sometimes Jenna was managing and sometimes she'd be unable to stop crying.

Jenna sank down on the sofa, her mother sitting beside her. "Didn't start out that way. I make the mistake of thinking I could actually start seeing someone. A very handsome, very kind cowboy named Diego."

Her mom's eyes widened. "What happened? You were honest about your needs and he couldn't handle it?"

"Oh, he could, actually. He could handle anything. The problem turned out to be me."

She told her mom everything, including that they'd spent the night together, two nights, but how *last* night, Jenna had given into her attraction and feelings. Until she'd woken up in the middle of the night.

Choking. Seized up. Scared.

Her mom took her hand and held it. "I know it's a cliché to say, but all love comes with risk, Jenna."

"I know that. It's why I'm backing out. Why I can't keeping seeing Diego. How can I let myself fall in love with someone when *anything* can happen? I have enough people in my life to worry about on a daily basis."

"I understand, sweetie. Of course I do. What I think you're really saying is that you're just not ready."

Jenna wasn't sure that was really the issue. "How can I ever be ready to fall for someone I could lose, though?"

"I wish I had words of wisdom for you. All I know is that this man must be pretty special for you to have gotten involved with him in the first place."

"He is," she said, trying to blink Diego's image from her mind. That face. The kindness. Memories of their night together.

She missed him so much already. How was she going to cut him out of her life?

They'd be friends. But how did you go from an intense attraction and deep interest to being platonic? How did you just shut off the romance, the sexual desire?

Maybe it would be easier than she thought. Because her fear seemed to trump everything else.

"Let's go bake something gooey and fattening," her mom said. "And eat every bit of it."

Jenna smiled. "Good idea."

But then her smile faded as she was reminded of Diego saying he had to pass on the red velvet cupcakes because he was bursting at the seams from dinner and the cookies at the dance. How nervous she'd been that he was making an excuse not to stay for their planned dessert. How thrilled she'd been when he'd asked for coffee.

All leading to a night she'd never forget as long as she lived. The passion, the tenderness.

She followed her mother to the kitchen, where she'd baked by her mom's side from the time she was three years old. The cheery room with the same white round table, the same wallpaper with its leaf motif, was so comforting that Jenna instantly felt better.

"All you can do is what feels right," her mom said as she started setting out the ingredients for Jenna's favorite cake: good old chocolate layer. "Whether that's spending the night with Diego or backing away because you're scared or anywhere between those two. Nothing you feel is wrong, Jenna. Just know that."

Jenna squeezed her mom's hand. "Thanks. Just what I needed to hear."

And it really was. A relief since following her heart, her head was all she *could* do.

CHAPTER TWELVE

ALL MORNING AT WORK, while Diego herded cattle to a different snowy pasture, while he'd checked over a Black Angus heifer that had been acting off, while he'd helped out the hands with a feed delivery that needed unloading, he'd been asked the same question: |*You okay?*|

He wasn't okay and wasn't surprised his emotions showed on his face. This morning had been rough. To the point that he barely felt the cold Montana wind whipping at his cowboy hat and trying to get through his leather barn coat and work gloves. It wasn't just the big change in Jenna from last night to this morning—especially right after he'd had a big change happening inside himself and in the opposite direction. But that he couldn't talk to her about it. Not till she got back from Bronco. He couldn't call or text her while she was visiting with her folks, and he certainly wouldn't interrupt her on a long drive. He'd just have to wait to hear what she had to say.

He'd had the same response for everyone who'd taken one look at his grim face and asked if he was okay—his dad, a few fellow cowboys, even the foreman. Two other cowboys had mentioned they'd seen him at the dance getting up close and personal with a pretty redhead—was she his new girlfriend?

Diego had answered honestly, which had surprised him: "I don't know but I hope so."

He'd never thought such a line would come out of his mouth, but there it was. Things could and did change. People could change.

Unfortunately, that didn't mean anyone else was in the same mindset at the same time.

He'd gotten tipped hats and claps on the back, which made him feel worse, since by tonight, it would be official that they weren't a couple.

And now, just past 1:00 p.m., he was keyed up and tense and needed to get out of here. Off the ranch. A change of scenery would do him good. He didn't have much of an appetite, but he could use coffee.

He got in his truck and headed into town, parking by the Silver Spur Café. As he was getting in line to order at the counter, he noticed a very familiar long dark ponytail right in front of him.

"Hey, Nina," he said.

His sister turned with a surprised smile. "You're here? You never come here."

His shrug must have been extra pathetic because she peered at him closely.

"Something's wrong," she said, studying him. "Is Dad okay? Mom? Luca?"

"Everyone's fine," he assured her.

"Except you." It was her turn to order. "What are you having?" she asked him.

"Large regular coffee," he told the waitress.

He was so distracted he hadn't even noticed Nina had gotten herself a coffee too and paid for them both. He'd get it next time. "Thanks."

They moved over by the window, which had a bar and stools.

"I'll assume this has something to do with Jenna Lattimore," she said, sipping her coffee.

Oh hell, he might as well tell her. He needed to talk to someone, and Nina was a good listener and always gave solid advice. "Just when I came around to taking things to the next level—"

Her mouth dropped open. "Wait, the next *level*? You're thinking of proposing?"

"The next level for me is an actual relationship beyond a few dates."

"I should have known. Sorry—continue. Just when you came around, she…"

"Changed her mind," he said. "I'm sure it has to do with her actually taking that next step herself and then getting cold feet. She and her husband were together since she was nineteen. He died just over a year ago."

"Must be very hard," Nina said compassionately. "She's also raising a baby on her own."

He nodded, picturing Jenna holding Robbie, snuggling her close. "I want to be there for her, take care of her—*them*. If she just wants to be friends, fine, I'll be the best friend she's ever had, though she has one of those already. But…" He let out a hard breath and hung his head back.

"But you have serious feelings for Jenna. And the baby."

He nodded again, that adorable little girl coming to mind with her big blue eyes and penchant for grabbing his nose and ear. "Robbie. She's so cute. Turns out I like holding a baby."

Nina was staring at him, wonder in her expression. "Wow, you have really done a one-eighty, Diego."

He really had. "I guess Julian was right. It just comes for you and that's that."

"By 'it' do you mean love?" She grinned but then looked at him thoughtfully.

Love. Was that what this was? Maybe. Love was a *big* word. He shrugged. "I just know that I've never felt this way before," he said.

She grabbed his hand and gave it a squeeze. "I'm so damned happy to hear that. And I think things will work out just fine. But right now, Jenna's going through some huge changes. Scary changes."

Scary changes. Like caring about someone else again.

"I know," he said. "I just hope she doesn't shut me out. I want to help. Without putting any pressure on her."

"She probably just needs time. For you, everything is brand-new. But for her, it isn't—and the last time she did this, she lost everything in the most painful way possible. She's going to react, she's going to freak out, she's going to retreat, but she'll likely come running too. Just let her do what she needs to—and when."

He nodded, taking all that in. "I will." He slugged down his coffee, the caffeine boost and Nina's excellent advice buoying him. "I owe you, *mana*. For the coffee and the sisterly wisdom."

"Anytime," she said with a smile. Her phone buzzed and she glanced at it. "Gotta run. Let me know how it goes. I like details."

"Will do," he said. "Though maybe not the details."

She squeezed his hand and left. Diego sat for a few more minutes, finishing his coffee. He checked his own phone as though there would magically be a text when there was no notification.

There wasn't.

He wanted to hear from Jenna so badly. But at least when they talked tonight, he'd be a bit more grounded. It had helped to talk it all out with Nina.

Would Jenna come running? He wasn't so sure of that. Come inching toward him? Maybe. But it opened the possibility that he had a shot at keeping her in his life.

JENNA COULDN'T RELAX. She was pacing around the living room, clasping and unclasping her hands, straightening perfectly straight photo frames and candlesticks on the mantel.

Diego would be here any minute.

She'd texted him right before she'd left her parents' house a few hours ago.

Can we talk tonight? After Robbie's bedtime at 8:30?

He'd texted back in three seconds. I'll see you then.

She was not looking forward to this conversation. But she *was* looking forward to seeing him. For what might be the last time.

She bit her lip and rearranged the order of the items on the coffee table, then put them back the way there were. It would be just her and Diego. Robbie was asleep in the nursery, so there would be no stalling to put her to bed, no buffer of small talk over how Robbie had fallen asleep early or how cute the new Valentine-themed footie pajamas were that her parents had insisted on buying for their granddaughter during a trip into town.

Jenna heard the pickup truck pulling into the driveway and her heart rate sped up even though she knew exactly how this would go. She would tell him how she felt. He would tell her it was okay, he understood, no worries. He'd give her a hug. That was Diego. And it wasn't fair that someone so supportive was being treated this way. After that beautiful night together.

She closed her eyes for a second, not used to feeling like a heel. *I'm sorry, Diego.*

While she and her parents had been at Sadie's Holiday House, a gift shop in Bronco, something had occurred to her: that Diego might actually be relieved. He was at the "trying" stage, going from his usual casual dating to keeping an open mind about a real relationship between them. Perhaps he'd feel a weight off his shoulders, a pressure gone when she told him she couldn't do this after all. They had gotten to a point where he had to be feeling uncomfortable. Especially because they'd slept together.

She remembered his face this morning, his expression when it was clear that something had changed for her. It was the look of a relieved confirmed bachelor.

Her phone pinged with a text. I'm here. Didn't want to ring the bell and wake Robbie.

That was Diego Sanchez. Summed up right there in the tiniest gesture why she'd felt so safe, so cared for, so supported that she'd slept with him.

And the moment she opened the door and saw him, she remembered the other part of why she'd taken him into the guest room. That handsome face. His deep brown eyes. The tall, muscular body. She had to suck in a breath at his effect on her. How she wanted to grab him to her and kiss the living daylights out of him.

But a second later, she envisioned him on a horse near a steep drop. Behind the wheel of a car on a slick road. Just going about his daily life when anything could happen, anytime. Rain or shine.

And her resolve strengthened. That she was intensely attracted to him and had very strong feelings were not in question.

Nor was her ability to deal with loving and losing all over again.

Because it was out of the question. She'd done a lot of thinking on the long drive back from her parents' house and she'd come to some important realizations. She'd share them with him tonight.

"How was the drive there and back?" he asked. "Any traffic?"

"Not at all," she said, shutting the door behind him and leading the way to the living room. Neither of them sat, though. Jenna stood kind of awkwardly by the fireplace, and Diego was beside the sofa. "I made good time and I *had* a good time. Seeing my parents was just what I needed. And they doted on their grandbaby, of course."

"I'm sure," he said with a half smile. Then he looked at her intently. "Jenna, I want to tell you something. Whatever you're feeling, whatever you need to say to me or do, it's okay. I understand. Whatever you need from me, that's what I'll be. But... I just don't want something to get lost or unsaid, so here goes."

With everything in her she had to fight the urge to close the few feet between them and throw her arms around him. Hold on for dear life. Because it didn't work that way. There *was* no holding on.

She'd learned that the hardest way possible.

"I want this," he continued. "*Us.* I want to be with you. I want to be there for Robbie in whatever way you feel comfortable with. I'm in this one hundred percent. There's no more trying. There's no need to try. I'm *there*, Jenna."

Oh, Diego. Her heart squeezed so tightly that she had to press her hand to her chest. He *wasn't* going to be relieved to hear what she had to say.

"I won't speak for you," he said. "But I think I understand what happened between the time we dozed off and this morning. Or the middle of the night when you left the bed."

He paused for a moment, looking away and then back at her. Her heart went out to him—at how hard he was fighting for this. For them. At how much he *had* changed.

There's no more trying... I'm there...

This wasn't fair to him at all. And she couldn't do anything about it.

"You lost your husband, your partner of almost ten years," he continued. "And now you're involved with me and it's calling up all those scary, painful feelings. You don't want to go through anything like that again."

That was exactly right. It almost helped to hear him say it.

"I *can't*," she said. "I realized something on the ride home from Bronco. That I'm finally in an okay place. It's why I was able to be romantically involved with you in the first place, to sleep with you. In those early months after I lost Rob I was a wreck who sobbed constantly and needed to hold my infant daughter to get through the day. I'm okay now, Diego, except for the occasional time when I need a half hour to sit with it. And I want to leave that alone, leave myself in peace. For me and for Robbie."

He seemed to be taking that in and was quiet for a moment. "I'm not going to stand here and try to convince you to let me in, Jenna. I refuse to pressure you. You have every right to your feelings. I won't lie—I want to fight for you. But the cowboy code has a clause about that."

She managed to smile through the tears suddenly stinging her eyes. "I'll keep being honest here. All I want right now is for you to hold me. I need you, Diego. But *you're* the one I'm in danger from. How did everything get so upside down?" The tears started falling, and she wiped them away.

"Well, there's where I'll tell you you're wrong," he said, stepping toward her. "I'm not the danger. The fear is coming from here." He reached out his hand and pressed it to her heart. "I know what you mean, though. I'm scary. What we have is scary. And loss is heart-wrenching. Jenna, this is beside the point right now, but *you're* scary as hell to *me*. Because of how I feel about you."

She flew to him then, wrapping her arms around him. He held her tightly as she cried. "I do need you, Diego. I need you, but I can't have you in my life." She wasn't letting go, though. She couldn't seem to do that, either.

"I have an idea," he said gently. "What if we take this so slowly that you don't even know there's an us?"

She leaned her head back and looked at him, her expression brightening just a bit. "What do you mean?"

"What if we just go minute by minute, Jenna? At the core, we have a beautiful, necessary friendship. If you want more in any given moment, any given day, great. If not, absolutely fine. We go at your pace so you can get used to dating, to letting yourself care about someone again. If it gets to be too much, just tell me and I'll back off immediately."

She bit her lip, his words making sense. She took a step back, leaning against the wall, needing a minute to let this all sink in. She *might* be able to do this—what he'd described. Minute by minute. No labels. No pressure. Friends at the core. Her deep need for him would be met. They could date. They could kiss. They could make love. She could sleep spooned against him. She could also leave in the middle of the night if she wanted. If she got scared and nervous at any time, she could retreat.

Right now, she felt more hopeful than scared. She could go with this. She didn't have to shut out what she needed. *Don't turn away this wonderful man. Try.* Like he did—like he was right now. "This sounds good to me, Diego, except for the part where I get everything I need and you're out in the cold."

His dark eyes sparkled with the in she'd given him. "In the cold? Are you kidding? You've come to mean so much to me that the iceberg in my chest completely melted. I'm warm all the time. I'm also Latino—hot-blooded." He smiled.

She couldn't help but laugh. "Can we really do this? Just as you said?"

He pulled her into his arms again. "I absolutely can. Because like I said, the core of us is friendship. And friends are there for each other no matter what. If I can kiss you, if I can make love to you, all the better, but I just want to be in your life. Yours and Robbie's."

"I like the sounds of that," she said, so touched by him that her eyes misted up all over again.

She was still worried, though—deep down and right on the surface—but if she could keep Diego Sanchez in her life in a way that didn't scare her every other minute, she was taking it.

CHAPTER THIRTEEN

LAST NIGHT, WHEN Diego had been saying goodbye to Jenna at the door, they'd discovered they both had today off. A rare, happy coincidence. He'd invited her and Robbie on an outing, hoping she'd say yes. He didn't want to overwhelm her with his presence, considering he'd stayed for a few hours.

After they'd come to an agreement on their relationship, Jenna had suggested they finally enjoy those delicious red velvet cupcakes he'd brought over for Robbie's seven-month birthday. They'd had their treats while watching a rom-com that had them commenting through the entire movie. They'd laughed and chatted, keeping the conversation light—about the film, funny stories from their childhoods, and what kind of dog they'd each get if their living situation ever got dog-friendly. Diego liked Great Danes and chihuahuas and wanted one of each. Jenna liked medium-sized, furry, smiley dogs, like Australian shepherds. They'd both agreed that lonely mutts at the shelter who needed homes would win their hearts and they'd want to take them all home.

And then it had gotten late fast. Diego had said he'd better hit the road since he didn't want to overstay his welcome so soon, and when Jenna didn't invite him to stick around longer, he wasn't disappointed. He'd truly meant all he'd said to her when he'd first arrived. Her terms. Her timeline.

And now, at 10:00 a.m., the three of them, Diego, Jenna and Robbie, were headed to the Tenacity Town Hall to see a special art show that Jenna had suggested. The show featured art from kids of all ages, from toddlers to teenagers. The daycare where Jenna worked had part of a wall devoted to their kids' work, including baby Robbie's artistic debut.

"We're here, Robbie!" Diego said as he turned into the parking lot. "I can't wait to see your handprints."

Jenna got out and unlatched Robbie's car seat, then snapped it into the stroller base. "Me too! I've seen it, of course, but not hanging on a wall! Robbie definitely liked having her hands plopped into the pink watercolor paint, didn't you, my little *artiste*?"

Diego smiled as he watched Jenna with her daughter. He'd never expected to be a dad, so he'd never pictured himself in the midst of something like this. As an uncle, sure. But this felt different because the tiny human having such an effect on him wasn't a relative who he adored simply because they were family. The intense protectiveness he felt for Robbie was brand-new to him.

As they headed toward the entrance, Diego was reminded of the Valentine's dance, Jenna in his arms and all the promise of that night—which had almost derailed. But things were back on track. He'd woken up feeling very positive about their talk last night. He'd been willing to go from zero to sixty because of how strongly he felt about Jenna, how much Robbie had come to mean to him, but he knew *he* should be going slowly for his own sake too. He hadn't let himself feel anything for a woman in seven years. And now he was spending the day with a single mom and her baby, a family of two who he'd do anything for.

This new plan of theirs was good for them both.

Inside, they waved and said hi to the few people milling around this early; the big crowd would come after school when the young artists came with their families. There was some serious talent among the children of Tenacity. Katie W., age 10, had sketched a drawing of a yellow Lab with such expression in the dog's face and eyes that Diego would have bought it were it for sale. A high school student painted her entire family with colored dots. Little Cowpokes Daycare Center had his favorite work, though. Various colored suns with long spokes around the orb, houses with no doors, lots of stick people. The art was beyond adorable.

"And the masterpiece," he said as they stopped in front of the pink watercolor. *Handprints by Robbie L, age 7 months.* "Great job, Robbie!" he said, bending down to shake her little hand.

Jenna grinned and took out a phone to snap a few photos of the artwork for her parents, then stepped to the side to text them.

He knelt down beside the stroller. "Love your use of shading, Robbie," he quipped, running a finger down the baby's soft cheek.

"Hey, Diego," said a male voice.

He turned to see a guy he'd gone to school with here in Tenacity. Linc Danvers, who'd been on the baseball team with him. A young kid was up on his shoulders, and his hands were on a stroller with a napping baby. Diego hadn't spoken to Linc since graduation. Tenacity was a small town, but there weren't many places to run into people. "Hey, Linc. Mini artist in the family?" he asked.

"Actually, no. My wife has a bad cold so I figured I'd get these two out of the house for a bit and this seemed like a fun activity. This big guy is Willis—he's four, and the baby is Sara. A year next month."

Diego smiled up at the cute blond boy, then peered into the stroller. "Happy almost birthday," he whispered to the napper just as Jenna came back over. "Linc, this is Jenna and the talented artist is Robbie. These are her handprints," he added, gesturing at the watercolor.

"Proud daddy," Linc said with a smile. "I know how that is."

Diego glanced at Jenna, whose expression tightened. "I'm actually a family friend," he said to Linc.

Linc nodded. "Ah. Well, nice to see you, Diego. And nice to meet you, Jenna. Enjoy the day."

As the guy headed down the hall, Diego was struck not only by what he'd said, but by the image of him walking with the little boy up on his shoulders as he pushed the stroller.

I actually do feel like a proud papa.

And I want to be wheeling Robbie about town. I want Robbie up on my shoulders, my hands around her ankles, someday.

And I want Jenna by my side.

He froze for a second at the realization that he was already quite serious about Jenna. It had happened without his awareness. Exactly like Julian had said it would.

"Cute kids," Jenna said kind of absently, her gaze on the next piece of art on the wall.

"Sorry about that." He had no doubt she'd know what he was referring to.

She was quiet for a second, then shook her head and touched his arm. "No worries, Diego. Really. I just reacted in the moment. You'd think I be used to it—Mike's been mistaken for Robbie's dad more than a few times the past seven months."

He smiled but there was a reason it didn't bother her until now, until Diego. Mike wasn't a love interest, a potential partner. Diego was.

"You have every right to feel protective of who her father is and his memory, Jenna."

She wrapped her arm around his and rested her head on his shoulder, surprising him. "You always understand me."

Because I love you, he thought out of the clear blue sky— and froze.

He did love her. *I love Jenna Lattimore.* He wanted to scream it down the hall, cupping his hand around his mouth like a megaphone.

If he could change to this degree, he had no doubt that with time and love and care, Jenna would fully welcome him into her and Robbie's life.

He was ready for it.

A COUPLE OF hours later, Jenna had just put Robbie down for her nap in the nursery when Diego came to the doorway. They'd had a great morning, enjoying the art show, then going for coffee and pie at the Silver Spur Café, something she rarely ever did given her strict budget. He'd insisted on treating—*I invited you out, so it's on me.* Then Robbie had started yawning so they'd brought her home. Diego had been about to leave when he said the squeaky bathroom door hinge was driving him nuts and it would take him two seconds to lubricate it. She'd jokingly mentioned she had a whole bunch of other little things that needed fixing, and he'd said he'd take care of it all and had gone to his pickup for his tool kit. She'd better watch out or he'd make himself a little too indispensable. Very nice and superhot was fine. But a man who could fix a leaky faucet was golden.

"Robbie asleep?" he asked, stepping inside to peer at the baby. "I love how she always naps with her arm crooked alongside her head, fist at her ear."

Jenna laughed. "My favorite thing is when she quirks her lip like Elvis." She gasped. "She just did it!"

Diego laughed too. "I have another invitation for you." He held up his phone. "Just got a text from my mom. Family dinner tonight. She's making her incredible enchiladas suizas and would love for you and Robbie to join us."

Surprise lit her face. "Really? That's so nice. Any particular reason or occasion?"

"Well, the whole family is invited because my sister Marisa and her husband, Dawson, are back from their honeymoon and everyone wants to see the photos. And I'll be honest about why *you're* likely invited—I was moping yesterday morning and I ran into my sister Nina and I might have told her I was worried about us. So she might have told my mom to add another plate at the table. Trying to do a little matchmaking, no doubt."

"Aww. We beat them to it."

He pulled her to him for a hug. "Yeah, we did."

She relished being in his arms. She'd been aware all morning that he'd been taking care not to overwhelm her. He'd been affectionate, but not overboard. And then there was the way he'd handled her reaction when his old school friend had mistaken him for Robbie's dad.

You have every right to feel protective of who her father is and his memory, Jenna.

They were taking their relationship minute by minute, and minute by minute Diego Sanchez was showing her that she'd been right about him all along.

"I'd love to go and meet your family. I'll put Robbie in her fanciest clothes."

He smiled. "I'll let my mom know," he said, sending a quick text back.

Over the next few hours, Diego took care of those issues around the house—the squeaky hinge, the leaky faucet, the bottom of a door that needed sanding, and since Jenna had wanted to move some furniture around, switching the desk and console table in the living room.

She looked around at the new arrangement and smiled. "I could not have managed that on my own. It's nice to have a brawny cowboy around."

He made a muscle with his arm and smiled. "So we'll leave in a half hour for my place."

They'd spent so much time together today, and with the exception of the art show and pie, they'd been right here, doing everyday things. In between his handyman fixes, he'd made a pot of coffee, looking like he belonged in her kitchen. And when he rooted around in the fridge to make some lunch suggestions—and then whipped them up sandwiches—she realized that he felt right at home and that it didn't make her feel funny. Instead, she felt...comforted. Excited.

"I'm really looking forward to meeting everyone," she said. "And to try those enchiladas. I'll just go get ready. Keep an ear for Robbie?"

"Will do," he said, dropping down on the sofa.

I trust you, she realized in amazement as she hurried to her bedroom to have this moment in private. She went to her dresser and stared at herself in the mirror, sure she must look different. Granted, she was just feet away from Robbie's nursery should Robbie suddenly start screeching out of control, but Diego had become a trusted person in her life the way Mike was.

And now she was meeting his whole family. Getting further enmeshed in his world. She knew she'd fall for this man fast and swift and hard no matter how slowly she tried to go.

One minute at a time, she reminded herself.

She freshened up her makeup and changed into dark jeans and her favorite emerald green sweater, adding gold earrings and a necklace to dress it up a little. When she came out of her bedroom, Diego had Robbie in his arms, swaying her back and forth by the patio door.

Singing her a lullaby that he clearly didn't know the words to and was adorably mangling.

She'd chuckle if she wasn't so touched. Did he know the way to her heart was through being this sweet and caring to her child?

"FORGET OUR HONEYMOON PICS," Marisa said as she oohed and ahhed over Robbie. "I could look at this precious baby all day."

They'd arrived a half hour ago, Diego getting more claps on the back and knowing looks in one five-minute period than he'd gotten in his entire life. Jenna had gotten a warm welcome, and everyone fussed over the baby. They were now seated at the dining room table, Robbie sitting in the playpen the Sanchezes had on hand for when Julian and Ruby visited with their little one. Little Jay was napping in his car seat, since he'd conked out in Julian's truck on the way over. Big sister Emery was sitting in her booster seat at the table with the grown-ups.

Diego's mother's gaze was soft on Robbie. "I'm always ready for grandchildren to fuss over," Nicole said. She didn't turn to look at Diego, but he felt as if she was—pointedly. Interestingly, he wasn't uncomfortable with the idea like he'd normally be.

"That goes triple for me," Will Sanchez said. His dad threw a grin his way. And instead of mock-coughing or changing the subject, Diego smiled back.

It was a lot easier being this new Diego.

"The more grandnieces and -nephews the better," Uncle Stanley added, wrapping his arm around his Winona, whose gaze was boring into Diego. As usual.

Trying to tell me something? he wanted to ask, but he knew better than to question the psychic. If she had something to say, she'd say it. And leave you to figure out what the heck she meant. All he knew for certain was that her pronouncements always came true.

Jenna sat beside Diego, answering Marisa's and Nina's barrage of questions about Robbie and what her favorite solid foods were so far and if she'd said her first word. He was aware of his relatives watching him—them—and listening closely. How he looked at Jenna, how he spoke to her, how he handled Robbie.

"Must be serious," Luca had whispered when he, Diego and Julian had gone into the kitchen to refill the bowls of their uncle Stanley's homemade salsa for their mother's homemade tortilla chips—Diego's favorite on earth. "You brought not just Jenna but her *daughter*." His brother was studying him for the real answer just in case Diego wasn't forthcoming.

"I'm very serious about them both," he'd whispered back.

Both Luca's and Julian's eyes had opened wide in such surprise that Diego had to laugh. Hey, he got it. He'd been Tenacity's unofficial most confirmed bachelor for years.

Now, as they were enjoying the delicious enchiladas, the conversation moved to focus on a different Sanchez every few minutes. Marisa's wedding and the honeymoon, Julian's plans for the ranch he'd purchased, which he'd named The Start of a New Day Ranch, Ruby's report of Jay's well-baby checkup—all was very well—and Diego's mom's amazement that her home business as a seamstress had tripled profits from last month since so many folks had hired her to have their Valentine's Day date outfits taken in or let out. Nina, though, was on the quiet side and seemed distracted.

"Nina, any word on your search into the Deroy family?" Diego asked, sensing she had that on her mind.

Diego recalled that Nina had asked their uncle Stanley to use his newly discovered sleuthing skills to locate the Deroys—particularly Barrett, her first love. He hadn't been seen or heard from since he was sixteen, when he and his family suddenly left town. Why and what had become of them was a total mystery.

Nina's shoulders deflated. "I haven't been able to find out *anything* about them and neither has Uncle Stanley—not for lack of both of us trying. It's like Barrett vanished into thin air. I just want to know what happened all these years ago to make him and his family leave Tenacity. And where he is now. What he's doing."

Stanley looked at Nina. "I'm surprised that I haven't been able to find out anything. I left the online searches to you and know it didn't get you anywhere, but all my chatting folks up on my walks and trip to the grocery store were a letdown too. Sorry." He seemed lost in thought for a moment. "Nina, I do have to caution you that when the Deroys left town, they were persona non grata. Folks turned against them for some reason. I wonder if the family purposely destroyed any trail that could lead anyone to them."

Nina frowned. "I just wish I knew what happened back then. What did they do that was so terrible?"

Uncle Stanley threw up his hands. "I wasn't around back then and neither was Winona. But I think it might have had something to do with Tenacity itself and the town falling on hard times." He turned to Diego's parents. "Will, Nicole, do you remember anything?"

Nicole shook her head. "Will and I talked about it after Nina asked you to look into it all. We can't remember why they left. In fact, we're not sure anyone really knows. It was all a bit of a mystery."

Stanley nodded. "So this really requires a lot more digging on my part." He turned to Nina. "I promise you that I'm working on it."

Nina nodded. "I appreciate your help, Uncle Stanley. I just wish I knew why Barrett left town without saying anything to me. It just makes no sense. I don't get it."

"Maybe he found it too painful to say goodbye," Diego said, thinking about yesterday morning, how hard it was to leave Jenna's house knowing that it might be the last time he saw the Lattimores.

All eyes turned to him. The family definitely wasn't used to sensitive insight about matters of the heart coming from him.

"Maybe," Nina said with a nod. "That would make sense, I guess." Again, she seemed lost in thought.

"It is written in the stars," Winona suddenly said.

Now all eyes turned to the psychic at the table. Everyone was clearly trying to figure out what she meant. What, exactly, was written in the stars? And when? Nina hadn't seen Barrett in fifteen years.

"What do you mean, Winona?" Nina asked with so much

angst in her voice that Diego knew this was really important to her. Finding Barrett. Getting to the truth.

"It's written in the stars," Winona repeated.

Written in the stars. Diego thought about the night in the guest room, when he and Jenna had stared out at the window at the stars and made their wishes.

His had come true. He'd tell her that sometime. When she needed to hear it.

If she needed to hear it.

"It's time to find answers," Winona added, and then sipped her wine. Her gaze bored into Nina's, then moved to Diego's.

Was she applying that to him too? At the moment, he didn't need any answers. He and Jenna were taking it slow, day by day, minute by minute. No labels, no pressure. He supposed he did have a burning question and maybe wise Winona knew it.

His question? If he'd be fully welcomed into Jenna and Robbie's life the way he hoped.

CHAPTER FOURTEEN

IN THE MORNING, Diego and his father were herding cattle into a farther pasture on the ranch, the bright sunshine warming up the cold temperature. He couldn't stop thinking about Jenna, wondering what she was doing right then. He knew she was at work at Little Cowpokes Daycare Center, maybe reading to the children in her group or leading an arts and craft activity. Maybe she was taking a break and visiting Robbie in the baby room, asking her daughter what she thought of the Sanchez family. He smiled at that. They'd both had a great time last night. He knew Jenna had because she'd said so and had clearly meant it—and had looked so happy and comfortable last night at his house. Chatting with his family, laughing, telling everyone about Robbie's latest milestones, talking about Bronco and how she'd just visited her parents there recently.

"She's lovely," Diego's mom had said right before they were leaving. "So warm and friendly—not to mention beautiful."

"A keeper," his dad had whispered when he and Diego had gone into the kitchen to get a second pie for dessert. The first had gone in minutes.

"Agreed," Diego had whispered back, and the happy look on his dad's face was something else. Diego had realized then that his parents had likely been really worried about him and his state of mind, and state of heart, the past seven years, the last few particularly after turning thirty, since he'd avoided commitment and love for far too long.

"Think you and Jenna will get married?" his father asked now, deftly directing his mare to herd the cattle to the left.

"I still can't believe that question can apply to me," Diego said, marveling at how much he'd changed. How much a woman and a baby had swooped into his heart and turned his life rightside up.

"Trust me, I know," Will said with a chuckle. "Your mom and I wondered if someone would ever crack open that stubborn heart of yours."

"Someone definitely did." He smiled, Jenna's beautiful face coming to mind. Her warm blue eyes, full pink-red lips that he'd kissed so passionately. Not in the last couple of days, but their night in the guest room would last him a while. There would be time for passionate kisses and much more when Jenna was ready. Right now, he was just glad she'd opened the door.

"You love her?" his dad asked, looking at his son intently.

Diego was once again in total wonder that such a question was being directed at him, the guy who never went on a fourth date.

"With all my heart," Diego said. "Robbie too. Crazy, right? What happened to me?"

His father laughed. "Love happened. I'm very happy it got you, Diego."

"Me too," he said. "I like it. Who knew?"

His father laughed again, but when a few of the cattle went a little rogue, the two cowboys stopped yakking and started herding.

A few hours later, when they were back at the barn with the horses, his dad said he'd make them lunch at the house if Diego was hungry yet.

But Diego had another idea for his lunch hour. Something that had been on his mind the past few hours ever since his father had asked if he thought he and Jenna would get married. If he loved Jenna.

Yes and yes.

Well, that first question relied on someone else and right now, marriage had to be the last thing on Jenna's mind.

But the second was all him and yes he did. Diego Sanchez loved Jenna Lattimore. Deeply. And he wanted to celebrate that. Quietly. Just by himself. It was a big deal and he knew it. And it needed a big gesture.

Which was why he found himself using his lunch hour to drive two towns over to where an online search had told him he'd find a nice jewelry store in Beaumont and Rossi's Fine Jewels. He wouldn't have the pick of the store, of course, but he'd find something just right and worthy of Jenna in his price range. He drove the half hour and parked in front, noticing a familiar blond and a tall, well-dressed man coming out of a restaurant across the street.

His ex. Caroline. She and the man got into a fancy SUV and drove off.

You'll never be more than just a cowboy on a middling ranch...

He waited a second to feel that old familiar twist in his gut, a rush of bitterness—something. But he felt nothing. A neutral nothing. It was as if he'd seen an old acquaintance whose name he could barely remember.

I'm over you, he realized. *Over the cruel things you said. I know who I am and what I have to offer. Jenna Lattimore taught me that.*

Damn, that felt good.

It's written in the stars. Winona Cobbs-Sanchez's words came rushing back to him. Maybe this was what she'd meant. That he'd come to this jewelry store. That he'd spot his ex. That it wouldn't affect him in the slightest. That all he'd have burning in his heart was his love for Jenna. And his very unexpected interest in buying her an engagement ring—which he had no intention of proposing with or giving her for a long time, of course—for two reasons. To symbolize how far he'd come and as tangible proof of his love for her, of his belief in them.

Proposing marriage to Jenna Lattimore was not an option—not yet. Diego might be ready for that major step, but she wasn't. He'd hold on to the ring for at least six months, maybe a year.

Maybe two years. Jenna was his woman. And when she was ready, he'd know it. Then he'd get down on one knee and ask her and Robbie to spend the rest of their lives with him.

He walked into the shop and looked in the display cases, eyeing every ring. Nope, no, not remotely Jenna-like. Finally, there it was. Jenna's ring. The twinkling round diamond on a gold band inset with tiny diamonds was the one, just like she was.

It would set back his bank account, but he'd been saving for years. He had nine months of an emergency fund. He had a solid nest egg growing for retirement. Nothing to write home about yet at thirty-three, but he was getting there. He had a steady, solid paycheck. He could afford the ring.

He was a cowboy and proud of it. Being a cowboy had always given him the life he wanted, what he needed. It just took him a long time to realize that. If he hadn't met Jenna Lattimore, hadn't fallen for her, he might still be the same old Diego.

The new Diego had marriage on his mind. Very much so. If he had to wait another seven years to watch the woman he loved walk down the aisle to him, so be it. He'd wait.

Fifteen minutes later, the ring, engraved inside the band with *J, all my love, D*, was in a black satin box in his coat pocket.

Would wonders ever cease? He sure hoped not. Because it meant that someday, he would be married to Jenna and helping to raise the baby girl who'd sneaked inside his heart.

A half hour later, back at work out on the range on horseback, he'd stuck his hand in his coat pocket a few times just to feel the ring box there. To know. To celebrate all he felt for Jenna. At home later, he'd hide it in the back of his closet for safekeeping.

He had his hand in his pocket when he saw something furry and tall-eared suddenly dart out from behind the stand of evergreens about a hundred feet away. Horses didn't like sudden movements, and Dusty, one of his favorite mares, bristled.

Coyote.

It stared at Diego with its amber eyes, then darted to another stand of trees a lot closer to him.

Before Diego could even blink, the mare reacted, panicking

and galloping hard with a sudden pivot. Diego was pitched forward hard—and that was the last thing he remembered.

Everything went black.

JENNA SAT AT a big round table at Little Cowpokes Daycare Center, leading the three-and four-year-old group in a fun self-portrait activity. The kids were having a blast. So was Jenna as she worked on her own drawing, coloring in her long tresses with a red crayon. She'd given her hair a little more bounce on the ends than it had, but hey, it was art.

She had an itch to draw Diego. She was no artist and she'd never capture his expression, let alone the shape of his eyes or nose or chin for that matter. She just couldn't stop thinking of him and how wonderful it had felt to be included in his family dinner last night. To be a part of all that love and conversation and good will. The Sanchezes were such a warm bunch, and there was no such thing as an empty plate or glass unless you were absolutely stuffed and couldn't eat another bite.

They'd both had to be at work early this morning, so by 10:00 p.m. last night she was in bed, thinking of Diego. How he'd deftly transferred a sleeping Robbie to her bassinet when he'd taken them home. How he'd pressed a kiss to the baby's forehead and just stared at her for a moment the way Jenna always did because sometimes she couldn't believe this wonder of a little human was hers. Diego had had that same look on his face.

Her head had been telling her one thing these past days. First to back away completely, then to take a baby step forward again. Extra slowly. But Diego was just too wonderful. Even with the family component, even with seeing Diego often, even with him holding her tightly, she could handle it. It wasn't too much. And it wasn't too little. Things were just right.

Last night, while she'd lain in the guest room bed to be reminded of her night with Diego, she'd thought for the first time that maybe in the future, maybe like a year from now, she could even see herself engaged to him.

She wasn't ready to call what they had *love*. That was too much. Much too much. But what they had was heartfelt and beautiful and filled her up.

As she gave her self-portrait some eyelashes, her phone vibrated in her back pocket. She pulled it out—an unfamiliar number. Ugh, probably spam. She ignored it. A minute later, her phone vibrated again to reveal a new voicemail.

"Back in two seconds," she said, stepping to the side of the table to listen to the message. "Keep coloring, kids!"

She pressed Play.

Jenna, it's Will Sanchez. I'm very sorry to leave this message but I know Diego would want you to know right away. I'll just say it plainly—his horse threw him this afternoon on the ranch. He's still unconscious and the hospital is running tests. We're at the Mason Springs Hospital ER, waiting and praying. Come as soon as you can.

Jenna's blood had run cold the moment she'd heard Will's voice, clogged with emotion, with worry and fear.

Oh God. No. No, no, no.

"Jenna?"

Was someone calling her name? She couldn't think, couldn't move. Her legs were shaking. Jenna was vaguely aware that Angela was at her side, saying, "Honey, what's wrong?"

Jenna finally looked at her boss, trying to find her voice. "It's Diego. His dad called. He got hurt. He's in the hospital in Mason Springs. It's thirty minutes from here." Her voice sounded both broken and robotic. She was going numb.

"Honey, you go do what you need to do," Angela said with a firm hand on Jenna's shoulder. "We'll keep Robbie here. If you're not back to get her by six, I'll take her home with me. No worries. Just go. Are you okay to drive?"

Jenna managed a nod and gave Angela a quick hug. "Thank you." A sob was rising up in her throat and she wanted to assure the kids—who were all staring at her—that she was all right. But she wasn't.

"Honey, go," Angela repeated. "I've got them. I've got Robbie."

Thank God for Angela.

Jenna hurried to the baby room for just a look at her daughter. Then she grabbed her coat and raced out.

She drove with two hands white-knuckled on the steering wheel the half hour to Mason Springs, two towns over from Tenacity.

She went slowly. Carefully. All she wanted was to get there.

Finally, she parked in the Emergency area and ran inside. She saw the Sanchez family immediately, some sitting, some pacing, his sisters teary-eyed. She rushed over to the group.

"Will, thank you for calling me," Jenna said in a rush. "Please tell me he's okay." *Please, please, please.*

"We don't know anything yet," Will said gently. "They're running tests, and then the doctor will come talk to us. He's still not conscious."

Her knees were shaky and she felt unsteady, her hands trembling as she reached for the armrest before she dropped down on the chair.

"He has to be okay," she said into the air. "He has to be okay."

His mother, on the other side of her, reached for Jenna's hand and squeezed it, but Nicole Sanchez seemed too emotional to speak.

If he was unconscious, he'd been thrown *hard.*

What if...

No, no, no, no, she silently chanted over and over. *Please let him be okay.*

She grabbed her phone and quickly texted Mike: Diego in hospital.

He called her back right away, and she stepped into the vestibule. She barely managed to get out what happened.

"I'll go pick up Robbie from Little Cowpokes right now," he said. "I'll take care of her as long as you need."

She knew Robbie would be fine at the daycare, but Angela and Elaina had enough to do without babysitting for Jenna, kind as they were.

"I appreciate that, Mike. I'll check in later."

She disconnected and went back to the Sanchezes. When one sat down, another got up to pace. Uncle Stanley and Winona both sat grim-faced, their arms entwined.

"Mr. and Mrs. Sanchez," said a woman in a white lab coat. Her face was unreadable. No assurance there whatsoever.

Everyone stood up. Including Jenna. Waiting.

"Diego is going to be okay," the doctor said. "He's awake and the scans are clear. He has a concussion and a nasty goose egg, and some bruising on his torso and legs. He'll have to keep to light activity for a week, depending on how he feels. No heavy lifting, mentally or physically. Not even a crossword puzzle for two weeks."

They all breathed a collective sigh of relief. There were hugs and crying. Nina was saying that she'd never seen Diego do a crossword puzzle in his life, so no worries there. That got a smile out of the group, and the mood changed from worry and fear to jubilation.

Diego was fine. He was okay.

Jenna wasn't, though.

Her heart rate was returning to normal, her mind was clearing, her hands stopping the constant trembling, but she wasn't okay.

She was aware of an awful numbness in her chest, a strange hollow feeling. She'd been absolutely right in the wee hours after she and Diego had slept together. When she'd known she couldn't possibly allow herself to love him. To date him. Be involved with him.

She could have lost Diego today. And she couldn't, wouldn't be able to take it. She knew that by how she'd reacted. The terror. Her heart pounding. Her legs shaking.

If something happened to Diego she'd be destroyed. A wreck of a person, unable to function as she lay under the covers, not eating or sleeping.

Or being any kind of a mother to her baby.

Love meant loss. Harrowing loss. And Jenna had to be done with that. It wasn't better to have loved and lost. Jenna knew that.

She *hated* that saying.

The strangest sensation came over her just then. Like her heart shrinking. Closing in on itself. Robbie was in there, she thought numbly. With her family. And her memories.

There was no room left.

She had to say goodbye to Diego. Forever.

CHAPTER FIFTEEN

DIEGO HAD BEEN cautioned not to think too hard because of the concussion. Good thing he didn't have to wonder why Jenna hadn't come to see him. He knew why.

He understood. He hated it, but he understood. Her worst fear about welcoming him into her life had come true for her.

Damn coyote.

He lay in his hospital bed, staring out at the overcast sky. That he was bruised and battered barely registered when his heart hurt like hell. The good news was that Dusty had escaped unscathed; the coyote must have slinked back into the woods. Dusty had made her way back to the ranch alone, which was how the foreman had known there was a problem. Diego had been lucky to be found so quickly.

He was stuck here overnight as a precaution, then he'd be sprung tomorrow if he could walk and talk well in the morning. He usually hated being in the hospital, but he still felt the remnants of the monster headache he'd awoken with, the over the counter extra-strength pain relievers thankfully doing their job.

Except for the ache in his chest, left side. That went deep and wouldn't be going away for a long time.

His whole family had come in, two at a time, which was the max allowed. The foreman and a couple of cowboys Diego was good buddies with had turned up with his favorite snack, a family-sized bag of Doritos. His dad had told him Jenna had been in the waiting room with them but had left after hearing from the doctor that he was all right.

He glanced at the annoying ticking analog clock on the wall. Vising hours were ending in twenty minutes. He longed to see Jenna's beautiful face, Robbie's bright blue eyes and wispy auburn curls. But he didn't expect Jenna to come. This whole experience had to be very rough on her. Ever since they'd had that conversation the day he thought she was dumping him, he'd actually taken notice of instances where he could be more careful. He'd stopped trying to get through a yellow light. He no longer jaywalked, even in sleepy Tenacity because you just never knew who was coming speeding from around the corner, who was backing out of a spot when you weren't paying attention. He'd taken greater safety measures when he'd been fixing the little things in her home—not just jumping down from the stepladder without a thought. He planned to avoid the open range during a thunderstorm, just in case lightning was looking for someone to strike.

But accidents happened. Period. Coyotes darted from woods and spooked horses.

Jenna knew that. It was why she wasn't here. Because any minute, any day, she could lose him. He'd been lucky today. He might not be tomorrow.

She wasn't coming. Ever.

Unless... He sat up a bit, his head not appreciating that. Maybe Jenna had left because she was thinking things over and just needed some time. Maybe she'd realized that yes, accidents *did* happen and that shutting out love wouldn't be much help.

He felt himself brightening. Until he knew otherwise, he was going with that.

There was a tap on the door. "Diego? It's Jenna."

His heart gave a leap at the sound of her voice. It was as if his wishing, his positive thoughts, had conjured her. This had to be a sign—a good sign—that he was on the right track with his assumption. That she was coming to tell him that she loved him and wanted him by her side, that his accident made her realize that. He was 51 percent sure, anyway.

But the missing ring was definitely a *bad* omen. He'd asked the nurse for the contents of his coat pockets. They'd given him a set of keys and his wallet, which had been zipped in the left pocket. There'd been nothing in the right pocket, they'd said. Where the ring had been. The ring box he'd been touching when Dusty had reacted.

He'd confided in his Uncle Stanley about the ring. If the little black box had gotten thrown with him, it probably would have landed somewhere near him, but the foreman and the cowboy who'd gone to look for Diego when the mare had returned alone hadn't mentioned seeing anything.

Maybe the ring box fell in a critter hole. Or ended up under some brush in the tree line. The coyote could have grabbed it in its mouth and run off with it, hoping it was a snack.

Nope, coyote, it's just a symbol of what I hope is my future. A forever love with the woman and baby I want to spend my life with.

Once he was healed up, he'd take a less easily spooked horse out to that area and look for it.

"Come on in," he called.

She came in tentatively, then rushed over to the bed, her hand on her heart. She seemed so flustered and emotional and wasn't saying anything.

"You should see the other guy," he said with a grin.

Not even a hint of a smile appeared on her too pale face.

"I'm okay, Jenna," he assured her. "Really. I am." The more he looked at her, the less sure he was of what she was going to say. "Where's Robbie? With Mike?"

She nodded, then let out a breath. "When your dad called and left me that message, I was so scared. And while I was in the waiting room, not sure if you would be all right—" She shook her head and stopped talking, dropping down on the chair beside the bed. "I'm so, so relieved that you're all right."

"I'm definitely all right," he said, reaching for her hand and holding it. "Just a headache. And I can't tax my brain for a solid week. Or do anything that might cause another concussion, like go about my daily life." *I could lay on your sofa and think about how much I love you. Hold Robbie and feed her spoonfuls of pureed sweet potatoes and little bites of scrambled eggs...*

She looked away for a moment, and the hope he'd felt just two minutes ago was dissipating. "Diego, I..." She got up and walked over to the window, staring out. "I wish I were a stronger person. I wish—" She looked down and wiped at her eyes, his heart breaking for her. *Oh, Jenna.* "I'm sorry," she said in a broken voice. "But—" The tears came then, and she covered her face with her hands.

"Sweetheart, it's okay," he said, a clump of sadness settling inside him. It wasn't okay, not for either of them, but he had to be gentle. He'd always known that. "Come sit next to me."

She sniffled and moved to the chair. He took her hand and just looked at their entwined fingers, the ache in his chest deepening, widening. What were the magic words? What could he say to make her stay in his life without pressuring her? He wouldn't do that. But he would tell her how he felt.

"Listen, Jenna. You're the best thing that's ever happened to me. You and Robbie. You changed my life. You changed *me*. You showed me that I do have something to offer. Myself." He took a breath, not sure anything he was saying could change things. "I love you, Jenna Lattimore. And like I said the day after we made love, I'm not going to try to pressure you. I love you too much for that. I want you in my life. But if that's not possible, then maybe it's a matter of time. I waited seven years to feel like this. I can wait another seven."

He had to pray that she just needed some time. To get over this awful experience. To get used to loving him. To accept that love couldn't be denied, no matter how scared you were of it.

He had to hope she'd come back.

Tears misted her blue eyes. "You're a dream man, Diego. Someone will snap you up by then," she said in an almost whisper, her voice cracking.

"Who can compare to you and Robbie?" he asked, trying to get a smile on his face, but this hurt so damned badly that he couldn't. His voice had shaken on the baby's name.

"I care about you too much to be at all wishy-washy," she added. "I can't be with you. I can't live in this state of worry-

ing twenty-four seven. Of being so afraid. I know it's weak.
But it's where I am."

"Jenna, you're not weak. You're actually one of the strongest people I know."

He could list twenty reasons how and why that was true. But
he said he wouldn't pressure her to look at things differently,
so he'd leave it at that.

Diego had never been much of an optimist. But now? His
hope was all he had. What he and Jenna had was pretty powerful. It might do the work for him. It might bring her back to him.

But right now, he had to let her go.

The wish he'd made on the star from the window in her guest
room wouldn't be coming true for a long time. That they'd become a family. The three of them.

"Do something for me?" he asked.

"Sure," she said, a bit nervously.

"Text me the photo you took of Robbie's pink handprints."

Tears streamed down her cheeks. She managed a nod,
squeezed his hand and then hurried out.

And his heart cracked in two so hard that he had to grab
the weird buckwheat pillow his sister Marisa and Dawson had
brought him and clutch it against his chest.

FOR THE NEXT WEEK, Jenna had gone to work and then straight
home. She'd tried very hard not to think of Diego. Not to wonder how his concussion was faring, if his bruises were fading.
She avoided the guest room, keeping the door closed against
the memories inside.

As promised, she'd texted him the photo of Robbie's pink
watercolor handprints, and it was the very bittersweet goodbye she'd needed. A final gesture. But that night, all she could
think about as she'd lain in bed was Diego seeing a text from
her, thinking that maybe she'd changed her mind about them,
and then it just being the photo. She'd kept her word, nothing
more. She could see him looking at the watercolor, wistful.
Missing her and Robbie. The pieces of her shattered heart still
managed to go out to him. *I'm sorry I hurt you, Diego. I know*

some wonderful people, and you are tops. You didn't deserve that. Not when you came so far yourself.

She hated that part. He'd changed because of her, *for* her. And she was running from him. For self-preservation.

It had been a rough week emotionally. She'd taken care of Robbie, she'd knitted hats and started a sweater for her mom's upcoming birthday, she'd made big batches of different soups to keep her distracted and eating, she'd had visits from Mike, who'd come by or texted every day. Even her parents had come for an overnight when she'd confided in her mother—crying through most of it—that she'd broken her own heart by needing to end her relationship with Diego.

Her father had taken one look at his saddened daughter and had pulled her into a hug, then said he was going to give it to her straight: She meant the world to him, he understood how she was feeling, but denying herself the man she loved wasn't the answer.

You love us, Jenna. Your mom and me. You love Robbie. You can't shut us out. You can't stop loving us out of fear that something will happen. So I don't think you should do that with Diego.

Steven, her mother had chastised her husband. *If you understand, then let Jenna feel what she feels.*

Her father had tightened his hug, comforting her with his support, even if he thought she was making a mistake.

Honesty is good, Jenna had said. *But I just can't, Dad. I can't.*

They'd made her tea and baked her cookies, doted on their grandbaby, and when they'd left the next morning she'd given some thought to what her father had said, made a little easier by her mom taking her "side." But there was a difference between her loving the people in her life and not shutting them out and doing that to Diego. He wasn't family, even if he felt like family. He hadn't been there all along. He was new.

And loving anyone new was out of the question. His accident had hit that home.

The doorbell rang. Maybe Mike or Angela, who'd stopped by a few days ago with a crock of her famed macaroni and cheese and a hug.

Jenna opened the door, surprised to find Stanley and Winona on her doorstep, bundled up in wool hats and parkas—Winona's in her trademark purple.

"I'm not much of a talker," Winona said, "but I have something to say to you."

Jenna almost jumped. Winona seemed serious. Jenna stepped back and welcomed them in, taking their coats and hats and hanging them up.

They accepted her offer of coffee, and the cookies she'd said her parents had baked the other day, and she brought a tray into the living room, where they sat on the sofa. She sat adjacent on the love seat, and they both turned toward her.

Winona's blue eyes bored into her. "You already love Diego so you might as well share your life with him. Why love him from a distance?"

She must have looked taken aback because Stanley suddenly said, "Diego didn't say a word to us. He must have confided in one of his siblings about why he seemed so miserable and word spread among the family so that we could try to cheer him up."

Jenna gave something of a nod, a little uncomfortable. But somehow comforted at the same time. Stanley and Winona had been a huge support to her at the Valentine's dance, and she'd never forget it.

She opened her mouth to try to explain why she had to send Diego out of her life, but it wasn't easy. "I just have to protect myself" was all she could manage.

"I know everyone's different, Jenna," Winona said. "But I'll tell you this. I've been through it all and then some. So has Stanley. But we're still here, living and loving because both are a blessing." Their wedding rings glinted in the afternoon sunlight coming from the windows. "That's all I wanted to say." She picked up her cup and drank, then took a cookie and sat back, staring straight ahead.

Jenna looked away for a moment, everything suddenly… jumbled.

Stanley cleared his throat. He suddenly looked a little nervous. Like he was debating whether or not to tell her something. "Jenna, I wasn't sure if I should do this or not, but... I feel it's right."

Okay, now *she* was nervous.

"Diego told me that when he got thrown," Stanley said, "there'd been something in his coat pocket that must have gotten thrown too. Took me a while, but I found it. I think you should know the story behind it."

Jenna tilted her head, wondering what it could be.

Stanley set a small black ring box on the coffee table and Jenna gasped, her eyes going wide. "I told Diego I found it and that I was surprised he'd buy a ring at this point. He explained that he had no intention of giving it to you for at least six months—that it was a symbol. Not just of how far he's come, but as tangible proof of his love and belief in the two of you."

Oh, Diego, she thought, deeply moved by *both* Sanchezes' intentions—Stanley at wanting her to know all this and Diego for the secret gesture.

"That's lovely," Winona said, nodding at her husband.

Stanley put his arm around his wife. "It is that. Jenna, he knew you weren't ready for a proposal. But he wanted to have it for when you were. I was about to leave it on his dresser in his room, but he asked me to hang on to it for him. Said I was lucky and he wasn't."

Jenna's eyes misted with tears. She stared at the little box.

The elderly couple stood. "We'll leave you be," Stanley said. "Thank you for the coffee and cookies. Oh—and rest assured that we won't breathe a word of our visit to Diego. We're meddling enough as it is, but sometimes..."

Jenna tried to manage a smile, but she was on the verge of breaking down. Her heart was thudding, her legs felt shaky and her mind was spinning. But she did have one burning question. "Can you tell me how Diego's doing?"

"He's doing great," Stanley said. "Going a little stir-crazy, but we've all been watching him like hawks to make sure he doesn't do anything taxing."

Relief flooded through her. "I'm very glad to hear that."

She walked them to the door. Stanley gallantly helped his

wife on with her coat, and Winona lovingly wrapped his red scarf around his neck.

Winona stared at Jenna, her blue eyes so intent on her that Jenna was almost mesmerized. "It's written in the stars. But you know that, dear."

Before Jenna could say anything—not that she had a thought in her head at the confusing, emotional moment—Winona put her arm around her husband's and they left.

Jenna dropped down on the little bench in the entryway, Stanley's words echoing in her head. *A symbol...of his love and belief in the two of you...*

She went back into the living room to collect their coffee cups and plates, eager to have some busywork to do so she wouldn't sit and ruminate on all Stanley and Winona had said and shown her. Their visit had been a lot. She was reaching for the cups when she gasped. Stanley had accidentally left the ring box on the coffee table.

She grabbed it and hurried to the door, but their car was already heading down the street.

Jenna bit her lip and closed the door slowly, then went back into the living room.

She sat down, setting the box back on the coffee table.

Open it, she told herself. *Do that, at least.*

She took the box in her hands. She sucked in a breath, then lifted the lid, and tears misted her eyes again. A round diamond on a gold band with little diamonds all around it. Just beautiful. She could see that something was engraved inside the band.

She took the ring from the box and tilted it to read the engraving.

J, all my love, D.

As she sat there, closing her hand around the ring, a barrage of voices entered her head. Her father telling her that she couldn't stop loving them and Robbie out of fear that something would happen. That she shouldn't do the same with Diego. Mike, just that morning, saying that while he'd always feel over-protective of her, he liked Diego for her. *No, scratch that,* he'd said. *He* loved *Diego for her.* For her and Robbie.

Winona's words. *You already love Diego so you might as well share your life with him. Why love him from a distance?*

Stanley's: *He knew you're weren't ready for a proposal. But he wanted to have it for when you were.*

Diego's: *You're the best thing that's ever happened to me. You and Robbie. I love you, Jenna Lattimore.*

And her own now: *I can't love you.*

And a smaller voice, from very deep down saying, *But I do.*

Winona's voice again, echoing: *Living and loving are a blessing.*

Yes, they were. She and Robbie were here. She knew what Rob Lattimore would want for them both. Happiness. Love. Support. Big strong arms that he could no longer wrap around them.

She *knew* it.

She froze, then her gaze shot to the stairs. She pictured Robbie sleeping in her bassinet, little fist by her ear. Lips making an Elvis quirk. What was she teaching Robbie about the blessings of life and love? To run from both the way she was doing now?

She bit her lip and sat there for a while, just thinking, looking at the photos on the mantel. Her as a new mother holding her baby, wanting to give her the world the same way that Diego wanted to give *them* the world.

Finally, she put the ring box in the pocket of her cardigan and went upstairs to check on her daughter. To *be* with her daughter was more like it.

No. To tell her something. Something she didn't understand or even think about until just now.

Her daughter was still fast asleep, her fist indeed up by her ear in the way that made Diego smile. Jenna's heart could burst any second it was so full.

"Robbie," she whispered. "I forgot something in all this. And it's about you and what I want you to know. What I want for you. If something terrible happens to someone you love, if you lose someone, I wouldn't want you to hide yourself away. I'd want you to see life and love as the blessings they are, like Winona said. Love is everything. It's *everything*, Robbie. And I need to show you that I'm strong like Diego said I was."

Robbie Lattimore opened her eyes. Jenna gasped in surprise. A sign, for sure.

So what are you going to do about it? she asked herself, putting the beautiful ring back in the box.

CHAPTER SIXTEEN

DIEGO WAS MAKING himself as useful around the house as he could. That primarily meant cooking, since he discovered he actually liked whipping up meals and there were three occasions to do it during the day at standard times, providing some much-needed structure. Over the past week, he'd made omelets stuffed with all kinds of interesting fillings and cheeses for breakfasts, piled-high sandwiches for lunch, and broiled steaks and baked chicken and even made his own pasta for dinners. Uncle Stanley had said it wasn't half bad, either.

Right now, an overcast Thursday afternoon, he'd just added the hominy and red chiles to his attempt at *pozole*, a beloved Mexican soup that was a favorite of Uncle Stanley's. Stanley had been a godsend the past week and deserved a special treat. Not bringing up Jenna when it was obvious Diego didn't want to talk about her, but plopping down next to his grandnephew in the living room to watch a game or movie or laugh over Bugs Bunny arguing with Elmer Fudd. The *pozole* was Diego's way of saying thank you *and* needing to kill a good couple of hours.

The kitchen smelled amazing. He had the house to himself, so there was no one to appreciate the fragrant aroma emanating from the big pot every time he took off the lid to stir the soup. His father was out on the range, his mother was delivering garments she'd worked on and Luca was working.

He'd had lots of time to think about Jenna this past week. Their last conversation. The two nights they'd spent together, one very passionately. Her beautiful face.

And Robbie too. He missed that baby so much. A couple of times he'd even opened the text with the handprint photo, just to feel connected to her.

Every day he wanted to get in his pickup and drive to Jenna's house. And every day he stopped himself. He had to let her come to him. He just wasn't sure she ever would.

He heard a car pulling up and went to the window. Finally, someone to appreciate his delicious smelling *pozole* and be his taste tester. He pulled aside the curtain to see who it was.

Whoa.

Jenna.

He went to the front door and opened it. Jenna was coming up the path, carrying Robbie in her car seat. He grabbed his jacket because it was freezing and met her on the porch. "Is everything okay? Is Robbie okay?"

She smiled and turned the car seat around so he could see Robbie's face. She was sleeping. "We're okay. I just wanted to come see you. Tell you something."

Maybe she was leaving town. Selling her house and moving back to Bronco to be near her parents. He was glad for them but sad for himself. Out of sight often meant out of mind. If and when she was ever ready to love again, she'd have forgotten all about him.

They came inside and he closed the door behind her, taking her coat. She unsnapped Robbie's fleece bunting, then picked up the seat.

"Follow me to the kitchen," he said. "I spent so much time on tonight's dinner that if it burns I honestly might cry."

And he'd done his share of crying earlier this week, not that he liked to admit it. In the shower. In bed at night. He'd stopped, the sadness so close to the surface moving down deeper, where it hurt even worse.

She sniffed the air. "Mmm, something smells amazing."

"Mexican soup called *pozole*. That's what I do these days. Cook. And start uninteresting conversations about whether tomatoes are a fruit or a vegetable. Did you know that cast iron pans are best for getting a good sear on a steak if it's too cold to grill outside? This is what happens to a cowboy with a lot of time on his hands. He starts googling."

She was looking at him with sort of a happy expression on her face. Not like a woman who'd come to tell him that she was leaving Tenacity. Or that they'd never see each other again.

"What did you want to tell me?" he asked, needing to hear it, get it over with.

She gently set the car seat down. "That I love you, Diego. I think you know that already, given that I was so scared I had to cut you out of my life. But I want to say it. I love you. So much."

He almost gasped. "You love me," he repeated, letting her words sink in.

"I had some help coming to a few important realizations. My father gave it to me straight, as always. Mike. And Stanley and Winona—just a couple of hours ago."

He mock-narrowed his eyes. "What did they have to say?"

"Winona reminded me that life and love are blessings. Sounds like something a person hears every day and already knows. But her words hit me hard. I'm not one to mess with blessings, Diego. I understand now that I'm always going to be nervous about bad weather and spooked horses and rickety ladders. Life is all about risks. But love is the greatest reward. That's what I want to teach Robbie. When I realized that, I understood. I finally understood."

Wonders *would* never cease. He was sure of that now. "You have no idea how happy you're making me."

"Good. Because I know I made this week even harder on you than it started out." She reached into the pocket of her thick black sweater and pulled something out.

The ring box.

He gaped at it, feeling his cheeks burn. "Um, first of all, how did you get that?" he asked, then his eyed narrowed again. "Stanley." He shook his head with a smile. "You're not supposed to have that for like seven years."

Jenna laughed. "Stanley told me the story of this ring. And he left it with me—supposedly accidentally."

"I know you're nowhere near ready for a proposal and a ring, Jenna." He held out his hand to take back the box. "I gave it to Stanley for safekeeping, but I feel so lucky now that I'm ready to hold on to it for when you are."

But instead of giving him the box, Jenna moved it close to her chest. "Actually, I thought maybe you'd slide the ring on my finger."

Now he did gasp. "What are you saying?"

"I'm saying I'm ready to have you in my life, full throttle. I'm ready to love you with all my heart. I'm ready."

Diego was so floored that he was grateful to get down on one knee because his legs were shaking. "Jenna Lattimore, love of my life, will you marry me?"

Tears sprang to her eyes—happy emotional tears, this time. "Yes. I will."

He stood and slid the ring on her finger, the diamond sparkling in the kitchen. "I promise to be the husband you deserve and the father figure Robbie needs. I promise to give you everything I am."

He wrapped her in a hug and kissed her.

"I don't want to protect myself from the man who makes me feel safest," she whispered. "And very loved."

He kissed her again, his heart thudding. "You know, I told Stanley he should hold on to that ring because he was lucky and I wasn't, and I'd probably end up losing it again somehow. But I'm the luckiest man in Tenacity. In Montana. Maybe the world. Because I'm going to marry you and help you raise Robbie. I love you both so much."

She leaned up to kiss him. "We love you back."

"No rush on planning the wedding, Jenna. We can wait a couple of years. As long as I know you're mine, I'm good. My wish on that star came true, after all."

She smiled and kissed him again. "Actually, I was thinking how cute it would be to have Robbie walk down the aisle at our wedding. Toddle down, really. That's just four, five months away. I can be a June bride."

His heart was overflowing. "I'm very happy to hear that. I

guess the Sanchez kitchen wasn't the most romantic place to get engaged. Sorry about that."

Jenna laughed. "I loved every second of that *pozole*-scented proposal, and I'll never forget it."

He tightened his arms around his fiancée and held her tight, then kissed her with all the passion he'd held back this past week.

Diego thought back to the after-party in the Tenacity Social Club, the night he saw Jenna for the first time. Saw Robbie in her yellow snowsuit. His two great loves.

He couldn't wait to tell his *tio* that he had an answer to his question about which Sanchez would be the next to get married.

TURNED OUT THAT Diego might not be the next Sanchez getting married, after all.

Because a week ago, the day after Diego was cleared by his doctor to resume normal activities—happily earlier than expected—another Sanchez had a big surprise.

Julian had proposed to Ruby—on Valentine's Day!

The eldest Sanchez sibling and his bride-to-be had wanted to keep their engagement to themselves for a bit, particularly to let four-year-old Emery get used to the idea and for Julian, Ruby, Emery, and baby Jay to just revel in the fact that they'd truly be a family soon. And when Diego had gotten hurt, they'd held onto the news for a while longer.

Now, the Sanchez family was gathered in the dining room at their home for a special dinner—to celebrate the two engagements.

Not only were Ruby's two little ones officially joining the family, but so was Robbie Lattimore.

The whole family had helped with this particular meal—everyone's favorite tacos, which meant every possible type of filling from carnitas to chicken to guacamole, and every type of topping.

Diego had just finished ribbing Julian about how he was on his third taco when they'd just all sat down five minutes ago. Beside Julian was Ruby with her twinkling engagement ring and baby Jay, and four-year-old Emery. Across the table were Nina and Luca, and Marisa and Dawson, and Diego sat next to Jenna, with Robbie in her highchair on her other side. The Sanchez *madre* and *padre*, Nicole and Will, were on Nina's other side.

"I have to ask this again?" *Tio* Stanley said with a grin, passing the big platter of the soft tortillas he'd made to Diego, who sat beside him.

Jenna took a sip of her sangria, also made by Stanley with his bride Winona's help. "Ask what?"

Stanley's brown eyes sparkled. "Which Sanchez is next to get hitched, as you say here in Montana."

Diego laughed. "Who knows? Maybe it'll be Luca. Maybe he'll beat us all to the altar." Luca was probably the most easygoing of the Sanchez siblings, but the bachelor cowboy wasn't even dating anyone.

Luca's gaze shot up. "Hey, find me the right woman, and who knows?" Ha. Like Diego said, easy-going. What a difference between the two of them. But hey, stubborn Diego had gotten where he'd needed to be. Right here with Jenna and Robbie.

Diego glanced at his sister Nina, sitting across the table. Nina was pushing rice around on her plate—and not saying much. She had a pleasant enough expression plastered on her face, but Diego had a feeling she was thinking about the guy who got away. Her old teenage love, Barrett. Now was not the time to tease her.

"Maybe we'll have the first ever Sanchez family double wedding!" *Tio* Stanley said, raising his glass of Sangria.

"Maybe we just will," his psychic bride, Winona, said.

What Winona Cobbs-Sanchez said was nearly always the case, whether in a week or a year, so they all figured there would be a very big family celebration in the coming months.

"I think Robbie wants to try a very tiny taco bite," Jenna said, "now that she's part of this big, wonderful clan, she'll get to try lots of Mexican specialties."

Diego got up and knelt down beside the adorable baby girl he loved so much, the child he would raise as his own, though he and Jenna would keep the memory of her birth father alive in her heart.

As his fiancée smiled at him, he took a small piece of tortilla and filled it with a tiny bit of shredded carnitas, a sprinkle of cheese, and held it front of the baby's mouth. "Try this, Robbie!"

The little lips parted and she took the bite.

Her blue eyes widened and twinkled and she opened up again.

"She loves tacos!" Diego said, grinning. "She wants more!"

Jenna laughed. "I love being part of this family."

For the next forty-five minutes, they ate, talked, laughed and made all kinds of wedding plans, from the outrageous to the simple. Stanley was saying something about a marching band down Central Avenue.

All Diego cared about was marrying the woman he loved, taking good care of little Robbie, and making good on his promise to be the man, husband and father this family deserved forever.

* * * * *

Don't miss the stories in this mini series!

MONTANA MAVERICKS: THE TENACITY SOCIAL CLUB

Welcome to Big Sky Country! Where spirited men and women discover love on the range.

The Maverick's Promise
MELISSA SENATE
January 2025

A Maverick's Road Home
CATHERINE MANN
February 2025

All In With The Maverick
ELIZABETH HRIB
March 2025

MILLS & BOON

Big Sky Bachelor
JoAnna Sims

MILLS & BOON

Dear Reader,

Thank you for choosing *Big Sky Bachelor*.

Danica "Danny" Brand is a fiercely independent real estate broker who has built an empire buying and selling houses for the very rich and very famous clients in the hot LA scene. As her fortieth birthday came and went, Danica was ready to marry Grant, her business partner and fiancé, so they could shift focus from building their empire to building their family. And then when she finds out that Grant had impregnated their office manager, Fallon, Danica retreats to Big Sky, Montana, her hometown, to recover and regroup. She isn't looking for love, but lightning strikes, and she finds herself deeply in love with the most eligible bachelor in Big Sky.

Dr. Matteo Katz is a family physician who is tired of being alone. After a difficult breakup, Matteo began to date the many lovely ladies in the Big Sky area. He found that all the women possessed their own individual wonderfulness, but none of them had felt like home. Then one day Matteo bumps into Danica Brand, a strikingly beautiful woman with intense blue eyes and a laugh that makes him smile. Matteo knows in his heart that Danica is the wife he's been waiting for. But can he convince big-city Danica to leave her fast-paced life in LA to become the wife of a small-town doctor?

You can connect with me via my website: joannasimsromance.love.

Happy reading!

JoAnna

JoAnna Sims is proud to pen contemporary romance for Harlequin Special Edition. JoAnna's series, The Brands of Montana, features hardworking characters with hometown values. You are cordially invited to join the Brands of Montana as they wrangle their own happily-ever-afters.

Books by JoAnna Sims

The Brands of Montana

A Match Made in Montana
High Country Christmas
High Country Baby
Meet Me at the Chapel
Thankful for You
A Wedding to Remember
A Bride for Liam Brand
High Country Cowgirl
The Sergeant's Christmas Mission
Her Second Forever
His Christmas Eve Homecoming
She Dreamed of a Cowboy
The Marine's Christmas Wish
Her Outback Rancher
Big Sky Cowboy
Big Sky Christmas
Big Sky Bachelor

Montana Mavericks: The Trail to Tenacity

The Maverick's Mistletoe Queen

Visit the Author Profile page
at millsandboon.com.au for more titles.

Dedicated to Angela T.

Thank you for your kindness and support
as I hung up my therapist hat.

You are a truly talented, intelligent, strong woman
who shares my love for education and writing.

You are a blessing and I hope our paths never *un*cross.

JoAnna

PROLOGUE

"YES, OF COURSE, Prince Aziz," Danica Brand said. "Full price cash offers only. You have an exquisite property, it's still very much a seller's market, and I am certain that we will get a buyer in record-breaking time for a record-breaking price."

Danica, Los Angeles Realtor to the überwealthy and celebrities, was on the phone with one of her regular clients, a Saudi prince, when she heard the distracting sound of a woman weeping loudly. Danica tried to focus on the call but after a few minutes of the grating sound, she told Prince Aziz that she would call him back, hung up the phone and then walked purposefully toward the wailing.

Danica walked quickly past her fiancé and business partner's office but then stopped in her tracks. She spun on the heels of her four-inch stilettos, pushed the slightly ajar door open and saw Grant holding their distraught receptionist, Fallon, in his arms.

She stood in the doorway, while her brain jumped from annoyed to confused and then quickly landed on shock. "What's going on in here, Grant? I had to hang up with Prince Aziz."

Fallon, a Farrah Fawcett look-alike aspiring actress and model, had her head buried in Grant's chest.

The receptionist looked up at her with swollen, doe-like eyes and then her face crumpled as she got up, raced past her to the bathroom and then slammed that door behind her.

Danica stared at her fiancé of nearly twenty years while her stomach began to twist. She stepped into his office and closed the door behind her. Grant Fowler was a fastidious man; he was trim and fit, and his clothing was always neat as a pin, and there wasn't a strand of dyed brown hair out of place. So the large wet area on his shirt left by Fallon's tears drew her attention while her mind quickly sifted through the possibilities and finally landed on the most plausible.

"Please don't tell me that you've turned us into a cliché, Grant," Danica said in a cool, even tone. Her heart was racing but her poker face, something she was known for in her industry, remained in place.

Grant didn't respond right away but it didn't matter. She already knew, first in her gut and now in her mind.

With a sigh that almost sounded like he didn't want to be bothered with this conversation, Grant leaned back against his imported, heavily carved desk, ran his fingers through his hair and then gave a little shrug. "She's pregnant."

Danica felt her knees to begin to buckle and tears wanting to form. She locked her legs and *refused* to let those tears manifest. Wordlessly, she stared at this man whom she had built a life and a business with, but now she realized that she didn't know him at all. Grant squirmed, broke eye contact and then retreated to his ten-thousand-dollar executive chair and sat down. He leaned back casually, and that made Danica narrow her eyes. There was a very real part of Grant that appeared to be enjoying this.

"She's twenty, Grant."

"Twenty-one." Grant frowned at her while brushing something off his desk.

Grant was an undeniably handsome man; he had the even features and bone structure of a male model, still looked good without his shirt on at the beach, and with a little help from modern plastic surgery and a strict diet, those looks hadn't faded yet.

"What now?" he asked her.

"I'm sorry," Danica asked, "are you asking me?"

He tapped his finger on the desk while the sounds of Fallon

gulping, coughing and then starting the crying all over again penetrated the door.

"Just hear me out," Grant said. "Fallon loves you…"

"Oh, please, Grant, do spare me," Danica snapped back. "Sleeping with my fiancé isn't exactly a love letter."

"Well," he seemed to concede, "she thinks the world of you. Respects you…"

"Quit trying to flatter me, Grant."

"She is going to have to give up a lot to keep this baby." He restarted, "She's very worried about her figure."

"Poor thing."

"That was sarcasm and I understand why."

"Thank you so much."

"You have always been a woman who thinks outside of the box." Grant made another thinly veiled attempt at flattery as he held up his arms and gestured around the room. "We've built an empire together."

And you and I both know that I own the majority stake.

"I love you, Danica," her soon-to-be ex said with a look in his eyes that had typically worked to earn her forgiveness when he needed to apologize for something. "I adore you."

Danica closed her eyes, took in a deep breath to keep her anger to a simmer before she picked up the nearest golf trophy and flung it at him. She had grown up in Montana and shooting guns, hunting, was just a part of the life; she was an excellent shot.

When she opened her eyes again, it did her some good to see that his smile had faltered; beads of sweat had formed a shiny mustache just above his now-quivering upper lip. He was nervous, as well he should be.

Grant leaned forward. "We've never found the right time to have a child."

She had frozen her eggs five years ago, but Grant had always pushed the timeline back. He always had reasons to *not* get married, to *not* have a child. Now that she was forty, she may have wasted years waiting for Grant and she only had herself to blame. There had been rumors and suspicions, but never any evidence. Now, a barely adult aspiring actress carrying Grant's child was undeniable proof. Two decades of her life, washed away like beach sand at high tide.

"If I recall, you had some doubts about carrying a child."

That's when the mask slipped. She took a step forward, and in a quiet, furious tone, Danica said, "Don't you dare, Grant. Don't. You. Dare."

Grant held up his hands in surrender. "Okay. Okay."

"How could you, Grant?" she asked him with a waver in her voice.

At the first sign of weakness, her ex stood up, rounded his enormous desk, and then crossed to her and tried to take her into his arms.

Danica stepped back, held up her hand for him to stop. "You will never touch me again."

Now Grant looked as if he was going to cry. But she wasn't naive enough to believe that it was sorrow for his mistake or some deep abiding love he had for her. No, Grant was worried about the business, the money and the possessions they had accumulated, like his prize yacht that he had named *Got It Made*.

"I don't want to lose you, sweetheart," he said with a pleading tone. He reached out his arms and then put them back down. "Can't we come to some agreement?"

There was a very real part of her that, as if watching it unfold for someone else, wanted to hear Grant's proposal for a path forward.

"Which would be?"

He dipped his head down, looked at her with his hazel eyes. "You want a baby. Fallon wants a career…"

Danica could not move or think for a split second while she processed what she thought was Grant's *everyone wins* plan.

"You want me to adopt her baby?"

"Oh, no. *No*. She wants the baby."

"Okay. Let me take another stab at this then. Fallon wants a career, your baby and *you*. What do I get again?"

"Well—" more lip twitching "—we will have a home together…"

His name wasn't on the deed.

"We still have our love," he said, "and our business."

"Are you suggesting," she said with a small, disbelieving noise, "because I can't believe you would. But are you suggesting that I *share* you with Fallon?"

Grant took a handkerchief out of his pocket and dabbed his forehead. "Is it such a crazy idea?"

Now, that made her laugh, out loud, held tilted back, grateful for this moment of levity in what was turning out to be a no good, rotten day.

"Yes, Grant," she said, "it *is* a crazy idea."

She turned on her heel and Grant followed her, reached out to touch her arm as she swung open the door to his office. She put her Pilates to use, spun around and glared up at him, "If you don't back off, Grant, I am going to jam my heel so hard into your instep that you'll be limping for a week. Not to mention the damage it would cause to your precious loafers."

Grant backed away, his cajoling mask slipping. "Now there's that ice queen mean streak."

She stopped in the doorway, looked at him. The man standing before her now seemed to have shrunken from his six foot four height and his features were noticeably pinched.

"I get it, Grant, you need to demonize me to make you feel better. I guess that bump of self-esteem after getting Fallon into bed wasn't lasting."

Danica headed to her office and began to pack up quickly, putting her laptop in her designer case, putting files away in a locked drawer, shrugging on her cashmere coat, and then shutting off the light and locking her door behind her, taking the only key with her. Grant was standing in the doorway to his office watching her as she stopped by the bathroom to rap on the door.

"Fallon?"

"Yes?"

"Open the door, please."

Fallon shuffled toward the door, sniffling loudly. When she opened the door, her lovely face was blotchy and red, and it did touch Danica in an unexpected way.

"I'm so sorry, Ms. Brand."

"I know you are," Danica said in a kind tone that surprised

her. "Unfortunately, most of us women have some version of this kind of mistake in our love lives. This one is yours."

Fallon blew her nose again loudly.

"Now, listen up, Fallon, because what I am going to say now is important." Danica felt Grant wanting to step in between them but he held back, watching her intently. "Grant has a very a huge golf memorabilia collection. It takes up two of my very large bedrooms, so I hope you have a good-sized home, because he will be taking those with him,"

"It's a studio, actually."

"Well," Danica said, "I suppose love will find a way.

"The Bentley is a lease," Danica continued. "Do you have reliable transportation?"

Now Fallon's eyes were wide as teacup saucers. "Well, actually, no."

Danica continued, "Now, Grant also has a very swollen prostate, it happens with men his age I'm afraid, and there have been many nights that I haven't gotten a wink of sleep because he's up and down and up and down all night. So my best advice is let him sleep on the bed closest to the bathroom so you can get your rest. After all, you are with child."

Fallon started to cry again while Grant appeared to be frozen in his spot.

Danica looked at Grant, threw her scarf over her shoulder with what she hoped was a dramatic flair, and then set off down the hall, chin up, head held high. Then she stopped, chuckled at herself with a small shake of the head, backed up a step, and then said with a sharp, decisive boss-lady tone, "And, Fallon, one last thing."

"Yes, Ms. Brand?"

"You're fired."

CHAPTER ONE

Big Sky, Montana
One month later

DANICA BRAND HAD arrived in her home state of Montana still stunned by Grant's betrayal. Instead of staying at their family's ranch, Hideaway, she had taken a rental in town, grateful that her Realtor connections allowed her to find a gem of a condo in the height of winter sports season in Big Sky. When she first arrived in Big Sky, she had given herself permission to grieve for one whole week; she drank wine, deleted pictures of Grant from her phone, changed her status on her social media and spent extra time in bed while she hugged a pillow and cried. After the week was up, Danica refocused her attention on her business and communicating with her attorney and financial advisers about how to untangle her life from Grant's.

One month post-breakup, Danica had established a routine that included taking power walks, which was her favorite form of exercising to reduce stress and to clear her mind. Big Sky Community Park fit that bill; they maintained their trails during snowy Montana winters. Now, weather permitting, she started her day with a brisk walk, exploring different trails for a change of scenery.

"How are you?" Leena, her junior Realtor, asked, concerned.

Earbud in her ear, her phone tucked into a pocket on her snugly fitting workout pants, Danica pumped her arms to propel forward with each long stride. "Right as rain."

"Fake it until you make it?"

"That's what I've told you. And that's what I'm doing. Don't *ever* let anyone see you sweat." Danica slowed down, feeling lightheaded. She still hadn't adjusted to the altitude and when she pushed herself, and she was *always* pushing herself, she felt dizzy and out of breath. This bout was different. This time, she had to stop, bend over, hands braced on her knees, eyes closed as she waited to catch her breath and let the dizziness subside.

Just as she was standing upright and while listening to Leena's litany of concerns about hosting an open house on her own for the first time, she heard a man's voice call out "Lu Lu" followed by a neon pink Frisbee flying over her head, and while her mind was occupied by that Frisbee for a nanosecond, a rotund pig, wearing a very chic pink-and-white polka-dot sweater with a matching toboggan covering her ears, dashed out in front of her, surprised her, bumped into her hard enough to get her off-balance, leaving her flailing her arms in an unsuccessful attempt to stop herself from falling. She twisted her body to take the brunt of the fall on her right side and her right hand, and she felt her ankle twist as she landed on the frozen rocky ground.

"Leena!" Danica interrupted her protégée's lengthy list of worries about the open house. "I've got to go. We'll talk later."

"Are you all right?"

"For the love of peanuts, Leena! Please stop asking me that!" Danica exclaimed, assessing the damage. "I'm fine! I just got blindsided by a pig in polka dots!"

The last thing she heard Leena say before she hung up was, "And I thought LA was weird." As she rolled off her right hip, that quip made her laugh while she rubbed her ankle.

"Are you all right?" A tall man rounded the corner taking long strides.

"Yes," she said, laughing. "I'm okay."

The morning sun made a golden halo around the man's body, the features of his face in shadow. When he blocked out the sun with his broad shoulders, his handsome features came into view, and she discovered that she was looking at one of the most beautiful men she had ever seen. Strong nose, strong chin, square jaw, deep-set brown eyes framed by dark eyebrows. He had the bone structure of a Hollywood leading man and a hot bod to boot!

The man knelt beside her and smelled of saddle soap and pine needles. *Hello, handsome.* "How badly are you hurt?" he asked.

It took Danica a split second to respond because she had been quite distracted by his kissable lips. "Not too bad. A scrape, a bruise, twisted ankle. I'm not a doctor, but…"

"I am," he said matter-of-factly. "A doctor. If you'd let me, I'd like to take a look at your injuries."

Her mind immediately started a checklist on the man. Handsome, check. Smells divine, check. Handsome doctor, check check.

"What happened?"

"A pig happened. Knocked right into me. I fell back, landed on my hip and my hand, with what I'm sure was catlike grace, and then I proceeded to twist my ankle."

"I am very sorry."

"It's not your fault."

"I'm afraid it is."

She studied him for a second as two plus two equaled four in her mind. "Oh. That was *your* pig in pink polka dots."

"I'm afraid so."

The man, still nameless, so in her mind, mysterious, helped her over to a nearby bench. When she was seated, she said, "Thank you. I don't even know your name."

"Matteo Katz," he said, before he whistled loudly, scanning the brush on either side of the rocky trail.

"Nice to meet you." She sent him a flirtatious smile that came out of nowhere, but she didn't regret it. After fifteen years, she was unexpectedly single, and she needed to dust off her "how to flirt" playbook and get some practice in. No time like the present. "Danica Brand."

"Hideaway Ranch?"

"Yes." She nodded. "Have you been?"

"No," he said, "but I've heard good things. And I've crossed paths with your sisters a time or two."

He helped her to a nearby bench and after she was seated, Matteo whistled the same whistle again and then soon after, Lu Lu the pig came out of the nearby brush carrying her pink Frisbee. She dropped the Frisbee at Matteo's feet, sat down with what Danica rated as a genuinely pleased smile and oinked loudly.

"Good girl, Lu Lu." He leaned down to give his pig a scratch beneath her ample chin.

Danica felt quite charmed by the man and his pig. She turned her body toward Lu Lu, leaned forward, and said in sweet voice, "Hello, Lu Lu. You are a very pretty pig. I'd go as far as to say that you are a fashionista. Your Frisbee matches your ensemble to perfection!"

"She picks the Frisbee that matches her outfit."

"Are you kidding me? I know plenty of people who can't do that," she said, her smile broadened as she looked up at Matteo.

"No, not kidding. She's very smart. She can be a real diva, I can tell you that right now. When she gets bored, and I try very hard to not *let* her get bored, she is two whole handfuls."

Danica leaned down and let the pig smell her hand with that large, round, wet nose. To Lu Lu she said, "It's okay to be a diva. I come from the land of divas. And I'll tell you a secret." She lowered her voice to a more private level. "Some people might even consider *me* to be a diva."

Lu Lu made some chuffing sounds in the back of her throat with her adorable curly tail wagging and hopped in a circle, which made Danica laugh more loudly and freely than she had in years.

"How does that ankle feel?" Matteo asked her, interrupting her good time with Lu Lu.

With a shake of her head and a self-effacing smile, Danica sat up and said, "I forgot all about it."

Now that it was back on her radar, her hip felt like she would have a large bruise in a bit, and her hand was scraped at the wrist and had taken the brunt of the fall.

Matteo knelt and motioned for her to put her foot on his thigh, but she hesitated. "Now, before I let you examine me, what kind of doctor are you, exactly? I mean, you aren't a gynecologist or a large animal vet?"

He laughed with a broad perfectly white smile. "General practice. Humans only."

"So, ankle qualified."

"Yes," he said, then nodded toward her injured foot. "May I?"

"Not so fast, mister," she said, sliding her phone out of her pocket. "Full name, please."

"Dr. Matteo Katz-Cortez."

Danica searched his name and then said, "Hmm. Four-point-eight stars, two hundred and eighteen reviews. Nearly all women."

"To be fair—" he caught her gaze and held it "—I am a big fish in a tiny pond."

"A pond stocked with only female fish."

And, because he was still smiling at her, she found herself smiling back at him again. Three honest smiles in a thirty-minute window! Her one week of grieving Grant had been the exact right amount of time.

"So," he prompted when she just stared at him without any words forthcoming, "may I take a look at that ankle?"

"Yes, you may," she replied in her most controlled, professional, not *at all* thinking about your sexy lips, voice.

Given the go-ahead, he gently slipped off her tennis shoe, putting the shoe down by Lu Lu, who had been grunting, oinking and talking to them nonstop, and then he carefully lifted her foot to rest it on his rock-solid thigh. While he was examining her, she was most definitely examining him. And she was really enjoying this moment until he palpated her ankle and asked, "Does that hurt?"

"Yes." She frowned. "It does."

"How about this?" he asked.

"Still, yes!"

He sighed, pulled her sock back up and very much like the prince seeing if the glass slipper fit Cinderella, Dr. Katz placed her tennis shoe back onto her foot.

"Well, you've got some swelling."

"I do?"

He nodded. "You'll have a bruise most likely. You'll need to wrap it, ice it and elevate it."

"You really did me in, didn't you?" she asked, teasingly. She had just met him, but she felt comfortable with him. It was easy.

Matteo's lips turned up in a small smile, letting her know that he had taken her good-natured ribbing in stride. Still kneeling, he reached for her hand. "Minor abrasion. Clean it with alcohol and apply an antibiotic ointment."

"Okay."

He sat back on his heel. "You said you also landed on your hip? Are you experiencing any pain?"

She raised an eyebrow at him. "Now, Dr. Matteo, you will not be examining my gluteus maximus on a public trail. Just suffice it to say that it smarts."

He stood up with a smile and then said, "Stand up and let's see if you can put weight on it."

"Oh, please!" she said. "I'm sure I can put weight on it. I'm sure I could finish my hike on it. I've worn five-inch stilettos up a long drive in the West Hollywood Hills with a bad sprain before with not so much as a limp!"

"Humor me."

She shrugged and then she stood up and when she put weight on it, she said, "Ow!"

At the same time she was standing up, Lu Lu was foraging in the brush next to the trail and every time she leaned down and tried to get whatever delicious thing she had found into her mouth, her back legs lifted into the air, she would shift her weight back to get her hind legs on the ground, and that cycle repeated.

So Danica was cringing from the pain in her ankle while laughing at the antics of the rotund, stubby-legged pig.

"I'd like to help you back to your vehicle," the handsome doctor offered.

"Thank you," she said. It was an unusual feeling, this dependence on another person. She had built her business, and had thrived, in a man's world by being fiercely independent. That was why Grant lived in *her* house and had been made a partner in *her* company at a sixty-forty split with her holding the largest share.

"It's the least I could do," he said, bending down to put the leash on Lu Lu's harness.

And then she did something she rarely did; she hooked her arm with his and leaned on him, just a little bit.

Danica had to smile at the little pig jauntily walking next to Matteo, talking in her language the entire time.

"She certainly doesn't lack conversational skills," she noted.

That made Matteo laugh. "You are correct. She does not. Not at all. Some of it's super-cute, but when she's mad? She goes from cute to bloodcurdling real quick."

She could feel his biceps flexing beneath her hand and it made her imagine what the gorgeous doctor might look like during the summer, in a clothing-optional situation.

"How long will you be in town?"

Still creating a rather racy image of Matteo in a shirt unbuttoned down to the waistband of snug-fit Wrangler jeans, her companion repeated the question and that time she heard it and responded.

"Maybe a month or two more."

"Business or pleasure?"

"Both," she said with a small sigh. "It's a long story."

"I like long stories."

She winced a bit; her right butt cheek hurt, her hand hurt, and her stupid ankle hurt, too! The best thing she knew to do was focus on her companions and push the rest aside.

"So, may I ask how you acquired your delightful pig?"

"That's a long story."

She glanced up at him. "I like long stories, too.

"Here's a question for you…does your wife, girlfriend, boyfriend or generally anyone who thinks they are currently in a relationship with you design Lu Lu's clothing?"

"Was that your not-so-subtle way of asking me if I'm in a relationship?"

"Yes," she said, "and just an FYI—that's as subtle as I get."

"I like direct."

"So do I," she said. "So many things in common."

"Seems like," he said with a rather sheepish smile, a small spark of unexpected shyness. "I'm not spoken for. You?"

She shook her head. "Newly *un*engaged."

Even as slowly as they had walked, they reached the parking lot much too quickly. She pointed out her rented Cadillac luxury SUV. She opened the door, wishing that the walk wasn't over.

"Well, Lu Lu—" Danica bent down "—I hope we meet again."

She started to scratch the pig beneath her chin and the pig closed her eyes and extended out her neck.

"If you scratch her chin, she will be your friend for life."

"Is that true, Lu Lu? Will you be my friend for life?"

"But when you stop…"

"Uh-huh?" she asked, while still scratching.

"She will get mad," he said, with a warning undertone in his voice, "and then you'll be very sorry that you ever started in the first place."

"Oh, nonsense," she said, standing up, "She's an…"

Danica never got the word *angel* out of her mouth because the horrid, ear-stabbing, mind-blowingly shrill shriek that Lu Lu was making made her plug her ears.

Matteo distracted Lu Lu by tossing her Frisbee a few feet, still out of the range of any vehicles that may pass by.

"Now do you see why I'm still single?" he asked.

"Yes." She nodded, and then said to Lu Lu she when the pig brought the Frisbee back, "Good girl, Lu Lu. Scare all of them away."

Matteo helped her into the driver's seat. Danica climbed behind the wheel with a promise to Matteo that she could drive with her sprain.

He shut the door behind her while she cranked the engine; then she rolled down the window. "It was a pleasure to meet you, Dr. Katz."

"Thank you," he said. "I'm sorry for the circumstance. If you decide you want to sue me, I know a reputable lawyer."

She looked at him and didn't look away when their eyes locked. "I find you very interesting, Dr. Katz."

"I feel the same." His smile started at his lips and ended in his deep brown gold-flecked eyes. "I'd like to call you, check on you."

She nodded and fished a business card out of her pants pocket; she always kept a couple handy. She handed it to the handsome doctor and asked with good humor, "Now, was this your subtle way of asking for my number?"

"Absolutely," he said. "Do you mind?"

"Not at all," she said. "I was just about to ask for yours."

He threw the Frisbee for Lu Lu again while he put her number into his contacts. Danica's phone chimed and she slid it out of her pants pocket and saw that she had a new text message. She read the message and felt giddy like a schoolgirl with her first crush.

Would you like to share our long stories over drinks and dinner this Friday? Six o'clock?

Still smiling, Danica typed her response.

Yes.

Now Matteo was smiling again as he caught her gaze and held it. "Text me your address and I'll pick you up at six."

"I'll be ready."

"WAIT, WAIT, WAIT!" her sister Charlotte exclaimed. "Are you telling us that you are going out on date with the most wanted bachelor within a one-hundred-mile radius?"

"And on a Friday? That's nearly a declaration of love!" Rayna's face was alight with happiness for her.

Danica was sitting in the living room of her family home with her ankle wrapped and elevated. When their mother, Rose, died, she, along with her sisters, had turned their family ranch into a corporate retreat. Even though she wasn't staying at the ranch, she spent much of her day at Hideaway Ranch with her sisters. Being with them always gave her a much-needed boost.

"I didn't know he was the most wanted bachelor." Danica took a small sip of the hot chamomile tea her identical twin sister, Ray, had prepared for her. "But I can certainly see why. He is the most beautiful man I've ever seen. And that's saying something—I live in the capital of beautiful men."

Charlotte, also known to friends and family as Charlie, leaned back against the butcher block island and said, "Now, Wayne is *the* most handsome man to me, but Dr. Katz? A very close, infinitesimal really, second."

Charlie, a cowgirl to her core, had been determined to keep Hideaway Ranch in the family by transforming it from a cattle ranch into a destination spot. Wayne Westbrook was a silver fox, jack-of-all-trades cowboy who had helped Charlotte reach that goal. Wayne was a perfect match for Charlie, on the ranch and in her heart, and they were the first romance to blossom at the ranch.

"Same." Rayna "Ray" was rocking in an old family rocking chair dated back three generations, under a quilt their mother had made just before her passing. "For me, Dean Legend is the most handsome man in any room. Tall, burly…"

Ray, a recently divorced empty nester, had moved back to Big Sky with a plan to figure out her next move. When she rekindled a love affair with Dean Legend, her first love and boyfriend all through high school, everyone knew what her next move would be.

"But if I *didn't* have Dean," Ray said with a sheepish smile, "I might've joined the hunt."

"He's smart, handsome, an animal lover," Danica said. "He's like a unicorn. Something *must* be wrong with him. Men like that aren't just roaming around like free-range chickens."

Charlie topped off her tea. "No one's without flaw obviously, but Dr. Katz is about as close as a human male can be to perfection. I've only heard good things."

Ray held up her own glass and said, "On these auspicious occasions, I propose a toast to our dear sister Danny, who managed to land the biggest fish in our Big Sky pond."

"And she doesn't even like to fish!" Charlie added with a smile.

Their conversation soon shifted from the hunky Dr. Katz to the changes to their website that highlighted the fact that "love blooms" at Hideaway Ranch. There was a number counter on the website now, one marriage, two engagements, one baby, and a long-distance romance that had inspired a cross-country move.

"I think it's perfect," Ray said. "I know when we started this venture we thought our bread and butter would be from corporate retreats."

"I did think that when I hatched the idea but looking at our bookings, these aren't corporate clients," Charlie agreed.

"No. They aren't. I believe our next guest is an author?" Danica asked Ray to confirm.

Ray nodded, "A *romance* writer, actually. We had a cancellation and Journey Lamar was the first name on our waiting list. I *love* that name."

"She might have seen our social media 'Love is always in season at Hideaway Ranch' advertisement campaign." The more Danica talked about it, the more excited she became about the ranch; she had handled the budget and the renovations of the main house remotely from LA. In person, where she could feel firsthand the energy of the place, now she understood that the intangible *something* happening on this land had to be *felt* to be understood. "I see us as a destination for weddings, anniversaries, honeymoons. The opportunities in the romance category are limitless! I can see people who are looking for love booking with us in hopes that some of our Hideaway Ranch love magic will align the stars for them. But we have to dig into the data regularly, analyze trend lines and shift our focus quickly, if need be, to reflect market demands," Danica explained to her sisters.

"I have no idea what you just said," Charlie laughed, "but I sure as heck agree with every single darn word."

"Me too," Ray joined in, "every darn word."

"Journey has us booked for two weeks. The beginning of the second week, her ten-year-old son, Oakley, will be joining with her."

Right as they were finishing up with a review of the website, their social media footprint and preparations for their guests, Wayne swung the front door open and slammed it shut in his haste.

"Is he here?" Charlie asked her fiancé.

"Heading down the drive as we speak," Wayne said before he tipped his hat to Ray and her. "Ladies."

Wayne noticed her ankle and asked, "What happened there?"

"I'll fill you in later." Charlie grabbed her cowgirl hat hastily before she looked at them. "We're done here, right?"

"Sure," Danica agreed. She was feeling unusually sleepy and could see herself curling up in one of the beds and taking a nap. Napping, generally, was not something she did.

"Who's coming?" Ray asked.

"Cody Ty Hawkins!" Charlie followed Wayne the short distance to the front door.

"I'm drawing a blank," Ray said.

"Me, too," Danica said. "Who is Cody Ty Hawkins?"

Before Charlie went outside, she turned and looked at them with a disappointed expression on her face when she asked, "Seriously? Who is *Cody Ty*?" She then shook her head. "How are we even related?"

CHAPTER TWO

"WHAT DO YOU THINK?" Matteo held up two button-down shirts for Lu Lu. "Black or purple?"

"Would you like the other person in the room to share an opinion?" his sister, Estrella, chimed in. "I think both of those colors are a bad idea."

He had a close relationship with his younger sister by two years and even though she lived in Baltimore, they video-chatted at least one time a day. Lu Lu approached the options and made her choice.

"Lu Lu voted for purple," he told Estrella.

"But of course she did."

Lu Lu headed over to her oversize bed with her name embroidered on it and promptly went to sleep.

"I guess that decision really tuckered poor Lu Lu out." Matteo turned the phone so his sister could see his swine companion.

"She may have sleep apnea," Estrella noted. "That's quite a snore."

Now with his outfit for tonight's date picked out, it was time to go to the kitchen for a quick protein shake and then off to work. Estrella kept him company while he gathered ingredients.

"Why are you so nervous?" his sister asked him. "You have nothing *but* gorgeous, googly-eyed women dropping at your feet on the daily! All of these women fanatical over my dorky brother."

"First of all, I'm not a dork."

"Uh, yes you are."

"And, second, this is different." He began to cut up his fresh fruit. "*Danica* is different."

"How? She's blonde with a stunning face. She looks like a fitness model, she's obviously accomplished, age-appropriate, which is more than I can say for some of your past dates. So I guess *that's* a plus."

"She's witty, intelligent. I love her laugh. There was a spark between us and I know she felt it, too," he told her, and then added, "I knew you'd look her up."

"Of course you did. And of course *I* did," Estrella said. "I actually like her for you, in theory. But her life seems to be very well-established in California, Matteo. Are you willing to break your ban on long-distance relationships?"

"*Hermanita*, let me get through the first date and I'll get back to you on that." Matteo finished cutting the fruit, put it into the blender and then added unsweetened oat milk to the mix.

"Okay, okay," his sister said, laughing, "at least you got the pig thing out of the way."

"Danica loved Lu Lu and the feeling was mutual."

"Maybe she is the one for you," Estrella said. "She met you while playing Frisbee with your pet pig? And she didn't sprint back to the Hollywood Hills?"

Estrella shrugged. "Maybe your crazy jibes with her crazy."

"Thank you, I think?"

"Call me after!"

"I will."

"No matter how late."

"I *will*."

"Okay." His sister blew him a kiss that he used his hand to catch and put on his cheek. "I've gotta go. *Te amo*."

After his sister signed off Matteo turned on the blender, which awakened Lu Lu, and soon her annoyed squeal overtook the sound of the machine. He shut it off, drank the shake right from the blender jar, rinsed it out and then stopped by Lu Lu to say he was sorry, and then he headed to the main bedroom. As he was getting ready for work, Matteo couldn't stop thinking about Danica. In fact, ever since they had met, she was a frequent visitor to his thoughts. It was the chemistry between them that had caught him completely off guard. It was undeniable, electric, that intangible connection that could not be planned, only experienced. And he had that with Danica, and he believed, to his core, that she had felt it, too.

He couldn't deny that he was apprehensive about his sudden-onset feelings for Danica. Ever since his last relationship ended, he had become a serial casual dater who preferred to spend his time with women who were in town for winter sports. They would have a wonderful time and then he would see them off at the end of their vacation, and the relationship would just naturally fade away. This lifestyle had suited him; was he lonely at times? Sure. But he loved his career, he loved his life in Big Sky, he had good friends and plenty of outdoor activities that kept his life full, and, of course, he had Lu Lu. His life was rolling along, and he didn't see any real reason to change it. Then Danica happened. He had a gut feeling, an intangible instinct, that no matter how much time he had with Danica, it would *never* be enough.

"WHAT DO YOU THINK?" Danica twirled for her sister Ray.

"Oh, Danny," Ray said, "it's simply gorgeous on you."

Catrin, Dean's ex-wife and mother of his two daughters, was a clothing designer whose business, Poem, had a global reach. The dress she was wearing for her first date in nearly fifteen years had been a gift from Catrin to Ray.

Danica looked at her reflection in the mirror; the figure-flattering sheath dress had a scoop neck and an hourglass fit. The sleeves were quarter-length; the skirt of the dress hit below the knees, giving the dress both a sexy and classic look. The entire dress was decorated with a hand-painted scene of the skyline of Paris. Each dress was a one-of-a-kind and Dean's ex-wife had been kind enough to give a work-of-art dress to Ray.

"She's a genius," Danica said.

"Yes, she is."

Danica met her sister's gaze in the mirror. "Are you sure you want me to wear this, Ray?"

There was no hesitation when Ray said, "Yes."

She sat down on the velvet bench at the makeup station in the large, ornate bathroom while Ray fixed her hair. The two of them fell into a familiar pattern even though their lives had taken them in wildly different directions.

When she was done, Ray had slicked back her icy-blond hair into a classic chignon and then her sister began to work on her makeup.

"I was blessed with two awesome boys, so I'm a little rusty in the makeup department," Ray said. Ray worked quickly and when she was done, Danica studied her reflection; the makeup was subtle and clean, and brought out her cheekbones and her eyes to perfection.

"You're a genius, too, Ray."

Ray shook her head. "No."

Danica stood up and hugged her twin sister, feeling nostalgic about all of the years they had lived their lives apart from each other.

"Thank you."

"Of course, Danny. Your happiness is my happiness."

They had picked out a strappy pair of heels that were a perfect match for the dress and then found a small clutch that she could use to carry her wallet, phone and a tube of matte lipstick.

Danica was walking around the bedroom and could only detect the tiniest twinge of pain from her nearly healed sprained ankle. She circled back to Ray for one final opportunity to edit the outfit when her sister received a call from Dean.

"Oh no," Ray said. "I'm leaving now."

Ray's face had just drained all of its color and she stood stock still, seemingly stunned by the phone call.

Forgetting about her outfit, Danica put her hand on her sister's arm and asked, "What's wrong?"

"It's Buck," Ray said in a monotone. "They're transferring him from the hospital to the ranch. He wants to die in his own house."

Buck Legend was a dear friend of the family, a neighbor, and Danica's soon-to-be father-in-law.

Danica knew that words could not help, so she simply put her arms around her sister and hugged her tightly.

Buck had always been as strong as a Cottonwood tree as long as she could remember. It was difficult to accept that the strongest of men would eventually slip away from them. Buck had been ill with lung cancer for several years and he hadn't been doing anything to prevent it from killing him, bit by bit, day by day. He had become a shell of a man after his beloved wife, Nettie, had died, and he wanted to be free of his body so he could be with Nettie in heaven.

"I have to go," Ray said, wiping the tears from her face.

"Of course," she said. "What can I do?"

"Pray for him," her sister said. "Pray for him."

"I don't have to go on this date, Ray. Actually, it feels really callous to go have a good time in light of…what's happening."

Ray gathered her things. "No! Please don't cancel. You need this, Danny, and there isn't one thing that you can do right now other than go have a much-deserved good time. It's what I want." Ray hugged her one last time, and said of Dean's daughters, Paisley and Luna, "Thank goodness the girls are in Europe visiting their mother."

"If you need me, call me," Danica told Ray. "Promise."

"I will."

Danica closed the door behind her sister, turned around and then leaned back against the door. She had spent the morning fighting with Grant via their attorneys about the business and the home they had shared. Now her sister was in crisis. It didn't feel *right* to be going out on a date. She sighed, picked up her phone off the coffee table and was just about to call Matteo to cancel their date when the phone rang.

"Hi, Matteo," she answered the phone.

"Hi, Danica," Dr. Gorgeous said in his silky baritone voice that should be banned as a secret weapon. It made her heart race accompanied by goose bumps on her arms, a shiver up her spine and a tingle in places on her body that hadn't had a *tingle* in quite a long while.

"I'm just calling to confirm our date."

She had full intention to cancel on him, but now that she was talking to him, she waffled and wavered.

"Danica? Are you still there?"

"Yes. I'm still here. Sorry. My sister just had some difficult news."

There was a brief silence from the other end of the line, and then Matteo asked, "Do we need to reschedule?"

"Yes," she said, and then, "I don't know. I mean, no, we don't. But I might have to cut things short if Ray needs me."

"I understand," he said. "So, I'll pick you up in an hour?"

"Yes. One hour. I'll look forward to seeing you then."

"Likewise."

MATTEO SAT IN his metallic gray Audi R8 sports car. He didn't often bring it out during the winter, but Danica was a luxury kind of woman and he wanted to show her that, even though he was a small-town doctor, he could do luxury just the same as any LA man.

Matteo pulled into a parking spot, turned off the engine and sat in the silence for several minutes. He was nervous. Really nervous. And he couldn't remember feeling this way *ever* in his life. Women naturally gravitated toward him, so he never had to put too much energy or effort into wooing a woman. And yet, even with her straightforward self-confidence and her willingness to ask for *his* number, he felt out of his depth. He wanted to impress her; he wanted to win her heart. He had just figured out *that* fun fact on his way over to pick her up.

Matteo took one last look in the rearview mirror before he stepped out of his Audi. He wore a long cashmere overcoat, black slacks, polished shoes and the purple shirt that Lu Lu had picked out.

"Why would you let a pig pick out your shirt?" Matteo asked himself under his breath as he walked to the front door.

Too late to change now.

After he rang the bell, Danica opened the door rather quickly wearing a slim-fit dress that hugged her modest curves in the best way. His eyes quickly followed the pattern of the dress before he said, "You are stunning."

"Thank you."

That compliment drew a small, pleased smile from Danica, whose full lips were perfectly colored a deep shade of matte rose red. And those lips looked incredibly kissable. His reaction to her, and the swiftness of his *body's* reaction to her, confirmed to him that Danica Brand was somebody special to him.

Danica slipped into a long black coat, stepped outside and locked the door behind her. Matteo offered her his arm and she took it. He puffed out his chest and felt like a very lucky man to have a woman like Danica by his side.

"I'm glad to see you," he said.

She looked at him, her lovely face, with its pert nose, high cheekbones and wide cornflower-blue eyes, turned upward. "Isn't that funny? I'm happy to see you, too."

"Well, good," Matteo said as he opened the passenger door for her. "I'm glad that I'm not the only one in this boat."

Once she was settled, he walked swiftly around to the driver's door. When he joined her, she said, "Audi R8. Very nice."

He cranked the engine, pleased that she appreciated his second "baby," only surpassed by Lu Lu. "I rarely take it out during winter, but I wanted your carriage to be worthy of you."

Danica had been rather subdued since he had arrived; she laughed her lovely, tinkling laugh and said, "I think you have a rather inflated opinion of me. I'm just a woman from LA."

"Who has built a multimillion-dollar business…"

"Yes." She gave a small smile. "There is that."

She glanced over to him. "Someone's been doing some research online."

He didn't try to deny it. "You can learn a lot."

"Yes, you can."

"What did you learn about me?"

"Who said I did any searching?"

Their eyes met and she confessed, "I did a little snooping. And so did Ray. And so did Charlie."

"The Brand sisters stick together. I wouldn't have expected anything less," he said, driving them toward one of his favorite places to eat. It did strike him that he never took other women he had dated to this spot. He'd eaten there with friends or alone. "Did you find anything useful to assess my character?"

"Well," she said slowly, keeping him in suspense, "seeing that all of us have a digital footprint dating back to our birth…"

"Oh, no."

"Oh, yes," she said with a sassy flair, "I was quite surprised and pleased to see that you were second runner-up in your elementary school talent show…"

"I will *never* live that down," he groaned. "My sister, Estrella, brings that up whenever she thinks I'm getting too big for my britches."

"Why do you have to live that down?" Danica said in teasing tone. "Ventriloquism is a very impressive talent. A little girl won *America's Got Talent* a couple of years ago. What was her name?"

"Darci Lynne," he said automatically. When he felt Danica looking at him, he glanced her way with a half smile. "I like to keep up with my other ventriloquist peeps.

"I was a big fan of Edgar Bergen. And my mom bought me a replica of his doll, Charlie McCarthy," he admitted. "Most people don't even know who he is."

"Do you mean the very popular entertainer from the 1920s who asked a wood-carver to make him a doll whom he later named Charlie McCarthy? They starred in fourteen motion pictures together, toured with the USO overseas during World War II, and had a career that spanned fifty years."

After a quick second, he said, "You looked it up."

"I looked it up."

They laughed together and he was happy that he chose the Audi; they were together in semi-tight quarters, and he could smell the fresh lilac scent of her skin. He pulled into a parking spot outside of the Block 3 Kitchen and Bar and shut off the engine before he came to his date's side of the vehicle.

"This looks nice," Danica said, popping the collar of her coat up.

"It's my favorite." He offered his arm again. "Shall we?"

"Yes." His date had a pleased expression on her face. "Let's."

IT DID NOT escape her notice that when they walked in the door, nearly every head in the restaurant turned.

"You know how to make an entrance," she said.

Her date leaned his head down toward hers and whispered, "Ten percent me, ninety percent you."

The hostess, who couldn't seem to stop blushing when she was talking to Matteo, showed them to their table and then glanced back several times to look at him before returning to her lectern. But she couldn't fault the women and the men who were struck by Matteo's handsomeness. He was simply too handsome to *not* look at him.

Matteo removed his long gentleman's coat, took hers and draped them carefully over the empty chair at their table.

"I love that purple shirt on you," Danica said. "You get high marks for that."

"This is all Lu Lu," he said.

"Lord, do I love that pig." She laughed. "She's got great taste in fashion and in men."

He sat down at their table and the expression on his face, and the way he looked at her with a spark of energy in his deep brown eyes, she could easily read his appreciation of her. It was there for anyone to see. "Thank you. Most women can't see what I see in Lu Lu."

"She's a good companion."

"Yes," he agreed, "she is that. Now, may I recommend the barrel-aged Manhattan?"

"Are you trying to get me tipsy, sir?"

"Maybe just a little bit." He winked at her. "And I'm driving, so…"

"Why not?"

"Exactly. Why not?"

They feasted on cheese fondue, grilled asparagus with oven-roasted tomato pesto, and chilled seafood platter. Matteo also ordered roasted chicken and sipped on water while she had a second barrel-aged Manhattan as they transitioned from the dining room to some comfy seating in front of a toasty fire.

"Did you enjoy your food?" he asked.

"Oh! It was positively delicious. Thank you so much." Danica felt her stomach pooching out a bit in the body-hugging dress but felt that the hand-painted scene provided some camouflage. "I hate to say this, but I wasn't expecting much. When I was growing up, Big Sky wasn't exactly known for its cuisine."

A waitress came by, and he ordered them both hot coffees before he said, "We do have some hidden gems.

"So." Matteo focused his attention on her, something he had done all evening. And his actions certainly made her feel special in that his eyes never once followed the several beautiful women who had walked by, looking at his face, perhaps hoping to steal his attention away. "Should we just get our long stories out of the way? That way, we won't have to deal with it on our second date. I would like to see you again."

She couldn't stop herself from smiling at him; he seemed to know exactly what she needed to hear, and his actions matched his words. "I would like that."

"Now that I've locked you down for a second date, would you like to go first? Or shall I?"

"You should go first. I've been dying to know the backstory of how Lu Lu came into your life. I have a feeling it has something to do with a woman. An ex-wife perhaps?"

"Not an ex-wife, but as close as I've ever been."

Danica finished her cocktail, feeling loose and languid and warm all over. She took her coffee in both hands and listened.

"I was engaged," he told her, "to a single mother."

"Oh. There was a child."

"There was." He nodded, and she saw the fleeting sadness in his eyes and the first frown she had seen on this man's handsome face.

Instinctively, she put her coffee mug down, turned her body to face him and put her hand on his arm. "You don't have to tell me that story. I'll go."

He put his hand over hers with a slight shake of his head. "I want to tell you."

"Okay. I'm listening."

"I met Lindsey at the hospital where I had my residency. She was a nurse on the graveyard shift, and we took our breaks together. I don't think either one of us thought that we would end up together. She was just coming off a divorce and I was a very sleep-deprived doctor. But one thing led to another, and we fell in love, or at least we thought we did."

He continued, "When I met Emerson, her daughter, I was a goner. Those big blue eyes, that sweet little face. She was just a joy. A light in my rather dark world."

"She must have loved you."

Matteo swallowed several times, and she felt the emotion rising up in his throat, but he stopped it from expressing as tears. She could feel his pain nonetheless.

He cleared his throat and then he continued, "I had a buddy who said that this region of Montana was desperate for doctors. After my residency, I came out here and fell in love with it. I asked Lindsey to marry me. I often wonder if we both were doing it for Emerson and not for us."

"So they moved here."

"Yes. They did." He nodded. "And my sweet Emy wanted a pig."

Danica let out a sigh she hadn't known she was holding. "Lu Lu."

Again, he nodded, pain naked in his eyes that he hadn't tried to hide from her. "Neither of us was planning the wedding, neither one of us had even talked about setting a date. And then one day, it was just over. Lindsey moved back to Baltimore, and I tried my best to stay in touch with Emy. But Lindsey got married…"

"Oh."

"And her husband officially adopted Emy."

Danica's heart sank for him, and she reached out for his hand. "I'm so sorry, Matteo."

"Me too," he said, and then tried to smile. "I'm sorry I've turned our first date into a bummer."

"I'm not. And it isn't," she said quickly to reassure him. "A bummer, I mean. It helps me understand you better—Lu Lu symbolizes your relationship with Emy."

"Yes. Thank you," he said, still holding on to her hand, "for understanding."

Danica was about to take her turn with her own long story, but a phone call from Ray stopped her.

"Danny! Call Charlie, tell her to come quick. Bring Wayne, and you come, too! Please come quick!"

"I'm leaving now!" Danica said in a rush before speed-dialing Charlie. "I'm sorry, Matteo. I have to go."

He helped her into her coat and paid the tab and they left the restaurant together. When she was in his car, it occurred to her that she had two strong drinks.

"I can't drive!" Danica said loudly. "I can't drive!"

"I'll take you," Matteo said without hesitation. "I'll take you."

CHAPTER THREE

DANICA DID NOT speak during their ride to the Legend ranch and Matteo didn't expect her to. Their connection was strong in a way that was inexplicable and yet very real and very tangible; when he reached over and put his hand on her arm occasionally to offer some comfort in this troubling time, she accepted that comfort, and even covered his hand with hers to signal to him that she appreciated it. The roads were slick with ice, and he had pondered switching out vehicles, but time was of the essence, and he didn't want to risk Danica arriving late and missing her chance to pay her respects to Buck Legend.

"It's been years," Danica said as he pulled off the freeway onto the winding lane leading up to the grand brick house with columns on the front porch and four chimney stacks.

"So much has changed," she said in a soft, melancholy voice.

Matteo parked his car while Danica quickly texted her sisters that she had arrived. Then Matteo met her at the passenger-side door, opening it and holding out his hand for her to take. Danica was wearing very sexy shoes, but they weren't designed for ice and snow.

"Thank you, Matteo," Danica said, taking his hand.

"I'm glad to be of service."

Danica hooked her arm with his and he ensured that she reached the front door safely. The front steps leading up the grand porch designed in an antebellum style had been recently salted; even so, he didn't let go of her until she was standing firmly on the welcome mat. Before Danica had a chance to ring the doorbell, the front door opened and Charlie was standing in the doorway, her eyes red from crying. Wordlessly, Charlie hugged Danica, and his date, who hadn't shed any tears on the ride over, began to cry.

"Tonight?" Danica asked.

Charlie nodded. "We think so."

Dean appeared behind Charlie and said, "Dr. Katz, please come in. Dad would want you here. You were the only doctor he respected, and he never forgot the way you took care of Mom in her last days."

Matteo entered the house, shook hands with Dean, and knowing that the look Danica was giving him had a question mark in it, he said, "I was Buck and Nettie's primary care for many years. It wasn't my place to divulge that."

He helped Danica out of her coat and hung it on a nearby coatrack. And together, they followed Charlie and Dean to the large library with floor-to-ceiling windows looking over hundreds of prime cattle pastures. Nettie had collected books, rare and beautiful, from nearly every genre from fiction to history and everything in between. When Buck became ill enough to need a hospital bed and round-the-clock nurses, Dean's dad insisted that he be moved from the first-floor primary bedroom to the library, Nettie's favorite room in the house. Matteo was there for that move but then he had to turn Buck's case over to an oncologist.

Ray saw her twin and she waved her over to where she was seated, holding on to Buck's hand. Buck appeared to be unconscious. Ray let go of Buck's hand, stood up and hugged Danica tightly. "He's leaving."

"I know he is," Danica said. "He's going home to Nettie."

Ray nodded, new tears following old, and said to Matteo, "Thank you for bringing her."

"My pleasure."

Matteo said his last goodbye to Buck, a man he had met soon after moving to Big Sky and had grown to respect—the man who had prioritized his wife and children and had built a legacy that could be sustained for generations.

He shook Dean's hand and excused himself. He was grateful to say farewell to Buck, but he wasn't family and didn't want to intrude. Danica saw him preparing to leave, left Ray for a moment to see him to the door. After he put on his coat, he took Danica's hands into his.

"I had a wonderful time," Danica said. "Thank you—for being so kind."

"You're welcome," he replied. "Thank you for letting me."

"I remember Buck the way he was when I was in high school," Danica said with a far-off look in her eyes. "When I see him…like that, I wonder why I stayed away so long."

"He is a great man. I have always admired him," he said with an emotional catch in his voice. Seeing Buck in his last moments on Earth had struck a chord; even incredibly strong, bigger-than-life men faced their own mortality at some point. And when he saw Buck listless in that hospital bed, and when he looked around at Danica's sisters and their men, it made him begin to reflect on his own life. What was he waiting for? Buck, he was sure, would remind him, as he had in every doctor's appointment, that nothing ventured, nothing gained.

"I want to see you again, Danica," he said, quite taken with her lovely face, and the depth and honesty he saw in her wide, blue eyes encouraged him to ask but then he said, "But I know family is first."

And, because Danica was a no-nonsense, no-drama, straight-forward woman, she didn't play coy. "I want to see you too, but—"

"Your family needs you," he filled in the blanks.

"Yes—" Danica nodded "—they do."

Matteo took her into his arms, held her tightly, and then took her slight hand in his and kissed it. "I'm here, Danica. If you need me, please call."

"I will."

After one last hug, Matteo said goodbye to his date and on the way back to his car, he felt a bit stunned. He hadn't ever fallen in love at first sight before, so he hadn't ever really believed that it was an actual thing. But meeting Danica Brand, blond bombshell, had made him rethink his long-held belief. Perhaps there was such a thing as love at first sight.

DANICA SAT BY Buck Legend's bedside, supporting her sisters and Dean in the wee hours of the morning. Their cat, Magic, a robust black-and-white cat with striking green eyes, had jumped up onto the bed, placed his paw over Buck's heart and purred nonstop for hours. Though Buck was not much of a cat person, Magic and his persistence had turned him into a cat lover, and it seemed fitting that Magic be a part of his final hours.

Wayne had joined them but had to leave at dawn to see to the animals and, just after Wayne's departure and as the sun began to rise, flooding the library with the beautiful morning light, Buck's eyes fluttered open, and they all stood up, surprised, and called out his name. But the look in his eyes was otherworldly, staring through them, not at them, and they read his lips as he whispered, *Nettie*, and then took one more breath; that one breath was his last. He slipped away on a long exhale, leaving behind a hole in their lives that could not be filled by another.

Danica sat down in her chair, stunned at the unexpected loss of a man who was an integral part of her most formative years. He had always treated the Brand triplets as his extended family, and she felt honored to be a part of his last moments. Charlie came to her side, and they held on to each other while Ray and Dean consoled each other. Danica leaned down to kiss Buck on the forehead. And the emotional and physical toll of sitting at his bedside caught up at once. She slumped down into a nearby overstuffed chairs that she had sat in many times before in her teenage years.

"Yes, Catrin," Dean said to his ex-wife, "he passed. I'd like to tell the girls myself." Dean paused then said, "Thank you, Catrin. Give me a couple of hours and I'll call back."

"They will be crushed," Ray said, refusing to leave Buck's side.

Dean was a burly lumberjack of a man, but in this moment, after he had held it together when he talked to his ex-wife, bent down to hug his father, his tears soaked his father's pillow.

"He loved you so much," Dean said to Ray. "I'm so glad he got to see us together."

Ray nodded. "Me, too."

"Our union inspired him to hang on just a little bit longer."

"He's with Nettie now," Ray said. "May he rest in peace."

Danica dozed off curled up in the chair; she awakened just in time for the funeral home to arrive and take Buck's body away to prepare for the burial. He would be laid to rest by his beloved Nettie. And then the machines were turned off and his morning nurse arrived to discover that the job was done. She gave her condolences to Dean and Ray before she began to wrap up cords and move machines to the side, out of the way. It was strange; these mundane tasks had to be done even as a giant of a man had left the world. Life did keep going.

"Let's head back home." Charlie helped her up.

They checked on Ray, who was keeping herself busy with the regular chores that kept a large ranch going.

"Will you be okay?"

Ray nodded. "Eventually."

The three sisters put their arms around one another's shoulders, heads touching in the middle; it was something they had done for as long as they could remember and even longer according to their dearly departed mother, Rose.

"Whatever you need. Whatever Dean needs, we are here," Danica emphasized.

"Thank you. I'll be over later," Ray said. "We have to make some final preparations for our guest. She arrives in one week."

"You let us handle that, Ray. You focus on Dean and his girls."

Ray, who appeared dazed and robotic, did seem relieved that she could step back from Hideaway Ranch while they handled the details. After another triplet hug, Danica and Charlie got into a truck and drove the short distance to their ranch. The Legends and Brands had shared more than just a property line; they had shared the good times, bad times, happy and sad times. Their families were irrevocably intertwined.

With a promise to touch base later, Charlie dropped her off at the main house while she headed to the restored 1900s cabin that had been built by their ancestors. That was the home she now shared with Wayne. Exhausted, Danica stripped out of her clothes, drew a very hot bath, and then, after she dried off, climbed in a bed that she had chosen and purchased from LA.

"This is very comfy," Danica said, as she snuggled down into the feathery mattress and the silky bamboo sheets. "Not too shabby, Danny. Not too shabby."

JOURNEY LAMAR TURNED onto the gravel road that would lead her to Hideaway Ranch. She was a Michigan gal, so ice and snow didn't scare her. But horses *did* and she was pushing through this lifelong phobia in order to do important research for her next book. She had always dreamed of writing romance novels and that dream had come true and her first book, *How to Wrangle a Cowboy*, had been published the previous year. It was wonderful and great and terrifying and deeply disappointing. Reader reviews had ripped apart her book, complaining about the characters, the dialogue, the realism. After the twentieth one-star review, written by a blogger with the handle Romance4Life, *and* who wanted to give her minus one star for the most annoying heroine in the history of her blog, Journey had turned her social media private and made a solemn vow not to look at *any* reviews so she could focus on her next book.

She refused to be a one-book writer, and this meant she needed to head west to Montana. She'd always loved a sexy cowboy, but Michigan wasn't part of the romantic West and other than some saloons and Little Leagues, her only way to research was online. She was the type of writer who needed the scents, the language, the grit of cowboy life in order to authentically tell a story the way she wanted to tell it.

"Hello?" She answered the call as she crept along the driveway wanting to absorb this first introduction to Hideaway Ranch.

"How do, little lady," Riggs, her best friend from elementary school to the present, greeted her in a manner not typical.

"Well, giddy-up, cowboy!"

They laughed together and then Riggs said, "Give me all the deets! Have you seen any sweaty shirtless cowboys yet?"

"It's January. In Montana. No one is topless."

"Ugh," Riggs said with a dramatic flair. "I hope the rest of your trip isn't a total snooze-fest. Why couldn't you set your book in someplace tropical?"

"Cowboys sell books," she told him.

"How am I supposed to argue with you when you're always right?"

"Bye, Riggs."

"Bye, gorg."

Riggs was perpetually single because he always wanted to mingle; he had inherited an obscene amount of money from his grandfather so didn't have to work. It seemed like an impossible friendship with her being a single mother to a ten-year-old boy and helping her mother take care of both grandparents. Somehow, it just worked, and they just were friends. And even though many people thought he was juvenile and careless, Riggs was the only person other than her mother who was always there; no matter what time of day or where he was in the world, Riggs was there. It was rare to find a friend like that.

After she hung up with her best friend as she drove through a gate with a rustic wood-and-metal archway embossed with *Hideaway Ranch* that led to the main house where she would be staying, Journey had to turn off the engine and just absorb the scenery. The log cabin was lovely and raw and made her feel as if she had just driven into a past that had long since gone away.

"This is absolutely perfect." Journey opened the car door, swung her long legs around and then stepped into a slushy puddle. The midafternoon sun felt warm on her cheeks just as it had warmed the brisk air and melted the snow from the night before. She walked behind the rental and saw a man working with a horse in a circular area that was called a round pen, a place to exercise horses. The cowboy in the center of the pen was wearing a well-loved brown cowboy hat and black jeans that were faded almost to a light gray, and he looked exactly like the type of man she had been hoping to study.

She snapped a picture discreetly and then posted on her social media, "*The Horse Whisperer*, circa 1998, Robert Redford," and then added several heart-eyes emojis. She was spinning around in a circle, trying to, all at once, process and file away every amazing detail in her mind.

"Journey?" asked a pretty woman wearing a mustard-colored coat with a sheepskin collar, jeans and tall brown boots, with a pair of the brightest blue eyes she had ever seen in her life.

"That's me!" She waved with a smile.

"Welcome to Hideaway Ranch! I'm Charlie. We spoke on the phone."

"Yes. Hello!"

Charlie waved her up to the porch. "Just leave your bags. I'll have my fiancé grab them in bit."

"Are you sure?" Journey asked. "I'm actually stronger than I look."

Charlie waved again, and Journey thought, *Well, why not?* She climbed the steps up to the wide front porch with the rocking chairs covered in layers of melting snow.

"Nice to meet you." Charlie had a strong handshake. "We're happy to have you."

"I'm happy to be had!" Journey said with a bright smile, and she couldn't seem to stop glancing over to the man and his horse.

Charlie noticed and said, "That's Cody Ty Hawkins. One of the greatest rodeo champions in the world."

Journey didn't know the name, but she intended to research him later on. Two strokes of luck! First on the cancellation list *and* a rodeo champion on-site?

"He's fascinating," Journey said, and there was a flicker of understanding in Charlie's eyes made her a smidge self-conscious.

"Yes, he is," Charlie said, opening the door. "He's the real deal."

Journey stepped into the cozy atmosphere of the main cabin. There was a fire burning in the fireplace, a faint scent of pine, and the minute she walked into the cabin, she felt at ease and at home as if she had been there many lifetimes ago.

"Make yourself comfortable." Charlie shrugged out of her jacket and hung it and her hat on the horseshoe hooks next to the door.

"Thank you." Journey hung up her coat as well and then sat down at the butcher block-style island.

"Coffee, hot cocoa, hot buttered rum?"

"Where have you been all my life?" Journey asked. "It's five o'clock somewhere. Hot buttered rum? Yes, please."

Her son wouldn't be arriving for a week, and she fully intended to delve into some self-care and let her proverbial hair down. Oakley was her heart and her world, but mothers needed a break, too.

Charlie joined her and together they enjoyed the warm drink and then had a second.

"So, you write romance?"

Journey put her mug down and held it to keep her hands warm. "Yes. I do. Well, really just the one."

"One's better than none."

"True." Journey loved Charlie's energy; it was such a good vibe.

"I love your hair," Journey said about Charlie's thick long silver-and-brown natural hair that was plaited into a long braid down her back.

"Thank you," her host said. "I just couldn't be bothered with it. I look way older than my sisters, but the horses don't care."

Charlie's sense of humor plus the buttered rum served to relax Journey and she could see herself feeling right at home in Montana.

"Let me show you to your room. Wayne just texted, he's on his way over to help with your bags."

Journey followed Charlie; she was interested in the photographs lining the hallway and stopped to ask questions about the people featured in them.

"So much history here," she said, awestruck. "Didn't the website say that this property has been in your family for generations?"

"Five." Charlie led her to a spacious room with a king-size bed and windows that overlooked expansive, snow-white pastureland.

"That is truly amazing. I feel honored to be here."

"We're honored to have you with us."

Journey took the tour and discovered a luxury en suite bathroom that had been completely updated and featured a soaker tub that had her name on it.

"This is all for me?"

"We only book one group at a time. When they arrive, your son and mother will have the rooms across the hall." Charlie smiled at her. "Wayne's here. Let's go meet him at your car."

"Oh! Wait a sec. I'd like my mom to have this room. I'll share the bathroom with my son."

"Okay by me." Charlie gave her a thumbs-up.

Wayne was her very first *real* cowboy experience. Button-down shirt, silver goatee, intense deep-set eyes; he wasn't much of a talker, but he tipped his hat to her several times and greeted her with a "how do?" That was also a first. She kind of liked it and was definitely taking mental notes to add some color to her cowboy characters.

"Ma'am." Wayne tipped his hat to her again after he brought her bags into her room that shared a Jack-and-Jill bathroom.

"Thank you, Wayne. Nice to meet you."

"Likewise." The cowboy headed out of the door, but then he stopped, turned and caught her gaze. "We'll be sitting around the campfire this evening. We'd be pleased if you'd join."

And there it was, cowboy magic! Anyone with just one eye could see that Wayne was a goner for Charlie. But when he gave her that direct look plus the set of his chin, the roughness of his hands, all wrapped up in cowboy boots, a silver buckle and that button-down shirt with some chest hair showing—she didn't have to wonder a moment longer. She was hooked on cowboys now. And in record time.

"Thank you." She gave him a nod. "It would be my pleasure."

A WAKE WAS held at the Legend home a week after Buck's death. Between her own issues in California, which seemed to be heading in the wrong direction, and supporting Dean and Ray, Danica only had time to text with Matteo. They had several short conversations, but he had a busy medical practice, and the planets didn't align for them. As it turned out, the next time they saw each other in person was at the wake.

"How are you?" Matteo asked her. "How are Dean and Ray holding up?"

Danica breathed in and let it out on a sigh. "Devastated. And the girls, Paisley and Luna, they are heartbroken. And Dean and his ex-wife Catrin don't agree on how things should be handled."

Danica lowered her voice and Matteo leaned his head down. "Catrin does not want them to attend the funeral. She follows her Buddhist tradition. The body should not be embalmed but should be cremated."

"I see."

"Well, that makes one of us," Danica said in a sharp tone. She was tired of fighting with Grant, she was tired of the tug-of-war happening with Dean's daughters. She felt angry that Dean's ex had refused to cut the girls' visit short to allow them to attend the funeral.

"I'm sorry," she said almost immediately, "I haven't had much sleep."

"I understand. Hard, emotional times," Matteo said, kindly, and that made her feel seen, heard and supported.

"Thank you." She put her hand on his arm. "I like you very much."

The smile he gave her made her spirit lighten for the first time since the night they lost Buck. "I like you very much, too."

The wake was an emotional roller coaster for Danica; so many people had traveled from around the state to pay their respects. The long driveway to the main house was used for parking on both sides with some parking on the berm of the highway and then walking the rest of the way in.

The wake, per Buck's last wishes, was not a downtrodden affair. Buck loved everything classic country music, so the house was alive with the sounds of Loretta Lynn, Johnny Cash, Garth Brooks, Dolly Parton and the Judds. All of Buck's favorite foods were prepared by Ray and Miss Minnie, a woman as round as she was tall, who had worked for the Legends so long that she was a valued family member.

"I miss that ol' curmudgeon," Miss Minnie said. "I truly do and I truly will."

Danica walked in just in time for a taste test after she hugged Ray. "Mmm. The taste of our childhood."

"It is," Ray agreed. Buck's all-time favorite was cowboy mashed potatoes with baby carrots, garlic, white corn, butter, chives and some shredded cheddar cheese. "It never tastes this good when I make it, though."

"If you don't mind, take this batch out for me." Miss Minnie had a sheen of sweat on her round face, standing with her hands on her broad hips. "My dogs are really barking today. Bad feet, bad hips, bad back."

Ray walked over, gave Minnie a hug. "Beautiful heart."

Miss Minnie smiled, pleased, and it seemed to give her a much-needed boost to keep her going. "All right now, we don't need to be sitting around blathering and blubbering with all of this work to do."

Ray and Danica took the mashed potatoes to the buffet-style setup. The main entrance and the library were filled with people laughing, crying and telling stories about Buck, a true man among men.

Charlie broke free of a conversation and joined them at the buffet.

"Buck sure did mean a lot to so many people," she said, then asked Ray, "What's the news on Dean's girls?"

Ray sighed. "Most of the time, Dean and Catrin can negotiate a middle ground, but both of them are in their corners just waiting for the bell to be rung."

After a few minutes watching the guests quietly, lost in their own thoughts, Charlie said, "What were you and Dr. Drop-Dead Gorgeous talking about?"

"Oh," Danica said, "he'd like us to get together this week, but..."

"But nothing," Charlie and Ray said in unison.

In a lowered voice, Danica answered, "It seems, I don't know..."

"Disrespectful to Buck?"

Danica nodded. "I suppose so."

"Look around, Danny," Ray said. "Does Buck want any of

us to hold back on living because he died? No. He wouldn't. So go out with your handsome doctor. And think of Buck sitting on a cloud, happy as a clam, with Nettie by his side."

CHAPTER FOUR

"IF YOU LOVE ME, please don't stand Dad up for Shabbat dinner again," his sister said. "I'm running out of excuses."

Their mother was from the island of Puerto Rico and their father's family had fled from Austria in order to escape persecution for being Jewish. The family practiced Judaism and still got together on Friday night via video chat for prayers and to eat challah—braided bread—and drink wine together. For their parents, it eased the pain of distance from their adult children, while ensuring that the family, and grandchildren if they should come, continue the Jewish traditions. This was, above all else, their father's wish.

"I'll be there," Matteo said. "It's been a tough week."

Matteo had learned how to bake challah from their grandmother, and it was one of his favorite things to make. He put the loaf of bread in the oven and then sat down at his dining room table. Lu Lu was snoring on her bed nearby.

"So, what's the news?"

Matteo leaned back against the kitchen counter, arms crossed casually. "I lost someone I admired. I attended the wake and I plan on going to the funeral."

His sister's expression changed from frustrated and annoyed to empathetic and concerned. "I'm so sorry. I didn't know. And here I'm bugging you about Shabbat dinner."

"You have every right to bug me. It's not fair for me to lean on you to play interference."

"Well," Estrella said, "I'm still sorry."

"Thank you."

"Changing the subject…" His sister had a glint in her eye when she asked, "How's it going with Danica?"

"Actually, I have to call and cancel our date tonight. You aren't the only one on my case about Friday evenings." Matteo worked half days on Friday so he could prep for the Friday night Sabbath.

"Mom?"

"Bingo. *And*, she was speaking in Spanish."

"No bueno."

"Exactamente," he agreed. "When Mom breaks out the Spanish, we know someone's in trouble."

"But why ask her out on a Friday? You know that's a conflict."

"Because," Matteo said, going to the fridge to pull out some vegetable snacks for Lu Lu, "Friday night is for serious dates, and I am serious about Danica."

"Saturday nights are the same as Friday night dates."

"I usually hang out with my friends most Saturday nights, but sacrifices will have to be made."

"Well," Estrella said, frowning, "you're rearranging your life for her. I hope she's as serious as you are."

"You let me handle my love life," Matteo said, before waving goodbye and ending the video chat. Lu Lu hoisted herself out of bed and did her waddle-walk, curly tail wagging, and talking in oinks and grunts all the way to her bowl. Matteo sat down on the floor with her. When she was done, she went outside to soak up some of the afternoon sun and he picked up the phone to reschedule the date. Eventually, he would like to invite Danica to their family Friday night dinner. For now, he would put a temporary hold on Saturday night hanging out with his buddies in Bozeman. He loved his tight group of friends; on the other hand, he had no idea how long he had Danica in Montana so he could successfully lock that down. He didn't want another long-distance relationship, but he had to make an exception for the beautiful Realtor.

Lu Lu finished her snack and then used her nose to flip his phone out of his hand, which was her way of saying *pay attention to me, not your phone.*

"Okay," he said affectionately, "let me make this call first and then you will have my undivided attention."

"HOW'S DEAN HOLDING UP?" Danica asked Ray, who had made a habit of coming over to her condo rental. It was nice for Danica to have their twin bond strengthened.

"Not good," Ray said, drinking down a green smoothie. "I've never seen him like this. He's lost his appetite. He's trying to solve everything through work. And, unfortunately, he's still going back and forth with Catrin."

"Did they at least find a compromise?"

Ray nodded while she made another green smoothie for her. "Catrin is borrowing her fiancé's private jet. The girls will be home in time for the funeral."

"Good. That will help."

Ray put the smoothie in front of her and she drank it down quickly.

"Are you still connecting with Matteo?"

She nodded. She had just spoken to Matteo, who asked to change their dinner to Saturday night and, not only did she agree, but she was also grateful. She had been fighting with Grant through their lawyers *every* day. And to make matters worse, many of the people she had counted as friends were trashing her on social media, taking Grant's side and wondering how he had managed to put up with a "cold fish" like her for as long as he did. She had blocked and unfriended so many people over the course of the week that it had taken an emotional toll.

"He's fantastic. But I'm not sure I can really be anything more than friends. The constant fighting with Grant is exhausting and maddening. He acts as if *I'm* the one who cheated. He's threatening to sue me for *emotional distress.*"

"Oh, you're kidding, right?"

"No. I'm not. I don't think it will go anywhere. I have no idea who this man is. Is *this* who he's been this whole time?"

Ray walked over and hugged her tightly. "I'm sorry, Danny, I really am."

Grateful for the hug, Danica said, "He's dragging my name through the mud, Ray. It took me over a decade of work to build my reputation and my good name. How can he begin to dismantle the entire structure with a couple of nasty tweets and putting our dirty laundry out at every party he attends? And I can easily see that some of my so-called friends were my enemies because they are inviting him and Fallon to their parties and plastering their images all over their social media."

"You might just have to sue him for slander or defamation of character," Ray said, then added, "You need a break."

"Yes. I really do. I think I'm still in shock. No one expects their lives to blow up the next day," she said with a shake of her head. "Maybe I should schedule a massage. Or a facial. Or a lobotomy so I can forget Grant ever existed."

"Or—" Ray had raised eyebrows and an overly excited and happy expression on her face that made Danica laugh "—you could join my goat yoga class. It's so much fun! I *promise* you—" Ray had her hands together in a plea and a prayer "—you will be saying *Grant who?* five minutes in."

And that was how she wound up being lovingly coerced into her first goat yoga class.

JOURNEY HAD QUICKLY developed a routine at Hideaway Ranch. In the morning, she made herself some avocado toast on wholewheat bread with a cup of black coffee. The Brand sisters had stocked the fridge and pantry with all of her favorite foods. She made the bed, cleaned up the kitchen and then put on her hiking gear and set out on foot to explore the wild land surrounding the inhabited area of the ranch. At night, she heard many nocturnal animal sounds, and she had already gone through Charlie's *How to Handle Wildlife Encounters* tutorial and had bear spray and air horns to scare off bears if they should charge. She also was taught how to handle bison, elk and wolves. Most people might have thought that her fear of encountering a bear was much less than the fear she had of horses. But then again, she hadn't had any bad experiences with a bear or an elk or a wolf; when she was a young child, she had a very bad experience with a horse and had feared them ever since.

When she returned from her walk, she saw Ray pull up to the main house and get out with a striking blond woman who Journey assumed was Danica Brand, the only one of the Brand triplets she had yet to meet.

"Journey!" Ray called out to her with a welcoming smile. "Come meet Danny!"

Journey waved at them and headed back to the house.

Danica Brand greeted her with the same friendliness Charlie and Ray had exhibited.

"Wow!" Danica exclaimed, "you are *gorgeous*. And so statuesque! Do you model?"

Journey smiled. "I did when I was younger. When I became a mother, traveling for photo shoots wasn't practical anymore."

"During the pandemic, I decided to give writing a chance. I was addicted to Harlequin books. I devoured them. Harlequin is the reason why I don't understand fractions."

"Did any of us really need to know fractions?" Charlie interjected.

Journey smiled and rolled her eyes. "So unnecessary. But at least it wasn't 'new' math that my son is being taught. It's a bunch of boxes."

"Tragic," Charlie said.

Danica had been listening but not really participating in the conversation; she examined her like a woman admiring a sports car she was interested in buying before she asked, "Would you consider modeling for our website and social media? You are so striking, I think everyone, men, women, and everything in between, would gravitate to you."

"I'd consider it," she said. "Absolutely."

Ray checked the time on her Apple watch. "I've got to get the goats ready for class. Are you joining us, Journey?"

"That would be a big fat yes."

Feeling accepted by the Brand sisters, Journey rushed to her room, changed out of her hiking gear to her yoga clothing. She swept her waist-length honey-blond hair up into a long pony and checked herself out in the bathroom mirror and then hurried out the front door. From the porch, she saw Ray leading five goats that were braying and hopping around. Ray promised, with a money-back guarantee, to work the zygomaticus major and minor, aka the smile muscles of the face.

One extra curious goat with black and white spots on its body and a lightning-bolt shape in white down its dark gray head made funny hopping motions on its way over to a persistent weed pushing through the melting snow.

"Hickory!" Ray called after the baby goat, who ignored her and kept on exploring.

"I can get him!" Journey said, wanting to get her hands on that sweet little goat.

"Are you sure?"

"Sure, sure," she said, taking the porch steps quickly and walking with her long-legged stride to scoop up the goat.

"I got you!" Journey picked up the baby goat and held him safely in her arms. "You are a handsome doll baby, aren't you?"

The goat went soft in her arms as he licked the tip of her nose and that moment meant so much to her that she felt a swell of emotion rising to the surface. "How can you be this cute?"

She took Hickory over to Ray and then followed the other goats into a walkout basement with floor-to-ceiling windows that let in the warm sunlight while giving the goat yoga participants an incredible view of the Montana mountains.

"Thank you," Ray said with a small laugh. "Hickory, Dickory and Dock are new yoga instructors."

Danica arrived with two more young goats by the names of Tick and Tock. While Journey helped the sisters to set up the mats for the class, and as guests began to arrive, the baby goats were running, headbutting, hopping and braying and as promised in the advertisement, her smile muscles had already gotten a workout and the class hadn't yet begun!

Once the mats were set up, and exactly at 1:00 p.m., Ray opened the doors and let in the excited group of women who were gathered at the entrance. The minute new people arrived, the goats ran up to them, stubby tails upright, all vying for attention.

"Come on in! Find a mat and let's get our yoga on!" Ray said, and Journey loved her upbeat, positive vibe.

"I'm going to stick with you." Danica took the mat next to her.

"I'm already having a great time."

"Me, too. Surprisingly."

"How so?"

"I'm not typically a person who exercises in a group, but I love this already. When Ray first came up with the idea, I was all for it. I had no idea that it would become one of the most lucrative ventures for this ranch."

Ray began to take them through basic yoga poses while the goats ran around, chasing each other, jumping on the patrons' backs while they were holding the table pose. The room was filled with laughter at the antics of the young goats.

"I invite you to keep your tabletop pose if you have a goat standing on your back!"

Dock kept right on circling back to her and she took every moment she could with him, loving the softness of his fur and the sweet, trusting blue eyes.

"I need to pack you away in my suitcase," Journey said when Dock walked beneath her while in the downward dog pose. "Take you home with me."

At the end of the class, Journey picked up Dock and cuddled with him.

"I didn't expect this," Danica said, snuggling with Hickory. "We didn't have goats when I was a kid. It makes me wonder how I managed to live forty-plus years on this planet without them!"

They helped Ray clean up the basement and then took the goats back to the warm barn. Two males had caught Journey's attention: Cody Ty and Dock. After she put Dock down in the clean, refreshed hay, Journey asked Ray, as casually as she could, about Cody Ty.

"I don't know much about him, really," Ray said. "Charlie is a better person to ask."

As if on schedule, Charlie walked into the barn, covered in mud and dirt, with patches of water stains on her coat and her jeans.

"Hey!" Ray called Charlie over while Journey tried to shrink down and wished she had never asked the question in the first place. "Journey has some questions about Cody!"

And just when she thought things couldn't get more embarrassing, Cody Ty appeared in the barn just as Ray was yelling that to her sister.

She was six feet even in her bare feet, so she had no way to hide. She held herself very still and hoped that he wouldn't zero in on her. But he did zero in on her and their eyes met, and when they did, her body felt like it had just turned into wobbly Jell-O, and she took an involuntary step back, as if the sheer force of that electricity between them had knocked her for a loop.

"Well, he's right here." Charlie turned around to gesture toward him, but he was gone.

Right before he took his leave, he tipped his hat to Journey, and that nearly made her hyperventilate. For the first time, she was experiencing that cowboy romanticism, the draw of women, regardless of the age or geography. That cowboy *thing* had just smacked her in the face, and she couldn't imagine writing a book without a cowboy as the hero.

"Well, he *was* there," Charlie said, laughing. "That man is always on the move. So, what's going on?"

"Journey was interested in him."

"For research," Journey was quick to add. "A secondary character."

Charlie looked at her like she had grown a flipper. "Cody Ty, as a character, has to be the leading man. Yes, he's clocked some miles, but he wears them well. I actually think he's more handsome now. He's rodeo royalty—if he was entered into a competition, everyone knew that he couldn't be beat, so they fought each other for second and third."

Charlie continued, "He's handsome, strong and kindhearted."

The three sisters and Journey walked back toward the main house.

"How's the book coming?" Ray asked.

Journey sighed and let it out on a long breath. "I was so inspired on day one that I thought I'd be several chapters in by now, but I have writer's block. I can't seem to get words on the page. So instead of writing, I hike, or organize my suitcase, or make some coffee. You guys get the idea."

When they reached the main house, Journey continued to the front door. She thought it might be rude to *not* invite the triplets for coffee and conversation, but she just couldn't do it. She needed to be alone with her thoughts; she needed to call Riggs because she had just been hit with a lightning bolt with Cody Ty's name on it.

BUCK LEGEND'S WAKE and funeral were held one week after his death. The Wake was held at the Legend ranch while the funeral was held at the Soldiers Chapel in Gallatin Gateway, a town that was a short distance from Big Sky. The church looked like a perfect fit for Buck; it was a rugged chapel, with a masculine flair of stone and wood, and had a circular window of stained glass just above the large orangish-brown entry doors. The chapel was sitting alone in a sea of white snow with a snowy roof and glorious snowcapped mountains in the background. They waited a week after his death to allow the many people in Buck's vast network of ranchers and farmers across the state of Montana to make travel plans to arrive in time for the burial. There would be overflow in the church parking lot and the service would stream live for those who couldn't make it. Danica was amazed at the sheer volume of mourners and relieved when she saw Matteo standing tall and cutting a fine figure in his somber black suit with a black shirt and a tie that had a matte and shiny black geometric pattern design—so much so that she naturally changed course and walked over to him.

Matteo saw her and he walked to meet her halfway. At the point where they met, Matteo hugged her. It was exactly what she needed. And it was just as natural for Matteo to reach for her hand, as she reached for his. Was this a declaration? She wasn't really sure, and she didn't really care about optics. She'd lost Buck, a man who had always treated her as one of his own, and the fact that she hadn't made a concerted effort to return home and visit her parents and the Legends cut deep. In her late twenties and early thirties, she had been focused on her career, to the detriment of most everything else, and now, looking back as they buried Buck Legend, it dawned on her that she had been misguided. No matter what her career demands, she should have made time for her family. She knew that her family noticed that she was holding hands with Matteo, but after an exchange of curious looks, her sisters returned their attention to the priest, who had been the Legend and Brand families' go-to for baptisms, weddings and, yes, funerals as well.

The Legend family members occupied the first three rows and then the next two rows were reserved for the Brand family. Ray was sitting in the first row with Dean, his daughters, and his ex-wife Catrin; Catrin had had a change of heart and flown with the girls from London to attend the funeral to support her daughters. Matteo quietly asked Danica if he should sit on the guest side of the church, but Danica held his hand firmly, so she sat next to Charlie and Wayne, and he sat sandwiched in between her and Wayne; his broad shoulders and height made him a tight squeeze for the rest of them. And she worried that he might block the view of the folks sitting directly behind them. She forgot about that concern and focused her attention on the priest.

After opening remarks, Dean walked up to the lectern. He looked somber and heartbroken as he began to give his eulogy. After several minutes, Paisley and Luna had begun to cry. Luna held on to Ray for comfort while Paisley had folded over with her head pressed against Catrin's chest. After Dean's remarks, several of Buck's best friends spoke about their friend; sometimes there was laughter and sometimes there were tears. Danica found herself solidly in the latter category; Dean's eulogy had gotten her crying and she couldn't seem to stop. Matteo offered her a handkerchief and she took it gratefully.

After the service was over, everyone piled into their vehicles and drove to the cemetery where he would be laid to rest next to his beloved Nettie. At the last minute, Danica decided to ride with Matteo. Yes, her sisters would have questions about the connection between the most eligible bachelor and her. And she would answer questions if she actually had an answer. From the very beginning, not very long ago, the electricity between them hadn't been planned for either of them. It just *was*. And ever since they had met, she was following her gut, her intuition, not her head.

"It was a beautiful ceremony," Danica said, riding in Matteo's GMC Sierra 3500 HD Denali.

Matteo nodded his agreement.

"I was happy to see you," she added.

"I was happy to see you, too." He looked at her with a smile before refocusing on the still-icy roads.

They both rode in quiet remembrance of the man they had just lost. There were profound shifts in her priorities, and she wondered how it would ultimately impact her life. Matteo followed the slow-moving procession following the hearse. Parking was easier with fewer people attending the burial. Snow was about to hit, and folks needed to get home while the roads were passable.

They huddled together in tents as they lowered the casket into the ground. Catrin had taken Paisley and Luna to the Legends' ranch; this was their compromise. The girls would attend the funeral service but not the burial. When the casket reached its destination, Dean placed his hands on the casket, telling his father how he loved him and how much he would miss him. Then this big, tough, burly man, rarely showing his emotions as his upbringing demanded, dropped to his knees and wept. And Ray, ever Dean's ally, knelt beside him and put her arm around him, her own tears streaming down her face.

Danica was triggered by Dean's sorrow, and she found it impossible to keep her fresh tears at bay. She spun around and left the tent, ignoring the fat, fluffy flakes of snow falling. Matteo followed her but this time she wasn't so sure she wanted him to. Her strength had come from being independent and self-sufficient, and leaning on others rarely. The heels of her shoes dug into the mushy grass as she headed down another row of headstones. At one point, the right heel of her shoe snagged on something, and that tweaked the ankle that she had twisted the day she met the handsome doctor and his adorable pig Lu Lu.

"Ow!" she exclaimed. "Gosh darn it!"

Matteo was at her side, offering his arm, and she accepted the help even as her brain was short-circuiting because she had already leaned on the doctor too many times already. For the love of peanuts, she had held his hand for over an hour! What was wrong with her?

"Getting soft," she muttered.

"What was that?" he asked.

"Nothing," she grumbled. "I seem to fall around you."

"Well," Matteo said, "I'd rather see you fall *for* me. But I'll take what I can get. Now where are we going?"

"Just up this row."

Together they walked toward a large headstone at the end of the row. Danica let go of his arm, bent down and brushed the snow from the headstone. Once the snow was gone, the names on the headstone were Butch and Rose Brand.

"My parents."

Matteo gave a small nod of understanding.

Danica was all out of tears, but her heart ached for her lost parents. If she hadn't been betrayed by Grant, how often would she have traveled to Big Sky to spend time with her sisters? Not a whole heck of a lot. She preferred to keep her involvement with the ranch while continuing her life in LA.

"They must have been lovely," Matteo said.

"Yes, they were," she agreed.

"Time goes by too fast."

She nodded, never taking her eyes off of her parents' graves. When she looked up, she saw Charlie and Ray heading their way. Matteo stepped to the side to make room for her sisters. Silently, and using their telepathic connection that had only grown stronger since they had reconnected after Rose's death, they found themselves in the same place. They put their arms around each other and touched their foreheads together as they acknowledged the parents, Brand and Legend, they had lost.

"May you rest in peace," Charlie said.

"Amen," Danica and Ray said.

And then, arms linked together in union, the triplet women walked back toward the burial site with Matteo following behind them.

"May I give you a ride home?" Matteo asked her once she had finished giving condolences for the Legend extended family.

"Yes, you may," Danica said simply. There was no sense trying to fight this connection between them. She didn't have a crystal ball, so she didn't know how this was all going to pan out. But for now, they were here together, and the future would just have to be handled when it became the present.

CHAPTER FIVE

THE SATURDAY AFTER Buck's funeral, Danica went to Matteo's house for an early dinner. His home was small and rustic with some acreage necessary to keep Lu Lu occupied with enough land for rooting, which was her nature. As a Realtor, she always believed that she could learn almost everything she needed to know about a client just by looking at the inside and the outside of the house. Matteo's house was decorated in an eclectic style and the majority of the odds and ends were from his travels. It was a masculine house with a masculine color palette of dark browns and blacks; wood was the dominant material with stained wood shiplap and high-end leather furniture. The kitchen was just as moody as the rest of the house; it was a chef's kitchen with professional-grade gas stove and double-wide refrigerator. The accent color, a sunburst orange, gave the eye somewhere to land. It was a sophisticated look that made her think that the handsome, much-sought-after bachelor had a deeper, richer side to him that in their short time together had not been tapped.

There were two walls of bookshelves, overflowing with books on art, horticulture, cooking, travel, martial arts and anatomy. Three shelves were dedicated entirely to how to raise a pig.

"Is this Emy?" Danica stopped to look at a picture on a bookshelf. "And is that Lu Lu as a piglet?!"

Matteo was cutting vegetables for the stir-fry dish he was making for them; he looked up and smiled. "Yes and yes."

"Emy is adorable. And so too is Lu Lu." Danica walked back to the large quartz island, picked up the bottle of wine she had brought for them and asked, "Do you need a top-off?"

"Sure," he said before he threw the freshly cut vegetables into the hot wok.

Danica poured another glass for herself, and then watched Matteo's mastery in the kitchen. She hated to tell him that she had used a personal chef for the last eight years and could not cook an egg. This was the one area where she was not as independent, but she had many restaurants on speed dial, so she wasn't in any danger of starving.

"You are accomplished," she said.

Matteo soaked in the compliment, giving her a wink and smile. "I considered becoming a chef, but my dad expected me to be an attorney or a doctor."

"You seem happy with your choice. Fulfilled."

"I am. Medicine wasn't my first choice, though."

She raised her eyebrows at him to let him know that she was listening and wanted him to continue.

Matteo drank some of the wine in his glass before he said, "I went to law school first."

Danica leaned forward, eyes wide open, and asked, "Are you an attorney, too?"

He laughed. "Yes. I went to school, passed the bar, had an internship with a big firm in Baltimore and found out real quick that I wasn't cut out for that."

"Well," she said, "I'm impressed."

"Good. I'm glad."

After a moment, she asked, "So when you said you knew a good lawyer, were you speaking of yourself?"

He laughed. "Yep."

They talked while Matteo cooked and while she set the table for them. He didn't have to tell her where everything was kept because she had a similar setup in her LA house.

"We are definitely a match when it comes to how to set up a kitchen. And a living room, actually."

"Lucky for me."

They sat down at his modern metal-and-glass dining table; the juxtaposition of the traditional, masculine dark wood with select ultramodern pieces such as the table and some of the light fixtures drew a picture of a man who was traditional, decidedly male, but forward-thinking, an out-of-the-box man. And she loved what she saw—in his decor and in the man himself.

"Well—" Danica put down her fork and looked at her empty plate "—that was the most delicious meal I've had in a very long time."

"Better than Block 3?"

She nodded.

"Better than anything in LA?"

"Let's call it a solid tie." She laughed. "I do love a man who can cook. Would you like to get married?"

She had said this in jest, but he sounded rather serious when he said, "Yes, I would."

They cleared the table, he put the dishes in the sink to soak, and they took their wine to his living room.

"I wish I had gotten to see Lu Lu," she said, feeling very comfortable in Matteo's house.

"I know," he said, "but it was better this way, trust me. If Lu Lu is in the room, she commands attention. And if she doesn't get it…"

"Ear-curdling squeal?"

"Exactly. So I fed her an early dinner and she is happily sleeping in her house."

He took his phone out of his shirt pocket and then showed her a video of Lu Lu happily sleeping in a giant, squishy pillow bed. And of course, she was snoring loudly with a content smile on her face.

"Oh!" Danica exclaimed. "She has pajamas!"

Matteo smiled.

"I love her," she told him. "I just adore her."

"Do you know, you're the very first woman outside of my ex who has taken to her?"

Danica shook her head. "Is that why the most eligible bachelor is still single?"

"Yes," he said bluntly, "and I'm not saying that she is as important as, or equal to, a child, but she is the closest thing to a child that I have. She's part of my family and I made a promise to Emy that I would take care of her always. And I intend to keep that promise."

Danica reached over to put her hand on his and said, "You are a kind, honorable man, Matteo."

"And you are an incredibly kind and beautiful woman, Danica," he echoed.

He reached for her hand and threaded their fingers together. The look of admiration in his eyes, the expression of pure acceptance and raw, unmistakable attraction from him to her, made Danica duck her head, blushing. She had forgotten what it was like to have this kind of interest from a man; the spark had gone out of the relationship with Grant years ago. But they had been comfortable and shared the same goals. Or at least she had believed that.

"Do you feel this *thing* between us?" he asked her.

She was too old to play coy. "Yes, I do."

"I'm glad you didn't say no," he said. "That question could've gone one of two ways for me," and then he asked, "It's magnetic, right?"

"Yes, it is."

Matteo dragged his fingers through his hair with a small shake of his head before he looked back at her with a steady, unwavering, gaze. "I've never felt *this* before."

"It's oddly comfortable."

"It *is* oddly comfortable. This is a first."

"For me, too." Danica tucked one leg under the other. "I feel like I've known you for years instead of weeks. It's *familiar*."

"Exactly." He nodded. "Exactly," then quickly added, "but not like brother-and-sister vibes."

"Oh, God! Why would you even *say* such a thing?" She hit him playfully on the arm. "Don't put that image in my head! What's wrong with you?"

"Platonic!" He laughed with that deep baritone laugh that made her smile. "I was going for platonic!"

"Okay. But in *that* case, you could have said that you don't want to be friend-zoned."

"I don't want to be friend-zoned."

"Well, neither do I," she said and then, as if to emphasize the silliness of his concern, she did something she hadn't done since she was in high school. She crossed her eyes at him.

That made Matteo laugh and because he was laughing, so did she. It was the comic relief that they both needed.

"You're beautiful, funny, intelligent," he said. "You're a triple threat."

"Was that a triplet joke?"

"I wish I had been that clever," he said. "I guess you're a triplet who's a triple threat."

Danica ducked her head, feeling self-conscious in that she wasn't used to being looked at the way Matteo looked at her every time they were together: appreciated, admired, attractive, and he always focused on her no matter how many wealthy knockout women were milling about in Big Sky. And there were plenty; this pond was fully stocked. The few times they were out together, his focus on her never wavered, and she had a gut feeling that he never would disrespect her that way. And it was something new, something rare and precious, because she had never experienced that with Grant; that man had an eye for the ladies and the older he got, the younger the women that caught his interest were. Fallon, case in point.

"I can't say where this might take us, though," Danica said, prepared to share her *long* story with him. He needed to know, particularly now that she knew he shared her feelings of undeniable attraction and chemistry that was also deeply quiet and relaxed. She had never been a romantic like Ray; she didn't believe in soulmates. Until now.

Matteo took a last sip of wine, put his glass down on the coffee table, and then took hers and put it next to his. He unthreaded their hands and then he closed the short distance between them, put his large, warm hands on her face, and said in a voice that sent shock waves of anticipation leaving a wake of goose bumps across her body, "I want to kiss you, Danica. Any objections?"

"Yes," she said in a sultry voice that was brand-new. Forty years and then suddenly she had a sultry voice in her repertoire! "I mean, no."

"No, I can't?" Matteo needed that confirmation, and she didn't blame him. "Or yes, I can?"

"Yes, you should." She melted into his strong arms, head tilted back, being enveloped by the woodsy scent of his skin, and then his firm lips were on hers, gentle, questioning and so sweet.

Matteo cradled her head in his free hand while he kissed her again, lovingly more than passionate, but these kisses held promise of steamier kisses further down the line. At this moment, these lovely kisses were exactly what she needed.

Matteo leaned back and Danica put her head on his chest and loved the feel of his strong arms holding on to her, and the feather kisses he was dusting across the top of her head. She didn't want this moment to end, but she also didn't feel right not sharing her long story. Grant was currently making her life miserable with no sign that he would stop, just to be spiteful. Many of the women she had considered friends had taken Grant's side. She wasn't emotionally ready to jump into another committed relationship when she was very much tangled up in the last one.

Danica pushed herself upright and looked at Matteo. "Can I tell you my long story?"

Cody Ty Hawkins had lived most of his life in the spotlight. He had been a top junior rodeo competitor with only a few rare losses on his score card. Then, when he aged out of the junior circuit, he went straight to adult rodeo and cleaned up there as well. That was his life for the majority of his adulthood, living on the road, staying in seedy hotels, too much drinking, too much fighting and too little time at home. He'd had a pretty young wife, Jessa, his high school sweetheart, whom he married the day they graduated, and instead of a honeymoon night, he headed off to the next rodeo. On one trip home, they made themselves a baby, and he was tickled about it. But he wasn't there for the birth, and he had missed nearly every birthday his daughter, Abilene, had.

When Jessa got pregnant with another man's baby, he had

only himself to blame. They divorced while he rode the wave of his success and celebrity as the reigning rodeo champion in the world. For a good long while, he was undefeated. Other cowboys vied for the second and third slot when he was at the event. Everywhere he went, someone recognized him, wanted to take a picture with him and get an autograph. Booze and women were in a seemingly endless supply, and he had been a greedy man. When the free booze and willing women began to taper off to a trickle and there weren't crowds of fans waiting to cheer him on, or grab those pictures and autographs, Cody had slipped into a deep depression that fueled the self-destructive drunken phase that had landed him in jail time and again.

The landslide from adored to scorned had been much quicker than the climb to reach the pinnacle. And then, when he'd thought he'd reached rock bottom, he found a new low. He was living out of his truck, doing odds and ends for local folks, making enough to fill up his tank, buy some cheap whiskey and maybe eat if there was money left over. At his very worst, he ran into an old friend by the name of Wayne Westbrook and that colliding of two lives changed his life for the positive and he hadn't let a drop of liquor or beer pass through his lips for a decade. He'd gotten back to his passion of gentling young horses and getting them under saddle, and he made a fine living, even put some money aside for his retirement. Perhaps he hadn't always made the best choices, but he'd always been loyal. He hadn't forgotten, and never would, how Wayne helped to dry him out, get him back on his feet and give him work on his crew in Wyoming.

So when Wayne called him to help train some young horses on a ranch in Montana, he hitched up his travel trailer and headed toward Hideaway Ranch.

"She's got a fine conformation." Wayne stopped by the round pen where Cody had been working with a red roan filly with a reddish-brown face, speckles of red and white down her back, and a black mane and tail.

"She's a good-looker and willing," Cody said, moving back a couple of the steps, removing his pressure on her hind end, signaling to her that she could stop trotting down to walking.

The filly, ears perked forward, eyes on Cody, halted and turned her body toward him and when he invited her into the circle, she walked over to him and put her head down for a scratch.

"Damn, Cody," Wayne said with appreciation. "Not one word was said, and she knew exactly what you wanted her to do."

"They read energy," Cody said, "and I thank you for the compliment."

"You're welcome," Wayne said, "and thank you. This is going to be another revenue stream for this ranch."

Cody walked forward and the filly followed him, accepting him as her herd boss. "You say you get these horses from Bozeman?"

"One of Charlie's kin, Jock Brand. Sugar Creek Ranch. They have one of the best quarter horse breeding programs I've ever seen."

"So he gets a cut," Cody said, "and you get a cut."

"The ranch really," Wayne said, "and you get a cut. Three-way split."

"Well, I appreciate it," he said, putting the halter on the red roan's head. "It's a fair deal. Maybe *too* fair of a deal."

"No—" his friend shook his head "—it's more than fair. No one else is better at this than you."

Cody Ty had learned over the last few years to smile. "Is it too late to renegotiate my fee?"

That made Wayne laugh. "I'm afraid so, my friend."

Wayne set off to his ranch chores; in this life, there was always more work to do than anyone had the time, or the energy, to do. It was an ever-updating list of "must-dos." Cody led the pretty red roan filly to the barn when he saw a tall woman, looked to be in her late thirties, come out of the main house to the snowy porch. Her loveliness slapped him in right in the face because he had lived his life out of a suitcase and he had *never* encountered a more beautiful woman in all of his travels; she resembled a palomino mare with her thick honey-blond hair that cascaded down her back to her waist; her skin was as golden as wheat growing in a field.

Not wanting to get caught staring at her, he made a quick turn to the barn with the rambunctious filly dancing around him.

"Now, that," Cody said to the filly after putting her in a vacant stall, "is a bona fide gorgeous woman."

Cody led a colt, a young male horse, out to the round pen and was both relieved and disappointed that the woman was gone.

"We don't have time for distractions, do we?" Cody said to the frisky black colt, with a white star on his face with matching white socks up to his knees. "We've got work to do."

"WHY WOULD ANYONE avoid you? You're the nicest person ever and if that cowboy doesn't get that, tell him to go kick rocks," Riggs said, while he used hair product to mold spikes all over his head. "Which do you prefer? Green or hot pink?"

"Neither."

"Spoilsport," Riggs said, painting one spike neon green.

"I don't know," she said about Cody, pulling her hair over her shoulder and twisting it while she thought, "maybe it's my imagination."

But even as she said it, she didn't think that was true. When their eyes met in the barn, he *noticed* her in the same way she had noticed him during her first couple of days at Hideaway Ranch. She had hoped to see him at the regular evening campfire singing and storytelling when weather permitted; her hope was dashed because he never came. All work, no play.

"Well, I do." Riggs took a short break from his hair and looked at her directly. "You either ignore him like a bad habit, *or* track him down and *make him* pay attention to you."

"I don't like either of those choices."

"I call it like I see it," Riggs said. "Wish me luck. I'm going to an art gallery and I hope I can find a buyer for my boat."

"You are very weird."

Riggs grinned at her, and that grin always took her back to the first time they had met as kids. Riggs was being bullied and her father, a man who had desperately wanted a boy, decided to make lemonade, and taught her how to box. She punched that bully square in the nose and then finished him off with an uppercut. She got sent to the principal's office and her father acted really disappointed in her. Once they were out of sight, he got her an ice cream cone. It was one of the best memories she had of her dad.

After she ended the video chat with Riggs, Journey sat for a minute to think about what her bestie had said. Maybe she should take the forward approach. Yes, there were other cowboys milling around on the ranch who could be her muse. But none of them drew her attention like Cody Ty. She had, of course, researched him and burned the midnight oil until she seemed to have found everything online that she could find. Now that she knew at least part of the backstory, she needed to meet the man *behind* those articles and old newspaper stories. Who was Cody Ty, really? She only had a one-dimensional, shallow view of him. She wanted to know the flesh-and-blood man behind the fame and, ultimately, the fall from grace.

"So, Riggs is right, *again*." Journey stood up, gathered her hair into a ponytail and put on her cowgirl boots, which were dusty and dirty; she was proud that her boots now looked like Charlie's and Ray's boots. "If I want him, I'm gonna have to put on my big-girl drawers and go get that cowboy."

CODY WAS BRUSHING down a blue-eyed, white-faced colt whose body markings looked like a black-and-white Rorschach test. He was a good one, this colt. Cody could already tell that this little guy was a hard worker and wanted to please.

"I might just ask Wayne if I can have you instead of my cut. You're a good boy."

"Hello."

Cody heard the voice, a light, melodic sound, and knew at the core of his being that it was his palomino. His hand kept on brushing the colt while his knees tried not to buckle. He caught her eye for the briefest of moments, registered that she was even more beautiful up close, before he said, "Howdy."

That made his palomino laugh. "Howdy. I wasn't at all sure if this was a myth or made up by Hollywood writers, but people around these parts, at least the locals, actually *do* say howdy."

She was so tickled by this minute detail that he found himself smiling. Just for a bit.

"Folks do, I suppose."

She got tickled again, rocked forward on her feet, and then said, "Folks. I love that."

"Can I help you, miss?"

"Funny you should ask," Journey said. "You *can* help me. I'm Journey, by the way."

"Pleased to meet'cha," Cody said and tipped his hat to her. "I'm Cody."

Journey clasped her hands. "And the tip of the hat. I love it. I wish more men in the city would wear a hat just so they could tip it at me."

Cody did his best to keep his focus on the colt, but the colt's eyes were wide, he was nervous, and he kept trying to see behind him.

"Miss," Cody said, unhooking the colt's halter from the crossties, "you're spooking my youngsters."

"I'm sorry." Journey's brow drew together. "How am I doing that?"

Cody let the colt face Journey so he could get a good look at her. "Horses read energy just better than about any creature on this green earth. If you're nervous, they're programmed to assume that you are dangerous. A predator."

Journey's blue-green eyes widened. "I'm not a predator. I'm petrified."

That unexpected confession made him chuckle as he put up the colt and it seemed to change the tension in the air for all of them.

"Now, why are you petrified of horses? They don't mean to hurt nobody."

Journey had her hands in her pockets and her feet were firmly planted in the middle of the aisle. This was the barn where the young horses were housed. She loved the goats and totally wanted to pack Dock into her suitcase, but horses? No, no, no, no, no. *No!*

"I don't want to bore you with my childhood trauma."

"When it comes down to horses, I don't bore easy."

"Well, that makes one of us," she said with a nervous laugh, hands out of pockets and her arms twisted together like a pretzel.

And because Journey was out of her depth in his environment, some of Cody's initial shyness with the lovely palomino had given way to his confidence when it came to horses.

"Can't hurt to tell me," he said, "and it might just help."

"When I was four or five, we went to visit my mom's sister on their farm. I loved horses, and really, I still do, they are one of nature's most amazing creations."

"Amen."

"My cousin John put me on one of their horses and he hit that horse on the butt with a crop and that horse took off with me, spooked at my other cousin waving a plastic bag, and then it bucked me off. I broke the fence with my body, broke my arm, and I had to get stiches under my chin." Journey lifted her head and pointed to her scar, then shrugged. "I wasn't afraid of horses before, but this *fear* of horses is so ingrained in my body now that I can't imagine ever overcoming it."

She was shaking, reliving the trauma, and she hugged her arms tightly to her body and finished by saying, "I'll just continue to love and admire them from afar."

Cody stared at her for a moment, and then he said, "I'm real sorry that happened to you. I truly am. If you give me two weeks of your time, I guarantee that you'll conquer your fear."

CHAPTER SIX

THE NIGHT OF their first kiss had turned into morning and Danica awakened in Matteo's bed. After a whole bottle of wine, and talking into the early hours of the morning, Matteo had given her the king bed in the main bedroom while he bunked in the guest room. Danica looked at her phone for the time, then checked in with LA and her sisters. It had felt good to share her "long" story with Matteo; he took it in stride and understood that she was mired in the recent split. His thoughts? Enjoy each other's company now and let the future take care of itself. She slipped out of bed and tip-toed into the kitchen. She did her best to be quiet while she searched for pots and pans and ingredients for the only breakfast she knew how to make.

"Good morning." Matteo walked out shirtless, showing off his sexy chest hair, muscular arms, his abs, and his beautiful broad shoulders. Just like Michelangelo's *David*, Matteo was made to be admired.

Matteo leaned down for a kiss and Danica's body responded, lighting up parts of her body that had been unused, and therefore nearly forgotten, for years.

"What are you making?" he asked her, fixing Lu Lu's breakfast.

"Well." She smiled at him. "I noticed some things in your house."

He raised his eyebrows questioningly.

"I did see the menorah on the bookshelf," she said, "and I found a freshly baked loaf of challah bread."

"So, on one hand, I see some clues that may point to Judaism. However—" she walked over, placed her hand on his chest "—you have a cross tattooed over your heart."

"I'm an international man of mystery." He smiled at her, taking her hand and kissing it.

"Yes, Austin Powers, you are. And I kind of like it."

"I also think you were looking for an excuse to touch me."

That made her blush because he was correct. "Maybe."

"Well," he said, "you don't need any reason to touch me. I give you a lifetime pass."

She was still beaming as Matteo put on his winter coat and rubber boots and headed out to Lu Lu's house with her breakfast. Danica didn't know exactly what had come over her, but she felt, in that moment, lighthearted with a positive outlook. Then again, meeting someone who just "got her," with whom she felt the same, who happened to have Cary Grant's and George Clooney's bone structure, who also was funny and kind and a doctor? Danica surmised that any woman's heart would be in danger of falling for the handsome Dr. Katz.

"How is she?" Danica asked after Lu Lu.

"Same Lu Lu." He smiled as he hung his coat. "Ready for food and love."

Danica was busy slicing the challah bread. "I'd like to see her in her own element after breakfast."

"I can arrange that." He sat down on one of the island stools. "Are you making French toast?"

"Guilty as charged." Danica smiled. "Your kitchen, wait, let me rephrase this, your *house* is set up perfectly. I have found everything I need without having to search."

"Don't go giving me the credit. I had a designer. A woman."

"Well, bless her. She knows what she's doing and is worth every penny you paid."

Sadly, Matteo put a shirt on for breakfast while she set the table and brought a heaping plate of challah French toast. They sat down together, each using butter and the syrup sparingly.

"Mmm." Matteo looked at her with a renewed admiration.

"This is a good as my mom's. Not gonna tell her that, or she might never accept you."

Danica's brain temporarily short-circuited when Matteo brought up a possibility of her meeting his parents. She wasn't anywhere near that page; she was still trying to unravel her life with Grant. She simply couldn't see a scenario in which she found herself winding down one serious relationship just to jump into another.

"I'm glad you like it," she said, turning the conversation to safer waters.

She ate one last bite of the French toast, knowing full well that between the alcohol she had consumed and her "throw caution to the wind" diet, there were going to be some pounds to work off in goat yoga.

"So," she said after she dabbed her face with a napkin, "if you don't mind me asking…"

"Shoot."

"Are you Jewish or are you Christian or are you a hybrid?"

That made him smile, and after he finished chewing his bite, he said, "Hybrid."

"Explain yourself, man!"

"Well." Matteo put his napkin on his empty plate, drank a full tall glass of orange juice and said, "My mom, Mariposa, grew up on the island of Puerto Rico. She was bilingual from jump street and a very devout Christian."

He continued while she listened, truly interested in him. "My dad, Ezra, was Jewish by birth and wished that his children also be raised in the faith of Judaism."

"Two religions," she said, and then asked, "How did they navigate that?"

"Well, for my sister and I, we celebrated Christmas and Hanukkah. What kid *doesn't* want more gifts? But beyond that, sometimes the navigation was successful and other times, not so much. It's kind of a miracle that they had my sister and me and it is a testament to their love that they are still married."

"Absolutely."

"So I was raised in both religions and both cultures. I am fluent in Spanish and Hebrew and I did have a bar mitzvah."

"A coming-of-age ritual."

"Yes. Exactly." He nodded, starting to help her clear the table. "And I have a hyphenated name, Dr. Katz-Cortez, for my mother's culture. Most people just use Dr. Katz and that's fine."

Danica laughed, "Actually, I've heard you referred to as *Dr. Drop Dead Gorgeous* more often than Dr. Katz."

Matteo had a surprised expression and then he looked embarrassed.

"Surely you know this?"

"No one calls me that to my face, no."

She wrapped her arms around him, in a casual but completely comfortable manner, and looked up at him with a smile. "You can't blame people, really. You *are* spectacularly handsome."

He hugged her back and seemed more at ease with her light ribbing. He leaned down, kissed her on the lips, and then said, "And you are spectacularly beautiful."

DANICA LEFT MATTEO'S house feeling rejuvenated. Her time with the handsome doctor and his companion pig gave her joy in her life that had been absent for so long that she didn't even recognize that it was missing. And she couldn't blame Grant for that; she had been a dog with a bone when building her career and business and she rarely indulged in extracurricular activities. The only "hobby" she had was strategizing how to beat out her competition in the number of houses she sold and breaking dollars-per-square-foot records for her clients. As she pulled up to the main house on Hideaway Ranch, it did occur to her, upon reflection, that perhaps Grant had been lonely in their relationship. Not that this excused his tryst with Fallon, but did she have any responsibility in the initial breakdown of their relationship? Yes, she did. There were many times, too many to count really, that Grant had asked her to go sailing on his boat and take a mini vacay to the mountains. Her answer to these suggestions? One hundred percent, *no.*

When Danica arrived and parked her rental, she noticed that Charlie and Ray were standing near the firepit with Wayne and

Wayne's brother, Waylon. Just by the body language alone, this didn't seem like a "good" conversation.

She debated whether or not to join them, but then she decided that it might be something to do with the day-to-day operation of the ranch. Waylon was an invaluable member of their team.

"I would've preferred some notice, Waylon," Wayne said in a stern voice she had never heard him use before.

"I gave you notice." Waylon threw a packed duffel bag into the bed of his truck. "I told you I was going to be with Dasi."

Their first guests ever at Hideaway Ranch were a family of three and, as was the way at the ranch, Waylon and Dasi fell in love. The fact that Dasi had a neural diverse Autistic brain, high-functioning, didn't matter to Waylon; he knew that he'd have to take things slow and on a timeline that made sense for all of them. He needed to be in the same city with her, so they could date and get to know each other better.

"This is a hell of a deal." Wayne had his arms crossed in front of his body, his legs planted apart. "One hell of deal."

Charlie said, "Wayne, he did tell us that this winter would be his last in Montana."

"It's still winter the last time I checked. And I still don't know what the gosh darn hurry is all about."

Waylon had packed up the tent that had been his solitude since he came to Hideaway Ranch. Waylon was the second oldest after Wayne with Wade and Wyatt bringing up the rear. They all shared a father who was often absent, and Wayne had stepped into the role of both older brother and fill-in father.

Waylon closed the tailgate of his truck and then walked over to face his brother. "I love her, Wayne. No doubts. And when you find the person you love, being apart from them is an ache that can't be willed away."

Still sour, Wayne accepted his brother's hug before he said, "Keep me in the loop."

"I will," Waylon agreed. "And Wade is heading back here from Texas, so he can pick up any slack."

"What in the hell is going on here?" Wayne asked, exasperated. "When did I become the last person to know anything?"

Waylon hugged Charlie, Ray, and then even hugged Danica. She could see tears forming in Wayne's eyes; he turned on his heel and walked away while his brother climbed behind the wheel.

"I have to do this, Charlie," Waylon said.

"I know you do."

"Help him understand."

"I will," she said. "I promise."

Behind the wheel, Waylon rolled down his window and said, "Oh, one last thing. Wade is bringing his daughter, Phoenix, and Jillian here."

"Here?" Charlie went from completely calm to caught-off-guard in two seconds flat. "He's bringing Jillian *here*?"

"I know it's a shock," Waylon started.

"A shock? That's not a shock, Waylon, it's a dirty bomb! How long have you been sitting on this information?" Charlie asked and then held up her hand. "Never mind. I don't want to know."

"You're the best one to tell him, Charlie. Everyone knows that you are the Wayne Whisperer."

"Don't try to flatter me," Charlie said with a frown, "when you know you just dropped a steaming pile of manure at my feet."

"I'll be in touch." Waylon waved as he shifted into Drive.

When they could no longer see Waylon's taillights, Danica asked, "I take it this isn't good news."

"Nope," Charlie said, hands at her waist, a frustrated expression on her face. "Wade was supposed to get a divorce, but they just can't seem to live *with* each other or *without* each other. And now that drama is heading our way."

"We don't have to have them on the ranch." Danica said the unvarnished, practical thing. "Just because he's a Westbrook doesn't give him a free pass."

"That's tricky," Charlie said.

"Real tricky," Ray echoed.

"I don't see it that way at all," Danica said. "This is *our* land, *our* ranch and *our* livelihood. I don't particularly care that Wade is Wayne's brother and nor should you. If Wade and Jillian can't hold it together, they'll have to go."

"THERE'S MY HANDSOME BOY!" Journey smiled lovingly at her son, Oakley. "Are you doing all of your homework and listening to G-Ma?"

Her mother, Lucy, had picked out that name, G-Ma, when she found out that her daughter was expecting.

"I'm being good." Oakley grinned at her, and his sweet smile, as it always did, melted her heart.

"And your homework?" she prodded. As Oakley approached the age for him to be enrolled in school, Journey made the decision to homeschool him instead. She found that this format was the best idea for her smart-as-a-whip son, and it gave her a sense of satisfaction that she hadn't expected but loved.

"I'm ahead," her son said proudly, puffing his chest out.

"Good boy," Journey praised him. "Are you excited about coming to Montana?"

Oakley bounced out of his chair and hopped up and down in excitement. "I want to ride a horse!"

"Whoa, there, cowboy! Riding a horse? I'm not ready for that."

"But *why*?" he asked.

She didn't necessarily have a good reason and telling him that he couldn't ride because she had a scary event in her childhood didn't seem like the best idea, so Journey said, "Let's see how it goes. When you meet a horse, you might change your mind."

"Nope!" Oakley shouted. "I'm going to be a cowboy! I'm going to ride a horse!"

Oakley spun around in a circle, making himself dizzy with excitement, while Lucy appeared on the screen.

"It was your idea to write about cowboys." Her mother smiled at her with a wink.

Lucy Lamar was a stunning woman who had worked as a model in her early twenties. She was a Christie Brinkley, girl-next-door type beauty who never lacked work in her chosen industry. She had met Journey's father, Giovanni, in Milan and after a whirlwind romance, Lucy found herself pregnant by a man who was incapable of monogamy or honesty. She returned to the States, modeled as long as she could, and then moved back to her family's farm in Omaha, Nebraska, far away from the fast-lane life of a model that had taken her around the world.

"Cowboys sell," Journey said, her mind, as it was wont to do, returning to an image of Cody Ty, "and now I know *why* they sell."

They spoke for a few minutes more before Journey put on her outerwear and headed outside. Every day she added to her notes about Montana and ranch life and the way cowboys walked, how they talked and what made them tick. Her plan of getting a head start the first week before her son and mother joined her was nearly over and she felt frustrated and overwhelmed. The option book was due, and she hadn't written her first word.

She opened the door to find Danica about to knock.

"Hey!" Danica smiled at her. "I was just coming to check on you."

"Thank you," she said, stepping out onto the porch. "I think I'm good."

"I know your son and mother are joining you next week. Anything special you need for them? I'm heading into town now."

"I can't think of anything right now," she said, "unless of course you can buy me a couple of extra weeks in Montana at the grocery store."

Danica stopped in her tracks. "Is that what you need?"

Journey cracked a smile. "I'm just behind on my book."

"Do you need an extra week or two here?"

For a moment, Journey wasn't sure they were understanding each other when it hit her. "Can I stay for an extra week or two?"

Could she be that lucky?

"Give me one sec," Danica said, taking her phone out of the back pocket of her jeans. "Hey, Charlie, did anyone book the weeks reserved for family?"

There was a pause and then Danica said, "Okay. Good. Journey would like to stay an extra week or two."

"Two would be great!" Journey interjected.

Danica ended the conversation with Charlie and then said to her, "Ask and you shall receive."

Journey was so excited that she flung herself at Danica, the prickliest of the Brand triplets, and hugged her tightly.

"You have no idea what this means to me!"

"You're welcome," Danica said rather stiffly. "Are you going to attend goat yoga today?"

"Definitely," she said, feeling like the weight of the world had just been lifted off her shoulders. "I had no idea how much I needed goat yoga in my life!"

"Preach," Danica said.

"And thank you again. I can't express what this extra time means to me."

"You're welcome. I'm happy to help," Danica said. "But we're good with just the one hug."

MATTEO HAD BECOME a friend. That meant something to her. They agreed to meet each other at the hiking trail when they had first met as many times as they could manage, and his easy-going, self-assured manner was something she had begun to count on. This wasn't like her at all, but she couldn't regret it.

"Hey there." Matteo found her waiting for him in her rental.

"Hi!" She knew her eyes and face lit up when she saw him, heard his voice, and she didn't try to hide it from him.

She got out of the SUV, hugged him, and then knelt down to give Lu Lu some love. "I see that she's in purple today."

"Yes," he said, "it was a rough start of the day because she doesn't have a purple Frisbee."

"That's a travesty. How dare you?" she teased him. "What was the solution?"

"After a very long talking-to, she decided to forgive me and accept the white Frisbee because, and I'm just assuming this was her logic, the white matches her lace collar."

"I love this pig."

"You love her now," he said. "Just wait until she ruins one of your peaceful mornings. Let me tell you, Lu Lu can ruin a morning, afternoon *or* evening in five seconds flat."

"She's a princess, Matteo. What do you expect?"

"I don't know," he said in a playful manner. "A little more support from you."

"If you want me to take sides, I'd have to go with—" She always seemed to laugh when she was with the doctor and his pet pig.

"Princess Lu Lu," Matteo said in a defeated tone.

"Obviously, Princess Lu Lu."

He offered her his arm and she hooked hers to his.

"You look particularly lovely today," he said.

"Thank you. You, too."

They walked together as a family of three and this stroll through the woods was exactly what she needed to clear her mind. The minute the week started, she had been bombarded with several legal headaches relating to her home and her business. Grant wasn't about to go quietly; he was going to land as many emotional and legal punches as he could, and it made her wonder if she had ever really known the man who had been a fixture in her life for years.

"You're quiet," Matteo noted.

She sighed, not wanting to infect their good time with Grant. If she let him *ruin* every single moment, or any moments for that matter, he would win. And she couldn't allow that to happen.

"It's been challenging, but I don't want to talk about it now. Is that okay?"

"Sure," he said easily. "I'm more interested in making plans for this weekend."

"Oh yeah? What did you have in mind?"

"Do you dance?"

"Not really," she said with a self-effacing laugh. "Two left feet. Do you dance?"

"Do I dance? I salsa, merengue, tango *and* Texas two-step."

"That's way out of my league. I've been known to sway side to side before." She laughed. "That's what two left feet can accomplish."

"I can't hear anything but the sound of Latin music!" He gave a little demonstration of how his hips moved. "Will you let me teach you?"

"Sure," she said. "Why not? I'd follow those hips of yours anywhere you want me to go."

CHAPTER SEVEN

MATTEO HAD WAITED impatiently for Saturday night. He was back to his Friday night Shabbat dinner with his family, which kept the parents and his sister happy, but Saturday night was reserved for Danica. He understood the risk of getting closer and closer to Danica; she was in the middle of a messy breakup, her business was in LA, her entire life was in LA, and one of the last places in the world he would want to live was| |LA. Day by day, he was giving little pieces of his heart to Danica and there was a very good chance that he might wind up nursing some deep emotional cuts. And yet he couldn't, wouldn't, stop seeing Danica.

"Where are you taking me?" Danica said, letting him lead her to their destination.

"To a magical place," Matteo said, guiding her inside and shutting the door behind them. Then he took off her blindfold and let her see where he had taken her.

"This is your house."

"Yes, it is."

"But this is your house."

"Yes, I know," he said, "but tonight, it's not just my home. No! This is the space where I will teach you to dance."

He swayed his hips, took steps forward, two steps back. "Can you feel the energy in the room, *mi corazon*?"

"I feel something in the air but I'm not sure it's energy."

Matteo laughed, and then swung her into his arms, twirled her several times under his hand and then he captured her, dipped her back, and leaned forward and kissed her exposed neck. He lifted her back upright, spun her several more times, then brought her close, leading her through the basic steps. Her lovely face was alight with joy and fun and, yes, love. He saw it as much as he felt it in his own soul. He loved Danica Brand and she, in turn, loved him.

"Whoo!" Danica's typically perfectly coiffed hair was wispy and mussed in the sexiest of ways. "Now, that was a first."

He held her still in his arms, lifted her chin, and kissed her deeply, trying to tell her, with his lips, that he desired her, that he wanted to make love with her.

"Do you like salsa?"

"Whatever that was? I love it," she said, winded. "I didn't have to do anything but follow your lead."

"And how does that make you feel?"

"Total transparency—" she put her hand on his cheek "—that doesn't come naturally to me."

"But…?"

"I'm willing to give it another go."

Matteo picked her up and then swung her around before putting her down, twirling her again and then slowing down the pace so he could teach her the basic steps.

"Right foot, left foot," he said to encourage her. "You just needed the right teacher."

He could feel her body melting, becoming pliable and willing. Danica was a quick study and he loved to have her in his arms. He dipped her again, kissing her neck, her ear, her lips. When he lifted her up, her eyes were half-mast, with a mixture of desire and need.

"Danica," he whispered into her ear.

"Yes, Matteo?"

"I want to make love to you."

"Okay."

"Do you want to make love with me?"

"Yes."

Matteo lifted her into his arms and carried her into his large main suite. Layer by layer, he unwrapped her clothing like he was unwrapping a present on Christmas morning or the first night of Hanukkah.

He followed her into the bed, drew the covers over their naked bodies; his hands needed to explore, to touch, to feel. Her skin was silky and warm; her long legs naturally intertwined with his as they kissed, slowly at first.

"Danica?"

"Hmm?"

"Open your eyes, please."

Danica's eyes drifted open.

"Can you see on my face that I am in love with you?"

"Well," she said after a lengthy pause, "I'm really farsighted, so everything close-up is really fuzzy right now."

Matteo lowered his head and shook it. "I was setting this up as a tender moment and you ruined it."

"No, no, no. Let's get it back. Sexy dancing, awesome seduction, the best really, and then you declare…"

And that's when her voice trailed off and it must have dawned on her as she was recounting the events and what he had confessed.

"You said that you are in love with me."

"Yes," he said, "I am in love with you. I want you to know that yes, of course, my body wants you. How could it not? But so too does my mind, so too does my soul, so too does my heart."

"Oh, God." Danica held his handsome face in her hands, kissed his lips and his neck and his chest. "Where have you been all my life, Matteo?"

He captured her hand, kissed it lovingly. "I've been right here, waiting for you."

DANICA AWAKENED IN Matteo's bed feeling womanly, well-loved and satiated. They had made love three times, savoring each other until the early hours of the morning. She leaned back against the pillows, stared up at the ceiling, hands behind her head, breasts barely covered with the sheet. This was living.

This right here, right now, this was living. So many years she had been living half of a life.

She heard Matteo whistling in the kitchen, and she was lured out of bed by the smell of strong coffee. She picked up his shirt that he had thrown on the back of a chair in the corner, put it on, smelling his scent on the collar, rolled up the sleeves and, feeling decadent, she left the bedroom. She hadn't worn a man's clothing after a night of lovemaking since she was in graduate school. And it darn well felt fabulous.

"Good morning." She padded in her bare feet over to him.

"Good morning to you, my love." Matteo put his arm around her shoulders, hugged her close and kissed her sweetly.

"I like that shirt on you," he said.

"Would you mind if I keep it?"

"Of course not," then as an afterthought, he said, "As long as it isn't some souvenir."

"Please." She made herself comfortable on one of the stools at the bar. "I put notches in my bedpost for that."

He smiled at her, winked, and then asked, "How did you sleep?"

"Do you mean when you let me sleep?"

Another wink and a smile.

"Like a baby." She smiled back, reaching in her purse for her reading glasses to take a look at her phone. "What are you cooking? It smells divine."

"Plantains. My great-grandmother's recipe."

"I can't wait," she said, turning up the volume on her phone, and that's when emails, text messages and DMs in her social media began to blow up. There were so many dings and pings and chirps, some from the few true allies she had left from her female group, but most from her CPA and her attorney.

"Wanted lady," Matteo said with a question in his voice.

Danica began reading the messages and she stood up, still scrolling, with each message building on bad news on top of more bad news and still more bad news. Matteo was watching her with curious eyes. Under any other circumstances, she would have skipped breakfast, gotten on her phone and focused on the battle with Grant back in California. This time she didn't;

that said volumes to her. Matteo appeared to be occupying a space in her heart, her life, that hadn't been occupied before. With Matteo, she was learning how to focus on the moment, finding joy in that moment, and then dealing with business later. The elusive work-life balance.

"Need to talk?" he asked her.

"No." She put her phone down. "No. I don't want to infect our time with this *nonsense* back home."

"I'm here if you need me."

She nodded, watching him take the plantains off the skillet, flatten the slices on a chopping board, then dip them in a bowl of cold water. Then, Matteo turned up the heat on the skillet, cooked the plantains about a minute on each side. He transferred the plantains onto two plates, lightly salted, put the plate in front of her, and then joined her with his own plate.

Her first bite rocked her world. She didn't, as a rule, eat anything battered or fried. And she knew that Matteo avoided greasy or fried food because the man was muscular and fit.

"Well?" he asked her.

She nodded, made a noise while she was chewing to indicate that she was loving what she was tasting.

"Mmm." She nodded again.

That brought a smile to his face as he made short work of his own plantain. A moment later, her plate was clean also.

"Hats off to your great-grandmother!" She patted her stomach, which was rounder than when she had arrived in Montana. Emotional eating was something, over the years, she had deliberately avoided. When she was facing a crisis, she turned to exercise, not food, for the simple fact that her fit body was as much a part of her "uniform" as were her nails, Botox, her perfectly blond hair and her spray tan. The competition was vicious in the LA real estate market, where youth was always prized over wisdom.

"Coffee, tea or me?" he asked.

"Coffee and you," she said with a smile, bringing her plate to the sink.

They took their coffee to the couch where they had their first kiss. Their shared a comfortable silence, something that

Danica had only imagined was for couples who had been married for decades.

"Penny for your thoughts," he said.

She put her empty coffee cup on a coaster on the coffee table.

"Nothing earth-shattering," she said. "We've been pretty fast and loose with our food and drinks."

He nodded.

"If I keep going down this road, all of my clothes, which were custom-made to fit me like a glove, won't fit."

"Agreed," he agreed. "I'm not ready for a dad bod just yet."

That made her laugh, and her laugh made him smile at her with so much *love* and admiration that it made her feel self-conscious in the very best of ways. He reached for her hand, and she slipped it into his, a perfect fit.

"Any regrets?" he asked her.

She knew what he was asking, and she gave him her honest answer. "No. Not at all."

He squeezed her hand. "I'm glad. This thing between us seemed to be on overdrive."

Danica had thought something similar, but the time she spent with Matteo had been quality, well-spent time. Could the same be said about her time with Grant? Now that she was experiencing this romance with Matteo, wanting to be in his presence, wanting to soak up all of the way he made her feel inside with his feelings laid bare before her, the answer was no. Matteo had told her he loved her. It had been a shock, yes, but it also enhanced the specialness of their lovemaking. Still, she also felt a sense of being out of control, being swept up in the allure of this whirlwind with Matteo. In her mind, there would be an end to this shooting star relationship with the handsome doctor. Her life was in LA—her house, her business, her connections, and her track record had been built over a decade; yes, things were murky with this conflict with Grant that she was navigating. But she was still going back when the timing was right.

"Do you want to see Lu Lu?" he asked, and she was glad that he had changed the subject.

"Did you really need to ask that question?"

"No," he laughed, giving her his hand in a gentlemanly manner, and helped her up.

Coffee cups in the sink, Danica helped Matteo prepare Lu Lu's breakfast. First, they added pellets to her large breakfast bowl. Then, they added celery, cucumbers and some pumpkin. Matteo cut up some carrots to hide in the yard for Lu Lu to encourage her to forage as was her nature.

They put on winter gear and went into the massive fenced-in area for Lu Lu. Closer to the main house, there was an eight-by-eight tiny house with a front porch and climate control.

"It cracks me up that Lu Lu is a homeowner," she said.

"It's over the top," he said, "but she just can't be inside the house for most of the day. She needs to have more freedom. More stimulation, less boredom. This was the best solution I could think of."

"Well, I love it."

Danica followed Matteo into Lu Lu's house; it was toasty warm, and Lu Lu had a giant, fluffy bed upon which to lie. When Lu Lu saw her, she oinked excitedly and waddled over for a quick chin scratch before she began to devour her breakfast.

"Well, that's another first of many firsts," Matteo said to her as she followed him out the door.

"Lu Lu never goes to anyone else before she comes to me." Matteo had the slightest ring of injury in his voice.

"Are you jealous?"

"A little, yes."

She hugged him spontaneously, loving his honesty. "I'm just the flavor of the month. She still loves you the most."

They hid carrots throughout the yard and then Matteo checked to make sure that a puzzle toy that opened different doors where a pellet was hidden inside was still there. There was also a ball that when rolled by her nose, produced a treat.

"I just love her," Danica said, standing next to Matteo, putting her arm around him as he was putting his arm around her.

"Everyone here loves you," he said, matter-of-factly.

And there it was, a feeling of dread that manifested as a queasy stomach. He was brave, this man, telling her that he loved her without any expectation for a verbal confession of her love for him. It was a gift that he gave freely, no strings attached. It brought joy into her heart but sheer panic to her mind.

"I'd better get going." She moved away from him. "I do need to answer some of these emails."

She said goodbye to Lu Lu, kissing the little pig on her snout, before she followed Matteo inside to the welcoming, warm house he called home. She got dressed with a sense of purpose and then met him at the front door. He drove her back to her condo and at the door, kissed her with a kiss that was over much too quickly.

His hand on her face, he asked, "When will I see you again?"

"On the trail?" she asked. "Tomorrow around seven?"

"It's a date."

"Will Lu Lu join us?"

Matteo looked at her with a very upset expression when he asked, "You aren't just using me to get to my pig, are you?"

That made her laugh. "I don't think so, but *maybe*?"

Matteo returned to her side, kissed her lovingly, and then said, "I love you."

He said it as if they had always said it, with such certainty. She didn't, couldn't, say those words back to him. In her mind, though, the words *te amo, I love you* in Spanish, *were* thought.

Had she fallen in love with Matteo with lightning speed? Was this a rebound? She couldn't answer those questions, so she did what she always did when something in her private life was complicated or emotional: she buried herself in her business. This lucrative distraction was her go-to, but this time, when she began to answer the flurry of emails and placed calls to her CPA and attorney and her Realtors who were struggling without her, it didn't help. And that was the confirmation of her feelings for Matteo that she hadn't really been looking for.

"I love him," Danica said, sitting still at the desk, staring at a large picture of an elk in the snow on the wall in front of her. "I actually do love him. How could I have let that happen?"

She wasn't easily scared, but her feelings for Matteo Katz-Cortez surely did frighten her.

JOURNEY WAS SITTING on the porch at high noon, in a spot where the sun shone down and warmed her up while also melting the snow on the ground. She had her laptop open to Chapter One and there wasn't anything written after that. The more she tried to get out of her block, the worse it seemed to get.

"At this rate, I'll be a one-hit wonder," she grumbled to herself, feeling frustrated and annoyed by her writer's block. One of the authors she admired had said in a podcast that how she dealt with writer's block was to sit at the desk, hands on the keys, and wait. So that's what she had done. Hands on the keyboard awaiting inspiration.

On her character sheet, she had fleshed out the hero of the book, Billy Dean, who had evolved since she had arrived in Montana. That was probably her biggest accomplishment to date; she knew who the hero was now—he made more sense. Billy Dean was older, with some deep lines on his face and around his gray-blue eyes. He had gray hair mixed with brown-black and he was in his mid to late fifties; he definitely had more miles on that speedometer. The hero had completely transformed, a real overhaul to fit more in Cody's image with threadbare jeans and a Stetson hat and boots that needed replacing. And yet even with all of those outward appearance changes, Billy Dean still seemed flat, lifeless, a shell of a man, and she just couldn't seem to fill him in no matter how many hours she had watched Cody go about his business at the ranch. And, yes, of course, she had taken bits and pieces of other men on the ranch, but Cody was still her muse. She was attracted to him in every way a woman could be attracted to a man, and it caught her off guard. Ever since Oakley, she had hardly dated at all. A romantic relationship didn't even make her list of priorities. Now that Oakley was ten, it had, every now and again, hit her that she was lonely for a man. Someone to hold hands with, someone to lean on when times were rough, and someone for her to love. A friend as well as a lover.

Still not inspired to write, Journey's mind went on a winding trip with images of her with Cody and her son in a park, playing and laughing, and loving each other. Did this daydreaming help with the book? Doubtful, but perhaps.

CODY TY HAD done his darnedest not to think about Journey. When he saw her, he was cordial as he went about his business. Almost every day, he noticed that she would sit on the porch, in the frigid cold, and watch him work with the horses. He knew that she was at the ranch, doing research on her next book. If she was going to do real research about real life in Montana, she was going to have to get off that porch and get her hands dirty. Cody finished his training with a solid black colt with a frisky, playful personality, and after he put the colt back into the barn, he walked a direct line from the barn to the porch. The closer he got, the wider Journey's eyes were. Big, beautiful eyes, surrounded by a thick fringe of dark eyelashes creating the perfect frame. She was a beauty; rare, mesmerizing, with an electric draw for him that could no longer be ignored.

When he reached the porch, Journey had the look of a skittish filly on her face, and it seemed like she was trying to figure out an avenue of escape.

"Howdy," he said with a tip of his hat.

"Howdy," she said, then immediately chastised herself. "Darn it! I wasn't going to pick that up!"

"You can't cure your fear of horses if I can't get you off this porch."

"Oh," Journey said, and then asked, "You were serious about that?"

"Of course I was."

"Well—" the woman he had nicknamed Palomino in his mind looked around again for some sort of escape "—I appreciate it, Cody, I really do. But I don't really feel like I want to get over my fear. I mean, at least not on this trip."

"If you want to write about cowboy life, you've got to understand the one animal that has allowed cowboys like me to exist. You don't have a cowboy without a horse."

After he said those words, something seemed to dawn in Journey's mind, which showed on her lovely face. With what he read as a newfound resolve, Journey got up out of the rocking chair, crossed to the porch steps and met him on the ground. She had those long legs, and she was darn near close to looking at him eye-to-eye. But he didn't mind. He was drawn to her, and he wanted to get to know her. It was as simple as that.

"Where do we start?" she asked him, matching his purposeful stride.

"Barn work."

She seemed to falter before catching up.

He continued, "You can't know life here without getting your hands dirty."

"Well…" Journey appeared to be having second thoughts.

So he stopped. "If you don't want this kind of training, that's fine by me. But if you want to write about Montana cowboys and cowgirls, life out here in the shadow of mountains, you need to feel it, smell it, experience it, taste it. Experience firsthand what it's like to work in the snow, get up at the crack of dawn to get the animals fed hours before you've had a chance to sit down with your first cup of coffee. It takes true grit, determination, gumption and a whole lot of stupid to choose this life."

"You chose it."

"Yes, ma'am, I surely did. *And* it chose me," he said before he asked, "Question is, will you choose us?"

CHAPTER EIGHT

DANICA FELT LIKE a new woman; her time in Montana, her time
with her sisters, and her time, most certainly, with Matteo had
given her the space and the break to get in the right headspace
and figure out her next steps forward for her business and personal life in California. A renewal had occurred rather quickly.
And for the short term, she was able to manage her business
remotely but that was not sustainable. The only real dark cloud
in her expansive blue Montana sky was, of course, Grant. This
Grant was vindictive and angry, and had convinced himself as
well as many people in their orbit that he was the victim. He had
been forced to seek solace with Fallon. What else could he do?
He was in a long-term relationship with an ambitious, driven
woman, a cold fish, who was never truly ready for a family, and
he had suffered in this state for over a decade. For those who
had bought into that narrative, at least she knew who to weed
out of her life when she returned to LA.

For now, and at least for the next few weeks she had allot-
ted to be in Montana, she was living her best life, with a thriving ranch business with her sisters, and having a romantic tryst
with the most eligible bachelor in a one-hundred-mile radius,
who just happened to believe that she was a catch! And even
though she still didn't know beyond this day, this hour, these
minutes, what that budding relationship would hold for them in

the future, she was determined to savor every single moment she had with Matteo.

When Danica arrived at Hideaway, she had been listening to salsa music and doing her best to remember the steps. She got out of her SUV, found a spot of ground near the firepit that wasn't a soggy mess, and then tried to remember the beginning steps Matteo had taught her.

"Okay, legs together, back straight, three count, step forward with the left foot, lift up the right foot, then place it down and return the left foot to its original spot."

She practice that several times, sort of getting it correct. Then she attempted the next six steps by bringing her right foot back. "Four then right foot back, five, lift the left foot, put it down and then bring my right foot back, six."

"What is happening here?" Ray and Charlie came out of the chicken coop together holding a basket of fresh eggs.

"I'm practicing salsa."

Ray and Charlie exchanged questioning looks and then Charlie asked, "Will the real Danica Brand please step forward!"

That made Danica smile and Ray and Charlie laugh.

"Okay," she admitted, "I rarely dance."

"Rarely?" her sisters asked in unison.

Now she was laughing at herself. "Okay, *never*. Until now, I suppose."

"I take it this is the doing of Dr. Dreamboat?" Ray asked.

"Oh, my Lord, that man is chiseled to perfection!" Danica had to admit.

"You're glowing," Charlie noted, then said to Ray, "She's glowing."

"Did you?" Ray stepped forward and lowered her voice.

Danica tried to keep a straight face, but failed miserably. "A lady never tells."

"That's a big fat *yes*," Charlie said.

"I can't affirm or deny," she teased them, but she knew her broad, happy smile, combined with her unusual, relaxed vibe, answered the question without any words needed.

"But—" she wiggled her eyebrows suggestively "—we

have had hours and hours of riveting, amazing, mind-blowing, life-altering..."

Her sisters leaned in, waiting for some saucy secret to be shared.

"...conversations."

"What?!" Charlie shook her head with a frown.

Ray elbowed Charlie. "I suppose *conversation* is a new euphemism for sex."

Danica shrugged with a very happy smile. "I suppose it could be."

"You go girl." Ray gave her a high five. "You damn well deserved it."

Danica had to agree. This romance with Matteo was what she needed to repair her deflated ego, but she knew, in her heart, that this connection to Matteo ran deeper than a fling. He had captured her heart, along with her body and her soul. Even if they couldn't make a full-time relationship work, how she felt inside would not change. In fact, Danica was absolutely certain that this love she had for Matteo would never fade, that even if she met another man in LA, she would always carry Matteo in her heart.

They headed toward Charlie's renovated cottage that had been the cabin their great-great-grandparents had built and with Wayne's help, Charlie had lovingly restored. She lived in that cabin now and everyone who knew Charlie knew that she would live the rest of her life in that cabin.

Bowie, Charlie's beefy, muscular pit bull–rottweiler mix, met them at the door, wearing a plastic collar around his neck.

"Hi, good boy." Ray leaned down to pat Bowie on his head. "He looks so miserable."

"I know." Charlie stripped off her coat and hung it on the horseshoe-themed coatrack that Wayne had built for her. "He's always been so active, this surgery on his leg has been really hard on him, and it's been hard on us. He whines, he barks, I think he feels that if he has to be miserable, then so too should everyone else in his orbit!"

"Hi, there, Hitch." Danica reached down to pick up the older cat that Wayne had with him for several years while he traveled from job to job, never settling anywhere until he found a forever home with Charlie at Hideaway Ranch.

"Hitch is the only one who can suffer Bowie now." Charlie let them into the small quaint entryway. There were many parts of the cabin that were original, including the stone hearth built by their ancestors, and much of the wood on the walls was salvaged.

"It amazes me what you've done here, Charlie." Danica sat down at the small square table that Wayne built using some of the wood from felled trees. At one time, this cabin was in horrid condition, taken over by trees, animals, vines and weeds.

"Coming from you," her sister said, "that's high praise."

"I mean—" Danica ran her hand over the butcher-block table handmade for the home "—Wayne is a master carpenter."

"Coffee?" Charlie asked them.

They nodded yes, so Charlie put on a pot before joining them at the table. Bowie, looking depressed about his collar, lay down on the floor and Hitch sat in a bread loaf position next to him.

"Good boys," Charlie said. "Such good boys."

When the coffee was ready, Charlie delivered three piping-hot coffees in chunky mugs for her sisters to enjoy.

"Now it's time to discuss some business," Danica said. "I've been looking at real estate prices in Big Sky, and I can't believe what I'm seeing. There have to be more multimillionaires *here* than in California, period."

"What?" Ray asked, looking stunned.

"Take a look at this." Danica pulled up one of the popular sites for advertising homes for sale. "Fourteen million, twenty-two million. The only property under one million is a studio condo. I can only imagine what our ranch is worth."

"No," Charlie frowned severely. "No."

"I'm not saying sell, Charlie," Danica said firmly, "but we must raise our prices. We are leaving money on the table, and we can't."

"Okay," Charlie said.

"And we have to build more cabins," Danica added.

"Summer is really short," Ray said, "so we'll have to be ready the minute the weather takes a turn toward spring."

"Let's get set up with our architect and figure out locations, layouts, designs," Danica said.

"It makes sense." Charlie uncrossed her arms.

"I promise you, Charlie," Danica said, "I'm not angling to sell. I just want us to be profitable, and looking at what's available, with these celebrity mansions eating up the small amount of land there is to be had around the ski resort, we can ask for more. We've got to be competitive."

All three of them agreed on that and then tied up any loose ends regarding the ranch.

"I'm excited to have Journey's son and mother to arrive at the beginning of next week," Charlie said, "and they have extended their stay for two weeks."

"Oh!" Ray exclaimed. "I ordered her book! It's really good. I'm going to ask for her to autograph it."

"She's our first author, so that's supercool," Charlie said. "A feather in our cap."

They closed the minutes for the ranch; after their business was completed, and after a coffee refill, Danica asked, "How's Dean?"

Ray sighed heavily. "Devastated. He just seems *lost*. The girls, especially Paisley, are taking it very hard. We've lost both of our parents, and we know how it feels."

"Horrible," Danica said.

"Unmoored," Charlie added.

"Nothing I say seems to help," Ray admitted. "He's barely eating. He's barely sleeping. He's lost a lot of weight."

"Do you think he'd seek help?" Danica asked.

Charlie nodded and added, "I was thinking the same thing, Ray."

Another deep breath in, Ray said, "I've thought about that, and if he doesn't rebound—I just want him to mourn the loss of his father without losing touch with his own life."

"Of course not," Charlie interjected.

"I think we will have to figure something out. He needs to be there for the girls. As much as I love them and they love me, they need their father. This is the first major loss his girls have experienced. Paisley was two and Luna was still in the oven cooking when they lost Dean's mother."

"It's so hard," Danica said. "I just hope that Dean can find a path back."

"Let us know if there's anything we can do to help," Charlie said.

"Yes, please do," she agreed.

They finished their coffees, put on their winter gear, and then headed back outside. Ray asked, "When are you heading back to California?"

"Kicking me to the curb already?" Danica laughed.

Ray put her arm around her shoulders, "Never. I would actually like for you to move back. It would be wonderful to have all of us back in the same zip code."

"Well, I don't imagine that will happen," she said. "I think that I will have to head back in a week or two. Grant is being awful, just awful, and I have to show up and show him that I'm not afraid of him or his lawyers. I have to get into the ring so I can pull a Rocky move and knock him out!"

"You can do it, Danny," Charlie said encouragingly.

"Not even a fair fight, really," Ray agreed. "You can run circles around him while wearing stilettos and a pencil skirt."

Danica stopped, asked for a group triplet hug, and realized in that exact moment that she had built what she still loved in California, but Hideaway Ranch, for the first time in the longest time, felt like home to her. Her sisters felt like home. And so too did Matteo Katz-Cortez.

JOURNEY FELT SWEATY underneath her winter clothing and when that cold Montana air hit her exposed skin on her neck or her nose, it actually hurt. She hadn't been exactly sure what Cody would be like up close and personal, and now she knew. He was serious, goal-oriented, often abrupt and unsmiling, and he was proud of his cowboy lifestyle.

"Let me show you how to use that pitchfork," Cody said,

reaching out for the rather heavy pitchfork in her hand. "You've got to put some muscle behind it."

"I was putting muscle behind it," she objected to his characterization.

"You've got to be efficient and quick, because all of these here animals are eating and getting ready to make some manure and you'll still be on the first go-around."

Journey frowned at him. "I think I was doing the exact same thing you were just doing."

"Nope."

She took back the pitchfork and did the *exact same thing* she was doing before the demonstration, and scooped up some manure from the goats' stalls, put it into a wheelbarrow, and wished she had chosen a different muse. As it turned out, Cody Ty could be grumpy, annoying *and* bossy. He was, admittedly, very handsome in a rugged, rough-around-the-edges cowboy way; she liked the experience on his face. His hands were often ungloved, large, and calloused. But—and this was very important—he was a royal pain in the backside.

"What now?" she asked with an attitude that would rival her ten-year-old when he didn't want to pick up his room.

"Water buckets need to be dumped and cleaned."

She was already tired, but now it was a challenge and she refused to give in to the need to take a hot shower and crawl into bed for the rest of the day.

She went back into the goat stalls, grabbed the water buckets, which were heavier than they looked, groaned when she lifted one up, waddled toward the gate, spilling water along the way, and then she tripped over the water hose, dropped said bucket, and the dirty water in the bucket spilled out on the gravel aisle of the barn.

Cody gave her the side-eye and she really, truly and honestly wanted to throw that bucket at him. No one, not even her ex-husband, had gotten under her skin as quickly as Cody Ty had managed to do.

When he came over to help her, she held out her hand, and said, "Back off, cowboy, I've been given a job to do and I'm gonna gosh darn do it!"

That was when the tiniest glint of respect came into his deep-set eyes as he held up his hands in surrender. She had put a point on the imaginary scoreboard as she little by little, inch by inch, cleaned all of the buckets and put them back, and then filled them with water. By the time she was done with that chore, the goats had already left her some manure and urine. And then that was when she broke down.

"What kind of life is this, anyway?" she asked no one in particular. "This isn't romantic! This is dirty and smelly and exhausting."

In her moment of frustration, she had backed up and then she felt a nibble on her ear. She screamed, jumped, spun around, and realized that one of the horses had tried to turn her into a snack.

"Okay! That's it. You win." She leveled Cody with her best stern mother look that she had honed over the years. "I'm out of here!"

"Whoa, whoa, whoa," Cody said. "Don't go."

She crossed her arms. "Why should I stay? I'm not here to be the butt of your jokes. I have a book to write—my son and my mother are coming at the beginning of next week and I haven't written one word!"

"Now, just take a minute to cool off. I was just giving you a taste of reality."

"Okay. I get it," she said sourly. "Nothing but hard work, more hard work and more hard work."

"That's the life," Cody said, "but is that all you got?"

"What do you mean?"

"What do you smell?"

"Seriously?"

He nodded. "What do you smell?"

"Besides manure?" she asked. "A sweet smell."

"Alfalfa," he said. "Good fiber for the horses and the goats. What do you hear?"

"Other than you bark at me?"

"Yes. Other than that."

She closed her eyes and listened, and then opened her eyes. "Chewing. The sounds of the animals—the horses blowing air through their noses, the goats talking to each other."

"What do you see?"

"Beauty everywhere," she said softly. "The horses are beautiful, the goats are adorable, and the donkeys have those amazing ears."

"What do you feel?"

She thought about it, and then she realized, besides exhausted, sweaty, cold and frustrated, she felt "free."

"That's right." Cody nodded, and he seemed pleased with her thoughts. "It's a hard life, but it's a good life. This is one of the last places in this country that a man—or a woman—can feel *free*."

Journey felt oddly *changed* from this exercise with Cody. This was impactful and while she certainly wasn't going to puff up his already high self-esteem by telling him this, ranch life felt four-dimensional, not one-dimensional.

"I suppose I should thank you," she said begrudgingly.

That was when he smiled at her and she could see that smile reach his eyes. "Don't thank me if you don't want to."

"Okay," she said, "I take it back."

Then he laughed and she liked the sound of it, but she now was pretty sure she needed a different muse.

"That's all right." He nodded, leaning against the pitchfork. "If you learned something that helps you along the way, that's good enough for me. I've always loved to read and being that you are an author, that's impressive to me."

And there it was, Cody flipping the script and making her feel bad for being salty.

"Well, thank you."

They stood in silence for a second or two and then Cody asked her, "Was this a onetime deal or do you want to learn more?"

The next words came out of her mouth without much thought behind it. "Actually, I'd like to learn more about you."

He stared at her, and she stared at him, and then he broke eye contact, coughed a couple of times and said, "Well, I'm flattered. But you can probably find out all you need to know about me on the internet."

"No. I can't."

Cody looked down at the toe of his boot, seeming to mull something over. "If you need to know more, you'll have to get to know horses."

"I know that this one—" she pointed to the small sorrel horse that had tried to take a bite out of her ear "—tried to bite me."

"Rose?" he scoffed. "She wasn't trying to bite you. She was saying 'hi.'"

Journey didn't believe that for a second, so she just shook her head.

"They're herbivores."

"Okay, so maybe she didn't try to bite me—"

"She most definitely didn't try to bite you."

"Why is it so important for me to learn horses to know you?"

"Because," Cody said sincerely as he rubbed Rose's ears affectionately, "they are as much a part of who I am as my name, the color of my eyes or the wrinkles on my face."

"One doesn't go without the other."

"That's right."

Journey said, "Okay. How do I get started?"

"You already did," he said. "I just wanted you to be with them, look at them, see how they moved, how they spoke to you and to each other."

"Impressive," she said. "You got me to start without the anxiety."

"Yes, ma'am," he said. "You'll need steel-toed boots."

"Okay."

"Then I'll see you tomorrow," he said, "not on the porch."

"Yes." She nodded, feeling that she had just been in the company of greatness. "Thank you."

"It was my pleasure."

She raised an eyebrow at him and asked, "But was it, though?"

CODY FELT LIKE a real heel. All of his defenses were on high alert. He hadn't been involved with a woman in a very long time, not that he hadn't had options. There were always plenty of options. And he'd even tried his hand at marriage a time or two. Even though most people would assume that champion cowboy

Cody Ty Hawkins was a ladies' man, sleeping his way through the women at the rodeo circuit who just seemed to get younger and younger with each passing year—that wasn't him. He was a romantic, in it for love, and he had his heart squashed by a woman he had loved from the time he was a teenager in Tennessee. Lola Wilson, his second wife, had run off with his best friend while he was on the rodeo circuit. He lost his best friend and his wife all in one shot. So he did what he did best—he cut ties with the past and moved on into his future. The divorce was quick, and he didn't get invited to their wedding. He supposed he drank himself into a stupor a time or two until he finally dried out and a chance meeting with Wayne Westbrook, one of the finest cowboys he had ever met, changed the direction of his life.

"How are the babies coming along?" Wayne stopped by the barn to say hi.

"They're a fine group," Cody said. "I've given my heart to too many women, but I have to say, this little filly right here? I've gone and done it again."

"Love's like that, isn't it?" Wayne said. "You don't know when it's going to strike."

Cody's mind immediately went to Journey Lamar. That woman had run over him with a steamroller and flattened him but good. "It sure does."

"Well," Wayne said, "if you've got to have her, just let me know. We'll work something out for you."

"I just might," Cody said. "I just might."

Wayne shook his hand and then headed off, but Cody called him back. "I've offered to work with the author."

"Journey?"

Cody nodded. "She's researching ranch life."

"I heard that," Wayne said, his expression registering confused. "If you have time, I've got no objection."

"I just wanted to keep you in the loop, is all."

Wayne gave him a nod. "Consider me in the loop."

Cody put a harness on the little filly that had caught his eye and walked her out to the round pen. She was a real good-looking horse, and she was willing, curious and intelligent. In the best of ways, this little filly reminded him of Journey. She had some grit; he wasn't so sure there for a minute or two, but when she was getting hot under the collar, he saw a woman who would fight her way to the top, like the cream that she was.

She was dangerous to him; he didn't need another heartbreak. And yet he was drawn to her like that bee to honey. When Charlie told him that the author wanted to get to know him better, to understand cowboy life, he had been flattered but not at all interested. He'd already had his life dissected, shredded and thrown out to the sharks who took a kernel of truth and turned it into a scandal. He was famous; had been for more than half of his life. But fame was an illusion, and he never found any happiness in it. So, it was a "thank you but no thank you" situation. And then she caught his eye and, yes, of course, she was beautiful. He saw her outer beauty; he was more impressed with the kindness, the honesty, the vulnerability in her eyes. She was, to his mind, an open book. She wore her heart on her sleeve, and it made perfect sense that she was a romance author. Journey Lamar wasn't jaded like him; in fact, he believed they were polar opposites. He believed she was resilient in a way that he could never be.

When they reached the round pen, Cody forced his mind to the present moment so he could give his full attention to the lovely filly prancing about, snorting, kicking up her heels and then racing around him while he waited patiently for her to get her abundant energy out. When she slowed down, he caught her eye, and then backed up, giving the filly an opportunity to willingly come to him as he stepped back slowly. Horses were herd animals with a hierarchy; in the round pen, it was his job to show the horse with him that he was the leader of the herd.

"Good girl," Cody praised the filly when she stopped, looked at him, and then turned her body toward him, and then she walked over to him.

"There you are, sweet one." Cody scratched her behind her ears, speaking to her in soft tones.

"I think I'm going to have to declare my love for you, my beauty," Cody whispered to the young horse. "I'd rather give up a month's pay than lose you."

And that was settled; he would claim her tomorrow and then he would be thinking on a name. The filly rubbed her head against him; for him, that was her accepting him into her life.

"We belong to each other," he told her as he put the halter back on her slender head. "I promise to take care of you for the rest of your life."

CHAPTER NINE

"I LOVE HER," Matteo told his sister. For as long as he could remember, Estrella was the one person he told his deepest thoughts and secrets.

"I'm sorry, what?" his sister asked in a raised voice. "That's too fast, Matteo. Way too fast."

"You said that you fell in love with Lars the first time you met."

"Well, yeah, I did," she admitted, "but I…"

She stopped, thought for a moment, and then said, "Okay, you have me there. But this feels different. Lars and I hadn't built lives on polar opposite coasts."

"And what if you had?"

Estrella thought for another moment. "One of us would have to move. Are you willing to give up your practice, something you have built for nearly two decades?"

"I don't know. I'll cross that bridge when I get to it," he said. "For now, I just want to enjoy this feeling I have for Danica without putting a bunch of obstacles in our way."

"You know I support you. I always support you. I'm just worried," Estrella said. "What do you think the folks will think?"

"They'll love her."

"I hope so."

"They'll love her," he said again, "because *I* love her."

He said goodbye to his sister, understanding Estrella's concerns, and thinking maybe he should discuss moving the relationship forward; maybe he should consider moving this relationship with Danica to a more defined place. Yes, it was very early, and yes, Danica was in the midst of a messy breakup. But they had a soul-to-soul connection, one that he had never experienced before. And he believed that Danica, while perhaps less certain, returned his feelings.

Matteo prepared a health-conscious meal, a cauliflower steak with Thai-inspired sauces cooked in a skillet, flavored with olive oil, cilantro, a pinch of brown sugar and, for a taste bud surprise, finely chopped peanuts.

When the doorbell rang, he felt unusual nerves in his stomach; his sister, who historically had been correct in all things, had gotten into his head. He did feel rushed in that Danica's stay in Big Sky was most likely coming to an end sooner rather than later, and he felt compelled to formalize their relationship because, in his experience, distance did not make the heart grow fonder. He opened the door and was greeted with the woman who had stolen his heart. Matteo could see in her face that she was as excited to see him as he was to see her. The moment she stepped out of the cold into the warmth of his home fueled by a lovely, romantic fire, he took her in his arms and kissed her.

"I'm glad to see you," he said, helping her out of her coat.

Once free of it, she turned back to him, put her hand on his face, looked at him with an expression that he read as budding love, and she kissed him, with the same passion he had just kissed her with.

"I'm glad to see you, too," Danica said, walking into the living room. "It smells delicious. And the fire. Thank you."

"Of course," he replied. "I want to keep you coming back for more."

"Between the ranch and your place, I've barely spent any time at the rental," she said, then added, "Not that I'm complaining."

"I'm glad to hear that." He poured her a glass of wine.

Danica picked up the wineglass, swirled the white wine

around, sniffed it and then gave it the tiniest of tastes. "It's dry. It's a bit spicy. Austrian gruner vletliner?"

Matteo laughed, amazed at her palate. "Ten for ten, currently undefeated.

"Here's to you, Danica." He held out his glass to her.

"Here's to us," his date said, gently touching her glass to his.

It was a moment like this, a phrase such as this, using the word *us,* that gave him hope that he wasn't rushing things. And yes, he had said the L-word already, but it hadn't scared her off. They had met regularly for a hike on the trail where they first met, she absolutely adored Lu Lu, and Lu Lu returned that feeling to Danica. They texted several times during the day and they had shared a *physical* chemistry unlike anything he had experienced before.

"Dinner is served," he said after he plated the dinner fare.

"Matteo," his date said, "this is beautiful."

"I hope it tastes as it looks." He joined her.

Neither of them wanted to overindulge on the wine, so after one glass, they both switched to water with lemon.

"Mmm." Danica took her first bite. "Mmm!"

He took his first bite and he had to agree; this was one of his best meals.

Danica laughed and he loved to look at her beautiful face with the deepest ocean-blue eyes, a pert nose, and her signature ice-blond hair. She was stunning, a knockout, but her looks were only a small part of why he loved her. He loved her kindness, her intelligence, and yes, her ambition. She loved her work and so did he. And she loved Lu Lu. She understood why the adorable, but naughty and difficult-to-raise, pig held a special place in his heart. And because he had a lot of first dates that never turned into second dates, meeting Danica was the lightning bolt he had been waiting for. A big flashing sign with blinking lights and a red arrow pointing to Danica, saying *this is the one, Matteo.*

They finished their meals and transitioned to the living room to sit in front of the fire. Danica naturally sat close to him and leaned her back against his body. He kissed her cheek, and held her in his arms, and it felt like the right time to express his desire to define their relationship. But Estrella was in his head, holding up a yellow caution light, and that gave him pause. Estrella was his biggest fan, and she was never one to deliberately put up stumbling blocks in his way. Perhaps he *should* slow down, enjoy each moment with Danica without the added pressure of formalizing a relationship. She was, after all, going through a stressful breakup. And while Danica preferred to keep her legal and financial wranglings with Grant away from their time together, he was noticing subtle signs of frustration and anger that gave him a clue to her inner thoughts when it came to her relationship with Grant imploding.

Danica sighed happily in his arms, and he kissed her on the top of her head and drew her in closer.

"Thank you," she said to him.

"What for?"

"Everything, really," she said. "When I walk through that door, I can leave everything in my life in California at the doorstep. Your home, your arms, are safe places for me."

"You're welcome," he said, his mind circling back to what Estrella had said to him just a couple of hours ago. He felt ready to take things to the next level, but now, hearing how Danica felt about him, about his house, about his company, it didn't sound like a permanent home for her. In fact, it sounded as if she wasn't thinking of him seriously at all.

That night they cuddled, he held her in his arms until she fell asleep, and then he got out of bed, feeling like a lovesick fool. He needed to slow down, way down. And he might as well get started with that new leaf right away. He had told Danica that he loved her, but she had never returned that sentiment. He had put his heart out there, but he was alone in that risk.

Matteo donned his winter clothes, walked out to the small cottage built just for Lu Lu. He opened the door, walked into the warmth, and then sat down on the ground. Lu Lu, always willing for snuggles, got up, came over to him, and then plopped down next to him, rolled to the side, and asked for belly scratches.

"You've always been my girl, haven't you, Lu Lu?"

As if she understood him perfectly, she oinked a couple of times and then took her scratches quietly. After an hour of belly scratches, Matteo returned to his own bed, without a clue how to move forward with Danica but knowing that it was time for them to at least have a conversation about whether a long-term relationship was even on the list of possibilities. Or was he just a diversion for Danica while she ended her relationship with Grant? Either way, the dawn of the next morning would be, quite possibly, a pivotal one.

DANICA AWAKENED FEELING refreshed from a night of sleeping in Matteo's king bed. They hadn't made love but that didn't matter. Her feelings for Matteo certainly went beyond the physical, but admittedly, the handsome doctor did have an incredible physique and she liked it particularly when he wore a form-fitting T-shirt that showed off every bulge of the biceps and the curves of his pecs. He was a truly fine example of a chiseled man from his face to his form. She swung her legs out of bed, ran her fingers through her hair, put on his pajama top as was a new habit for her, and then padded out to the kitchen, lured by the smell of strong coffee.

"Good morning," she said to Matteo, walking over to him with a hug and kiss.

"Morning," he said, but seemed a tad standoffish. "How'd you sleep?"

"Like a very happy log." She took the offered coffee with a spritz of cream and no sugar. "But I suppose, technically, a log doesn't have feelings."

Matteo laughed at her joke, but that smile disappeared in record time. "Is everything okay?"

"Well, there is something I need to speak with you about."

"Oh, God." Her fingers on the mug tightened noticeably. "You're married."

"No," he said, and then repeated, "No."

"You got someone pregnant?"

The expression on Matteo's face made her immediately want to take that back.

"No," he said, "I'm not Grant."

She looked down at her coffee for a moment and then met his gaze. "Sorry. That was so...wrong."

He nodded, but there was definitely something serious on his mind and her body defaulted to the recent trauma of Grant and Fallon, and she just wished that Matteo would cut to the chase.

"There is something I want to discuss, but it doesn't involve another woman. Or another man, I suppose I should say."

She breathed in deeply, let it out, and then sat up straight, shoulders back, prepared to hear something she did not want to hear.

Matteo was about to tell her what was on her mind when her phone started buzzing and moving across the marble island. She looked at it and so did Matteo.

"I'm sorry," she said, "I have to take this."

She answered the phone, stood up, and listened to her attorney tell her the latest in the negotiations with Grant regarding the business and her estate.

"What are you saying?" she asked, pacing now. "Are you telling me that he isn't willing to let me buy him out?"

"Yes," her attorney said.

She felt her throat closing, her temperature rising and her mind short-circuiting. "Why?"

"He believes that the business has been undervalued and he wants more."

"He wants more?!" she asked, her voice raised. "He wants more?! Well, I would like him to be out of my life! That's what I want."

"Danica," her longtime attorney said calmly, "you need to be here, in LA, so we can fight this together. The longer you are away, the longer Grant seems to be digging in his heels."

"He wants a face-to-face with me?"

"Yes," he said, "and so does the arbitration judge. You need to fly back today."

Danica was quiet while her brain tried to digest what her attorney had said. Every day seemed to bring her one step closer to her return to California, but there was a part of her that didn't want to go back to that life. There was so much pain attached to it: feelings of betrayal, heartbreak, disbelief and pain without description for the children that they had planned to have with each other. How many people did she have to "unfriend" or "unfollow" on social media when they "liked" pictures of Grant's sonograms of the baby he was now having with Fallon? It was a kick in the gut, and it caused a new level of emotional pain that she hadn't known existed.

"Okay," she finally said, sinking into Matteo's couch. "I'll catch a flight today."

"None available," he said, "I already checked. I've arranged for a private jet. A driver will take you from Big Sky to Bozeman. You'll catch your jet there. Paramount Business Jets."

"Okay." She sounded as deflated as she felt.

"I'll send a driver to pick you up when you arrive in LA."

The call ended, and Danica just sat still, knowing that she had to move quickly, go to the condo, pack up her necessities and then head off to Bozeman.

She was staring at her phone, dazed, when Matteo joined her on the couch and put his strong arm around her, giving her the comfort she so desperately needed.

"What can I do?"

She shook her head, wanting to stay in this moment instead of heading back to LA. "Nothing."

Matteo was a man, a doctor, who was used to being able to solve problems. But this was a problem only she could solve, along with her team of attorneys and CPAs. She stood up, as did he, and she accepted his hug for a few minutes before she stepped away.

"I…" she began, and stopped. Then started again. "I can't—" she pointed to him "—be…" She stopped again, and then she shook her head, with what she knew was a sorrowful expression. "I have to go. I'm sorry. I am."

Danica raced to the bedroom, stripped off the pajama top and quickly dressed. She ran out of the bedroom, looked at Matteo, before she pivoted, returned for the pajama top that still smelled like him, and asked, "Can I take this with me?"

Until that moment, until that question, Danica could see Matteo drawing back from her. Her life was a mess, but the times with him were small pockets of joy and she didn't want this *entanglement* with Grant, a man who she now understood had an axe to grind with her, to ruin her relationship with Matteo. Their relationship was pure and lovely and uncomplicated and other than her sisters, Matteo was the only one she felt that she could trust. That made him invaluable to her.

"Will you come back?" Matteo asked as he enveloped her in one of his amazing hugs.

"Yes," she said. "I'm only packing a carry-on. Grant is still living in my house, and we have yet to agree to the terms on that property.

"I have to go," she said, fighting back tears. "I will miss you."

Matteo took her face in his hands and stared into her eyes with nothing but care and acceptance. "I am only a phone call away. If you need me, call, text, video chat."

"You promise that you're okay to drive?" Matteo asked. "I can drive you to Bozeman if you'd like."

"Thank you, Matteo, You are such a thoughtful man. My CPA is sending me a driver."

He helped her into her thick coat and scarf before she put the strap of her purse over her shoulder.

"Until next time," she said, accepting one last sweet kiss from her charming doctor.

"Let me know that you've arrived safely," Matteo said.

"I will," she promised before she backed out of his drive, then she stopped, remembering something important.

She rolled down the driver's window, and called out to him, "Give Lu Lu kisses for me! And please send videos!"

That was the moment when Matteo appeared to be his normal self. Whatever subject he wanted to raise had seemed to disappear when she needed comfort. And once she mentioned Lu Lu, his smile returned to his face.

"I will," he promised, standing in his driveway until she could no longer see him in the rearview mirror.

Even though she hadn't been able to put voice to it, she did feel genuine love for Matteo. It was too soon to know how things would pan out between them, but that didn't take away the feeling she had for him in her very bruised and trampled heart.

"As soon as humanly possible, I will be back." She said aloud to herself the words she hadn't been able to say to him. "And next time, I hope to have excised Grant from my house, my business, my mind *and* my heart. I deserve that. And so does Matteo."

"HI, MY HANDSOME boy!" Journey said when Oakley answered her video call.

"Hi, Mom." Oakley grinned at her. "Three more days!"

"I can't wait. I miss you too much."

"I miss you!"

"Do you know what you want to do when you get here?"

Oakley jumped out of his chair and hopped up and down in excitement. "I want to ride a horse!"

"No," she said quickly and emphatically.

"Hi, sweetie." Her mom came into view. "How's the book coming along?"

"Okay. At least I've got some words on the page."

"That's awesome! I'm proud of you."

"Thanks, Mom," she said. "What's up with Oakley's idea to ride a horse?"

"Well, I made an error," her mom said with a guilty look on her face. "I might have mentioned Cody Ty's name."

"He's incredible, Mom," Oakley said, squeezing in between her grandmother and the iPad. "I've watched almost all of his videos!"

Journey didn't know quite what to say. She was happy that Oakley was still excited to come to Montana, but the idea of him wanting to ride a horse because of Cody Ty made her ill.

"G-Ma! Can I go play video games next door with Misty?"

"You've finished your schoolwork, so yes."

"Bye, Mom!" Oakley said with his endless well of energy.

"I'll see you soon!"

"Okay!" he yelled out of the frame.

"I love you!" she called out just before she heard the front door slam.

"Mom—" she dropped her head into her hands "—I don't want him on a horse."

"Look," her mother said, "I'm sorry that I mentioned Cody Ty and now he's Oakley's hero. But I don't think it's a good idea to make him afraid of horses because you had a traumatic event."

Journey breathed in through her nose and then blew it out slowly from her mouth. "I suppose you have a point…"

"I know you want to put him into a hermetically sealed bubble. But you can't. He's got to navigate this world just like anybody else."

"I suppose."

"He'll be fine, sweetie. And I could think of tons of people he could look up to that we'd disapprove of. From what I've seen of Cody Ty, he promotes the value of hard work, perseverance and family."

"He's not a saint," Journey said, now having mixed feelings about the champion cowboy.

Her mother had a keen eye and asked, "So no longer your muse?"

"Well, I wouldn't go that far."

"How far would you go? Is this still a safe place for Oakley?"

"Yes, of course it is," she said quickly, "and spending time with Cody has helped me break through my writer's block for now."

"So what's the problem?"

She shrugged, wishing she hadn't even given her mom an inkling of her feelings for, and about, Cody.

"He can be…" She paused, and then said, "Abrupt."

"Okay."

"And bossy."

Her mom raised an eyebrow at her, and no words were needed.

"And he's always pushing me to get my hands dirty, get a full picture of ranch life, etc., etc.!"

"He sounds like a good man who's trying to help you out."

"How can I be losing this contest with a man you've never even met!"

"I didn't raise you to be a snowflake, Journey."

"How do you even know that term?"

"I know things," her mom said with a wink. "Now get back on that book."

"I will. I am. But…"

"But what?"

"I think it sounds stupid."

"Journey?!" her mom exclaimed. "Why would you even think that?"

Journey didn't want to admit that the reader reviews had been so harsh. Her first book felt like the best she could have written; she wanted her characters to feel as if they could be the reader's best friend, or sister, or mother.

"I just have lost my confidence, I suppose."

"No," her mother said. "No, ma'am. I know exactly what is getting into your head and you need to put those reviews in the trash where they belong. Your editor loved your first book, so much that she's willing to buy another!"

Journey nodded, and she knew that her mother had a point, but the reviews were stuck in her mind, and it was difficult to eject them from her brain.

"Don't let people live in your mind rent-free, Journey." Her mother added, "This is your chance to live your dream and write for Harlequin. If you give the power to these unknown people, who may have motives for rating your first book so low that have nothing to do with the quality of your book and everything to do with their own jealousy, they win and you lose!"

After a moment of reflecting on her mother's words, she looked up, nodded her agreement, and said, "You're right, Mom."

That made her mother laugh. "Boy, would I love to have pushed Record on this conversation!"

"I'll never admit to it, Mom. I'll take this conversation to the grave."

"Well," her mother said with the unconditional love she had always given to her and to Oakley, "just as long as you take it to your heart first."

CHAPTER TEN

"WHERE ARE YOUR steel-toed boots?" Cody asked her in that razor-sharp tone that he used all of the time.

"Still at the store, I suppose," she replied, chin up, hands resting on her hips, and looking him right in the eye.

Her stance only served to tickle him, not annoy him, and Cody surprised her, as he often did, when he said, "Come on, then. I'll take you to Bozeman."

Now frozen in her spot, she couldn't quite figure her next move. Yes, he was bossy, annoying, frustrating, but he was a nice man underneath his gruff way of being in the world. She did have him at a disadvantage because she knew more about him from researching him online than he most likely would ever know about her.

He waved at her to follow him, and she decided to accept the ride. Steel-toed boots weren't a regular fashion need in her wardrobe. Also, whenever she spent time with Cody, no matter how prickly he could be, she was given insight into her cowboy character. That was invaluable to her.

Cody walked with a slight limp and his legs were more bowed than she'd ever seen. You could imagine a life in the saddle for a man with that bow at the knee. His eyes crinkled deeply when he thought something was funny, and his bushy handle-bar mustache, a relic of the past, seemed to suit him particularly well. He was brutally honest, up early, to bed late, and he had a connection with the animals in his care that she had never witnessed before. She had tried to piece together a whole picture of Cody with the man she was getting to know now with the man she had researched online. But Cody was still a mystery that kept her intrigued and coming back for more.

"This is an impressive truck." She climbed up into the passenger seat.

"Thank you kindly."

His truck was a forest-green GMC Sierra 3500 Duramax Diesel V8; the inside was luxury from the stitching to the power seats that offered a massage. Cody Ty seemed to her to have few worldly desires and he certainly didn't match the glitz and glamour country celebrity he had apparently been in his younger years. He was humble in that way, but when it came to creature comforts, that's where the money was spent. His decked-out travel trailer was impressive from the outside and if it had any upgrades similar to the truck that hauled it from place to place, it had to be impressive on the inside.

"Are you sure you have the time to take me?"

"I've got all the time in the world if I say it's so," Cody said. "I don't punch a time clock. Never have—if God blesses me, I never will.

"How's the book coming?" he asked.

She breathed in and said on a sigh, "I started, so that's an improvement."

"Have I been helpful?"

Journey glanced over at him, wondering how honest she needed to be.

Then he chuckled at her silent thought process, and he added, "Besides the fact that I'm a pain in your hind parts."

"You are," she said, "a pain in the hind parts. In more ways than one."

He went straight from a chuckle to full laugh. "I knew you had it in you."

"Had what?"

"Fight, gumption, whatever you want to call it." He clarified,

"A cowboy—or cowgirl—can't make it in life if they don't have it. Make sure your characters have it."

"I will."

They rode in silence for a mile or two, listening to a country music station that she wouldn't have listened to on her own, but she discovered that she liked it, and she said as much to Cody.

"It's good music. I was raised on it," he said, "but I like symphonies and operas the most."

Now she was actually staring at his profile.

He glanced over at her with a smile, and said, "Doesn't fit the image?"

"No," she agreed, "but it makes you even more interesting."

"Happy to help."

And she could tell that he meant it. The more depth she could find with Cody, the more round, balanced and believable her character could be.

"My son, Oakley, he's coming out with my mom next week."

"That's real nice."

She hesitated and then added, "You are his latest idol."

Cody Ty considered this information and looked at her with an expression she hadn't seen before. He was pleased.

"Well, how 'bout that?"

"He's watched all of your videos."

"Well, that's real nice," the cowboy said. "I look forward to meeting him."

"He wants to ride."

"And that doesn't sit well with you."

"No," she acknowledged, "but my mom doesn't want me to put my trauma on him."

"She's got a point."

"Yes, she does," she said, "but that doesn't mean that I want him to climb on the back of an animal, while admittedly beautiful and magical and graceful, that runs first and asks questions later."

He listened without much response, until she asked, "Why do you love them so much? Maybe hearing it from you would help me understand my son better."

"Horses gave me my career and a purpose. So many people say they love these animals, who are, from my view, one of the most beautiful creatures made by our God in heaven, but they fear them. And because they fear them, they handle them roughly or cruelly. They'll speak to you if someone is patient enough to listen."

Journey wanted to believe Cody; she wanted to understand the draw the animals had because now her son seemed to have the same pull to these animals. But she hadn't lost her fear, even though she did feel less fearful than when she started working with Cody in the barn. And this turn in her thinking to her own son made her curious about Cody's childhood. From what she picked up online, it wasn't an easy one.

"You grew up in Alabama?"

"True."

"Is that when you developed this love for horses?"

"I didn't develop much love for anything back then. Alabama was poor in general, but my family was dirt poor. I worked when I was a kid for peanuts. Scorching hot and dry as a dust bowl during the summer, and all I knew is that I wanted out. I didn't have much use for school, and my mom, raising a pack of kids while working a couple of jobs, didn't mind me working instead of learning."

The minute Cody began to tell her about his past, all of those tidbits she had learned seemed woefully bland or full of too many holes.

"It sounds like a hard upbringing."

"I 'spect so, but it made me who I am today. I understand the meaning of hard work. Watching my mother struggle, while my dad spent too much money on booze, and going without meals or missing school so many days that you could never catch up," he said. "That has kept me humble, no matter how famous I got. No matter how many years go by, I'm still that kid who had one pair of pants that my granny sewed material onto the ends of while I grew. My shoes had holes in them, but I was grateful to have them."

Journey turned her body toward Cody. "So when did horses come in?"

"Well," the cowboy said, "I loved Clint Eastwood, and so did my daddy. My brother and I used to sneak into the movie theater and watch him on the screen. Bigger than life, in the saddle more than he walked on the ground. That was what I wanted to be. A cowboy. Just like John Wayne."

"And now my son wants to be a cowboy, just like you."

Cody parked in the lot outside of a country-western store; he shut off the engine and looked her over with a keen expression in his eyes. "You remember the wisdom of Willie Nelson?"

"Yes, I do know. But the way Oakley is talking, I may not have much of a choice."

He winked at her with a smile. "Let's go get you some real cowgirl boots."

DANICA HAD BEEN in LA for a couple of days; she had opted to take a suite at a hotel; Grant still lived in her house, and even though the early agreement between them barred him from moving Fallon in, her ex's desire to move his now-fiancée into the house and set up a baby room in one of the guest rooms was common knowledge. As much as she loved that house, she could not, would not, live beneath the same roof as Grant.

After a long day of negotiations, Danica could not stomach any of the offers proposed by the other side.

"This is my home!" she said to Ray and Charlie on a video call. "I built it. Every single tile, every single fixture, every window, stone, door handle, came from my brain! All he did was show up later and now he wants it for Fallon? I can't." She tried to locate a clean tissue. She had been crying so much that she had already run through one box.

"I'm sorry," Charlie said.

"We are." Ray nodded.

"But once the emotions settle, what is the best path forward for you?"

Danica blew her nose loudly. "I don't know. I'm still shocked that I could lose my home and my business."

"Okay, don't kill me for asking this," Charlie said. "Is there a possibility that you could work with Grant?"

Danica looked horrified and then furious as she shouted, "No! No! *No!* I will not work with that womanizing coward." She pointed to her chest. "I'm the one who started the business. He was just another pretty face that I hired."

She yanked another Kleenex from the box. "How could this be? How could I lose everything I worked so hard to build? I've lost friends…"

"Not actual friends," Ray interjected.

"Okay, yes, you're right. But those were close contacts that greased the wheels of my business. And now they are raving over Fallon's perfect little baby bump?"

There wasn't much her sisters could say in general, and nothing they could say to make it better. Nothing would ever make this better; it was a wound that would leave an emotional scar and that would last a lifetime. She would never forget this for as long as she lived.

"I need to stop crying," she said through her tears, "pick myself up by my bootstraps and figure out what to do next."

"We're here for you, Danny. We're always in your corner."

"Thank you," Danica said. "I'll call you guys later."

When she hung up, she rolled into the bed, covered her head with the comforter and tried to put the horrible news of the day out of her mind. When she heard the ringtone she had programmed in her phone just for Matteo, she reached her arm out from under the comforter, grabbed it and brought it into her cave.

"Hello?"

"Hi." The deep timbre of Matteo's voice washed her body with a feeling similar to sinking down into a hot tub.

"Hi."

"How are you?"

She sounded stuffy like she had come down with a bad cold. "Terrible."

"Tell me what's wrong, Danica."

And so she did, every last horrible thing. Her business, her contacts, her home, were all on the line. And it was inconceivable to her that she, the victim, was ending up on the losing side.

"I need to see you," Matteo said. "I'm going to switch to video. Pick up."

This was a new level of intimacy for her with anyone other than Grant and her sisters. She had worked for decades to cultivate and curate a very polished image of Danica Brand, business owner, Realtor to the rich and famous, "it" woman. Flawless makeup, age lines erased with any and every trick in her plastic surgeon's toolkit. And she had been fighting and winning the race against the clock; many women who had youth on their side had not been able to beat her. Had it been increasingly difficult to stay at the top? Yes, it had. But she had still been able to hold onto that crown she had fought to earn.

A few moments later, Matteo video-called and when she answered, she was greeted by an enthusiastic oink from Lu Lu.

"Oh, Lu Lu!" Danica forgot about her appearance and just focused on her adorable friend, Princess Lu Lu. "I miss you."

"She misses you," Matteo said, "and I miss you."

Danica caught her picture in the small square; her eyes were swollen and red, her waterproof mascara had run and looked like she tried to imitate Cleopatra. Her hair had been pulled up into a clip, but most had escaped while she was hiding under the covers, so she looked like she had porcupine quills.

"How can I help?" Matteo asked her.

"I don't think anyone can help, really," she said, downtrodden. "I either accept working with Grant for the rest of my career and split the house in two and live with him while he raises his baby. The baby *we* were going to have together..."

"That wouldn't be healthy for anyone."

"Or, I can just hand him the key to the castle and the business! How is any of that remotely fair?"

Danica reached out from under the comforter again, searching for that box of Kleenex. She blew her nose without any concern about how it sounded; Matteo had already seen behind the curtain. This was her as a hot mess.

"I need you to sit up and get yourself into a shower," he said with a layer of authority in his tone.

"Are those doctor's orders?" She couldn't believe she had it in her to actually flirt with Dr. Dashingly Handsome.

"Yes."

She frowned at him, thought it over, and then threw the comforter off of her body and pushed herself upright.

"Listen to me, Danica," Matteo said, "you are the strongest woman I have ever met."

"I thought you were going to say beautiful."

"That goes without saying."

"Well," she said, moving her hand in a circle around her puffy face, "if you think this is attractive, you must truly love me."

"I do," he said without a moment of pause. "Love you. And I need you to get out of bed and rinse yourself off. You're too good for this, *mi amor*, and you're a damn sight too good for this Grant guy."

"Mi amor," she repeated the sentiment. "I like that."

"Well, we like you," he answered. "I'll call you later."

Danica hung up with Matteo and actually felt better. So she did get out of bed and she did get into the shower. And afterward, things didn't look so grim. She had her sisters' love and support and she had Matteo and Lu Lu's love and support. With their help, she could find a way to step back into the light after coming through a dark tunnel.

With her hair in a towel, wearing a thick white hotel robe, Danica ordered a healthy meal and then watched back episodes of *Star Trek: Discovery*. And she was just getting ready to watch season three when Matteo video-called back as he said he would.

"What are you doing?" he asked, "besides being gorgeous."

She smiled shyly; her face completely devoid of any makeup under bright lights made her feel almost more naked than when she was actually naked with him in low light. She turned the camera around so he could see what she was watching.

"Are you serious right now?" he asked her.

"What?"

"You're a Trekkie?"

Danica nodded.

"How did I not know this about you?" Matteo seemed rather shocked.

"Well, we haven't known each other long enough to know so much."

"You should have started with this first." He held up his hand in the Spock salutation.

She held up her hand also and said, "Live long and prosper."

"Lu Lu loves *Star Trek* too. All of them except for *Star Trek: Enterprise*. She thinks it's super chauvinistic."

"And gives real pigs a bad name." She laughed. "It's hard to believe that it was made on 2001. There is some truly cringe-worthy dialogue."

"Agreed."

Danica, Matteo and Lu Lu watched the entire season three of *Discovery* and when she was unable to keep her eyes open, and Lu Lu's rhythmic snoring lulled her to sleep, Matteo ended the call and she groggily turned off the TV and then fell into a deep, restful sleep and didn't open her eyes again until her alarm went off at five in the morning.

As she got ready to hit the gym, she thought to send Matteo a good morning text, knowing that he would already be awake to exercise as well.

"Good morning, Matteo," she wrote, and then added an emoji blowing him a kiss.

"Good morning, *mi amor*," he texted right back.

Danica left her hotel room feeling upbeat, grateful that she had met Matteo. No matter what happened in the future, she would never forget his support and kindness during this most difficult time in her life.

JOURNEY WAS WALKING beside her cowboy muse in the town of Bozeman, and at first, she didn't really notice anything differ-ent. But then people were pointing at Cody, taking pictures and videos of him. Cody took it in stride, nodding his head, waving a bit, while he kept on moving along.

"Man, you're amazing." One man walked right up to Cody, shook his hand and then asked for a selfie.

And then it was just a *thing* that happened. Kids, parents, *grand*parents, saw Cody, recognized Cody, and then wanted attention from him.

"Sorry 'bout this," he said sincerely. "I was a pretty big deal here in Bozeman at one time."

"It looks like you're still a big deal here."

Journey stood back and watched Cody with his public. They were dedicated to him; generations of family members knew him, respected him and wanted to thank him for the years of entertainment. Then she noticed that some of his fans just happened to have Cody Ty hats on and T-shirts with his face or a scene when he was riding a bull. She knew that Cody had been popular back in the day and she supposed she thought of him as sort of washed up; she couldn't have been more wrong if she put some effort into it.

After he had given the group of fans autographs on their shirts or hats, took a bunch of selfies and said his catchphrase, new to her, into the videos, "Cody Ty wild," he put his arm around her shoulders so he could move both of them forward from the crowd.

"Does that happen everywhere you go?"

"Nah." He took his arm away. "Some places more than others."

"When's the last time you rodeoed? Is that even a word? Rodeoed?"

He chuckled and smiled at her. "It is a word and it's been too many years to count."

"And still." Journey couldn't help it, seeing all of his fans dedicated to Cody years after the peak of his career, that was something special. This man had something special and maybe that "it" factor that a person either had or didn't have, Cody Ty had in spades. And now her laser focus on Cody as her muse made all of the sense in the world.

"Here we are." Cody opened the door for her. "We can find you boots here for when you're working with the horses, and they step on your foot, and they will step on your foot because it's gonna take a minute or two for you to know how to not get your foot stepped on."

"You just said a whole lot of words without making a whole lot of sense."

He laughed, a nice, robust laugh, as he followed her inside the store.

"Cody Ty Hawkins!" The owner of the shop spotted him, rounded the counter and stuck his hand out for Cody to shake. "Welcome!"

Cody posed for yet another picture and then said to the owner, "My friend needs a pair of steel-toed boots."

"I am tickled, truly tickled that you have brought her to us," the owner said, beaming with what Journey could only describe in her head as a fanboy moment.

The owner of the store left them in the hands of a salesperson who didn't know Cody, which was nice because she wasn't trying to take pictures that would capture her trying on boots. She had always had giant feet and it took a while for her legs to catch up with those feet; she was teased mercilessly in junior high school. And when she got her first catalog spread in the local newspaper, instead of making her "cool," the teasing only got worse. So she was sensitive and didn't want her feet spread all over social media as the backdrop for a pic of Cody.

"How do you deal with this?" she asked, pushing her foot into a boot.

"Oh, I don't mind it, really," Cody said, sizing up the boots she had on. "My fans are dedicated to me, and I'm dedicated to them. When I was down on my luck, and there's been a few occasions of that, they've done what they could to lift me up and not tear me to pieces.

"How do those feel?" he asked, watching her walk.

Journey stood in the boots, kicked the heels, pushed her foot forward in the toe of the boots. "Pretty good, actually. I can definitely feel that there isn't any give in the toe of the boot, but I think it works."

"Good."

"I still don't think I need them because I'm not going to be close enough to a horse for it to squish my toe."

"Humor me."

"Okay," she said, "I'll humor you."

"Thank you." Cody stood up, got a bit creaky halfway up, put his hand on his knee and then pushed through what looked like a flash of pain on his face.

There was a moment when no one was trying to take a video or a picture; no one was asking him to say his catchphrase. And Journey was glad for the reprieve. She had a short-lived career in modeling and had landed some big campaigns before she got pregnant. But she had certainly not achieved notoriety in that profession. Seeing Cody's fans, it was both annoying and impressive all in one bundle.

"Cody Ty!" the owner said, coming through the front door of the store with a chubby woman with an amazed look on her face and her hand over her mouth as if she was rendered speechless.

"This is my wife, Mary. She's your biggest fan," the owner said. "I'd really appreciate it if you'd let us get a picture with you."

Cody agreed and took the picture while she paid for her boots. The salesperson handed her the receipt and the bag. The salesperson leaned forward and asked, "Who is that guy, anyway?"

"That's *the* Cody Ty Hawkins," she said with an unexpected defensiveness in her voice. "Rodeo royalty."

CHAPTER ELEVEN

DANICA AWAKENED FEELING a mixture of emotions. She had a meeting with her team of attorneys; she was a wealthy woman, yes, but there were limits. Having this many attorneys on retainer, sending a bill every month for a file review, needed to stop.

"Good morning," she said to the new receptionist, Brindle Huckabee, when she walked through the door of her business for the first time since the day she left for Big Sky.

"Good morning, Ms. Brand!" Brindle jumped up, closed the gap between them, grabbed her lightweight coat and her floral motif blue-and-white Prada bag.

"I'll keep my bag," Danica said, rather curtly. It felt odd to be back. It had been a relatively short time away but this, somehow, no longer felt like her home away from home. It was seventy degrees and it felt too hot!

"Any messages?" she asked Brindle.

"No, ma'am." The earnest young woman, seemingly starstruck, was shaking with excitement or fear and maybe she needed the restroom. Either way, Danica put her out of her misery.

"That will be all," she said to Brindle, and then walked the long hallway to her expansive office.

On her way back, she stopped by the room, a shared space, meant for the junior Realtors.

"Oh! Ms. Brand," Leena exclaimed, flew out of her chair, and flung herself at her. "I've been so worried!"

After Danica extracted her body from Leena, she said, "I'd like to meet with you in my office in ten minutes."

"Yes, ma'am, of course."

Now that she was in town, through their lawyers, Grant and Danica had come up with a schedule at the office until they could decide on a course of action. Today was her day and she fully intended to make the most of it.

"Brindle!"

"Yes?" The young woman popped her head in her office door.

"Do we have some sort of disinfectant wipe?"

Brindle nodded. "Yes, we do."

The office manager was back in a flash and tried to wipe down the desk for her; Danica thanked her and then did the deed herself. Nothing in the office looked disturbed, but she knew every centimeter of her office. Every knickknack, every picture, every pen, she knew the placement. And she knew that Grant had been using her office while she was away. And Fallon and he might have been doing dirty things on her desk and the thought made her nauseous. She wasn't a germaphobe really, but some things were a bridge too far.

Leena knocked on the doorframe to her office and Danica waved her in. After she had disinfected her desk, her chair, and any other surface that may have been used by Grant and his new fiancée, Danica sat down at her desk chair, annoyed that she had to adjust the settings to fit her needs, and then asked, "Fill me in."

And Leena did.

"I've had three open houses this week," Leena told her.

"Good," Danica said. "Are you feeling more confident?"

"Yes, I am."

"Glad to hear it. What else?"

There was a pregnant pause before Leena asked, "Can I speak candidly?"

"Of course."

"I don't like working for Grant."

Danica sat forward and listened.

"He's really harsh in his critiques of my job."

She raised her eyebrows, letting Leena know that she was listening.

"And he lets Fallon boss me around."

Danica had never felt firsthand the meaning behind the phrase "hot under the collar." But she did now. She did her very best to hide her frustration and focus on the work. Leena was going to make an excellent Realtor; she had the look, the brains and the enthusiasm for the job. And Danica wanted to make sure that Leena had the best chance, the well-deserved chance, to transition from a Realtor in training to a full-blown Realtor.

"Do you think you'll come back?" Leena asked her. But the honest truth that she shared with Leena was, *I don't know.*

After her meeting with Leena and touching base with the other Realtor in training, Aditya, who was rather cold and distant, which signaled to her that Aditya had hitched his wagon to Grant's fading star, she began to answer messages that had been neglected while she separated herself from reality in California. The Montana time in her life was bizarre to her and would be for those who knew her in the California setting. Would they recognize the pig-loving, salsa-learning, throw-caution-to-the-wind and canoodling-with-the-most-eligible-bachelor-in-Big-Sky-and-beyond woman?

No, they wouldn't. She was known as the ice queen in her Realtor circles; not only for her ice-blond signature hair, but because she never cracked during negotiations, and she always picked closing the deal over building potential friendships. Danica wasn't proud of that label anymore. She had been until she had time to reflect in a setting polar opposite to LA. Watching so many of her contacts align their loyalties with Grant was a slap in the face. And it occurred to her that perhaps pouring her entire self into her career and chasing that epic closing that kept on propelling her to the top of the LA heap was misguided.

Everyone had left for the day, and she was alone in the empty office that she had built from a one-room business to an empire that was housed in one of the most prestigious office buildings in LA. That meant she had arrived.

She was standing in her office, looking out of the floor-to-ceiling windows, feeling melancholy. She had brought a box with her; just a plain moving box that would be used to take her most valued personal items with her. Even this had been agreed upon by arbitration.

Her phone rang while she was catching tears with a Kleenex under her lower eyelashes.

"There she is!" It was Matteo. God bless his excellent timing.

"Hi."

"What are you doing?"

"Just wrapping up some loose ends at work." She leaned back against her massive desk.

"Any news?"

"No," she said, "not yet."

"Okay," he sounded in a hurry. "I'll call you later."

"Please do," she said, feeling a calm wash over her just by hearing his voice.

He had become important to her and being in LA had made the depth of her feelings easier to understand.

After she hung up with Matteo, she carefully wrapped the awards that had come down off the wall. She took Swarovski crystal animals out of the curio cabinet, something she had been collecting since her midtwenties. And besides that, everything else could stay. It was difficult to see her life distilled down to one cardboard box. But like it or not, this was her new reality until she came to terms with Grant. When she had retreated to Montana to get her head screwed on straight, the idea of *not* going back to her business and her estate had seemed so implausible that she hadn't even considered it.

With her box in her arms, she waited for the elevator to arrive and then pushed the button to the main floor. Her head was lowered, and she was feeling very blue, but when the door slid open, she put on her social mask and walked out of that elevator like a woman on top of the world. Then she saw Dr. Matteo Katz-Cortez standing in the lobby, awaiting her arrival, holding a bouquet of red roses.

And that made her mask crumble as they walked toward each other to meet somewhere in the middle. He took her into his arms, strong, muscular arms that made her feel safe and protected, something she hadn't imagined she needed since she was a little girl in her father's safe arms. But right now, in this moment, she did need that comfort and Matteo gave it to her without question.

"I can't believe you're here!" Danica held the red roses, breathing in their sweet scent.

Matteo picked up the box of her belongings and walked beside her, past the lobby desk and into the revolving door and the light of a sunny California day.

"Do you have a car?" she asked.

"No." He smiled at her. "I could use a lift."

MATTEO DIDN'T TAKE leaving Big Sky to show support to Danica lightly—not even when he knew that his partner, Dr. Brown, who typically covered the Bozeman area, could see his patients. This was something he hadn't done since he helped his ex-fiancée and her daughter move out of his house. He didn't think anything else could be more important than his track record; at that time, he hadn't known Danica was going to come into his life and turn things on its head.

"I took a room in the hotel," Matteo told her in the hotel elevator.

"No."

"No?"

"Yes. No," she repeated, "I'd like you to stay with me. I've taken the penthouse."

"I didn't want to assume."

"I understand, thank you," Danica said, "but you came all this way to be with me."

He had.

"So, be with me."

"Okay."

Matteo got off at his floor to gather up his belongings and then rode the elevator up to the penthouse, used the spare key and walked into luxury that was not his norm. He was comfortable financially, but he wasn't so wealthy that taking this penthouse would be a regular occasion. Seeing this penthouse helped him understand Danica outside of Montana.

"Hello, *bonita*." He put his arms around her, called her pretty in Spanish and kissed the side of her neck. She put her hands on his hands and leaned back on his body. This was more than just a body movement for her; she was leaning on him both physically as well as figuratively. And he felt honored to have gained Danica's trust.

She turned in his arms, arms that had ached for her after only a few days apart, and he saw her lovely face bathed in the sunlight, her ice-blond hair recently trimmed and tucked behind her ears. Large glinting diamond studs adorned her ears and a collar of diamonds hung around her slender neck. Her makeup was flawless and so too was her suit, which appeared to have been made for her, it fit so perfectly. Montana Danica was more relaxed, comfortable, with less makeup and no flashy jewelry. LA Danica was different, quite a bit different. But Matteo believed that his Danica, Montana Danica, was a truer version of herself.

"Thank you." She looked up at him with her large blue eyes. "It must have been so difficult for you to get away on short notice."

"It was a challenge, but one that I believe was worth it," he said, running his hand over her silky hair. "I hope you are happy that I'm here. This could have given off a weird vibe showing up unannounced."

"No." She put her hand on his chest. "You showing up here when I was feeling so alone was exactly what I needed."

Grateful to hear that his big, romantic gesture was received in the manner it had been offered, he leaned down and kissed her, drawing her closer into his orbit.

"Mmm," she murmured against his lips, "I've missed these lips."

"They have missed you."

Danica took his hand and led him to the main bedroom and closed the double doors to block out LA. They stripped out of their clothing, met in the middle of the bed, and their bodies naturally intertwined, lips upon lips, hands exploring, until their union created one body, one soul, one mind. Making love with Danica had been something he didn't even know was absent in his world. Of course, he had made love since his breakup, but it wasn't as frequent as folks outside looking in would think. Lu Lu was frequently his late-night date after all of the first dates ended without a connection. It was notable that so many women wanted to move fast with him; first date, then hop into bed and then get engaged, and now he wanted to move fast with Danica. However, seeing her on her own turf, seeing her dressed in her armor, threw ice-cold water over him. In spite of his drive to lock her down and commit, he could see her devastation, live and in person, and he knew, down to the core of his being, that Danica didn't need any more pressure on her, especially from a man she counted on as a safe, uncomplicated space.

After they made love, they showered and donned the plush bathrobes, and ordered room service. They feasted on relatively healthy food, with a promise to hit the gym before the crack of dawn the next day.

"I'm stuffed." Danica flopped backward on the bed.

"Stuffed. Yes."

She rolled over, propped herself up onto her elbow and smiled at him with what he was sure was love, and kissed him on the lips.

"Gosh darn it, Matteo, you are so handsome."

He reached up to put her hair behind her ear. "Gosh darn it, Danica, you are so beautiful."

They went out onto the terrace with a glass of wine and kissed with the bustling cityscape in the background as dusk gave way to night.

"I do have a present for you," he said, kissing her neck, feeling the need to make love to her again.

"A present?" she asked, and that's when he saw the tiniest of slivers of the kid in her.

He laughed, put down his empty wineglass and walked over to his carry-on bag. She followed him, curious. He pulled out a wrapped present and handed it to her.

"I saw this, and I couldn't pass it by."

Excitedly, she started unwrapping the small box.

"It's not an engagement ring," he added, "just in case you were worried."

"I wasn't."

Matteo waited patiently for her to slowly unwrap the present, put the bow on the table, along with the ribbon, and then the paper was methodically removed, folded and put next to the bow and ribbon. *Finally*, she opened the box, stared at its contents, while a smile began with her lips, broadened and then reached her eyes.

"What a perfect gift," she said, emotionally, while she carefully took the crystal animal out of the protective foam.

"It's Lu Lu!" Danica said. "I only told you about my collection one time."

"I only need one time."

Danica admired the chubby crystal pig with a metal curlicue tail and black eyes.

"Thank you," she said, "for the gift, of course, but also for *seeing* me."

JOURNEY HAD DEVELOPED a routine of helping Cody in the barns—there were other cowboys available to handle the mundane chores of cleaning buckets, mucking, turning over stalls with fresh bedding and refilling hay bins—but he still wanted to keep his hands in the pie and, as far as she could see, he didn't shy away from those chores. In fact, now that she knew him better, Cody kept himself humble and grateful by doing the jobs typically handled by the cowboy, or cowgirl, last in line to eat at the trough.

"I just figured out something." She leaned on her pitchfork, an implement she had recently developed a relationship with.

"Oh yeah?" Cody hoisted a new bale of hay into a cart. "What's that?"

"You've been desensitizing me."

Cody stood upright, sweat on his brow, and asked her, "How do you figure?"

"This entire time, I've been under the impression that you wanted me to experience true ranch life, so I can taste it and smell it and feel it."

"Sounds about right."

"But," she said as if she was about to solve a mystery, "you've

been getting me to work around the horses, so I could feel relaxed around them."

Cody chuckled, and she loved to hear that rare sound from
a man she had grown to both like and respect. So much so that
she was tempted to buy some Cody Ty swag and get him to
sign it for Oakley.

"Did I get it right?" she asked.

He looked up at her, head cocked to the side, looking a
smidge guilty.

"I did get it right!"

"Did it work?"

Journey sat down in a nearby chair, looked at the sweet-faced
mare across the aisle, and realized that she *could be* calm around
a horse. This was a huge leap for her, and she couldn't believe
Cody had masterfully gotten her to this point while distracting
her by giving her grunt work in the barn.

"Yes." She smiled at him. "It did, actually."

He smiled with a nod. "Well, that's all right."

Cody sat down in another chair, slumped down a bit, legs
out in front of him, his ankles crossed. Completely comfortable in his own skin.

"Can I ask you something?"

"You can ask, but that don't mean I'm gonna answer."

She smiled, knowing that about him already. "How old are
you?"

He looked down at his crossed hands resting on his flat stomach before he lifted his head just enough to see her, she sus-
pected, without allowing her to see his eyes. "You can't figure
that out on your fancy phone?"

"First, it's a smartphone, not a fancy phone," she said.

"I don't have any use for them."

"Second," she continued, "I have looked you up on my fancy
phone and you have way too many birth dates floating out there.
Why is that?"

He pushed his hat back on his head with his forefinger so
he could look at her. "No one knows, that's the short version."

"And the long version?"

He took off his hat, raked his hand through his salt-and-pepper hair, then put the hat back in place. "The long version? I was born at home, parents couldn't afford a doctor. Mom nearly died while my daddy was out doing only the good Lord above knows what. Time got the best of us sometimes. One hard day would blend into the next hard day. We didn't celebrate our birthdays and Mom had so many youngsters roaming around that she couldn't remember who was who and which was which. My birthday is just a guess. That's all. Just a guess."

"I'm sorry."

"Don't be." Cody's shoulders tensed along with the muscles on his face. "My life has turned out as it was meant to and I don't have one ounce of regret about anything I did or anything that was done to me," he continued, "and with everything my mama had to endure, and every dawn-'til-dusk job she had to work, and every beatdown my pa gave her when he came home drunk, I'm lucky to be alive. I don't much give a damn if anyone knows my real birthdate. Makes no difference to me."

"I've upset you," Journey said. "I'm sorry."

"Don't spend another second worrying about it." Cody stood up. "I've already forgotten it."

"Okay," she said, also standing up. "How old do you *think* you are?"

"Relentless, aren't you?"

She nodded. "When something's important to me, yes."

"My age is important to you?"

Again, she nodded.

"How about this, I'm stove-up and beat down," he said in blunt manner, "and if that don't satisfy you, I'm sure as heck old enough to know better."

CODY DIDN'T WANT to admit it, but Journey had hit a sore spot with all of her questions. He'd been asked before in a multitude of venues, but she was the first to truly get under his skin. He liked Journey, more than he should, actually. She was a big-city girl, still young with her whole life ahead of her. The die had set on his life, and he accepted it. No matter how attracted he was to her, and he was plenty attracted, he had to keep her at a distance. Admire her from afar was his way of thinking about it.

But it was tough. Damn tough. Every day he told himself that he was going to spend less time with the beautiful blonde palomino, but when the next day arrived, he'd end up spending more time, not less. He'd let her lead him down a path, asking him questions about things in his life that he'd long since forgotten. And in those moments, he remembered why he could never be with a woman like Journey. He'd led a reckless life full of fame, fortune, beautiful women, and all of the trappings of success that a boatload of money could buy. But all of that had come with a cost; he was stiff as a board, rickety and crotchety. He'd made a life on his own terms without having to ask anyone for permission.

He'd given up on finding love. And he had made his peace with it. A woman like Journey—lovely, intelligent, educated, a single mother who adored her son and was trying to live her dream of being a successful romance author—was not in his wheelhouse. He admired her and he wanted to help; she was the type of woman not found in country dive bars while moving from one town to the next. And, yes, he had seen some feelings for him in her eyes, but when the balance sheet was completed, Journey Lamar was just too damn good for him.

JOURNEY SAT DOWN at the desk and began typing. At times, the words poured out of her, but more often than not, she ended up with her head in her hands, trying to figure out what needed to be said next.

"Stubborn man," she muttered, walking over to the window to watch Cody working with one of his young horses.

Why did she care two hoots about his age? She could answer that question easily. She liked Cody. She respected him. And he was the first man since her divorce from Oakley's father that she had any interest in whatsoever!

She pinned him somewhere in his late fifties, but he was more alive and vibrant and talented than any of the men in her age range. And she found herself falling for him without any way to resolve their Grand Canyon–sized differences. It wasn't just about age.

"Damn it, Journey, *focus* on the book."

Sitting down at the desk again, Journey did realize that the more time she spent with Cody, the more her hero of the new book resembled the famous cowboy. The way he walked, the way he talked, the clothes that he wore. Her hero was being shaped to resemble Cody because of her own attraction to him. She had a secret, one that she didn't know if she would share with her best friend and mother. Oakley wasn't the only admirer of Cody Ty Hawkins in the family; she had become a total fangirl, too.

CHAPTER TWELVE

MATTEO WAS GOING to be with her over the weekend and Danica felt grateful for his support. She had contacted several of the friends in her corner, which made LA seem less lonely, less isolated. But no matter who the small handful of people standing by her were, she was the one who had to ultimately decide what to do with her entanglements with Grant. Sitting across from Grant for the last several days had been painful. This was to be the father of her children; now she realized that her slow walk to children with Grant had been a gift. As horrible all of this was, and how unfair it seemed, at least they weren't fighting over custody of a child.

"You look beat." Matteo had been working at one of the three desks in the penthouse suite, but he stopped to greet her.

"I am."

"Do you want to talk about it?"

She breathed in deeply and then after a long exhale, she said, "No. Maybe later. Just not now."

"That's okay," he said. "Why don't you sit out on the terrace, and I'll bring you a healthy juice. Crafted just for you by these hands." Matteo managed to make her smile, even in her worn-down, exhausted state, no matter how weakly. She changed her clothing, putting on shorts, a tank top, and a headband to hold her hair away from her face. After some sunscreen on her face, arms, hands, and neck, she slipped on designer sunglasses and leaned back in one of the lounge chairs and shut her eyes. This was exactly what she needed; a sunny day, relaxed clothing, with *Dr. Dangerously Handsome* making her a healthy juice.

Matteo's button-down shirt was left open, showing off his developed pecs and six-pack abs. Eye candy.

"Hope you like it." He handed her a tall glass filled with a green concoction.

While he took off his shirt and took the chair next to her, she tasted a tiny bit first. "Mmm!"

"You like?"

"How do you do this, Matteo? You're so talented!"

"Thank you."

"No, Matteo, thank you," she said, "for being here for me."

"That's what friends are for."

"Well—" she frowned at him "—I hope we're more than friends."

He reached out, took her hand, gave it a gentle squeeze. "We have time to figure that out later."

"Okay," she agreed, "you're right. My mind seems to be scattered, like a one-thousand-piece puzzle thrown into the air with pieces flying everywhere."

"Well," he said, letting the rays of the sun turn his skin a golden brown, "I do have one thing that may help get your head back in the game."

"What's that?"

"Salsa."

"Salsa?"

"Salsa," he confirmed. "I found a club where we can dance. I'd like to get you out of my living room and onto a real dance floor."

"Do you know what?" she asked. "A couple of months ago, you couldn't get me into a club, much less for dancing. But I like the idea."

"Good."

"I don't have anything to wear, I don't think. I brought casual and business."

"Hold that thought." He got up and went back inside. When he returned, he had a bag with him.

"Is this a dress?"

"Open it."

So she did. Inside the bag was a slinky little black dress with an open, plunging back and a tulip skirt meant to create a dramatic flair with the movement of her hips.

"It's gorgeous," she said, not sure that this was her type of dress or not.

"Full disclosure," he said, "I did consult with your sisters."

"It's…" She paused and then said, "Thank you. It's very thoughtful."

"Uh-oh." He frowned. "Not sure I like all of this thanks for being so thoughtful. What's wrong?"

She looked down at the dress in her lap. "Do you mean besides the ten slices of cheesecake I've eaten since I've been here?"

"Wish I'd been here to join you," he said. "I love cheesecake."

"Me too, obviously," she said, shrugging, "but that's not it, really. I'm just not…"

Matteo watched her and waited for her to continue.

"I'm not really the sexy type," she said, feeling rather shy. "Tough businesswoman, check, Realtor to the stars, check, and a decent sister, check, check. But, sexy? No."

Matteo looked at her as if she had just confessed to being an alien from a faraway galaxy.

"Okay, first, you *are* sexy, and two, you can be all those things you just listed. Only now, you can add sexy salsa dancer to the list."

Danica told him that she would at least try on the dress, put on some strappy heels and then decide if salsa dancing was going to be in her immediate future. It was strange how she had compartmentalized her life—sister, Realtor, community leader, businesswoman, globe-trotter. Matteo may have pointed out something important for her; who was she without those rigid frameworks she had erected around herself? And who would she be if one of those narrow definitions went away? Honestly, she just didn't know.

JOURNEY HAD MADE progress on her unexpected quest to get over her fear of horses. That didn't mean she was going to ride one, but being able to lead them, groom them and be in the stall with them to muck seemed like reachable goals. She wanted to show her son that it was never too late to grow and change. And that if she overcame her fears, then he could also conquer his.

"How does that feel, sweet girl?" she asked Rose, an older mare who was petite in stature, calm and gentle.

Cody was standing nearby, working with a colt, while she brushed Rose. And while she brushed the horse, she found herself talking to her. The mare, as she had soon discovered, loved to be spoken to in a soft, gentle manner. And when she was successful in making the mare feel relaxed around her, the mare would lick and chew and then her large brown eyes would droop to half-mast. There was a sense of self-pride that she was able to be near a horse and feel safe, confident and knowledgeable.

"These animals are a reflection of who we are," Cody had told her. "They read energy, they read your heart, and some folks don't like what they see reflected in a horse's eyes."

Journey did her best to keep her toes out of the line the horse would step on should it need to change position or if it was spooked by something.

"These here animals are prey; that's why they have eyes on the side of their heads so they can see predators. If your energy is off, if you approach them with fear, they're gonna think that *you* are a predator, and you'll see the horse get real animated."

Cody had continued, "If a horse is nervous, edgy, worried, that's on you and your energy. Most folks want to blame the horse, but there's a whole lot of idiots out there."

Journey did her best to be a good student, enjoying her time with Rose. She learned how to groom her, pick out her hooves, comb her mane and tail, put the halter on her head, and lead her to and from the stall. And she couldn't deny that this relationship with Rose had changed her for the better; it had also given her writing a sense of authenticity. She now knew how a horse's body moved, why they shook their heads, what to look for when picking out the hooves, and she had become a talented manure mucker. She had to thank Cody for this; he was the one who basically booted her off the porch and into the barn.

"My mom and son are arriving tomorrow," she said, combing Rose's long mane.

"I've heard." Cody smiled at her.

"At least two times from me today." She smiled fondly at him. "Just fair warning, Oakley is going to want to tag along with you. Lately, all he wants to talk about is you."

"I don't mind if your son wants to learn how to be a cowboy. But I won't have you micromanaging the situation. If you don't trust me with your boy, then best not get started in the first place."

She stopped combing and frowned at him. "What makes you think I would micromanage?"

He looked at her and she looked at him and then she said, "Fine, you have a point."

"I know I did," he chuckled.

After she combed Rose's mane free of knots and tangles, she moved on to the tail. She loved brushing that tail, starting at the end and working her way up. She had wanted a girl because she had always been a girlie girl. But she was blessed with a son, and she embraced it with her whole heart. And yet she still longed to comb a little girl's hair, sweep it up into a ponytail or French braid it. Rose was the closest to that experience, and she was grateful for it.

While she was slowly working her way through the tangled tail, she did broach a subject that had been on her mind. If Cody did work with Oakley, she needed to warn him about something many people couldn't seem to overcome.

"I did want to share something with you," she started, still, after ten years, having difficulty talking about it.

"Ears on."

Cody's little quips always made her smile and lightened her mood. "My son, Oakley, was born with a genetic condition."

The cowboy stopped what he was doing and actually gave her his full attention. "Is that right?"

She nodded. "And in a world that puts such a high value on beauty, his condition has made it, at times, unbearably painful."

He was leaning over the top board of the stall, waiting on her to continue, and she truly appreciated him caring enough about her, about her son, to let her get it out on her own timeline.

Instead of spending a whole lot of time explaining it to Cody, Journey scrolled through her pictures of Oakley and selected her favorite one.

"This is Oakley."

She had learned to watch the faces of people who first see a picture of her sweet boy.

"Nice-lookin' boy," Cody said, and she couldn't believe it but she heard the ring of truth in the cowboy's voice. Truth, she believed, had a resonating tone.

"Thank you," she said.

"Now, what's goin' on with him? What's it called?"

"Treacher-Collins," she told him, still looking at her son, who was now, and had always been, her handsome angel.

"And what's that mean?"

"Um, there's varying degrees of facial deformities, from cleft palate, receded chin, ears malformed or missing. Oakley doesn't have a left ear, and is deaf on that side, but we are working to get a prosthetic. Poor kid, he's had so many surgeries already." When she realized he wasn't recoiling like some did, she felt encouraged to tell Cody, "Some do think that he might be challenged intellectually, but that's not the case with most people with TC. He's such a smart boy."

"Well," Cody said, "I'll look forward to meeting him."

Journey had to turn away and press her fingers into the side of her eyes to stop tears of relief at Cody's reaction. His kindness was such a testament to who he was as a man, and it occurred to her that this was the reason he still had so many fans years after his career as a world-renowned rodeo cowboy had ended. Beneath that surly, rough-hewn exterior was a man among men: kind, hardworking, dedicated, with more emotional intelligence than she had ever seen.

She turned back to him. "Thank you."

"What for?"

"For being decent."

"Ain't no reason *not* to be," he said. "And yes, I'm aware of the double negative. But that's how my kinfolk talked and that's how I talk every now and again."

"You allow them to live through you."

He looked at her with what she could only describe as admiration. "You certainly do know how to turn a phrase, Journey."

She smiled, her emotional meter starting at ugly crying to incredibly flattered.

"Now," Cody said in his abrupt manner, "just because your son has some challenges that life's given him, that does not mean you can hover and mother hen while I'm working with him."

"I will watch from an appropriate distance, I promise."

"We'll see about that," Cody said. "You've proven yourself to be a big ol' thorn under the fingernail."

Even though he was basically calling her a pain in the hind parts, when he was coming out of the stall, she met him there and flung herself at him. And instead of rebuffing her, he, as he always seemed to do, accepted the hug, and hugged her real tight, too.

She hadn't been in a man's arms for so long, it felt scary and wonderful and every other emotion in between. He was strong, burly, and the miles he had clocked on the odometer didn't matter. He was handsome—undeniably—but what she had grown to love was his honesty, his character and the heart he brought to every single thing that he did, no matter how big or how small.

"Well—" Cody cleared his throat several times "—work's still got to be done."

And she knew Cody Ty well enough to know that this was his way of saying the hug needed to be over.

"Finish cleaning up this mare," Cody said before he walked with his familiar limp out of the barn.

"Can I confide in you, Rose?"

The mare opened her eyes and used her lips to play with the cuff on her jacket. "I've got a crush on Cody Ty Hawkins. And maybe, just maybe, Cody Ty has a crush on me. Sounds like an epic Harlequin romance in the making."

MATTEO TIED THE straps of the little black salsa dress he had purchased for Danica. He ran his finger down her back to the deep vee right above her compact derriere.

"You were made for this dress." He kissed her bare shoulders. "Turn around and look at yourself in the mirror."

Danica turned around and looked at her reflection. She had never seen herself in this type of dress; she had worn thousands of demure cocktail dresses designed by the top designers in the world. Up-and-coming designers had lobbied to have her wear their designs when she went to New York Fashion Week or to the governor's mansion. As a part of her persona, she was always elegantly dressed and put together to perfection.

She moved her hips one way to make the tulip skirt dance; this was a very clingy material that showed every possible bulge, and she couldn't wear her regular underwear. A thong or nude were her two choices.

Her entire arms were exposed, her neck, most of her legs, the majority of her back. The only thing that she had in her closet that was a close comparison was lingerie.

"Dare I?" she asked herself, not Matteo.

Matteo took her hand, twirled her under his arm, caught her, dipped her and then kissed her passionately before bringing her back up.

"Well?" he asked her. "What does your heart tell you?"

"My heart is telling me to—call my sisters."

Matteo was kissing her neck up to her chin and down to her bare shoulder.

"If you keep doing that, Matteo, we won't be going to any club."

He smiled and stopped his amorous moves. "That is for dessert."

She video-called her sisters. Ray and Charlie were together and when they saw her, they both yelled, "Jennifer Grey, Patrick Swayze, *Dirty Dancing*!"

Then Ray added, "No one puts Danny in a corner!"

"So this is a yes?"

"That's a hell yes!" Charlie said loudly.

"You look frickin' amazing, Danny," Ray said. "Wear it, own it, and have the best darn time you've had in years. You deserve it!"

She hung up and looked at Matteo, who was leaning against the back of a chair, sexy himself in black slacks, a bright blue shirt unbuttoned enough to show off his fabulous pecs, looking at her like she was a snack, jacket thrown casually over his shoulder.

"I believe that's a yes," he said.

"I think so, too."

Matteo crossed to her, took her in his arms and kissed her in a way that really made her waffle between salsa or the bed.

"Let's go." He helped her into her coat. "I want to show you off."

GOING TO THE salsa club was one of the best decisions she had made in her life. There, she was anonymous, out of the public eye but out in public. She had danced for hours, learning new steps, following Matteo's lead. He was not only a doctor, a lawyer, an excellent cook, animal lover; she could add incredible dancer. And again, it only confirmed why he was the most eligible bachelor in the land of movie stars and multimillionaires crammed into a very small radius.

They closed the bar, caught an Uber, and then made love in the shower. Being with Matteo couldn't take away the pain she felt over her unraveling life in LA, but it certainly stopped her from winding down into a pit of despair.

Naked in Matteo's arms, she felt at home, but she couldn't make any decisions about this new relationship when she was still so mired down with the old.

"You're leaving today," she said, running her hand over his chest.

"Yes."

"Thank you for coming."

He kissed her hand and then placed it back over his chest. "I'll miss this."

She nodded and then said, "But I bet you will be happy to see Lu Lu again."

"Well, yes." He smiled. "Of course. I will look forward to a time when both of my girls are under one roof again."

They made love one last time before she helped Matteo pack up his few belongings and then saw him to the lobby.

There, they hugged tightly. "Come home to me soon, my flower."

She truly didn't know what to say, because her life was in free fall. The thought of closing up shop in LA to make a move to Montana wasn't even on her list of possibilities. She could imagine a relationship with Matteo in which they spent time in both places. And the idea of him shuttering his thriving medical practice? She would never want that for him, knowing how much time, sweat and sacrifice he had made to build that practice.

They kissed and then she waited for him to be out of sight before she went back into the hotel and rode the elevator to the penthouse. And, as if on cue, one of her attorneys called.

"There's an offer and I, we, are recommending that you take it."

"Okay." She sat down, put on her reading glasses and opened her email to quickly read over the main content.

"This isn't serious, is it?"

"It is."

"He wants to buy *me* out? And buy the house?"

"He thinks it will be a wonderful place to raise a child."

That knife was stabbed into her gut and twisted. "Yes, I am aware. We were going to raise our children there!"

She was yelling at the man she was paying to give her good, unemotional advice, and she didn't want to hear it. She didn't want to take it. She wanted to turn back the clock all the way to the point when she had met Grant at an entrepreneurs' conference where he charmed everyone with his California looks, his pearly white smile and his sense of fashion. He talked a good game, but when push came to shove, he had ridden on her coattails all the way to the present. And the kicker was, she knew it for years and she was too busy, too complacent, to do anything about it.

"I need to think about this."

"We understand," her attorney said, "but this could wipe the slate clean, you will have enough money to do anything you want in your life."

After she hung up the phone and spent time thoroughly reviewing the offer for her business and her home, Danica sat at the desk, head in hands, her heart in her throat, crying uncontrollably for what seemed like hours. She was mourning her business, her house, her life, and it all seemed like a bad dream. What would her act two be? What would she do?

She finally sat up, dried off her face and then sat on the terrace to find some clarity. If she signed the agreement, Grant would win. He would have her business, her home that she designed with an architect, every lovingly selected stick of wood, tile and window treatment. It had been home for such a long time, and she had imagined raising her children, taking pictures of their sons or daughters on the winding, sweeping staircase, and growing old there. How could this be? How could it be that those moments would be for Grant and Fallon?

"Hi, Matteo."

"Hi, sweetheart," he said. "I just got home. Are you okay?"

"No. I'm not," she said. "Would you please look over a settlement document? My attorneys think I should take it."

"I'm only an attorney on paper," he reminded her. "I haven't actually practiced law in years."

"I know. I trust you."

There was a pause and then he said, "Thank you. I'll look them over right now."

They hung up and between phone calls, Danica paced around the large suite, her stomach in knots, gurgling, and she felt nauseous. If she agreed, this would sever all ties with Grant, but it would also be severing the life she had built for over a decade.

When Matteo called back, she fumbled with the phone, dropping it on the ground, and she was unable to hit the green button in time. Annoyed, she hit Redial.

"So? What do you think?"

"I think your attorneys have a point," he said seriously. "If you don't, you have to contend with Grant because he doesn't seem like he's leaving anytime soon."

Danica knew it already, but the confirmation was difficult. She slumped down into a pillowy oversize chair, unable to think, much less find words.

"As a fellow Trekkie..." Matteo said after the moment of silence.

"Live long and prosper." When she finally found words, these were the ones that came out.

"If all the variables were the same," Matteo asked, "What advice would Spock give to Captain James T. Kirk?"

CHAPTER THIRTEEN

THE DAY THAT Oakley and her mom arrived at the farm was a happy day for Journey. There was magic on this land; she felt it, and she knew it, and she could see Oakley thriving on this ranch. He would relish the freedom he could never have in the city. When Oakley sent a text saying that they were turning onto the long drive to the main house, Journey put on her winter layers and raced down the steps, grateful she didn't slip and land on her tailbone. She wanted to be there the moment Oakley and her mother arrived.

Waving her arms in greeting, Journey cried happy tears for being reunited with her son. The SUV parked, and then Oakley opened the door and rushed over to her and hugged her. She could pick him up just a little and swing him around, but these days were ending.

"Are you taller?" she asked. "You're taller!"

Oakley's eyes looked like they were being pulled down and to the side, his chin was very recessed, and he had some scarring from when they fixed his severe cleft palate. And as his mother, none of that mattered. All she saw was her perfect son.

"Is Cody Ty here?" Oakley asked.

The driver had put the luggage on the front porch while she greeted her mother.

"How was the flight?"

"Good," her mother said. "This is more beautiful in person."

"Isn't it?"

Then Oakley asked again, "Is Cody Ty here?"

And this time, as if on cue, Cody Ty walked out of the barn and headed straight for them.

"There he is, right there," she said, pointing.

That was all she needed to say for her son to run at record speed toward Cody. Inwardly, she cringed, always nervous when someone new met her son, especially when he was about to hurl himself into the cowboy's arms.

Cody, as she had witnessed firsthand in Bozeman, let Oakley hug him and returned that hug. Over Oakley's head, Cody caught her eye and winked. That was when all of her anxiety and fear went away. And it was that very moment, with Cody walking toward her, arm around Oakley's back like they were pals from way back, that Journey realized that she had fallen in love with Cody Ty Hawkins.

"Cody says that he'll autograph my hat!" Oakley said in a voice fused with excitement and disbelief. How many times did people actually get to meet their idols?

"This is my mother, Lucy," she said.

"Ma'am—" Cody lifted up his hat for a second, accompanied with a nod "—my pleasure."

"Thank you. Likewise," Lucy said. "I've heard wonderful things."

Cody helped them get the bags into the house and then he headed back out to the barn. He heard Oakley ask his mom if he could follow along and that made him turn around and stop. Cody and Oakley were both waiting on her answer, and she could see her mother in her periphery nod her head.

"Are you sure you don't mind?"

Cody said, "I can always use a set of strong arms. Flex those biceps for me, son."

Oakley laughed, raised his arms like he was a bodybuilder in a competition, and Cody said, "Come on and bring those guns with you."

Journey hugged her son, made sure he made eye contact and then said, "Mr. Hawkins…"

"Cody."

"Mr. Cody is a very busy man, and you need to listen to him very carefully."

"Okay. I will." And then the reunion was over, and Journey couldn't stop from feeling let down because Oakley was enamored with Cody, and she said as much to her mother.

"Oh, let him be, Journey," Lucy said, unpacking her toiletries. "I haven't seen him this excited *ever*. If working with Cody can give him confidence, what's the harm in that?"

"You're right." She sat down at the end of the bed. "I just don't want him to get hurt. He's got so much against him."

Lucy sat down next to her. "You can't protect him from everything, Journey."

"I know."

"And I like this Cody Ty fellow. He's got a nice way about him. Humble. I didn't expect that from someone as famous as he is or has been."

"He is a very nice man," Journey said. "I have grown very fond of him."

"I could see that," Lucy said, "and I believe he's grown very fond of you."

Then Lucy yawned and Journey wanted her to rest after taking on the full-time job of watching Oakley for the past two weeks. Journey got her mother settled into the main bedroom, but her mind was on her son, and she just felt like she needed to see him working with Cody.

"I do think I will take a nap," her mom said.

"Yes, please do. It's so peaceful here." She hugged her mom. "After one week, you'll never want to leave."

CODY TOOK AN immediate liking to Oakley; yes, he could see that he had a different look about him, but he had no difficulty looking past that. The horses gravitated to Oakley and that was a sign of a good soul. Oakley was kind, gentle, soft-spoken, and the horses responded to that.

"Bring that wheelbarrow over here, son," Cody said to Journey's boy.

Oakley did as he was asked. "Do you think I'll be able to ride while I'm here?"

"Well—" Cody gave a shake of his head "—I'm not sure we'll be able to get your mom on board with that idea."

Oakley's shoulders dropped. "Just because she's afraid of horses doesn't mean that I have to be."

"That's right," he agreed, "but she's the boss applesauce and she gets veto power. But I'll put in a good word or two with her."

"Thank you," the boy said. "Maybe coming from you, she'll agree to it."

Cody didn't want to ruin it for him, but he didn't think he had much sway with Journey. She had taken major steps forward in her relationship with Rose. But he didn't imagine he'd ever see her in the saddle and that was okay.

When Cody was done mucking, he showed Oakley where to dump the manure and then they went back inside the barn. When they returned, Journey was in the barn scratching Rose's ears. And just as usual, the moment he laid eyes on her for the first time and every day since, his knees got week, he felt dizzy, with his throat closing in. If that wasn't a sign of love, he surely didn't know what else would be. A big barrier here was the matter of age; he wasn't sure of her age, but they weren't from the same generation. So as much as he had grown to care about Journey, and the waters did run deep, he had worked overtime to stop any feelings he had for her from getting in the way of teaching her about the majestic animals he had loved for his entire lifetime.

"How's it going?" Journey asked.

"Mom! Cody taught me how to muck stalls!" Oakley was overjoyed, as if Cody had bestowed a great honor upon him.

Journey gave him a playful raise of the brow. "You do know that there are still child labor laws in place."

"This isn't labor, Palomino," he said without stopping to choose his words carefully. "This is character-building."

The minute his private nickname for her was spoken aloud, all he could do was hope that she hadn't noticed. If she had noticed, she was playing it cool.

"We need to let Mr. Cody get his work done," she told her boy.

Oakley appeared crestfallen but didn't argue the point.

"I'll be working some young horses in the round pen for the next couple of hours. You're welcome to watch."

Oakley's eyes turned hopeful as he sought out his mother's gaze.

"Okay," Journey said, "but only if you promise to watch quietly."

Oakley made a cross over his heart, hugged his mother tightly and then turned his attention back to Cody.

"You're sure?" Journey asked him.

"I like the company," he told her, and it was true.

Oakley did have a unique face that he was certain drew unwanted attention from strangers. Behind those facial features was a golden heart. And perhaps it was because of his unusual features that Oakley seemed to have an old soul. A gentle soul that the horses gravitated to. A boy like that deserved to be taught how to work with horses, and once his mother saw that Oakley was building self-esteem, he was darn sure that Journey would approve. He could see how dedicated she was to her son, and he admired it.

"Thank you." Journey had some unshed tears in her eyes. She hugged her son one last time, and when he began to wiggle out, his mother let him go.

"I'm going to be okay," Oakley said. "Mr. Cody will watch out for me."

"That's right." Cody nodded. "Now, we've got work to do. Come on over here, Oakley, and I'll teach you how to put a halter on."

He did take a moment to watch Journey walk away, a sassy swing in her hips, her thick wheat-blond hair in a braid, and her long legs that reminded him so much of a gangly filly not even a month old. She was a beauty. And he knew that when it was time for Journey to leave the ranch, he'd miss her like he'd miss a limb. There would be phantom pain for years, of that he was certain.

IT TOOK ALL of Journey's willpower not to spy on Oakley and Cody. She did satisfy her curiosity by peeking out the window, but she realized that she didn't feel overly anxious when it came to Cody working with her son. This feeling of calm confidence she had with Cody had only happened with her mother. And this security, unexpected but welcome, only validated her growing romantic feelings for Cody.

"What are you doing?" her friend Riggs asked on video chat.

"Looking up a palomino."

"What's that?"

"I don't know," she said. "That's why I'm looking it up."

"Okay, while you do that, you'll be happy to know that I sold my boat."

"That does take a load off," Journey said with playful sarcasm. "Is that why've you been MIA?"

"Have I though?"

"Yes. You have." She looked at the pictures of the most beautiful golden horses with light blond manes and tails. "He does have feelings for me!"

"Rewind," Riggs said. "When the cat is away, Journey will play."

"Cody Ty Hawkins," Journey said. "I sent you links to videos."

"And I watched one or two before I had to turn the attention to me again," Riggs said. "I will say this, he's good-looking. Kind of old, but still doable."

"He's not old," Journey said defensively. "He's more productive than most of our friends."

"Whatevs." Her friend frowned and was beginning to look very bored. "Why do you think this very *youthful* cowboy has a crush?"

"He called me *Palomino*."

"Not ringing a bell on my end."

"I just sent you a link."

Riggs opened the link and then he said, "He has a crush. Big-time."

"Wow." Journey sat back in her chair, looking at the wall, stunned. "I would never have known except for his slip of the tongue."

Riggs's keen eyes were on her now and this is why he asked, "Do you want him to have a crush on you?"

Journey was silent for a second and then she said, "I'm in love with him."

Riggs's eyes widened, his jaw went slack, and he appeared to be completely shocked. "I leave for a couple of days—"

"Seven."

"...and you go off the rails! I have to go buy a boat."

"You just sold your boat."

"But I'll work you into my *schedge*," Riggs said with a dramatic sigh. "You need me more than I need sushi today."

"Was it a close call?" she asked with a laugh. "Me or the sushi?"

"A *very* close call."

After touching base with Riggs and tiptoeing past her mother's room, she sat down at the desk in her room, opened her laptop, pulled up the Word document, and typed the words *Chapter Two*. And then she sat there for what seemed like an eternity, but it was only ten minutes when a knock at the front door gave her the excuse she needed to avoid writing. When she wrote her first book, it had come easily. Now she could barely get through a sentence without putting her head into her hands and trying to think of the next bit of dialogue or a scene in general.

Journey opened the door and found Ray and Charlie on the threshold.

"Our sister needs us in California," Ray said.

Charlie added, "We are catching a plane today. If you need anything, please get in touch with Wayne."

"I hope everything is okay," she said. She really liked each Brand triplet.

"It will be," Ray said. "Once we get there, it will be."

She was shutting the door and the sisters had taken the porch stairs down when Ray stopped and called her back.

"Totally off subject. But I bought your book, and I loved it! When I get back, I would love for you to sign it for me."

"And my copy, too," Charlie called over her shoulder.

And then the sisters were gone, leaving her standing just inside the cabin, feeling shocked with her spirits raised. Perhaps those one-star reviews had gotten into her head and decided to build a permanent residence there. But Ray and Charlie were cowgirls at the core, native Montanans and fifth-generation ranchers.

"Well," she said, "what do you know?"

She walked back to her computer with her head lifted, shoulders back. One five-star review from Charlie and Ray meant more to her than one hundred one-star reviews.

Fingers on the keyboard, with a new resolve, and the feeling that the block was a thing of the past, Journey drew from the ranch, the Brand sisters, her newfound horse sense, and of course, her time with Cody Ty, while her fingers began to fly and all of the words she had pent up inside her came pouring out.

"ARE YOU SURE you don't need me to come back?" Matteo asked, looking dapper in his white coat and a stethoscope around his neck.

"No, thank you," Danica said, her nose stuffy from all of the crying she had done over the last couple of days. She hadn't cried this much as an adult and couldn't remember crying much in her childhood, either. But then again, she had never had to sign away everything she had built just to get Grant and Fallon out of her life.

"Okay." He sounded unconvinced. "If you need me, I'll hop on the next flight."

"I know you would," and as she said it, she knew it was true. Matteo had proved his feelings for her and his willingness to come to her when times were tough. "Thank you for giving me access to Lu Lu's cameras. I can't be sad when I watch her and it's certainly better than raiding the hotel bar."

"I'm glad it's helped," he said. "She misses you. When she hears your voice, she runs around oinking and her little curly tail just wagging a mile a minute."

That made her laugh through her fresh tears. "I know! That's why I don't talk to her through the camera because she tries very hard to figure out where I am!"

There was a knock on the hotel door, and that's when she

saw that her sisters had texted that they had arrived. "Ray and Charlie are here."

"Okay, keep me posted."

"I will."

"I love you," he said.

And with an automaticity that caught her off guard, she said, "I love you, too. Goodbye."

Danica didn't have time to dwell on that slip of the tongue. She needed to pull it together and go to the house that she had named *La Dulce Vida*, the sweet life, and pack up her personal belongings and other items that were agreed upon during arbitration.

"Hi," Danica greeted them, so relieved to see her sisters. For many years, they had each focused on their own lives taking them in opposite directions. Now she couldn't imagine going through anything without them. As were their parents' wishes, the ranch had brought them back together and cemented their bond as triplets.

They got into their triplet hug, touching foreheads, before they broke apart, knowing that they needed to get to *La Dulce Vida* to meet the movers.

"Oh, my." Danica looked at her reflection in the mirror. Her nose was red as Rudolph's and her skin was blotchy. Her eyes were puffy and resembled an inner tube.

"Don't worry your pretty little head over it," Ray said. "We are going to fix you right up and you'll face this next challenge looking like *the* Danica Brand."

Danica let her sisters fuss over her; she lay down on the bed and let Charlie put a damp cloth with ice in it over her eyes. After they depuffed some, Ray put some caffeine cream around her eyes.

Feeling more like herself, she fixed her hair and then put on her makeup. She put on one of her "boss" tailored suits in deep red. She turned in a circle for her sisters' approval.

"Two thumbs up," said Ray.

"*Four* thumbs up," Charlie said.

Hiding her still-puffy eyes behind stylish sunglasses, Danica walked out of that hotel with a carefree attitude on display that she did not feel inside. She was well-known in prominent social circles in LA and, not completely surprising, there was a photographer she recognized from a news rag, and she looked at him, smiled, chin up, confident, and then she disappeared inside an awaiting SUV with her long-standing driver.

Her driver took them to her estate in Beverly Hills.

"We're so sorry, Danny," Ray said.

"Thank you for coming." Danica took off her sunglasses. "I couldn't face this alone. And I don't know who is a friend anymore."

"We wouldn't want to be anywhere else," Charlie said, her jaw set. "This is a raw deal."

Danica shook her head, still in disbelief. "It seems like a dream."

"Nightmare," Charlie said.

"Everything I fought so hard to build, gone."

"You'll rebuild. Bigger and better." Ray reached out to take her hand.

"I don't even know what I want to do."

"You don't have to know right now," her identical triplet said. "You'll come home, regroup, and then you'll know."

"And whatever it is that you want, we will be here to support you."

"I love you both very much."

"And we love you," Ray and Charlie said in unison.

The rest of the ride was quiet. What could they say that hadn't already been said? When the car pulled up to her gate and the number was punched in, the wonderful world she had created unfolded before them. She heard both of her sisters gasp and it struck her now that her sisters hadn't seen it before.

Along a winding drive, up the hill, the Mediterranean-style home was revealed. The house sat on one acre and was built to maximize the views of the LA cityscape.

"How big is this place?" Charlie asked.

"Thirteen thousand square feet, nine bedrooms, twelve bathrooms."

"That's a lot of toilets to clean," her tomboy sister added.

"It is, but I didn't." She smiled at the thought. "We run a full staff here. I hope Grant keeps them on. Most of them have been with me since I built this house."

They stepped out of the SUV into her private sanctuary. Behind those gates, she had felt free to leave the stress of her job at the curb and enjoy the fruits of her success. As they walked through the front door, a grand staircase was the star of the show, leading up to a second story. Imported marble was on the floor of an entertainer's kitchen where various chefs would cook for her parties. An imported chandelier twinkled in the sunlight flooding in from a massive picture window.

"Why did you need all of this?" Charlie asked.

Danica looked around at her beautiful house filled with everything she had loved and cherished and couldn't give her sister an answer. Now, having stepped back from her fast-paced life, where keeping up the Joneses wasn't good enough, where she needed to overtake the Joneses and leave them in the dust—second place was for losers—she couldn't really remember needing all this.

"It's impressive." Ray always tried to sugarcoat things and put a positive spin on it. "Look what you achieved, Danny! It's amazing. *You* are amazing."

The movers arrived and her sisters followed her around the house, starting with her closet and her home office, and then they headed downstairs to the kitchen. The walls of the house were filled with an art collection that she had started with a small Picasso. The collection had grown as she and Grant picked out paintings together. The only painting she wanted was that Picasso. The rest of the collection would be appraised, and she would be reimbursed. She didn't find anything in the kitchen of use to her but there were several items that her sisters spotted that had come from their childhood home in the library.

"I've never seen this many books in one place other than the public library." Charlie looked around, hands on her hips.

"I love it," Ray said. "Will you be taking anything from here?"

Like every room that she had entered, she didn't want much out of the library either. It was odd, this detachment that she felt for her own home, her own belongings. But that was how she felt. She just didn't want it anymore.

Danica walked over to one of the shelves, slid a book out of its space, closed the protective glass door and then opened the book in her hand to the title page. She looked at her father's inscription, ran her finger across it, and then carried it with her as she left the library, knowing that this would be the last day she would see it.

"I think that's it," Danica said quietly.

"Mom and Dad would be so proud of you," Ray said.

"Yes," she said with a waver of emotion in her voice, "they would. But do you know what I regret now?"

Her sisters waited for her to continue.

"I regret that Mom and Dad never came here for a visit. I regret that neither of you came here—" she shook her head "—because I didn't invite you."

"It's okay, Danny." Her sisters were at her side.

"The things in life that I had placed so much value on seem like bottom-shelf items now," she told them. "Thank you for helping me on the next chapter in my life story."

Then, they joined together for their triplet hug and Danica could feel that she was on the right path, doing the right thing, at the right moment. This newly found bond with Ray and Charlie was her home. For now, and forever.

CHAPTER FOURTEEN

"YOU'RE REALLY THAT CERTAIN?" Estrella asked him.

Matteo had put on his best cowboy duds, with dark-wash Wrangler jeans and a blue-and-white Western-style shirt with pearl snaps, and felt ready to meet Danica at the private airport where she and her sisters would be arriving.

"I'm sure."

Estrella sighed but said, "If you're sure, then I'm sure."

"Thank you, *hermanita*." He called her "little sister" in Spanish, which always garnered a smile from Estrella.

"So," he asked, "how do I look?"

"Like a real cowboy."

"Well," he said, smiling broadly, "that's what I was going for."

He ended the call, grabbed his heavy coat, and then braced himself against the cold and the freshly falling snow. Once inside his truck, he backed out of his drive, and slowly, cautiously made his way toward the place where he would see his true love again. Yes, they spoke on the phone and video-chatted, but nothing could take the place of feeling her body next to his, holding her in his arms, and smelling the clean scent of her skin and her hair. He had missed hugging her, kissing her, and this "missing" her felt like an ache he'd never experienced in his life. And it confirmed to him that Danica was his person in this vast world. No matter how long it took for Danica to heal from this breakup with her life in California, he was ready to wait.

From behind the wheel of his truck, he saw the jet land and his heart began to pound like he had just run ten miles in a minute. He watched impatiently for the door to open and for the stairs to descend. And then, finally, Charlie appeared at the top of the steps, followed by Ray, and then his beloved appeared. She looked for him, and when she saw him, her smile was as big as his. He jumped out of his truck and walked quickly toward the jet.

Charlie and Ray also smiled at him; he had to believe that his care and concern for their sister had earned him a treasure trove of "attaboy" tokens.

The ground crew appeared and opened up the baggage compartment. Charlie and Ray hugged him tightly and then he had Danica in his arms again. Still with that broad smile of happiness to see him again, Danica stepped into his arms, and he picked her up and swung her around.

Laughing, Danica said, "I'm happy to see you, too!"

The three women, followed by their baggage, and with him holding Danica's gloved hand, made their way to his truck. Baggage had to rough it in the bed, while they piled in, and he cranked the heater.

"Thank you for picking us up," Ray said. "Cows love to have babies in a snowstorm."

"And horses," Charlie added, "and goats."

Danica had her body turned toward him, her face alight with joy, and he would bet that this joy was also reflected in his expression. He took his hand off the steering wheel for a moment, reached over, took her hand, and said, "I've missed you."

"Me, too," she said.

"Oh, Lord almighty," Charlie said, "get a room."

"Leave them be," Ray said. "I think it's magical. I love the two of you together."

"I guess Journey isn't the only hopeless romantic at Hideaway Ranch."

"Guilty as charged," Ray said. "Lightning struck me twice."

Charlie slumped down in her seat, crossed her arms, pulled

the knit cap she had on her head over her eyes and then began to lightly snore a minute later.

"Charlie can literally sleep through a blizzard." Danica turned around so she could meet Ray's eye.

"Especially when uncomfortable subjects are broached."

The remainder of the ride was quiet. There were so many things that he wanted to say to Danica, but those words were for her ears only. He turned off the highway onto Hideaway Ranch land. Soon he reached the common area that included the barn, main house and a large structure that once was Butch Brand's workshop.

Ray tapped Charlie on her thigh, and she pushed up the cap, opened her eyes a crack, and then, realizing that she was back home, she quickly unhooked the seat belt, mumbled thanks to him and then hauled her travel bag out of the back of the truck.

"Hideaway Ranch meeting tomorrow!" Danica called after her sister.

Not turning around, Charlie lifted her hand and made the thumbs-up sign.

"Broke the mold," Ray said about her sister with an affectionate smile.

"Agreed."

Next was the Legend family ranch, where Ray had been living with her fiancé Dean.

Ray had texted Dean that they had arrived, and he came out to help her with her bags.

"I'm so glad to see you." Ray hugged Dean tightly and then hugged Dean's youngest daughter, Luna, who had launched herself into Ray's arms. With her arm around Luna's shoulders, and with Dean carrying her bags up the brick steps to the enormous, custom-carved, double front door, Ray smiled over her shoulder at them, just before she disappeared inside the sprawling house.

Now back in the truck, Matteo leaned over to kiss his beloved. Danica returned the kiss and then made a face. "Your nose is so *cold*!"

"Sleeping on the job," he teased her. "You need to warm it up."

She kissed him three times while his nose warmed up, and

then he said, "We've got to get someplace private. I don't think Dean would appreciate us making out in front of his house."

Danica laughed and it was a sound that he loved. "No. I suspect not."

Matteo asked, "Your place or mine?"

"Yours," she said. "Definitely yours."

He backed out, and then put the truck in drive while he asked, "Lu Lu?"

"Of course," Danica said, nodding. "Lu Lu."

DANICA HAD BEEN overwhelmed with emotion when she stood at the top of the jet's stairs and saw Matteo waiting nearby. He had welcomed her home and for the first time in over two decades, she did feel that Big Sky was her home. She certainly couldn't have foreseen the events that had led her back to Big Sky; it certainly was a twist of fate that had put her on an unexpected path. And on this unexpected path, she had found Matteo and Lu Lu. The timing of it all—the naysayers, and she supposed ex-friends, told her that it was too soon to get into a relationship. Or that Matteo was a rebound. Danica discovered, and was very pleased with this development, that the only voice in her head that mattered was her own.

"I love when you cook for me." Danica sank down onto the comfy couch where Matteo joined her after he built a fire.

"I love to cook for you," he said, inviting her to lean back on him while he held her in his strong, comforting arms.

Leaning on anyone, physically or emotionally, was not her way of being in the world. She strove for independence, full control, and did, at times, think poorly of women in her universe who leaned on others. Now she understood that to trust others enough to lean on them was a strength.

"I missed you," she said, resting her hands on top of his.

He kissed her on the side of the neck. "I missed you. Very much."

In silence, they enjoyed the warmth of the fire and then she got up, held out her hand to him, and led him to a soft rug in front of the fire. One garment after another, she removed his clothing as he removed hers. Lying in front of the fire, their bodies skin to skin, their arms and legs intertwined, and his lips kissing her neck, her shoulders as if she were the only dessert he needed.

He rose up on his arm, admired her face with his eyes, and he said, "I love you, Danica."

She put her hand on his face, loving every part from his soulful eyes to his strong chin and nose, and those capable lips.

"*Te amo*, Matteo," she said—*I love you* in Spanish.

She did love him. Did she know what that meant for the future? No, and perhaps that was part of the enjoyment with this handsome doctor. Her plan was to not have a plan. She wanted to live her life without a rigid schedule or the hunt for that record-breaking price per square foot for her high-end clients. She had been a tigress to be reckoned with in California; deadly claws, razor sharp teeth, and never one to back down from a fight.

Was she still all of those things? Yes, of course. They would always be a part of her. But now she didn't need that armor anymore.

Now, she lay next to Matteo, covered in a soft blanket, her nails lightly running through his chest hair, her leg over his and her head on his strong heart.

"This was worth the wait," Matteo murmured, drifting off to sleep.

"Agreed."

Something in her voice made Matteo's eyes open up. He looked down at her and when he caught her eye, he gave a small shake of the head and asked, "Lu Lu?"

Danica pushed herself upright quickly. "Is it okay?"

"Do you mean leaving me, leaving this fire, leaving this blanket, so you can go see Lu Lu out in the freezing cold?"

"If you don't mind," she said, starting to hunt for her jeans, socks and shirt.

"If I did, would it matter?"

She found her underwear on a nearby lamp. "No."

He laughed as he threw off the blanket and got up. "Then I don't mind."

The man was truly a work of art, chiseled and gorgeous, but even that recognition couldn't stop her mission to see the most amazing, fashion-forward pig in the world. Once dressed, she rushed over to her largest suitcase, unzipped a pocket, and then pulled out something she had had made for Lu Lu.

"Look!" she said, showing the matching crocheted winter hat with flaps and an under-the-chin strap that held it in place along with a matching sweater. "Do you think they'll fit? I sent the request to one of my childhood friends who makes just about anything that can be crocheted."

"Well." Matteo had his jeans on but still unbuttoned in a way that made the nerve endings in her body abuzz. "She loves you and she loves pink."

Danica smiled joyfully. "I can't wait to put them on."

Matteo grabbed his shirt, but before he could pull it on, Danica traced the outline of his six-pack and that brought a glint into his eyes when he asked, "Do you approve?"

"Please," she said in a teasing, disbelieving voice, "any woman would approve."

Matteo reached for her, brought her close and kissed her deeply. "You're the only woman in this world whose approval matters to me."

She rose up on her tiptoes and kissed him. "I'm glad."

"And now can you see Lu Lu?"

"Now can I see Lu Lu?"

Matteo pulled on his shirt. "I have to tell you, this is the first time I've been put in second place behind my pig."

Danica raced outside as if she had been living in the North Pole. She loved her roly-poly friend. She crossed the yard, slipping on a couple of steps that made her move more cautiously until she reached the front porch of Lu Lu's playhouse.

When she opened the door, the house was cozy and warm, and Lu Lu was sleeping in a fluffy bed with layers of blankets around her. When Lu Lu saw her, the pig got up, oinked and chattered on her way over, her curlicue tail wagging, and when the pig reached her, she flopped over, put her head in her lap and begged for some belly scratches.

"We haven't lost a beat, have we?"

Soon after their reunion, Matteo banged the snow off his boots and opened the door.

"I see the love affair continues?"

She smiled, in part because Lu Lu was smiling blissfully. "I know all the best places to scratch."

"Well, when you're done, I have a container of goodies that Lu Lu can find if you want to do the honors."

Danica leaned over and whispered to Lu Lu, "Do you hear that? Goodies!"

"Are you going to try her new sweater?"

"No." Danica went over to Lu Lu's closet, put the sweater and hat together on a shelf, and then selected Lu Lu's warm, "hanging in the backyard" clothes. Once she had dressed Lu Lu, she opened the door and picked up the basket of the pig's favorite veggies. Danica stood in the center of the snowy yard, bent her knees to get an extra oomph when she stood up quickly and tossed all of the veggies up into the air, letting them fan out around her.

Beside herself, Lu Lu's sounds were loud and grating to the ear, but Danica didn't care. She could learn to wear earplugs. But what she couldn't, wouldn't, do was to let her life, a mystery at the present time, get too busy to share these moments with Lu Lu and Matteo. All of the excitement of being back with Matteo and her most favorite pig made her feel carefree and grateful. These were not the feelings she had anticipated back in California when she was putting her electronic name and initials to the documents that transferred the home she had designed and the business she had built with hard work and gumption.

Danica bent down, made a snowball, and threw it with rather good aim, and the snowball found its target—the side of Matteo's handsome face.

"Did you just hit me with a snowball?"

She was busy making her second snowball. "Maybe."

"You've crossed a line, woman!"

While Lu Lu was on a vegetable hunt, Matteo defended himself against her snowball onslaught. He managed to land some snowballs as well, but she clearly dominated. So much so that Matteo crossed the designated boundaries, picked her up and fell back into a embankment that offered a soft place for them to land.

Laughing and winded, Danica said, "You had to resort to cheating! I won!"

"No." Matteo leaned down to look at her directly in the eye. "I won. I won because I have you."

"Where have you been all my life, Dr. Katz-Cortez?"

"Waiting for you."

THE WRITING BLOCK was over, and Journey was well on her way to finishing Chapter Four. It had taken her some time to trust Cody, but she did. She trusted Cody with her precious son. A blast of frigid air smacked her in the face when she opened the front door to the main house and stepped outside.

"Hey." Her mother was wrapped up in a thick, quilted blanket, sitting in a rocking chair that she had staked out as her own territory. "How's writing?"

She sat down in a rocking chair next to her mother. "I've finally broken the block."

"Good. Good."

"How's it going with Cody?"

Her mother nodded toward the barn. "I've cried."

"Cried?"

"Twice."

"Why? What's wrong?" Journey stood up, ready to rush to Oakley's side.

"Sit." Her mother gestured. "Sit, sit. Nothing's wrong. Everything's right."

As if on cue, Oakley came out of the barn leading a large horse to the round pen with Cody a couple of paces behind them.

In that moment, Journey was rendered speechless. Oakley had his head held high, and she could plainly see that his self-confidence, in record time, had skyrocketed.

"Do you see?" her mother asked her.

Journey's hand was over her mouth, ecstatic tears in her eyes, and she nodded as she sat back down.

"This is the third horse he's led to that area."

"The round pen," she offered.

"Well," her mother laughed, "that makes sense, doesn't it? It's round and it's a pen."

Her mother's jubilation caught Journey off guard; her mother wasn't one for overusing happy emotions. So Lucy's joy only added to her own joy.

"Cody's been teaching him how to lead a horse, stop a horse, have a horse back up from him."

"He looks so little."

"He's a natural, Journey," her mother said. "This is what our boy was made for."

Journey couldn't deny it. Oakley looked happier than she had ever seen him. "And Cody? Would you give him five stars?"

"Hell," Lucy said, "I'd give him ten stars if I could. That is a man among men, just like my dad."

"High praise."

"Well-deserved praise."

Then there was a small lull in the conversation when she saw Cody hand Oakley a long crop with a woven cord; Oakley and Cody stood in the middle of the round pen, and with Cody standing behind her son, with his arms on top of Oakley's, Cody used the crop to move the horse to the outer edge of the round pen.

"What's he doing?" Journey stood back up. "That's too much."

"Sit down, Journey," her mother said. "Cody's got him."

She sat back down, hands in lap, her eyes focused on Oakley. First, he showed her son how to make a horse walk near the edge of the round pen and then had him move the horse into a trot, using clucks and body position to increase the horse's speed.

"I can't believe this," she said. "I've never seen him this happy."

Her mother nodded and she could see more tears of joy; Journey reached over and grabbed her mom's mittened hand and squeezed it.

"You know," Lucy said, "I owe you an apology."

"No," she said. "What in the world for?"

"Because I thought all of this was a fool's errand. You wanting to write romance for a living—and yes, I was very proud when you published your first book."

Her mother looked at her with such sorrow in her eyes that

she hurt for her as Lucy continued, "I didn't believe that it could be a career. I was wrong for thinking that. I was just worried that you were going to use up your savings and then what? I should've been more supportive."

"But you *have been* supportive! You took care of Oakley so I could get some research done and some chapters under my belt before you arrived."

"Well, if I've been helpful then I'm glad," her mother said. "When we drove up to this place, I lost my breath. And I could feel that there was something special about this place. I got goose bumps up and down my arms. Oakley felt it, too. He said that this is magical, and I agree. I see it so clearly now—you will write this book. And then the next and the next."

"Thank you, Mom," Journey said, still holding her hand. "Thank you."

JOURNEY RETURNED TO writing with a renewed sense of energy. She had just finished the last page of Chapter Four when she heard the front door open and then slam shut. Her son appeared in the doorway, his face flushed and windburned, his eyes shining like blue diamonds. His face was smudged with dirt; he had dirt under his fingernails and dirt on his clothes.

"Mom! Guess what?"

"What?" She turned and gave her son all of her attention.

"I learned how to put a halter on a horse and lead it to where you wanted him, or her, to go. I learned how to make a horse stop, walk, trot and canter by clucking my tongue and walking closer or farther away! This is the best day of my life!"

Oakley ran toward her, hugged her tightly and said, "And everything's okay, Mom. Cody watches out for me."

"I know he does," she said, still hugging him, not wanting to let him go. "You smell like horse."

Oakley stood up and smiled at her broadly. "I know. Isn't it great?"

A COUPLE OF days back in Montana and Danica was working on finding a new routine now that the move was a permanent one. She was paying a pretty penny for her rental but was rather lucky to find a place at all. Real estate in Big Sky was extremely limited, and drew the very rich and oftentimes famous. She was, now that the sale of the business and *La Dulce Vida* were done, a wealthy woman, but she would not pay the inflated prices for a home. And this was one of the things that she wanted to discuss with her sisters at their weekly meetings about the ranch.

"How are you, Danny?" Ray hugged her tightly when she arrived at Charlie's home.

"I'm good," she said, and it was the truth. Once the fight was over, and the decisions were made, she was able to let it go, for the most part, and focus on the future that she could make of her own design.

"Coffee?" Charlie brought a pot over to the table.

"Absolutely!" she said.

Once they were sitting together at the table, Ray asked, "So how has it been with Dr. Make Me Feel Good?"

That made her laugh. Wherever they went together, women, and some men, would stop and stare at Matteo. And that was because he was undeniably handsome. The cheekbones, the jawline, the broad shoulders and the height. Matteo was a walking, talking, living, breathing example of male perfection, and of course women wanted those genes for their children. No different than lions: the one with the best mane has the pick of the pride.

"He's living proof that sometimes you *can* judge a book by its cover," she said, petting Hitch, the orange tabby that ruled the roost. "He's as beautiful on the inside as he is on the outside."

"I'm so happy for you, Danny. You deserve it." Ray had tears in her eyes when she hugged her tightly. "Is it serious?"

"No. Not yet," she said. "But it has potential. I have strong feelings for him and he for me. But for now, I just want to have fun with Matteo. Enjoy his company, date, without the stress of living together."

Her twin agreed. "There's something about dishes and laundry that sucks all of the romance out of the relationship."

After a minute, Charlie chimed in, "If you're in love, that means you'll be on hand to take Hideaway Ranch to the next level."

Ray sat back down with a disapproving look on her face. "It's not all about the ranch, Charlie. Why are you always so focused on the ranch? There is a world beyond our property lines."

Charlie was using her pocketknife to clean the dirt out from under her jagged fingernails; she put it away and said, "Because this ranch is our past, our present and our future."

"I can't believe that I'm saying this," Danica said, "but I agree with Charlie. We're here for the ranch, so let's get down to business."

The meeting was fruitful, and Danica understood now that her place was in Montana. And yes, she often clashed with Charlie because of how different they were and how they didn't have much in common other than sharing a womb and growing up in the same house with the same parents. But now she could see clearly that Hideaway Ranch was the business that needed her attention, and she respected Charlie's singular focus on the ranch.

"Are we done?" Charlie asked. "I've got a couple of irons in the fire."

"Almost," Danica said, sending a text.

A few minutes later, Charlie's fiancé carried a large box into the kitchen.

"What's this?" Charlie stood up to kiss her cowboy.

"That's a question for Danny," Wayne said. "I just carry the boxes around here."

And then Wayne, a man of few words, left.

"Ray," Danica said, feeling excited, "open it."

Charlie cut open the box with her knife and then Ray tugged the box open and took out one of the T-shirts she found inside.

She held it up so Charlie could see it. It read, *Goat Yoga, Hideaway Ranch.*

"Look at the back," Danica said.

Ray read the back aloud. "'Yes, I do need this many goats.'"

"Thank you, Danny." Ray hugged her again. "I love them."

Charlie had taken a shirt out of the box, checked the size, and tugged the T-shirt she was wearing over her head and off her body before putting on the new Hideaway Ranch goat yoga T-shirt.

"I like it," Charlie said. "Fits good."

And then Charlie left the meeting and headed back outside. "Do you love them?" she asked Ray.

"I do," her twin said. "You *do* love goat yoga."

"I can't deny it. I love it." Danica laughed. "I have no idea what's happening to me. I am quite perplexed. How did I manage to live without goat yoga and a pet pig?"

CHAPTER FIFTEEN

THE NEXT DAY, early in the morning, Matteo joined her for a hike on one of Hideaway Ranch's two small mountain peaks. Sadly, Lu Lu had to sit this hike out—the terrain would be too challenging for her. But Danica told her that she would join her on a fun forage when they returned. She had been spending some nights with Matteo, but she also valued her alone time, something that she rarely had in California.

"I like the color," Matteo said, while they were sitting on a bench placed there by her father, who enjoyed sitting in the woods to enjoy nature and to think.

"Thank you," she said, reaching for his hand. "I like you."

She had gone to a stylist that Ray had recommended, and she had changed the color of her hair from an ice-queen blond to a honey wheat. When she looked in the mirror, she didn't really see herself, so the hair color would take some getting used to.

"Are you ready?" he asked after they had shared a protein bar and some water.

"Ready."

Some areas were iced over and could be treacherous but with Matteo's support, they both reached one of the sights she had wanted to show him.

"Here it is." Danica touched a large tree growing precariously at the edge of a rocky cliff.

"See here." She pointed to a heart carved into the tree by her father. Inside the heart were their initials. "My dad asked my mom to marry him here."

Matteo seemed to be fascinated with the tree. "It's beautiful. Your father was a romantic."

That made Danica laugh. "Every now and then. He was gruff most of the time. But a good man, a hard worker and a wonderful father. He loved all of his girls deeply. My family calls this tree our Love Tree."

Matteo put his arm around her and kissed her beneath the bows of the tree.

"My nose is all runny!" She laughed again. She could probably count on one hand how many times she *genuinely* laughed in the last ten years. Now in Big Sky, she seemed to be laughing without reservation. It was a revelation to her. Had she been unhappy in California but just didn't realize it?

"I'm a doctor. It doesn't bother me," he said.

"Well, that makes one of us!"

Matteo ran his finger along the carved heart. "This is beautiful."

"My parents were engaged here. We spread my parents' ashes here. And this is where Wayne asked Charlie to marry him."

"Thank you for sharing this with me."

She smiled as they headed upward to the pinnacle—a small area of quartz and rock faces. Some trees had been fighting to break through the rock and that always made Danica feel a kinship with these intrepid trees. She too had a desire to fight to break down barriers in her life. From the pinnacle, there was a bird's-eye view of a glorious valley that, during summer and spring, was filled with a carpet of wildflowers.

Matteo had packed some waterproof tarps upon which to sit but she was too busy using his binoculars to look at the wildlife below.

"It's a moose!" Danica exclaimed. "But it's all alone."

Matteo smiled at her. "They don't travel in herds."

"Oh," she said with a smile of her own, "shows you how much I remember about moose."

She continued to watch the lone moose, with its enormous antlers and its thick dark brown and black coat.

"We have Shiras moose here," Matteo told her. "They're actually the smallest breed of moose. They also have these weird snouts that help them not get water up their noses when they eat plants they find in water."

"Now it's ringing a bell." Danica joined him on the tarp. "My dad gave all of us girls nature lessons about the wildlife on our land, but I haven't exactly needed moose knowledge or bear spray on Hideaway land."

"Oh yeah?"

She nodded. "Plenty of people wanted permission to hunt on our land but dad wouldn't allow it. That's why we don't offer hunting. The only hunting would be to reduce numbers if they couldn't sustain themselves due to lack of resources."

"I never knew your dad, but I think I would have really liked him."

"You would have," she agreed. "Everyone loved Butch Brand." Matteo offered her coffee and she accepted.

"Mmm," she said after her first sip. "What's in it?"

"Cinnamon. This is how my *abuelita* taught me."

"Well, your grandmother was a genius."

"My grandmother on my mother's side."

She kept her hands wrapped around the cup, feeling its warmth through her gloves. "You were a very good learner."

"Thank you," he said, leaning over to steal a kiss. "Sometime soon I will fix you some Jewish cuisine."

"If you want to win my heart, homemade matzo ball soup and latkes with applesauce and sour cream will be required."

"Well, I am trying to win your heart," Matteo said sincerely. "Next cheat-day meal."

Together, they sat, absorbing the peace and the quiet at the top of the mountain. Danica felt completely at home on that peak, which was unexpected considering her desire, when she was eighteen, to leave Big Sky as quickly as possible and never look back.

"Penny for your thoughts."

"Latkes, mainly," she said with a smile. "Nothing profound."

"I must disagree. Mulling over the awesomeness of the latke *is* profound. All of the great thinkers like Socrates and, more recently, Stephen Hawking, often opined about the latke."

Danica bumped her shoulder playfully against his. "Socrates? Stephen Hawking?"

"Just to name a few."

When the cold became too much of a barrier, they packed up their few items, put them in Matteo's backpack, and then began the slow and methodical descent. Matteo wanted to take a selfie of them in front of the Love Tree to post on social media. He wasn't shy about documenting their relationship, which meant that he was absolutely serious about her and their relationship that was still in its infancy. It was both exciting and nerve-racking at the same time. Exciting because she was in a new relationship with a wonderful man and nerve-racking because he seemed to be further down the road to commitment than she was. The last thing she would ever want to do was hurt Matteo.

Instead of continuing down the path, Matteo stayed rooted in his spot next to the Love Tree.

"Are you okay?" she asked, confused.

Matteo held out his hands to her and she naturally took them into hers and looked at him.

"I didn't know about this tree or what it meant to you and your family," Matteo said, and her heart plummeted into her stomach. "But I can't let this moment pass me, pass *us*, by."

"The tree has been here for seventy years, give or take, and unless something catastrophic happens like a lightning strike, it will be here another seventy years. No rush."

"No," Matteo said quietly, "this is the place, and this is the moment."

"I don't know that it is."

"Danica," the doctor continued undeterred, "I love you. I want us to be together. Build a life. Have children."

She was now in fight-or-flight mode, and it took all of her willpower not to find an escape route.

"I know it's early."

"Very early."

"And I know you have gone through a challenging breakup."

"It has been," she said. "Still is."

"But, having said all that—" Matteo sought out her eyes and held them captive with the mesmerizing brown-black eyes "—are you ready to say that we are committed to each other?"

She wanted to yank her hands away and scream "no" as loudly as she could, but that didn't happen. She *did* slip her hands from his, gently but noticeably.

"That's a *no*," Matteo said, frowning.

"No, it's not," she said. "It's an *I don't know*."

Matteo took a step back away from her, and that made her feel like a world-class jerk.

"Do you see yourself with me, Danica? Down the road?"

She couldn't seem to speak. Every thought that came into her shocked brain seemed like a horrible choice. Matteo was pouring his heart out to her and she wished that she could reciprocate, but she couldn't. She just couldn't. Not yet. And maybe not ever. The last long-term relationship she was in cost her everything. And no matter that she could see that this was a great change, a chance to work more closely with her sisters, it didn't change the real trauma she had gone through, and it wouldn't be easily forgotten. Did this make her skittish when it came to a committed relationship? Yes. Absolutely yes.

Matteo had his hands in his jacket pockets, pain was present in his eyes, and she hated it.

"What about children, Danica? Do you still want children?"

"Well—" she looked over his shoulder and not in his eyes "—I think I do, but everything in my life has been turned upside down. I'm starting over, really, and it's difficult to know, right in this moment, what my future looks like."

He stared at her, and she stared at him, and she wished she had a rewind button that would take her all the way back to when she suggested a hike on one of her family's favorite trails.

And then, feeling anxious in the quiet moment, she said one of the horrible ideas aloud. "If you need to have a child, Matteo, and it's a nonnegotiable, I may not be right or you. I care too much about you to hold you up. There are women in a fifty-mile radius ready to line up to give you a child."

"So let me get this straight. You want me to find another woman to give me a child?"

"Well, yes, but it sounded worse when I said it than when I thought it."

Matteo's face was drawn and tense; his lips, the very ones she had kissed in the selfie, were unsmiling. "It looks like this tree doesn't hold the same magic for us, Danica."

And with that said, he started off to a nearby trail. Neither of them spoke on the path back. Matteo, always a gentleman, helped her across some slippery ice patches, but that was the extent of their interactions. And this pattern continued until they reached the edge of the woods, close to Charlie and Wayne's restored farmhouse.

"I've got to get back," Matteo said.

"Matteo, wait."

He stopped, looked at her with shuttered eyes and waited.

"None of that came out the way I wanted it to," she said.

"I think it was the truth whether it came out right or not."

She couldn't deny it, so she didn't try.

"Danica, I love you enough to let you go," the handsome doctor said before he headed back to the main house where he had parked his truck.

Stunned speechless again, it took her a moment to think to say, "But I promised Lu I would go on a forage hunt with her."

Matteo kept on walking with long determined strides to his truck. Danica stopped walking, feeling too many emotions to unpack in this moment.

Ray came out of Charlie's house and asked, "Was that Matteo leaving?"

"Yes."

Ray put her hands on her hips. "Well, I was going to invite him to lunch. Vegetable soup and sourdough bread."

Danica stood in her spot and watched Matteo walk away from her until she could no longer see him. Ray came out of the screened-in porch, looked at where Matteo had gone and then looked at her.

"What's wrong?" her twin asked. "What happened?"

Danica put her face in her hands, shaking it and trying to

make sense of the terrible turn their hike had taken. Concerned, Ray put her arm around her and led her to the porch and then inside Charlie's house. Danica sat down on one of the kitchen table chairs and was immediately joined by Hitch. The rotund red tabby curled up on her lap and began to purr.

"Thank you, sweet boy," she said, feeling comforted.

"Here's a cup of coffee," Ray said, joining her. "Now what happened?"

Danica did her best to recount the disagreement, but her memory was spotty even for a conversation that happened moments ago.

"So he wanted a commitment?"

Danica nodded. "A promise of a commitment, I suppose, looking back."

"You have said that you have strong feelings for him."

She finished her coffee. "I do. I love him. But that doesn't mean I can commit right now or even anytime soon! I need to figure out who *I* am."

"And he couldn't accept that?" Ray asked. "I know we don't really know people when they are behind closed doors. But it's hard for me to believe he's so rigid."

"Well…"

"Oh no," Ray said, and then asked, "What did you say, Danny? When your mouth is a mile in front of your brain, you can say some really…"

"Stupid?"

"…things."

"I can't deny it."

Ray leaned forward, resting her head on her hand. "What did you say?"

She shrugged, not even wanting to repeat what she had said to him. She did already regret it.

"I told him that I don't know if I want to have children anymore."

"Oh, this is bad."

"And because of that truth, that I didn't want to hold him back." Ray groaned.

"And I can't remember every word."

Her twin groaned louder.

"But it was something in the neighborhood of choosing a mother for his child from the long line of women wanting to have his baby."

Ray shook her head, rolled her eyes heavenward, with an expression of complete bewilderment.

"And then he left."

"Yeah, I saw him leave," Ray said. "I can't imagine why. You only told him to go find another woman to have his baby. No biggie."

Danica had a clearer mind farther down the mountain than she had at the Love Tree. Could there be plausible deniability because of difficulty with the altitude?

"Not my best turn of phrase."

"No."

"In my defense, I didn't know he was going to ask me for a commitment and nail me down about bearing his children on our hike, which happened to have the Love Tree as part of the scenery."

"Danny!" Ray exclaimed. "Not the Love Tree."

"Again—" she pointed to herself "—caught off guard."

Ray sat quietly and that only made things worse, so she asked her twin, "Is it as bad as I think it is?"

"Yes. It is," her sister said honestly without a moment's hesitation. "And if you don't want to lose Matteo for good, you'd better figure out how to clean up your mess."

"G-MA!" OAKLEY RUSHED up the porch steps to where his grandmother often sat, bundled up in a thick blanket and drinking hot cider. "Guess what?"

"What?"

"Cody says that since I'm a real cowboy now, I need cowboy clothes!"

His grandmother reached out her arms to him; G-Ma, as he liked to call her, had been one of his best people. She always encouraged him, had a kind word for him, and was willing to watch every single documentary about cowboys, horses and the

Wild West. He was pretty sure that she didn't like those shows so much and that only made him love her more.

"Well, then," she said to him, "I think you'd better go ask your mom."

He gave one more hug to G-Ma, raced to the front door of the main cabin and pushed the door harder than he had intended. The door hit inside wall and the bell clanged loudly.

"Oakley?"

"Yes, Mom!"

"Are you okay?"

He ran down the hallway to the room where his mother was writing and crashed into her in his excitement.

"What is going on with you?" his mother asked, smoothing his hair off his face and back under his *signed* Cody Ty hat. "Is a bear chasing you?"

He shook his head, feeling out of breath. He loved Cody Ty and had dreamed about one day meeting him. Even in his wildest dreams, he couldn't imagine spending whole days with him.

"Cody says that since I'm a cowboy, I need cowboy clothes."

"He said that?"

"More than once," Oakley said, feeling like ants were in his pants that were making him sway back and forth, waiting for his mother to say yes.

"What kind of clothes?"

"Cowboy hat, button-down shirt, silver belt buckle *and* steel-toed boots."

His mother had always been thoughtful and, often from his view of the world, too slow in her deliberations.

"Well," his mother said, "I'm just finishing up a chapter."

His heart was beating so fast, like a hummingbird's wings, because she was using her "possible" face. "Let me finish and I'll think on it. Okay?"

Oakley's shoulders slumped forward and his face crumpled with disappointment. He wanted cowboy clothes now, not later! Being a cowboy was his calling and the sooner he began to look like a cowboy, the quicker his mother and his G-Ma would know this wasn't a fad. This was who he had always been and now he knew it for certain.

"He's coming over now, Mom!"

His mother's eyebrows drew together. "Now? Why?"

"Because he's going into Bozeman already, so I could go to the store with cowboy clothes then."

His mother didn't speak for really long minutes, which made him follow up with, "*Please*, Mom. *Please!*"

After another excruciating second or two, his mother smiled, and she closed the laptop and stood up. "Well, let's go get you some duds, cowboy."

Oakley grabbed her hand and led her to the front door. "Mom, could you please never say the word *duds* again? It's embarrassing."

"Okay," his mother said while she donned her winter clothing. "For you, I will try."

Good as his word, Cody was waiting at the bottom of the porch steps and had just tipped his cowboy hat to his G-Ma. He could tell his grandmother, who wasn't always the social kind, liked Cody. And he could also see that when Cody looked at his mom, his eyes got all soft and today wasn't any different. In his mind, if Cody and his mom got married, he'd be able to keep on being a cowboy.

"Hi, Journey," Cody said to his mom. "How's the writing?"

He looked from Cody to his mom; his mom kind of acted weird around Cody, kind of shy and flirty, and he hoped that was a good thing in light of his plan to get Cody Ty to marry her.

"Slow and steady."

"Good," Cody said. "Glad to hear it."

"Cowboy clothes," he said, wanting everyone to stay on track.

"Oakley said that you said that he needs new clothes?" his mother said.

Cody gave a quick nod. "He needs the boots right now. If a horse steps on his foot, it will keep him safe."

Oakley added, "But Cody also said that it wouldn't hurt for me to have a cowboy hat, a silver buckle and a button-down shirt right now either."

"It wouldn't hurt?" his mother asked Cody.

"It wouldn't," Cody said.

"Looks like we're going into town. Mom, do you want to come?"

"No," his G-Ma said. "I'm happy where I sit."

CHAPTER SIXTEEN

JOURNEY'S AFTERNOON HAD certainly taken an interesting turn. She had been on a good writing roll, and she hated to break before she had finished the chapter. But she also had picked up so many authentic ways a real cowboy moved in the world from Cody, and Wayne Westbrook, that moments like these enriched her writing.

"I told Cody that sometimes people stare at me kind of rudely, but that we do our best to ignore it."

Journey turned around, smiled at her eager son with a deep sense of appreciation and gratitude. *This* Oakley? This was her first time meeting him. Yes, he had built a thicker skin because of his facial differences and yes, he had to endure the pain of multiple surgeries as well as understanding that there were many more to come, and this had made him strong and mature, light-years past his same-aged peers.

"But Cody says that horses don't care about what we look like," Oakley said. "That's because Cody says that horses read our souls."

"Is that right?" She smiled at her son, and then to Cody, she said, "*Cody says* is a very big thing in our household now."

"I hope it's not a bother," Cody said from behind the wheel of his truck. Billy Dean, her hero in her second book, had a similar truck.

"It's not," she said. "And you will tell me if Oakley tagging along becomes a bother to you."

"It's no bother," he said. "He's a great kid with a heart of gold. That's why the horses take to him so quick-like."

"Then I guess neither one of us is bothered."

"Looks that a'way."

"And thank you," she said with a waver of emotion in her voice, "for seeing my son as he truly is."

"Nothing easier from my way of thinking."

Again, she said, "Thank you."

The drive into Bozeman was picturesque and it felt good to see new scenery. Cody focused on the road, and she did her best not to stare at him like a bug under a microscope. Even after their earlier trip to Bozeman, it was still odd to see Cody off ranch property, his habitat, like a real person.

And that thought made her chuckle, which drew a brief look from Cody, but she shook her head and didn't voice that thought. Her son was a talker and if anyone gave him a chance to take center stage, he was going to take it! Oakley told her, in great detail, everything he had learned from Cody. She was impressed by how much Cody had already taught her son, but she was also impressed with how much Oakley had absorbed. Her son was smart with a higher-than-average IQ, and this was a challenge for them during homeschooling because he raced through the content so quickly that he was closing in on finishing middle school. She had heard of many homeschooled communities in her area whose children had attended college four or five years before what was typical. Her son was likely to be no exception. And because of his high IQ, Oakley tended to get bored after the first couple of days of new content, but this wasn't the case with what Cody was teaching him. This cowboy life, Journey believed, was meant for her son.

"You've taught him so much," she said, after Oakley stopped explaining what he had learned for over thirty minutes.

"You boy's like a giant sponge," Cody said with a pleased, rare smile. "If I say it, if I show it, he'll learn it."

She looked at Cody's profile—he had a strong profile that had aged well; his day-old stubble was mostly coming in silver-white. Yes, he had lines around his eyes and beneath his cheeks, there were some folds of skin on his neck, but it didn't take away from his appeal. He had been a handsome man in his youth when she googled images of him; he was still handsome. She had already felt drawn to Cody, from the first moment she saw him. She hadn't known who he was or what he was about, so it wasn't his career or fame that had piqued her interest. Like what Cody said about her son's soul, Cody's golden soul had resonated with her.

"I'll just be a minute." Cody parked his truck in front of a post office.

Journey watched him take a large box out of the bed of his truck and continued to watch him as he walked up the steps with a stiff limp. He opened the door for two women coming out of the post office before he went inside.

"Cody got that limp 'cuz a bucking bronco landed on his knee, and busted it up but good," Oakley told her using some of Cody's phraseology. "The doctors said that he might never walk again without a cane and that he'd never rodeo for the rest of his life."

Oakley paused and then continued, "He won two more championships just to prove them wrong."

"He's tough like you."

Oakley nodded. "I'm tough like him."

"Now, don't bother Cody, okay? He's got a lot of work to do."

"Aw Mom, I'm not!" her son said, exasperated. "You just heard him say it himself."

"He's polite, Oakley."

"Not about this, though. Horses are everything to him and he sees that I'm interested and that I have talent with horses, so he says that he's proud to pass on his knowledge to young cowboys just starting out like me."

She turned her body to look at her son over her shoulder. "Oakley, I want you to remember that we leave in less than two weeks."

"I know." Her son frowned. "But I'll just find my way back when I'm done with school. I'll find Cody. I know I will."

She turned back facing forward, feeling sick in her gut. She had never seen her son so passionate about anything other than video games that allowed him to have online friends without them actually seeing his face. In those worlds, he had avatars of his choosing.

"We'll figure something out," she said, putting it on her to-do list to find stables and horses near their home.

"Cody's mailing that package to his mom. Her name is May Bell and she lives with her sister, Regina. His mom likes to do crossword puzzles and crochet. Cody sends money home to Regina every month so she can take care of their mother full time."

Journey was surprised at how much Cody talked to her son. When she was with the cowboy, he barely managed to get a couple of sentences out!

"When he was my age, he saw a palomino horse on a farmer's land about a mile from where he grew up. He fell in love with that horse, and he vowed that one day he would own a palomino." Her son leaned forward and asked, "Do you know what a palomino horse is, Mom?"

"As a matter of fact, I do."

"ARE YOU TRYING to make me have a nervous breakdown, Matteo?" Estrella asked him with an exasperated look on her face.

"No. Not intentionally."

"Well, you are!" her sister said, annoyed. "Why did you accept Mom's request to be friends on Facebook?"

"Why wouldn't I?"

"Because, *hermano*," she retorted, drawing out the first word, "when you post nothing but pig pictures and pictures of your poker team or hiking pics, and then you start posting selfies with a mysterious blonde? Mom noticed and she's been grilling me because you are out of range, playing doctor."

"I'm not playing a doctor; I am a doctor."

"Big whoop." She frowned. "I'm really tired of running interference for you. Seriously."

Estrella and he had always been very close and he could plainly see that this was taking a toll on her.

"I'll talk to her tonight."

"Tonight, tonight?"

"What other tonight could there be?"

"When you're involved, who knows."

"Te amo, hermanita."

"Besos." His sister blew kisses to him.

When he hung up with his sister, Lu Lu brought something to him and dropped it on the ground at his feet.

He bent down and picked it up. "Is this the custom beret Danica had made for you?

"Is every single woman in my life—my sister, my mom, my girlfriend, my pig—*all* mad at me?"

He asked Lu Lu, "How can I make this better?"

Lu Lu oinked at him twice and then started walking in a circle making that horrible, mind-numbing squeal that could wake the dead.

"That's not helpful, Lu Lu," he said, "not helpful at all!"

EVER SINCE HER conversation with Matteo, Danica was filled with regret, especially because he had been radio silent with her. She had slid into his DMs and nothing! She had texted, emailed, left a card in his mailbox, and all of her efforts to reconnect failed. She was never one to quit when it mattered and she realized, very clearly during their time apart, that Matteo meant something to her. Yes, she was still raw from Grant and everything that entailed, but that didn't mean that she couldn't forge a new path, at a snail's pace, with this incredible man she loved and who loved her.

"Did Matteo get back to you?" Ray asked.

"As a matter of fact, he did!" She said, "Finally! He made me work for it, I'll say that."

"And?"

"And he's coming for the campfire!"

Ray stopped peeling potatoes and hugged her. "I'm so happy. I know you've tried to hide it but you're my twin. I feel your pain and sadness as if it were in my own body."

"Me too."

About once a month, they tried to have a campfire cookout with stew wrapped in tinfoil, cooked on an open fire, cowboy coffee, and of course, toasted marshmallows and s'mores.

"I love him, Ray," she said, "really and truly. The timing isn't right, I know that. But the love is real."

"It's no different than Dean and me." Ray went back to peeling potatoes. "I thought I would be back here for maybe six months while I tried to figure out who I was after the divorce. And then I reconnected with Dean."

Dean had been Ray's first love, her first *everything*, and everyone had thought that they would get married after college. But that wasn't what happened. They both married different people, had wonderful children with those partners, and then found themselves back in love around Christmas time.

"And you're certain?"

"About Dean?" Ray asked.

She nodded.

"One hundred million percent," her twin said. "Like you, I didn't think the timing worked but it happened, and Buck was the person who really reminded me of how short life is. I didn't want to look back on my chance to rekindle our relationship. That would have been real regret."

Danica asked, "And how is Dean doing? I rarely see him."

"He rarely wants to be seen," Ray said, and then asked her to get another roll of tinfoil out of the cabinet. "But he will be at the campfire tonight."

"Good, I'm glad."

Ray nodded, focused on her work.

"Question."

"Shoot."

"Do you have a good recipe for black-and-white cookies?"

MATTEO PULLED UP to the main house on Hideaway Ranch, eager to see Danica again. His heart ached for her heart, her lovely face, her laugh and the softness of her skin when he held her in his arms. He looked back at the moment, and he wished that he'd never allowed himself to be inspired by the Love Tree. It was too soon to try to ask Danica to enter into yet another serious relationship after what she had endured and all that she had lost. He had another chance—she had given him another chance—he needed to practice patience and give Danica time. That's what she needed and as enthusiastic as he felt, finally finding that woman he had dreamed of—a woman who was intelligent, kind, strong, self-possessed and loved Lu Lu as he did—if he pushed her away, he would live in regret for the rest of his life.

"Dr. Dangerously Handsome, is that you?" Danica asked as she walked toward him with an open posture.

"At your service."

"Is that any service of my choice?"

Matteo smiled at her. "Your wish is my command."

Danica stepped into his arms and hugged him tightly, her head resting on his chest above his heart.

"I have missed you," he said quietly.

"I have missed you," she said.

She took his hand into hers and said, "Let's not do this again."

"Agreed," he said readily, "never again."

When they reached the campfire, he was greeted like a hero returning home. He had struggled sometimes to find his people in Montana, but Danica's ranch felt right to him. And he said as much to her.

"Have you thought about building here, at the ranch?" he asked, taking his stew to a nearby chair.

"Yes," she said, "I am gloriously wealthy. And I plan on putting a large chunk of it into building more cabins, brand expansion, *and* a forever home for me. But first, I have to figure out who I am and what I want."

"I love it here," he said. "I have peace here."

"So—" she touched his arm and met his gaze "—you would consider living here one day?"

"Are you asking me to move into your fictitious house?"

She laughed. "Yes, I suppose I am."

"Well, you'd have to put a ring on it first, Ms. Brand." He winked at her. "But if you *did* put a ring on it, yes. I would."

THE TRIP TO Bozeman had been one of the most important trips of Journey's life, only second to the trip to Montana as a whole. If she had any doubts about the integrity and decency of the man who had been her muse since the first day at Hideaway

Ranch, those were gone. Wiped away, like dirt on a glass window. She already knew that, like the last trip to Bozeman, Cody Ty would be surrounded by fans. She also knew, from ten years of experience, that Oakley would draw rude stares wherever they went. And as always, she had to do her best to not return the rudeness by telling them to mind their own darn business.

"Do you know what Cody says about that?"

"No, tell me."

"Cody says that in his day, if people were rude and stared, back in his time, he'd say, *take a picture, it'll last longer.*"

She laughed and looked at Cody who appeared to be rather sheepish. "Maybe that wasn't the best thing I taught your boy. Apologies."

"No need," she said. "It gets the point across."

Cody took a lot of pictures for the fans, and plenty of pictures were taken with Cody Ty with his arm protectively over Oakley's shoulder. And it struck Journey that this was the first time she'd seen someone other than her mother or herself protecting Oakley. It made her feel so grateful that she had to excuse herself to the bathroom to stop tears from coming. This was a happy day for Oakley, and she couldn't do anything to detract from that.

By the time they left the store, Oakley had three big bags full of his cowboy garb. The first salesperson to greet them appeared horrified by Oakley's appearance and Cody acted immediately and went to the store manager. Apologetic, the store manager helped Oakley's transformation and he turned into a cowboy, right in front of her eyes. Cody helped him find a cowboy hat that fit perfectly, Wrangler jeans like the ones he wore, a tooled leather belt with a nice-size silver belt buckle, and of course, steel-toed boots.

"Mom—" Oakley spun around for her to see "—do I look like a cowboy now?"

"You do." She got up, hugged him and kissed him. "You certainly do."

On instinct, she hugged Cody and kissed him on the cheek. "Thank you."

"I didn't do hardly nothing," the cowboy said, his cheeks a

bit flushed as he looked at the toe of his boot. "But if you need to thank me, then thank you and you're welcome."

That night, Oakley got to show off his new cowboy clothes and he was so proud, so happy and so handsome as a cowboy, that Journey knew that one way or the other, she had to find a way to keep Oakley in this cowboy life.

With a big dinner, good company around a roaring fire on a cold, clear Montana night, Journey sipped on a hot buttered rum while Wayne played his guitar and led the group in camp-fire songs. When Cody joined them, and she was worried that like the hermit crab he would disappear into his shell, she saw a man who had stolen her heart. Who he was, the way he moved in the world with integrity, honesty and honor, that alone would have attracted her. How he treated Oakley with love and accep-tance, that only confirmed for her the reason behind that deep, abiding love she had developed for him.

Cody pulled out a harmonica from his jacket pocket and began to play along with Wayne, and Oakley jumped up, clap-ping his hands and stomping his foot to songs.

"Where has our shy, introverted boy gone?" his mother asked.

"I'm not sure. But what I am sure of is that this is what Oak-ley needs to have to live his best life."

"I can't disagree," Lucy said. "Let's discuss it tomorrow."

"Take Oakley in with you?"

Her mother tapped Oakley on the shoulder, and of course, he was upset to be going to bed while his new friends, Paisley and Luna, were allowed to stay longer.

"Mom, *please*, Paisley and Luna are still here," Oakley begged her, and how could she argue with his logic. Not only had he discovered his inner cowboy, but he had made friends.

"Okay, son," she said. "You can stay up with your friends."

Thrilled, Oakley ran over to the other side of the fire where Paisley and Luna were sitting on a log, toasting marshmal-lows. He joined then on the log and, for the first time in such a long time that she couldn't even pinpoint the memory, Oakley was just doing what all girls and boys do at a campfire. Dean's daughters were angels as far as she was concerned. Made of great stuff.

"That is a sight," her mom said.

Journey stood up and hugged her mom tightly. "This place is magical."

"It is, baby girl," Lucy said, "truly magical. And is truly a match made in heaven for our wonderful, magical boy."

Her mother had a keen mind and an otherworldly connection to Oakley. If she saw what she was seeing, a move to a place that suited Oakley better would be on the table. But proximity to health care and his large team of specialists was crucial. One day, those specialists would be able to make Oakley's face look closer to the norm and that would make his life easier for sure. Now, this place, this life, would make Oakley's life more fulfilling and that could not be ignored.

AS THE FIRE died down, Cody knew it was time for him to head back to the bunkhouse on the property, the place he had been hanging his hat ever since he had come to lend a hand with the horses at Hideaway Ranch. Earlier in the day, he had spent time in Bozeman with Journey and her boy. Oakley was a good egg; gentle, calm and steady, that boy had all the makings of a world-class cowboy. And he was proud for whatever he was able to teach Oakley of the ways of the cowboy. Dean Legend and Ray took their girls home and Wayne and Charlie headed back to their house. Soon after, Danica and Matteo left the firepit and then the count was down to Journey, Oakley and him.

"I'll take care of this fire," Cody said, always having difficulty not to stare at Journey. She was always beautiful to him, but, tonight, in the firelight, she was more than beautiful, she was like an angel from heaven. He'd thought that he knew his own heart and he had certainly thought he had been in love a couple of times along the highway of his life. But he hadn't been. He couldn't have been. The love he had for Journey, for her boy, was selfless, gentle, and rocked him at his core. And because this love he felt was selfless, he knew that he could never let Journey know that he loved her. It would be unfair. She was still young, and vibrant, and had a lifetime to find love. He had it rough most of his life. Even at the pinnacle of his career, he'd played it fast and loose, drinking, womanizing, gambling. He'd lost more than he saved, and he wasn't a good risk for someone as levelheaded and exceptional as Journey.

No. He would love her from afar and help her son as if he were his own flesh and blood. And he was proud of Oakley and didn't give a damn what other people thought of him. The boy had a special heart, and he wouldn't hesitate to claim him as his own.

Journey stood up, stretched, yawned and said to her boy, "Say good-night to Cody."

Oakley had milked the staying up after bedtime for all it was worth; he'd managed to be one of three people left at the firepit.

"Thank you, Cody." Oakley hugged him so tightly, he felt touched by it. "This was the best day of my life."

"Good night, cowboy."

Oakley looked up at him with admiration that he wasn't all that certain he deserved. "Good night, cowboy."

Oakley then hugged his mother and asked her, "Hey Mom, can I get a harmonica?"

Journey laughed and met his gaze over the soft flames of a dying fire. "We'll discuss it in the morning. Run off to bed, sweet boy."

And then there were two.

Journey walked around the fire and so did he. They met halfway and he kissed her. Plain, simple and full of love. The truth was all of the conversations he had in his head about letting her go so she could find a love more suitable for her and for her son meant nothing. Because when his heart started beating like a drum, pounding so hard that his thoughts were drowned out—any thoughts other than the one that demanded he take his palomino into his arms and kiss her like a man who had everything to lose if he let her slip away.

"I'm old, Journey," he confessed. "Broke down, bad knees, bad back."

Journey put her hand over his heart. "Kind heart, kind soul and more of a man than I've ever met in my life."

"I've got bad habits."

"I'm obsessed with clipping coupons. I have a bookcase full

of them. They take up a lot of room and I always forget to take them with me when I shop."

He took his rough hands and put them on the soft skin of her face and once she looked up at him, he let her see his soul. "I have to tell you that I love you. I don't think it's a smart idea for a woman like you to be shackled to a man like me."

Journey held out her wrists, palms facing upward. "Put those shackles on me, Cody Ty Hawkins. Oakley and I, we love you, and want to go wherever *you* go."

CHAPTER SEVENTEEN

MATTEO WAS AT Danica's condo helping her organize her boxes. Even though this was a rental, she wanted to put her personal touch on the space to make her feel more at home.

"If I had any doubt of your affections, this has dispelled them completely," she told him, handing him a hot tea.

"How so?"

"Moving? Unpacking boxes? Hanging things on the wall with materials that won't harm the paint? Loathsome business. Only the truly devoted would sign on."

Sitting down on the couch, Matteo smiled at her with his ridiculously handsome face. "Why are you looking me like that?"

"Like what?"

"Like I'm a science project."

Then she laughed, because she was trying to put two and two together. "I was actually trying to imagine what our child would look like."

Matteo put his tea down and gave her his full attention. "And?"

"Well, it would have to be a boy if he got that bone structure. Tough for a girl, I think," she said, then asked, "How do you feel about a surrogate?"

His eyebrows knit together. "I don't feel one way or the other. Why? Is that what you want?"

"I don't know, really," she said thoughtfully. "I want to be a mother. I always have. And I love Diane Keaton and she first became a mother in her fifties like a boss. But she adopted and I want to use my eggs. Those suckers weren't easy to extract, let me tell you that."

"But not fertilized?"

"No," she said quickly. "Lord, I can only imagine the fight I could've had on my hands if we had."

She continued, "Now I'm almost forty-one, and I know that's not old in brain years, but the body doesn't bounce back so easily now. I mean, look at Serena Williams! She's a superstar and it was nearly impossible for her to get back into competition shape to get back onto the court to compete. I'm certainly not in the same league as her. How would I fare?"

"I'm not opposed to it, but just like moving in together..."

She smiled at him. "I've got to put a ring on it."

He lifted up his left hand and pointed to his ring finger. "Right here, baby."

They made some more progress on the boxes and then headed out for a well-deserved lunch at a local bar and grill that was healthy and fresh food–focused. Matteo ordered New Zealand green shell mussels while she selected a salad made with fresh fruit, vegetables and a blackberry vinaigrette, all handmade on-site.

"Hmm." Danica nodded her head while she chewed. "This is excellent."

Matteo agreed, digging into his mussels.

"You know what?"

He raised his eyebrows.

She leaned forward and whispered, "Why can't we open a farm-to-table restaurant at the ranch? Ray is able to make down-home, stick-to-your-ribs winter dishes and then lighter foods such as salads with veggies grown at the ranch."

"I love that idea."

"We can tap into some of that wedding destination money," she added. "I've got the money now to build a barn for a ranch-chic wedding venue. My mind is spinning with ideas!"

"I think it's a great idea."

They both finished their meals and then ordered coffee. A man came out from the back of the house, weaved his way to their table and then greeted Matteo. "Dr. Katz, it's such a pleasure to see you again!"

Matteo stood up out of courtesy, shook the man's hand and then introduced him to Danica.

"It's a pleasure to meet you, Ms. Danica." Oscar, the owner of the restaurant bowed his head. "I hope you enjoyed your food?"

"It was delicious."

"Thank you, thank you." Oscar bowed his head again. "But I would be remiss if I didn't mention that my daughters are very upset that you are off the market, is that what young people say now?"

"I am sorry to hear about your daughters' dashed hopes," Danica said, "because I am afraid that I am the woman who has taken Dr. Katz off the market."

"Well, it was such a pleasure to meet you, Ms. Danica." He shook Matteo's hand one last time, and then went on with his business.

"Taken me off the market?" Matteo smiled at her with a wink. "That sounds official."

She waited for the waiter to fill their coffee cups before she said, "That's because it is official. You are mine and I am yours."

"I am yours and you are mine."

They touched coffee cups lightly and then fell into an easy conversation while they enjoyed their coffee.

"I did want to mention something to you," Matteo said.

"Uh-oh." She put her coffee cup down.

"It's nothing bad. Don't look so worried."

"Okay."

"So, you may have noticed that you are a regular person on my social media."

"I noticed."

"As did my sister, my parents, all of their extended family and on and on," he said.

"Okay," she repeated, impatiently waiting for the other shoe to drop.

"I'm not one to really post pictures of women on any of my feeds."

"Go on."

"I only post pictures of my friends, or nature pics, Lu Lu of course."

"Of course," she agreed. "That goes without saying."

In truth, she wasn't one to spend time on social media for personal reasons, only professional. What Matteo posted was more a passing curiosity versus something she honed in on all the time, every day, all day long.

"And when I say that I rarely post pictures of women, I meant that I *never* post pictures of women."

"Never?"

"No," he said, "not since my last relationship."

Danica sat back, her mind now fully involved. "But you've posted my pictures."

"Yes."

"And your family is wondering who the heck is this woman all over Matteo's feed?"

"Yep."

"And?"

"And they want to meet you."

Danica thought for a minute or two, and then said, "Well, it was bound to happen."

"Yes."

"So, why not?" she asked. "I asked Ray for a black-and-white cookie recipe because I wanted to make some for your folks, when the time was right, and send them as a greeting."

"God, I love you." He reached for her hand.

She reached for his. "Did you tell me in a public place so I couldn't flee?"

"Probably, yes.

"Since we're asking questions, answer this one for me. Did you make up with me just so you could see Lu Lu?"

She smiled broadly at him. "Probably, yes."

THEY WERE SCHEDULED to leave the next morning and Journey knew that she wasn't ready to leave, and she knew that Oakley felt the same way. This morning, she had found Oakley in his bed, crying softly because he would be losing the horses, Cody, and his two new friends, Paisley and Luna Legend.

"I promise you, Oakley, we will be coming back."

"Do you promise?"

She wiped away his tears with a tissue. "I promise."

"How do you know?"

"Because I do," she said. "Do you trust me?"

He nodded and then used the tissue to blow his nose.

"Okay, cowboy, you'd better hop to it and get dressed. Isn't Cody getting you up on a horse?"

"Yes!"

Journey left her son's room wondering how she had managed to go from being terrified of horses to agreeing to put her most beloved person, her son, on the back of a horse.

She walked out to the barn where she found Cody tacking up Atlas, the biggest horse in the barn.

"Good morning," she said to him with a smile.

He left Atlas's stall to hug her and to kiss her. "I keep on thinking that this was all a dream."

"Me, too."

"You leave tomorrow."

"Yes."

"I want to show you something before you go," Cody said, "and your boy."

After one more secretive kiss, Cody swung a saddle onto the draft horse's back.

"Did you have to pick the biggest darn horse in the barn?"

Cody chuckled. "My dad was mean when he was sober, worse when he was drunk, beaten down by life, and he died angry and bitter. But the man did give some advice that served me well over the years."

"And your father's advice is the reason for putting my ten-year-old son on a massive animal that bolts first and asks questions later?"

"Yep," he said. "Pop always told me that if I was ever to get into a bar fight, go after the biggest one in the bunch. Even if you lose, it will build your confidence."

"I see the parallel, I really do. Let's just keep that story between adults."

He laughed, one of those rare moments. "Yes, ma'am, mama bear."

She stopped by to give Rose some love; this little mare had taught her so much about herself—that she was kind and gentle and Rose always walked forward toward her and had helped her move past some of the trauma from her past.

"I love you, sweet Rose." She kissed the mare on the nose. "I will miss you. But this isn't goodbye. It's see you later."

When she left the barn, she saw Oakley in the round pen with Cody and Atlas; her mother was videotaping from the porch, so she decided to take pictures to stop herself from screaming "no" at the top of her lungs and racing to her son's side to stop this madness! Oakley had traded his cowboy hat for a riding helmet for safety.

Oakley, of course, looked more excited than she had ever seen him and as difficult as it was to watch, she had to let him live his life without overlaying her issues on him.

"Mom! G-Ma! Watch me!" Oakley waved at her before he climbed up the mounting block steps, stepped into the stirrup while Cody kept the horse standing in its spot, and then it happened. Oakley swung his right leg over the horse's back and sat down gently in the saddle.

"I did it!" she heard Oakley exclaim, and sat steady in the saddle as Cody told him to click his tongue to let the enormous draft horse know he wanted him to walk forward.

Journey rushed over to where her mom was standing. "He's doing it, Mom. He's really doing it!"

And then it happened. Cody took his hands off the reins and stepped back, coaching Oakley from the center of the ring.

"Look at him, Mom," she said, in awe of her son's bravery and tenacity. "He's a cowboy."

"Yes, he is," her mother said, tears on her cheeks. "He surely is."

DANICA HAD NOT met anyone's parents for nearly two decades and it made her feel jittery with nervous butterflies in her stomach at the thought of meeting Matteo's family. She would be attending video Shabbat dinner with his family. Shabbat was the Jewish day of rest and began at sunset Friday until sunset on Saturday. Matteo's father, mother and sister shared Shabbat dinner Friday night on video chat.

"I hope the cookies arrived and are in good condition," she said nervously, feeling sweat form on her upper lip. She went into the bathroom, dabbed the sweat off her lip, reapplied her lipstick and checked her hair.

"How do I look?" She spun around in her navy blue dress with a simple strand of pearls around her neck.

"Perfect," Matteo said. "You look like my future."

"Oh, I just love you, Dr. Katz-Cortez!"

He went in for a kiss but she dodged it. *"After* dinner. And then you can mess up my hair and makeup as much as you like."

Matteo smiled at her with a sexual glint in his eyes. "I'll look forward to it."

Seated at Matteo's marble bar top, Danica felt horrible. Still sweating, her stomach now hurting, it only confirmed the fact that she loved Matteo. She couldn't put herself through this if she didn't. Matteo had donned a black yarmulke with a silver Star of David in the center; it was the first time seeing him wearing this traditional cap to keep his head covered.

"Hi, Mom and Dad!" Matteo's parents joined the meeting. "Shabbat shalom."

"Good Shabbas, son," Dr. Katz said, "and Good Shabbas, Danica."

"Thank you, sir, Good Shabbas."

"And this is my wife, Mariposa."

"So nice to meet you," Danica said, taking an immediate liking to Matteo's parents. "Shabbat shalom, Mrs. Katz."

"Oh! You are so pretty, Danica! So pretty," Mariposa exclaimed, raising her hands to the heavens. "Finally, I see a woman in my son's life. I've been praying and praying and look, Ezra, what beautiful babies they will have."

"Let's take this one day at a time, my dear."

"I only want to say that I approve," his mother said. *"Gracias a Dios!* Thanks be to God. So many prayers have been answered."

After his sister Estrella logged on, Shabbat candles were lit and "Shalom Aleichem," a song that welcomed angels to the table, was sung. Matteo's father blessed the wine and the bread, and then they were able to eat the wonderful-smelling challah bread that Matteo had baked. And then, finally, Matteo's family opened the boxes of cookies she had sent to them.

"These are your first black-and-white cookies?" Estrella asked.

"Yes," Danica said. "The kitchen is not usually my friend."

"For this cookie, it was!" Dr. Katz said, holding the cookie for her to see.

After an hour together, Estrella logged off and then it was time for his parents to leave as well.

"This was wonderful," Danica said. "Thank you for letting me join."

"I hope you will join us every Friday," Ezra said. "And maybe you can get him to attend Saturday services at the temple."

"No, no." His mother shook her head. "Don't listen to him, Danica. Please make sure my son makes it to Sunday services. There must be a Catholic church close by."

"Good night, Mom, Shabbat shalom, Dad." Matteo moved the mouse to the red "leave call" button.

"And those were my parents and my baby sister," Matteo said, with a curious look on his handsome face.

"I love them."

"They loved you—even Estrella, who can be tough on the women I've dated."

"And they loved my cookies!"

"Yes, they did." He pulled her into his arms, held her tight and kissed her. "And I love you."

"I love you, Matteo," she said, wanting more sweet kisses. "More than words can say."

"Where are we going?" Oakley asked from the back seat of Cody's truck.

"Cody says it's a surprise," his mom said, and then added, "Now *I'm* saying 'Cody says'!"

"It's catchy, I reckon." Cody had a small smile on his face.

Oakley felt sad, really sad, and he couldn't understand how anyone could feel happy when he had to leave Montana, the one place on earth he wanted to be, and leave the one man he wanted to be like and be with.

"Do you know that I'm leaving tomorrow, Cody?"

The older cowboy looked at him in the rearview mirror. "Yes, I do, son, and I'm real sad about it."

"Yeah, me, too."

His mother turned around so she could look at him. "We will be coming back."

"When?"

"As soon as we can."

Oakley crossed his arms over his chest and scowled at the scenery outside the truck window. He didn't want to leave but he was just a kid. He didn't get a say. If he did, he'd never leave. Not ever!

Cody asked his mom about the book.

"I don't know what happened," his mom said. "I was on a roll and then something just—held me back and I don't really know what it is."

"Tell me more about it."

"Well, the hero is based on you, so that part's good."

"Happy to help."

"And it's not even the characters, really," she said. "I think all of the bad reviews of my first book still get to me, as much as I try to forget them. I'm actually surprised my editor wants to see a second book from me after those horrible one-star reviews."

"You know what my old man used to say?"

"What did he say?"

"Don't let people rent space in your head. And I've taken that advice in my own career. People want to build you up and then knock you down. So I don't let nobody rent space in my head and neither should you."

Oakley listened to them talking and couldn't understand how they could talk about trivial stuff when his life was unraveling! How could they? How could Cody?!

Cody turned off the highway onto an overgrown drive that didn't hold any interest to him.

"We're here," Cody said, putting the truck into Park and shutting off the engine. "We'll have to hoof it. No way to get the truck back there."

"Come on, Oakley," his mom said.

"No." He crossed his arms over his chest. "I'll wait here."

Cody Ty opened his door and unbuckled his seat belt. "Come on, cowboy, I promise you, you won't want to miss it."

"Okay," he grumbled, getting out of the truck.

Together, the three of them picked their way through winter brush that seemed to match his depressed mood, with brown and black foliage and the crooked branches of trees that had died years ago.

"What is this place?" he asked Cody, doing his best to keep pace with his idol.

"This is my place," Cody said, stopping at a bluff that over-looked a small valley with a hill on the other side.

"There's a building site over there." Cody pointed. "I reckon we could build us a two-story house. Enough room for all of us and a spot for your mother when she visits."

Oakley was aware that adults had conversations without him knowing about it and he was very confused. "Wait a minute. Did you say that you are going to build a house for us here?"

"If your mama will have me."

His eyes darted from his mother's face to Cody's face like a pendulum on a clock, back and forth, back and forth.

"Well," his mother said with an odd flush on her cheeks, "I suppose you should ask me."

Cody turned to his mother, and he asked, "Journey Lamar, would you do me the great honor of being my wife and build-ing a home right here, on this land?"

And to his total amazement, his mother said yes and then, still in shock and confused about what he had just witnessed, Oakley saw Cody and his mother lean toward each other to seal the deal with a kiss, nearly directly above his head, so he had to cover his eyes.

"How do you feel about this, Oakley?" his mother asked him.

"Are we really going to live here with Cody?"

"Yes," his mother said, "if you're okay with it."

"I'm okay with it!" Oakley shouted, sending some birds up into the sky.

"Then it's a done deal," Cody said to him. "Let's shake on it."

After they shook hands, man to man, cowboy to cowboy, Oakley waggled his head, his eyes wide open, trying to burn as much of this future home into his brain as possible.

"It's beautiful," his mother said, brushing tears from her cheeks.

"I'm glad you like it."

"I do," she said. "It's perfect."

"Is this my life?" Oakley asked loudly.

"Yes," his mother said, "this is your life."

Cody knelt down beside him and pulled the harmonica out of his pocket and handed it to him.

"Are you giving this to me?" He turned the instrument over in his hands.

"Nope, I'm not. That there is a loan. Just so you know that this here land is your home, and you can return it to me when you come back."

Oakley put the harmonica in his shirt pocket and hugged Cody like he never wanted to let him go. "I love you, Cody."

"I love you, son."

"For keeps?"

"For keeps."

And on that cold afternoon, as the sun slowly disappeared on the horizon, Oakley held Cody's hand while the cowboy held his mother close, the three of them quietly daydreaming about a life they would forge together, as a family, on this pristine Montana wilderness that stretched out before them.

EPILOGUE

Valentine's Day 2025

MATTEO AWAKENED ON Valentine's Day to the smell of challah French toast cooking. He threw off the covers, stood up, stretched and then pulled on his pajama bottoms after he retrieved them from on top of the lampshade.

"Hmm." He walked up behind his woman, wrapped her up in his arms and kissed her on the neck. "Good morning."

"Good morning," Danica said, looking sexy in his pajama top. "Happy Valentine's Day."

"Did you feed Lu Lu?"

"Yep," she said, "already done."

"I should have known." He sat down at the kitchen island and looked at Lu Lu, who was upside down in her bed with a smile on her face. "She never looks this content if she's hungry."

"True." Danica emphasized her point with the spatula.

"So you've raided the challah for Shabbat tonight."

"I won't tell your dad if you don't."

Matteo twisted his fingers over his lips like he was locking them. "It will go to my grave."

They ate together at the island, cleaning their plates and drinking orange juice. After Danica cleared the dishes and loaded them into the dishwasher, Matteo watched her, loving this ritual of her making breakfast for him with the challah bread he always made. He usually cooked for her, and it was special that she wanted to cook for him as well.

He took a shower and shaved, and then waited for Danica to shower as well. She emerged from the bedroom with her hair worn loose to her shoulders, a more carefree look for her that he loved. She was so beautiful and sweet and talented that he counted himself fortunate to have found her and to have won her heart.

With a playful expression on her face, she pulled her arms from behind her back and presented him with a small box. "Happy Valentine's Day."

"Ah! We are of the same mindset," he said, accepting the small present. "Check Lu Lu's collar."

"You didn't!" Danica exclaimed, kneeling down by the happy pig and unhooking a small box from her crystal-encrusted collar.

Danica brought her small box over and put it next to the small box she had given to him. "Who goes first?"

"Ladies first."

Danica slowly untied the ribbon, set it to the side neatly, and then one piece of tape at a time, she methodically unwrapped the paper.

"It's almost time for Shabbat dinner," he said.

"Oh hush," she said. "You open your present your way and I'll unwrap mine my way."

With the paper finally off, Danica opened the lid and took the small black ring box out and placed it on the island.

"It's not a ring," he said, hoping to waylay any anxiety she may have.

"It's not?"

"No."

Danica cracked open the velvet box and stared at the present he had gotten her for their first-ever Valentine's Day.

"It's…" She shook her head, and then continued. "It's so lovely, Matteo. Thank you."

"You're welcome, *mi amor*," he said, and then asked, "Would you like for me to put it on?"

She nodded as he took the large heart-shaped locket, made of platinum on a heavy platinum chain. There was a heart-shaped diamond in the center of the platinum.

"Is there a picture inside?"

"Open it and see."

Danica opened it and then she laughed. Inside the locket was a picture of Lu Lu in the crocheted outfit Danica had made for her.

"God, I love you, Matteo."

"Lucky for me," he said, putting it on for her.

She touched the locket. "It's perfect, Matteo. I love it."

After he received his kiss, he said, "My turn."

He ripped off the paper and ribbon in one fell swoop, then shook the outer box to get the small ring box out. Then he opened the box and his smile faltered and his heart started racing.

"Is this what I think it is?"

"What do you think it is?"

Matteo looked at the platinum ring, with a large bezel-set diamond glimmering in the early morning light. "An engagement ring?"

"I'm putting a ring on that," she said, smiling that loving smile he would never get tired of seeing.

Matteo put on the ring and looked at it. It looked foreign to him even though it was the perfect fit.

"Thank you." He stood up and drew her to him. "Happy Valentine's Day."

"Happy Valentine's Day to you, my love," she said.

After they shared a kiss, Danica asked, "You do know what this means, don't you?"

"What's that, *mi corazon*?"

"The Big Sky bachelor is officially *off* the market."

* * * * *